Farah Cook is a Danish writer of Pakistani descent. She grew up in Copenhagen with a creative and explorative childhood spent mostly outdoors. At the age of twelve, she began writing several short stories to fuel her passion for storytelling. Later, Farah graduated with a BA in social science from Sweden, an MA in arts from London and an MA in creative writing from the University of Surrey. Farah has lived in many countries, including Germany and New Zealand, but settled in London where she worked as a marketing manager for a large financial conglomerate. Her passion for storytelling remained, and at night she started to write all the things she'd imagine.

An alumna of the Faber Academy in London, Farah now lives in Bad Homburg, just outside Frankfurt, with her husband and two sons. She speaks six languages fluently including Danish, Swedish and German, and writes full-time.

Farah Cook

Care For Me

HODDER*studio*

First published in Great Britain in 2021 by Hodder Studio
An Imprint of Hodder & Stoughton
An Hachette UK company

1

A CIP catalogue record for this title is available from the British Library

Paperback ISBN 9781529364682
eBook ISBN 9781529364668

Typeset in Sabon MT by Hewer Text UK Ltd, Edinburgh
Printed and bound in Great Britain by Clays Ltd, Elcograf S.p.A.

Hodder & Stoughton policy is to use papers that are natural, renewable
and recyclable products and made from wood grown in sustainable
forests. The logging and manufacturing processes are expected to
conform to the environmental regulations of the country of origin.

Hodder & Stoughton Ltd
Carmelite House
50 Victoria Embankment
London EC4Y 0DZ

www.hodder-studio.com

To Chris, Ben and Noah
because of you, I am

PROLOGUE

She comes down the hallway, leaving the front door open. I stand poised and watch her throw her bag onto the floor. Jennifer Rush's crooning from the radio in the kitchen. She walks right past me. She doesn't meet my gaze. I'm not sure she even knows I exist. The pressure cooker whistles and a starchy smell of rice moistens the air.

'Where were you?'

No answer.

I catch a glimpse of her reflection in the mirror at the other end of the hall. I catch my own gaze in it as I stride in her direction.

'Answer me. Where did you go?' She turns into the dining room, pulls back a chair and sits at the table set with empty plates and glasses. Her fingers toy with the table cloth, twisting it into a tight knot.

'Don't pretend you don't know where I went.' The candle flickers, casting a shade on her face, which has turned pink. 'You've known all along, haven't you?'

'Badtameez ladki. That's not the way to speak to your mother. Didn't I tell you I don't want you to—' I fall silent and watch her watch me.

'Don't you tell me what to do.' Anger lingers like phantom threads between us.

'What did you say?' I loom over her, but she stands up and pushes the chair away with her foot. The table shakes, knocking over the candle. Thick smoke is coming from the kitchen. The smell of burning rice. But that's not all. Something else is burning. I look down. Small ribbons of flames rise from the table top.

1

'From now on, you don't have to worry about me.' She's at the window looking out. The hazy summer light slips through the shutters, leaving shadows on the floor.

'Why did you have to go with her?' I go to stand beside her and place my hand on her shoulder. It feels warm, smouldering. Hot air begins to envelop us, makes its way into our lungs.

'Tell me, why?' I adjust my wool kameez.

'Because,' her beady eyes look directly into mine. 'You stopped loving me.'

PART ONE
Mother
Daughter

1

AMIRA

Thursday, 25 April 2019

It's a dull day, rainy and wet. I park the car outside the local church, which is lending its room to the Carers Support Group. The woman at the Alzheimer's Society office scrawled the address on a piece of paper when I went to see her. I crease it up and throw it inside my handbag.

I don't even know why I am here. That's a lie. I am here because Meena suggested I speak to a care group. It's done wonders for her. I should turn around, it doesn't feel right. Neither did chatting to strangers in online discussion forums. But being anonymous comes with its perks, and strange friendships can be found, like the one I formed with Meena. I don't know her, but I instantly connected with her online and even gave out my real name, instead of holding onto my identity as *Nursemira*. It just seemed so impersonal. Now we chat every week and have become so close through exchanging daily episodes about our parents. I tell her personal things about Mum I never dreamed of telling anyone. She trusts me with things about her father. Sometimes I think that without Meena I'd have been lost.

When we last spoke, Meena encouraged me to contact the Alzheimer's Society. 'Do it for your own well-being,' she said. 'Or you will go insane.'

She has been a great support, and I don't know what I would have done if I hadn't found her in the forum for carers. Two words lit up my screen, brightening my day: 'Hello lovely.' I'd know it was her – *Thelonelymouse* – and would proceed to pour my heart out, tell her things only another carer would understand. I realise burdening one person with the same issue is unhealthy. I need to talk to somebody other than Meena, who is going through what I am. Somebody who understands my situation. That's why I need to attend the Carers Support Group.

I head through an arched corridor, gently knock on the door to my left and enter. Five people are sitting in a circle of chairs. An older man in a shirt, bow tie and trousers introduces himself to me as John Buchanan. He immediately pulls out another chair as if he's been expecting me. It's a cosy room, lit with bright fairy lights that fill the space like shimmering glitter. There's a table in the corner with tea, coffee, water and biscuits. I make myself a cup of tea, take a seat and listen to the man in his mid-forties talk about his mum. He scratches at his beard the entire time, looks down at the floor. When he's done, a woman, perhaps younger than me, starts talking about her dad. She dabs her eyes and blows her nose with a Kleenex. Tells the strangers in the room how much she loves him, but that she simply can't care for him all by herself anymore.

'It's just so hard, d'ya know what I mean? I'm so drained most days – physically and emotionally. I hardly have any contact with my friends. Dad needs constant attention. I worry that he'll hurt himself, d'ya know what I mean?' She pauses and looks at John, who nods understandingly. 'I'll never be able to forgive myself if anything were to happen to Dad. Never.'

'What are you going to do?' asks the man sitting next to her. He reveals a forehead full of deep creases as he pushes back his hair. A woman with a short crop leans in and asks the same question.

'My brother has agreed to move in with us. He wants to help care for Dad.'

'Good for you, Susan,' says John. 'You're finally getting the support you need.'

Susan wants to go on. But now John looks over at me. He expects me to introduce myself, and confess the thoughts that I carry around like a bag of bricks.

I inhale the stale air and take a good look at the unfamiliar faces. They suddenly don't seem so unfamiliar anymore. They must feel the same way I do, otherwise they wouldn't be here. I get an *it's OK* nod from John. I clear my throat

'Hello, my name is Amira Khan.' I pause. I always forget to use my maiden name. 'Malik. I'm Amira Malik and I'm thirty-eight. I have been caring for my mum for about seven years since she was diagnosed with dementia. I have lived with her ever since my dad died.' I pause again, feeling the relief easing from my chest. I don't mention the time I lived with Haroon. That time is a distant memory.

'When she was diagnosed, they said she might have had dementia for longer, but the signs could have just been related to her age. Mum turns seventy-six this year. I don't have siblings or relatives. We are alone and have been ever since my teenage son decided to move in with my husband. Ex-husband, I mean.'

'What was the reason your son—' John furrows his brows. 'What I mean to ask is did he move because of your mother? Teenagers can be quite sensitive to people with dementia.'

'No, I don't believe him going had anything to do with Mum. Nothing like that,' I hear myself lie. Shafi *was* annoyed. He was devastated that Nano was becoming forgetful. *She's stopped recognising me*, he used to say.

'It was getting too cramped for us all living under the same roof in a small, two-bedroom house. He's a typical thirteen-year-old and needed space, a room of his own. I'm sure you all understand—'

'Aye, I get that,' says Susan. 'My boy lives with his dad, too. And I was never married. Tony is my ex and—' Susan pauses, catching herself. 'I'm sorry, Amira, you were talking.' She gestures for me to continue, her face screwed up in apology.

'It's OK.' I need a break. But really, I want to go home. I feel guilty for being here. Meena told me not to let my guilt get to me. Haroon said that too. I can't help it. Talking about Mum in a support group makes me feel I am doing something terribly wrong. 'Actually . . . where is the loo?'

'To the left in the hallway,' says John.

As I leave, an echo of Mum's voice rings in my ears.

'Where is Shafi? And who is that boy?' She'd point a sharp finger at him. 'Don't want him in the house. Tell him to leave.'

She started to forget that Shafi had grown up. She never grasped the concept that he was no longer the sweet little boy stuck in her memory. Shafi started to spend more and more time away, making excuses not to come home and staying at Haroon's place more often. And whenever I'd ask him what was going on, he ignored me. But I knew he was frustrated with Mum who had started to treat him like a stranger.

'Get out,' she'd say when he'd come home. 'Out of our house.'

'Make Nano stop, please,' he would plead. How could I? The only thing I know how to do is making sure Mum is alright. I never saw that Shafi wasn't. And neither am I.

The corridor out of the room is dark, and the tube bulb in the ceiling is flickering. At the far end of the exit a shadow stands watching. Then I hear the clacking of heels start to echo down the corridor. The shadowy figure is getting closer. I spot a dark grey door to my left pressed into the whitewashed walls. I jerk on the handle and rush into a storeroom, full of boxes and cartons. A statue of Virgin Mary holding baby Jesus sits on the floor.

My heart pounds faster. The clacking stops. I place my ear on the door and hear a loud, heavy breath coming from the other side. Like something is out to swallow me. The air catches in my lungs. Beads of sweat trickle down my face. I step away from the door and manage to grab hold of Mary's head with the tip of my finger as it tips over. The sound of footsteps fade and somewhere a door slams shut.

I twist the handle open. The hallway is empty and the light from the ceiling no longer flickers, but illuminates down the long corridor. Did I imagine somebody was here? Whenever I am alone and in dark places, I tend to imagine things that aren't real. It started when I was little, alone in my bed. I used to scream and

Mum would come running. I used to think spiders crawled all over my bed.

I gather myself together, pulling back my hair, breathing deeply. I decide to go back to the room, even though my heart is still racing. I take a seat back in my chair and feel John's gaze deepening. He takes a sip from his cup and encourages me to go on. I hesitate. Can I trust that what I say will stay sealed between these walls? John assures me that everything we choose to share is confidential.

'How's your social life?' he asks. 'Do you see your friends much?'

'When I told my friends that Mum was diagnosed,' I say, wringing my hands, 'they felt sorry for me – said it's going to be hard caring for her full-time. I don't speak to any of them anymore.'

'That's just like my friends. D'ya know what I mean?' Susan asks. John stares at her. He signals that she should let me continue. 'Sorry, go on Mira or is it A-mira?' she glares at me with wide eyes.

'*Amira*,' I smile.

'Sorry.' Heat flashes to Susan's cheeks.

'Lately, I feel more and more frustrated. Mum's condition worsened. She won't let me help her in the bathroom. She doesn't want my help showering. She shuts the door right in my face when I try to.' I am trying to follow Meena's advice, I'm trying to open up. It does feel cathartic. 'She often walks around wearing her nightgown. Sometimes for days because she refuses to get changed. Drawers are left open, clothes will be on the floor. She stopped wearing underwear, says she can't find any. But I always find them stuffed underneath her pillow.' I stop myself from saying more. Looking around, I realise I don't need to reveal the reasons why Mum does what she does. They understand. They've been down that road.

'How are you helping your mum overcome some of these issues?' asks John.

'I smile when I speak. I try to remain calm. But it's not easy.'

Meena says *Smile and the world smiles with you*. I'd heard this quote before. I can't remember how it feels to be truly happy, or the last time I *really* smiled. I don't know if Mum and I feel anything for one another. Love, hate, disgust even.

'And what are some of the things you do that could improve her memory?'

'I'm helping her do Life Story Work, which helps her recognise her past. I've hung pictures of us in her bedroom. I plan to put up more. Perhaps a picture of my dad and my son. Mum doesn't remember them. I also want to write down her favourite foods and music. Perhaps familiar places she feels connected to. Anything to evoke her memories from the past. She can't remember what happens day to day. Isn't able to grasp time, as in, when things have happened. Mum refers to today and yesterday as *the other day*. And any *the other day* is the same. I want to give her a journal. She likes to write things down. Likes reading. I want Mum to use it so that she doesn't have to repeat everything. Even the smallest things she writes on her hand.'

'What does she like reading?' asks John.

I pause, blow at the surface of my tea before I take a sip. He offers me a biscuit, which I take.

'The newspaper. She is obsessed with reading it. Mum doesn't watch the news on telly, and I know it's because she can't recall anything she sees blinking on the screen. But I can't drive to town to get her the daily newspaper, I simply don't have the time for it. The *Inverness Courier* is biweekly. She'll read it and highlight all the headlines in yellow marker, often. She's searching for a fictional story about a young girl she says went missing—'

'Me dad cuts papers,' the heavy man sitting on the far left of the room says. 'Newspapers, letters, cards. You name it, he keeps all the scraps and bits.' He coughs. 'He don't live with me and me family no more. It's his carer who tells me he won't stop cutting things.'

'Anything else you want to share with us Amira?' John rolls the 'r' in my name as if he knows me well already. I feel like he's giving me special attention. Perhaps it's because I am new.

'Mum likes food. She used to be a wonderful cook, but I can't let her do the grocery shopping. She forgets things and buys too much, and it goes to waste. We've also had incidents where she picked food up from the store and started eating it right there and then. So I try to go during her afternoon naps. That's the only time I have to get things done around the house. She always wants to know what we're eating. Refuses to eat takeaway. Insists she has to do the cooking herself. We've had some minor accidents in the kitchen. Nothing serious. I wouldn't allow her in there cooking on her own.'

'I try not to leave Mother alone anywhere around the house,' says the woman with short blonde hair. 'She empties Nutella out of the jar with a spoon and then there's the honey pot—'

'Thank you, Bridget,' says John. 'For sharing that with us. Shall we, um, let Amira continue where she left off?' He sends me an approving nod.

'I no longer ask Mum what she wants for her meals. I give her what I know she needs, even when she refuses to eat what I plate in front of her. It doesn't always work. Sometimes I find that she makes her own meals when I am not around. She goes to the shop without my knowledge. Once, she left the shopping in the back of the car. I've had to throw meat away several times because she leaves it out for too long. I want to stop buying it. I want Mum to eat more vegetables.'

'She's forgotten how to cook, hasn't she?' asks Susan.

I nod. 'Yes, she no longer remembers the recipes.'

'My mum does something similar,' says the man I took to be in his forties. 'Once, she woke up early, took all the meat out from the freezer and left it on the counter, where it sat for the whole day. She said she wanted to prepare Christmas dinner for the family. I said to her, Christmas isn't due for another six months. She didn't believe me. I get that a lot and—'

'Thank you, Tom, for sharing your insights.' John looks back over at me.

I go quiet. Look down at my thumbs and twirl them round and round.

'I appreciate coming here today to share my experiences. Caring for Mum the past couple of years has been hard. And it's getting harder. I'm not sure how long I can manage to look after her. I'm terrified that some day something will go wrong.'

'What do you think might happen?' John grabs a biscuit for himself. 'If you were to leave your mother all by herself, is there a risk of danger?'

'The house is secure. I've had fire alarms installed. But I worry she'll forget what she's cooking and burn things.'

'Me dad's carer makes what he likes. Neeps and tatties. Boiled eggs and toast,' says the heavy man. 'But he burns the food when she's gone and eats all the black bits. He says it's delicious. I told him it's dangerous and that he'll end up causing a fire.'

'Mum is terrified of causing a fire,' I say. 'She's always been worried about it, ever since I can remember. I contacted her doctor, and spoke to a memory loss clinic that was recommended to me. I told them about Mum's condition. She should be due for an assessment soon, and one of the nurses said she might be better off living in a care home. I'm not sure I agree with them.'

'And why is that?'

I shrug. I don't tell him that in Pakistani culture the children are obliged to care for their parents. That we simply do not put our elders in a care home. It's considered amoral.

'My neighbour told me she doesn't like Mum wandering about the neighbourhood peering into people's houses. She said, "Why don't you place her in a care home? It's where she belongs." I think she called the social services. They almost took Mum away because she was shouting at pedestrians passing by our house to help put out the fire. People thought she was crazy. Our house has never been on fire. Mum has a phobia of lots of things. Loneliness, losing her jewellery. Fire is also one of them.'

John makes a note in his book of what I've just said. 'Go on, Amira.' He rolls the 'r' again.

'Earlier this year, I felt more tired than usual. I started to sleep in for an extra hour in the morning. Some days, I could barely get out of bed, let alone take care of Mum. I don't want her to go into a care home. I can't afford to put her into one. But I also have to think of what's best for her. I have to think about her safety.' I look over at Susan. 'I would never be able to forgive myself should anything happen to her.' She nods.

John thanks me, says I shouldn't worry. There's help if I need it. And I can tell by the look on his face that he thinks I need it.

I fold my hands and place them in my lap. I can't finish my tea. It's cold anyway. So is the room. Everyone is staring at me. No one says a word. I don't think they expected me to say this much on day one.

Before I go, John pulls me aside. He gives me what looks like a leaflet. Ravenswood Lodge Care Home. 'Speak to them. They are like no other facility. They might be able to help you.'

'How?' I ask.

'They offer grants for special cases,' he says, before he leaves.

I look at the glossy brochure in my hand. There's a picture with tall trees and a Victorian house on a cliff top, sleeping like a silent tomb.

I recognise this place. I've driven the long route to the rural Highlands, with its curved lanes bouncing over ruts and channels. The loose gravel spraying from beneath the tyres and wearing them out. And the deer, there must be thousands of deer out there in the wilderness roaming free.

One misty morning I remember driving past these large gates and the twisted driveway that leads up to the old manor. Beyond the hedgerows, I caught a glimpse of the sea. There was something beautiful and dangerous about the way the house stood there swallowed by dark woods and quiet hills facing the ocean. Powerful, and with a real presence marked by two tall turrets, it seemed out of my reach. I wondered who could live in a place like this. I imagined a wealthy family, or someone who wanted to live off-grid, undisturbed and in peace.

But now I know it's just some fancy care home I would never be able to afford to put Mum into, and Mum is not a special case. Just an old woman with dementia.

I flick through the brochure. Happy faces of elderly people selling false hope. Mum wouldn't be happy living in a care home anyway. I throw it in the bin and walk out of the building. I don't look back. I feel the guilt creep under my skin.

It was a mistake coming here.

2

AFRAH

It's a raw, stinging pain I feel each time I bite my nail to the nub. When there's nothing left to chew, I move on to the next and start all over till I see pink flesh. I spread out my hands and stare for a moment. Wiggle my fingers once, twice. I don't like what I'm looking at. The faint blue veins pattern my hands like fish scales.

Gold bracelets rub against my wrist. I used to have six, now I have four. One is elegant – ladylike, says Nisha – but I know she likes it when I wear four, two on each wrist, the way she does. She's one of those friends who'd never truly express what she really thinks. Nisha wouldn't want to hurt my feelings. Unlike my daughter, Amira, who says (often in a serious tone) that I shouldn't wear any of my jewellery because I'll end up losing it. She may be right. I hate to admit it, but she is so often right. At times, Amira wears the two gold bracelets I gave her. Mostly, though, she doesn't.

I open the bedside drawer. What I am looking for is not in there. My reading glasses, my diary – I must have left them by the wash basin. I fold back the cover and sit on the edge of the bed staring at the blank wall. I push my feet into a pair of velvety slippers. They envelop my mottled skin that stretches over lumps that have deformed my knobbly feet. Shoulders slumped, I go into the bathroom, unable to straighten my hunched back, with its sore, pained muscles. I use the toilet, flush and pull off my stained underwear.

I halt on seeing my own reflection. The face in the mirror doesn't look too well. I suppose I am not. I am a frail woman with bony shoulders. Pretty, perhaps, in my youth, I now feel washed out and hollow. Stone-grey eyes, with swollen lids sitting in pink crests, glare back at me. Snowy hair with no volume nests over a messy head, giving it the appearance of a sack. I try to keep it neat, braiding it tight. The strands spindle loose and smudge like ashes against my forehead. Coconut oil is rubbed into my scalp, the fragrance slightly bitter and helping to tie my hair in a knot the size of a walnut. A birthmark speckles my neck, ringed with lines. In the dim evening light, I memorise the features of my face. The fair skin on my cheeks and under my chin jiggle. Lips dry and thin. A proud looking nose. Several milia dot the dark circles under my eyes, which appear darker each day. Bright are the gold studs that glint in my saggy earlobes. I'm not a young girl. I am fifty-five years old.

What am I doing in the bathroom? Was I looking for something?

Sometimes I leave the house and forget what I went out for, or I switch on the television with no recollection of what programme I've just seen. Of course, I can't admit any of that to Amira, who has noticed that I am forgetting things more frequently now. No longer just misplacing my jewellery and my reading glasses. Once, I left grocery bags at the back of the car for hours.

The milk had turned sour, the ice cream had melted. I didn't say a word when the thick veins in her neck pulled hard like wires. I don't remember going to the supermarket. I don't remember buying anything. I wanted to cook korma, the way Amira likes it with coconut and poppy seeds. The raw chicken sitting on the counter for too long had turned bad. A feast for flies, and a little bit for the stray cat that's moved in with us.

I pinch the dirty underwear between the tips of my fingers and go back to the bedroom and hide them behind my pillow. On the wall, there is a string with clothes pegs holding photographs. Some of them are curving at the edges. I pick one at random of me and Amira. We look so happy sitting in the kitchen eating breakfast. I have trouble remembering that we ever were so carefree. Next to the pictures the board says Life Story Work. It shows different range of foods, music, literature and locations. I go through the list of dishes. Korma, saag aloo, tandoori chicken. Titled tracks of Qawwali songs, Urdu books and poetry, Bollywood films. Lahore, it says in big letters. The name of the city in Pakistan in which I was born followed by a map of Inverness with an arrow pointing to the Highlands. I read the collage again. The props are familiar, filled with forgotten memories. Is this my life, my story? I don't know. I feel as if I am floating, lost from the existence that belongs to me. My mind settles on the memories that sum up *my* life the way it used to be. Some I know, others flutter away like butterflies.

Edging closer, I glance at the pictures again. Looking back at me is the face of a child. Chestnut brown eyes. I recognise the Kashmiri features: aquiline nose, high cheekbones. Could this be Amira? Riding a bicycle, strolling along the windswept beach collecting broken seashells. Playing in the garden with sticks and rocks wearing wellies and a yellow raincoat. I remember a pair of wellies leaving a trail of sand and mud over our kitchen tiles. I don't remember the raincoat. There's another picture of a dashing looking man. I feel like I ought to know him. With a thick moustache and jet-black hair, he is leaning against an apple tree, in an orchard. What's that handsome Hollywood actor called again, Daniel Day-Lewis? That's him.

The moon throws shafts of silver through the gap in the curtains into the gloomy world that surrounds me. The curtains ripple and a draft of the summer breeze slips through. The wind howls over the trees in our garden, the trees sway over the pond. I don't like these awful sounds, they keep me awake. Howling like screams from a grave. It reminds me of something bad, very bad. I mustn't think about that. It's the one thing I must forget and yet I cannot. Grief latches onto me. My chest feels heavy. I step back, feel the wall against the knobs of my spine. I know I shouldn't chew at my nails. Amira stopped asking about the pink flesh visible around my nubs and replaced her questions with sighs. I can't tell her the reason I bite my nails.

* * *

The bed squeaks each time I turn from one side to the other. My skin is clammy with sweat. I look at the digital clock. The bright red colour shows 02:38. After a while, I look again. 03:06. I try to go back to sleep, but I can't. I roll onto my side, then my back, then to the other side.

The dream I just had twists like worms inside my head. I need to jot it down so I don't forget. From the desk drawer, I take out my reading glasses and my diary, the black leather smooth against my dry palms. I push on my glasses and turn the pages at random. I use coloured bookmarks in my diary to jump back and forth in time. The yellow bookmark placement marks a lot of joyful memories, reminding me of my summers spent at sea, walking along the shoreline. The blue bookmark section mentions numerous arguments I had with Amira. There's a lot of sorrow and a lot of pain in the pages. We disagree. We never agree to disagree. I turn to a grey bookmark. I have a lot of grey bookmarks in my diary among which I've written down the web of dreams troubling me.

In my dream a distant, familiar voice calls for me. Leaving the house barefoot, I go outside and pass the rose bush in the garden. A sharp sensation prickles my skin, holding me back. The spine of a stem is outgrowing like tusks. It's clutched onto my leg and I shake it off, leaving behind withered leaves. I push open the gate and enter a mossy track that leads me straight to the misty graveyard where a tombstone sleeps beneath a yew tree, its branches stretched out like claws. They reach for me with their hooks. Grab and pull me towards the open grave. I do not want to look and yet I do. A blackened corpse rises from the dirt, eyes hollow, hair thinned and flaring in the wind. It is rotten and has been dead for decades, but still it comes to life most nights in my dreams. It looks at me and cackles, saying the same thing over and over. *Now look. Look what you did to me.*

Wednesday, 21 August 2019

An echo crawls through my bedroom. It sounds like laughter coming from downstairs. I'm fully awake now and look for my reading glasses. They are not on my desk, not on the shelf, or on the stand next to the chair. Without them I can't read the newspaper strewn across my bed. I need to go through the headlines. I don't want to miss anything that's been written about her in the papers. It was front page news for a long time. It screamed at me from every street corner. Everyone wanted to know how it happened, who did it. It was unexpected and sudden. A '*tragic accident*'. I still keep some of the old news clippings in the box in my wardrobe.

Tossed into the bin basket is the journal Amira gave me. She asked me to keep track of what I do every day. *What do I do every day?* Every day is becoming more unfamiliar.

The journal is for taking note of the amount of fluids I drink in a day.

No, it's for drawing.

Or perhaps it is to record the number of times I visit the bathroom in a day. That's what Nisha uses her journal for, under doctor's orders.

I'd ask Amira again what the journal is for, but I try to avoid confrontation. Nisha says that's because being confrontational is inappropriate in Asian culture. She avoids it with her own daughter, too. But I remember an ill-mannered skinny girl with dark skin and button-black eyes calling Nisha silly and careless in front of others without showing trace of guilt or shame. If I am to believe the blue bookmark of my diary, my own daughter is no different.

Wasn't I looking for something . . .? What could it be? I walk around searching the room.

'—Ouch.'

I feel a stinging in my foot.

I look down. Caught between the knots of the rug is a small metal screw. I pick it up and place it on the bedside table. Could this belong to the hinges of my glasses? Where *are* my glasses? I look across the desk, open the drawers and empty the contents of my handbag onto the bed. I move the coins, receipts and scrawled pieces of paper, among which I find a set of keys. No, that's not it.

My glasses are sitting next to a pile of books on the bedside table. The lenses are dirty. I clean them against my nightgown. The left temple is slightly bent and the hinges are loose. Where is the screw? I had it a second ago. I am sure I did.

Never mind.

I adjust it so that it fits snugly behind my ears. Now I can read the headlines of *The Inverness Courier* scattered on my bed. One of the headlines is highlighted in bright yellow marker.

Woman killed in a hit and run. A 52-year-old Scottish woman was struck and killed while crossing a road near Beauly.

That's not far from where we live.

Amira doesn't like it when I highlight articles in the papers. She wants me to stop worrying about the terrible things happening in the world. But I can't. What if something were to happen to her? The fear of losing her terrifies me. On my left palm I write, *get today's paper.* I must jot this down so that I don't forget to ask Amira.

I need to know if they have caught the killer.

I look up and see Amira standing in the hallway, letters from the post in one hand. She stares at me as if I were a ghost.

'Are you alone?' I say. 'Who's there with you? I heard laughter. Voices.' I try to look past her, but she blocks my view. Now beside me, her hand rests on my arm.

Her expression turns into a cloud of confusion. 'No one is here.' She looks over her shoulder. To assure me that she is right and I am wrong. 'Are you hearing strange sounds again?' She raises her voice even though she's right next to me.

'I am not.' I look at her, but she is busy examining the post. 'Anything for me?' I notice my name on one of the envelopes.

'No, nothing,' she says while opening a letter.

'Are you sure? Because that one has my name on it, see, it says Afrah Malik. That's for me.' I point at it.

'It's nothing.' Amira opens another addressed to Amira Khan. I don't think she has noticed her surname is wrong. 'You can't go about looking the way you do,' she glimpses at me and smiles. 'I'll iron your shalwar kameez.'

'What's wrong with what I'm wearing now?'

'Ami, you are still in your nightgown.'

'And, so?'

'Well,' she smiles again. 'I thought that today I could help you to a shower.'

She knows how much I hate taking showers with her hovering over me, telling me how to apply soap and water on my skin. I don't want an argument. It makes me feel disoriented. Too often, I lose my words.

'Are we going somewhere?' I ask, and suddenly feel as if I'm the child here. 'Because if we are I'd like to make a stop at the super-market first.'

'No Ami, we're not!' She puts the sheaf of mail on the table without a glance. 'You've got to stop buying things and ordering Tesco Clubcards. It's the third in a month.' She waves the white sheet of paper with my name on it.

'There *is* a letter for me then.' I say. Amira's cheeks flush, she doesn't reply. I look at it closely. 'I've never ordered any Clubcards from Tesco.'

'Never mind, I'll prepare your breakfast and—'

'What did you want me to do again?' I ask.

Amira's nostrils flare. I smile tentatively, wishing I could wipe away the cold line between us. Too much time has passed to know when it began to form or if it was always there to begin with.

'Ami, perhaps you should go to the stimulation therapy group.'

'What sort of group?' I feel my face shrivel up like a raisin.

'I told you before, it's a special treatment that will improve your memory.'

'Mimi, there's nothing wrong with my memory, thank you very much.' She cringes. She hates it when I call her by her nickname.

'You are forgetful.'

'No, I'm not.' Silly ladki, why does she tell me I am forgetful when I am not. She thinks I am senile. That I am losing it.

'You don't remember things the way you used to. You need to exercise your memory. Write things down much more.'

'Says who?' I remember things, I remember them fine. 'You need to exercise yours.'

'Ami, sometimes medicine isn't always enough. Give the therapy a go.'

'If Pakistanis heard I was going to therapy, they would think I have failed. They'd think I'm mentally ill or, even worse, they'd say I've gone pagal – mad.'

Amira frowns.

'It will be our secret,' she says in a low whisper. 'Promise.'

'What secret, Mimi?'

'No one will ever need to know you're getting treated for your condition.' The tone of her voice remains adamant. Why does she insist I should go into therapy and what does she mean by my *condition*? Does Amira think I am pagal? Being a little forgetful is normal and doesn't mean I should expose it to the world. The next thing she'll suggest is that someone else should start to care for me or that I should be sent away like Nisha to one of those places far, far away that no one ever visits.

'Therapy isn't for people like us, Mimi.' I know of no immigrants who are in therapy. 'It's what the goreh do. White people! Why else did that woman report me to the social services? She thinks I'm pagal. Wants me gone. I'm telling you.' I've seen that woman watching me. She lives across the road. What's her name again? She used to look after Amira when she was little. Now she never speaks to me.

'Ami, you were wandering around the neighbourhood in your nightgown at six in the morning pulling on other people's door handles. Mrs Nesbit came out because she thought you were acting shifty. She was trying to help. And besides, we don't know if she was the one who called the social services. It could have been anyone living on the street.'

'I wouldn't have gone out if you weren't keeping me locked inside the house all day.' I don't think I've been out in months. 'I'm not pagal, Mimi. Do you hear me? I'm not pagal.'

I'm facing Amira's back. Her hair is twisted into a rope, black strands falling loose. She walks, her posture rigid, breath heavy, and without turning around she motions for me to follow her into the kitchen where I take a seat at the table. Feeling exhausted, I glance at the clock on the wall. It's nearly eleven-thirty. What was I doing until now?

A crusty slice pops up from the toaster. Amira puts it on a plate in front of me, slicks it with butter and cheese. But I never asked for it. The cupboard opens, cups clink and teabags release a dense herbal smell. Nothing fragrant. Amira wouldn't want to make me Kashmiri chai. She says it takes too long.

'No, it doesn't,' I say. 'Just add milk, pink tea leaves and cardamom seeds.'

'What's that?' she puts on the kettle, doesn't meet my eyes.

I shake my head. A plate of jalebi would be nice. Chewy and sticky, and dunked into cold milk. The other day, Amira bought mithai. I can't remember what the occasion was, only that it was special, and that I strictly wasn't allowed to eat it. But I did. I'll never forget the feeling of shame and humiliation when she caught me picking barfi from the box like a child.

She swivels around, conducting a culinary orchestra. The pan is crackling and plates are rattling. It smells buttery. She's making herself fried eggs and baked beans. Licks her fingers while eating it hot from the pan, and moves her hand to pour hot water into two cups, one she places on a coaster in front of me. I don't touch the toast she's prepared me. Instead I take out a peeler and knife from the drawer and reach for fruit from the basket.

Sticky apple skin scatters onto the table. I smack my lips, drying the sweet juice from my mouth, wondering if it's Pink Lady, Gala or Honeycrisp.

Amira turns towards me with her hands on her hips. 'What's this now?'

'Try one, it's delicious.' I say giving her a piece. 'It's definitely a Pink Lady.'

She glares down at me, doesn't take the apple. Heat rises to my face and I feel stricken into shame. What did I do wrong?

'Please don't do that.' She cleans the table with a cloth. 'How many times have I said not to leave a mess when you eat. Yesterday you left sticky mango peel everywhere. That's the reason those flies keep coming back into the house.' She moves the plate closer, which I stare at with distaste.

'I don't want cheese on toast.' I push it away. 'I want to eat fruit.' Or dried fruit from the jar she keeps hidden from me. I take whatever I can get from the basket. Green and red grapes, purple plums, and pile them in front of me. 'Silly ladki.'

Her arms cross over her chest and something tells me that we've done this many times over. I think her patience is running out.

'Ami!' Her voice is laden, shoulders broad. 'I know you have a sweet tooth, but . . .'

Do I have a sweet tooth? I am not sure.

Her mouth is still moving, lips twisting into a curl, but the sound muffles in my ears. She's waiting for me to say something, but all I can think of are the ripe bananas sitting in the fruit basket with brown patches on their skin, perfect for a fruit chaat. I wonder if we still have the sauce from the Asian market? Amira must have put it away. Where I can't see it. 'Where's that sauce for chaat? I had it the other day.'

'What?' Her pupils go wide. 'Did you actually hear what I just said?'

I adjust the glasses sitting on the tip of my nose. 'Say that again?'

'I'm not going to repeat myself.' She steadies her breath, maybe to calm herself down. Why is she so upset? Her face swells. Now *I* feel upset.

My palms flatten against the table. The veins under my skin bulging. Wiggle once, wiggle twice. She's shaking her head, looking down at my fingers. Heavy blows of sigh.

'If you carry on like this I'll have you wear gloves.'

'White ones like the Victorians?' I smile.

She doesn't return my smile. 'Such a bad habit. It needs to stop, OK?'

'You make me feel so bad,' I say.

'Me?' her forehead crinkles.

'Who else?' I look around. It's just the two of us.

'I don't, Ami.' Her eyes are bright. She shakes her head lightly. She seems sure.

'You make me feel awful, like I am a bad person.'

She makes me feel like shit.

I pull back my left hand and notice the words written in blue colour on my palm.

'Mimi, when you go out can you get me the newspaper?' I eat a handful of grapes and peer out the window. A bird with white cheeks is sitting on the branch of the tree in our garden, craning its rufous neck.

'I bought it last week and it is still in your bedroom, remember?' she says the last word slowly, as though I have difficulty understanding it. But I don't.

'I want to read *today's* paper.' I say and rub out the ink smearing my palm. 'Get it.'

'I told you many times. What you get is the biweekly newspaper.' She brings the cup to her lips and slurps the tea slowly. Curls of steam dampen the air. 'Should be enough.'

'But,' I pause and draw in a deep sharp breath. 'I need to know if anything has been written about the young girl. The one who went missing after that terrible accident.'

The incident still has an effect on me. A part of me is screaming out to forget, to let go. Another part of me needs to know what happened to her.

Amira's face turns dark red. 'I will not be going out to get the newspaper. I have so much to do. Laundry, hoovering, dusting. Scrubbing the bathrooms.' Her tone is clipped. 'I do everything around here. And your bedroom, Ami . . .'

'What about it?' my feeling of shame surges once again.

'It smells,' she creases her forehead. 'And needs airing.'

Badtameez ladki. That's not the way to speak to your mother. 'That's not necessary.'

I remind myself that Amira cleans the house often, too often. I told her to leave my bedroom the way it is and not to move anything around. I don't want her in there going through my personal belongings. Removing my clothes. I'd be ashamed if she finds my underwear. I don't want her to know they're stained with pee.

'Spring cleaning is overdue,' she says. 'I was hoping to go through all that clutter you've been hoarding. I want to clear the boxes in your cupboard. They have been in there for years. What do you keep in them anyway?'

'Nothing,' I coil my hand into a fist and stare at her. 'Nothing that should concern you.' But she never listens and urgently speeds around with that noisy hoover, up and down the stairs, plastic bag in one hand. God knows what things of mine she's thrown out.

'You must keep precious things in there since you insist on holding onto them.'

'It's no business of yours, do you hear me? Stay away from *my* personal belongings. You have no right to toss anything of mine away.'

Face towards me, she watches me with caution, as though she's a child about to get smacked by its mother. Her arms fold over her chest. She seems a little hesitant to be asking me the question. 'I have been meaning to ask, the stack of newspapers in your room . . .'

'What about it?' I furrow my brows.

'Can I get rid of it, please? You've marked every single headline in yellow. It's rubbish.'

Amira's own bedroom is neat and tidy. Books in alphabetic order. Folders and pens properly arranged. A colour-coordinated wardrobe of clothes, sliding the hangers along one by one. White shirts, followed by grey then black. No wonder she thinks my room is a mess.

'What? No,' my words come out in a mumble. 'Did you know a speedy driver ran that poor woman down? Did you? She was around my age, fifty-five, and it happened right by our neighbour-hood.' What was the name of the town again?

Amira laughs, shakes her head.

'What's so funny, Mimi?'

'You are not fifty-five, Ami. You are seventy-five. It's your birthday soon. I've booked your favourite restaurant, Anaya. Shafi said he'll be there.'

What is she talking about? 'I'm not seventy-five, silly ladki. Get me the newspaper.'

'Are you still playing detective.' She looks at me with a careless glint in her eyes.

'Searching for a fictional story about the young girl that went missing?'

Fictional. It's not fictional. 'Yes, I am.'

'Don't know where you read it. I've still not heard a thing in the news about it.'

My mind goes blank and I forget what I was saying. I look at my daughter for some kind of clue, but her expression is cold. 'Say that again?'

'Why do you keep newspapers? Her voice has risen louder than I have ever heard it.

'Because I want to.'

'You must have had them for years. All stupid little stories highlighted in your stupid little yellow marker,' she mutters.

'So what, Mimi?' I wring my hands. I'm not entirely sure why we're having this discussion. 'What's so bad about it?' It is clear to me that she is the mother and I the child.

'I don't see the point! The articles feature people dying a horri-ble death.'

'No, they don't.' She detects the trace of anger in my voice. 'I need to know if there's news about the young girl. She was only fourteen. It was a terrible accident.'

'Yes Ami.' She rolls her eyes as if what I said makes no sense.

'Don't get why you even read such a load of rubbish.' Amira's words begin to slur like a pearly white line of froth on a windy beach. Time stands still, dissolves my current existence as waves wash up old memories. I dive into them, swim through the lost ocean of my mind where I discover another version of myself. Back then I was different. I was respected, a woman with integrity.

Sunday, 8 September 2019

Today I will cook Amira's favourite dish, korma, which I haven't made in a while. I'll also prepare some tandoori masala and then go buy the chicken fresh from the butcher. Where to begin? Where are the canned tomatoes and all the fresh herbs? I need garlic, ginger and turmeric. Rice – I need basmati chawal.

The room spins. I've lost my way. Why am I in the kitchen? What could I possibly be looking for?

'Mimi, where are you?' No answer. Where could that silly ladki have gone again? I open the cupboards. My fingers push the plates, glasses and cups around. Where has she put all the masalas? She always puts things away where I can't find them. My head goes dizzy, my vision blurs. I bend over and turn to the freezer, yank out the drawers. Thick pieces of ice scatter across the floor.

'Where are the samosas I made and filled with mincemeat and peas?' A loud beeping sound disturbs me. I lean against the door to the freezer, it shuts, kills the annoying sound. 'Why are there none left? I am certain I made a whole batch the other day. Teacher Sahib, are you listening?' Of course he isn't. I laugh. Silly me. My husband is not here. Nadeem has been gone for decades.

I take out the vegetables from the fridge and begin to chop them with a sharp knife. Steam rises in the large pot simmering with water. How did it get there, and what should I do with it? I turn around to find something to toss into the pot, anything to keep the water busy. What's this, dhal? I fidget hesitantly before turning back to the gas hob. The blue flames rise. How do I switch it off? My hand shake violently as I turn all the knobs from one side to the other. How do I turn the oven back off? Never mind. I'll leave it for the tandoori chicken to roast.

I cup the vegetables, chunky, not fine, and throw them into the pot, keeping my distance. Half get wasted on the floor. I wave my arm and something breaks, the sound of shattering. It's the tea mug. I squat to pick it up, a piece of sharp glass cuts my finger. Blood streams down my wrist. I pull out the shard stuck in my finger and suck the tip, which leaves a taste of bitter metal in my mouth. I hear a noise coming from the hallway. Keys rattle in the lock.

'It's only me, you OK?' The front door slams shut and I jump, my heart racing inside my chest.

'No, I'm not OK. Who is in my house?' Before I get to it, the kitchen door swings open. A woman with a horrified face comes in holding net bags filled with groceries. She drops one, then the other.

'Ami, what on earth have you been doing?' She yanks a plaster out of the first aid box.

'Who are you?' I say. 'And where is my daughter?' I push her, she stumbles and looks taken aback.

'What are you saying? 'I am your daughter.' She peels the two sheets of paper away and attempts to seal my wound.

'No, you're not,' I pull back my hand. 'My daughter is five years old and not a grown-up woman.' Blood splatters onto the floor. The cut on my finger is deep, but I feel no pain. There's an awful metallic stink. I feel nauseated.

'Ami, why don't you sit down,' This woman places her hand on my shoulder. 'How many times have I asked you not to cook anything? It's dangerous.' She switches the gas hob off and removes the pot of simmering vegetables. 'What if—'

'I didn't do anything.' The walls appear blackened and close in on me. I inhale the smell of burned wood and shiver. There's smoke everywhere. 'It was an accident, an accident!'

A hot stream of tears run down my cheeks. She regards me with a tilted head.

'Ami, calm down. Nothing happened.'

'How do you know? You're just a silly ladki.'

I begin to bite my nails. I taste raw and tender flesh. And warm blood. She says nothing. Just stares at me, her expression blank.

3

Wednesday, 15th January 1986

Dear Diary,

Today was interesting. Naima brought along colourful cigarettes hidden inside a velvet case. Purple, yellow, pink. So beautiful, so soft. I held a purple one between my fingers, giggling as she watched me light it and puff in smoke. It nearly chocked me. I kept coughing and she laughed. 'Dummy, do it this way,' she said. She took the cigarette and pressed it to her lips, inhaling and exhaling slowly. She told me they were French and that her boyfriend brought them over from Paris.

I asked her what he was doing in Paris, and she said that he goes every year with his family for Christmas. They stay in this cool château in the countryside. Naima wants to go with him, but she knows that's not possible.

Naima is so pretty and so glam. I adore her. Of course she has a boyfriend. She is good at keeping secrets and has been with this cute French guy Oliver for one year without her parents even suspecting anything. Naima slipped the cigarette between my lips and I copied her style. She looked every inch like a chic French girl. Milky white face, straight brown hair. Glowing green eyes like a cat's. I can see why boys swarm around her. And that small nose with a piercing. I wish I could have one too, but Mum would never ever allow it.

After school Naima and I went down to the beach with Oliver and his friend. He always stares at me. I look away. My heart flutters inside my chest like some crazy bird. I don't look at him. Well, I do, but when he isn't looking. It's silly really. I don't even have a crush on him. Besides, Mum would kill me if she found out I was hanging out with Naima. We didn't stay for long. It was freezing.

Naima gets bored quickly and likes to try new things all the time. She challenged us all to skinny dip. The water was ice cold. I dipped my toes and the cold rattled my skinny bones. I was not going into the water. No way! No one dared except for Naima. She's so cool. I wish I was more like her. Brave, careless.

I didn't go home after the beach. I wanted to be with Naima. We were in her room and I was admiring the dolls she never plays with. She has so many different ones from all over the world. She said she was too old to play with them now. Her dad doesn't understand she doesn't want them. Naima thinks it's stupid he still brings her one every time he comes home from his travels. It makes her feel like a little girl. She told me several times, 'Have them. Take them all.'

I looked at all the beautiful dolls. I thought of Mum in that moment and how she'd react on seeing me in Naima's house. Her face would shrink like a crinkly piece of paper. She doesn't want me coming here. Not since the fall out. I told Naima I couldn't take them because Mum would know I've been with her.

Naima rolled her eyes and pressed her cute little chin against her chest. She does that a lot, and when she does her high pony tail swishes, side to side. She said that Mum is such a control freak and laughed. Naima wanted to know if I was scared of her. I'm not! I'm not scared of my own mother I told her repeatedly. I don't think she believed me because she suggested I stay for dinner. Naima's mum was going to order pizza. She asked me if I wanted some. I totally wanted to stay and have pizza with Naima and her parents. But I also knew I'd get into trouble if I stayed longer.

Mrs Singh was going to a party or whatever. The little brat would need babysitting again. But I really didn't care. Let Mum look after her. Why should I help out getting her dressed, tidying up the mess she leaves behind? I do not want to care for her. Sometimes I think Mum likes the little brat more than she like me.

I looked at Naima and nodded.

I just knew that we were going to have an exciting time.

4

AMIRA

When I was little, I used to dream about my father. The twinkle in his light brown eyes, and the way he held me in his arms when I was born. A gratified image of a proud looking man. The only picture we have of my father was framed in cheap glass, collecting grease and dust over the years it had been hanging on the living room wall. Some time ago, I took a copy, framed it in a wood-carved frame made in India and put it on the bookshelf in my bedroom. I hung up the original on the string in Mum's bedroom. She looked at it and asked who the man in the picture was. Repeatedly, I told her: it's your late husband Nadeem. She brushed me off the way she does when switching into speaking Urdu and said in a small scold, 'Areee, don't be silly. That's not your father. It's that handsome Hollywood actor, Daniel Day-Lewis.' It didn't upset me, her words. But lately she is delivering more misery than joy.

Mum keeps forgetting. No matter how much I try for her to remember the past, it slips away in the whim of a moment. I used to talk to her much more in the hope she would remember the life we had. Nothing. Her face puts on a frown. Her words a cocktail mix between English and Urdu, where every sentence ends with, *silly ladki*. That's what she thinks of me. Amira, the silly girl.

In the picture my father leans against a tree wearing a wide-collared shirt, bell bottom trousers and platform shoes. Tall and handsome, his black moustache stretches over milky-tea skin, covered in little spots. Behind him, there's an orchard yard with fallen apples smudging the grassy ground, and others rotten in the nearby water creek.

I don't dream of my father anymore. Instead I dream of strange and vivid things. But last night as my body drifted in and out of slumber and I thrashed around, I caught a glimpse of him somewhere between sleep and wakefulness. He was smiling and waving at me from the window of our house while I stood on the other side of the garden fence. I wanted to go to him but I didn't. I was terrified of the ghostly girl beside him, who looked just like me.

The lamp by my bedside table casts a pool of light on my tea which has turned cold. I am too tired to get up and make myself another. Lately, I've been sleeping in. Mum has been to check on me for the fifth time possibly in the last ten minutes. She said she is bringing me a refill but she keeps forgetting it. What she didn't forget was to bring me breakfast in bed. A bowl of dried fruit, which means she either found the jar I've been keeping from her or she went out and bought some more. I have little or no patience with her lately.

I never suspected matters getting worse, not even when she started wandering around the house late at night, opening and closing the doors, checking on me as I lay half asleep. I would see her shadow and pull the duvet over my head when she'd ask for random things. 'Mimi, get up!' I hate it when she calls me that. It reminds me of the good girl she wanted me to grow up to be.

'She took my bracelets,' Mum was shouting. 'We must go to her house and get them back. Hurry now and get up.'

I have to accept Mum's behaviours about her jewellery. She says it's a woman's security in times of financial crisis. She insisted I have two of her gold bracelets, the pearl maang tikka, and the gold necklace with matching earrings. She wore them when she married. I don't think I will ever wear any of it. Maybe the large nose ring to make up for the fact that she never allowed me to have my nose pierced. 'Ami, who took them? No one was here.' Forced to get up, I looked for her gold bracelets. 'See, they are right here, in your bedside drawer where you left them.' She ignored me and delved into her own little world in the way she does. I imagined where she was in her mind, imagined a sad memory or perhaps a fabrication like the story about the missing girl she talks about. Mum keeps secrets. Sometimes I wonder what it is from her past that she isn't telling me.

When picking up Shafi, Haroon would bring it to my attention again and again. He told me Mum seemed unwell and suggested she see another specialist for check-ups, and even recommended a new one. I told him it wasn't necessary. I didn't want him to think she was deteriorating. It was then he looked at me unbelievingly. I should have known not to lie.

I couldn't bring myself to tell Haroon I took Mum to see the specialist he had recommended in the beginning. I had taken along my own research on dementia. The specialist asked me kindly to put the papers away when suggesting treatments that were effective. I felt stupid when he said I should consider seeing a therapist. 'Being a carer is stressful. I've seen many suffer more than the patients.' He thought I was incapable of caring for my own mother.

'There's a memory loss clinic next to the hospital,' said Haroon. 'With a new ward. No one would need to know she's been there. Why don't you take her next time? Dementia causes depression, high blood pressure, strokes and heart attacks, and you wouldn't—'

'Thanks, but I think I am capable of making decisions on my own.' I felt pressured. After missing several appointments, in the end I swallowed my fear and decided to have Mum assessed. Nothing has changed. She still forgets things and it's getting worse with each day that passes by.

'Sorry, I didn't mean to interfere—' Haroon squinted, trying to remember more about it. 'Make sure she has a hobby. Something that keeps her busy.' I told him how she enjoys to read the newspaper and follows a story about a young girl who went missing. Mum gets obsessed with things easily. It's her way of being in control of the pieces of her life she is forgetting.

I shrugged, didn't raise my eyes to look at Haroon when he asked how *I* was doing. He gave me the name of a site recommended by a friend of his family and said I should speak to someone, join an online chat forum for carers. I am glad I did or else I wouldn't have connected with Meena.

Meena looks after her father. She quite often confesses she doesn't always know how to react when he pushes her around, telling her what to do in his demanding voice. She also makes all of his appointments with doctors, clinics, specialist. Cleaning, shopping, cooking. It's exhausting. I share her frustrations. I don't think it's any easier caring after one's father. Although, I wish I had known mine.

Laying here in my bed, I close my eyes and imagine my father in a way that is similar to how I used to dream of him. He is strolling next to a teenage version of me, pushing a buggy down the street where we live and wearing clothes to the time and era as in the framed picture on my bookshelf. Long hair flows around juvenile features. Well proportioned with broad shoulders, he carries an air of self-esteem like he knows exactly who he is. He's tall, and wears a moustache under his nose, the ends curled upwards, tips shaped into round loops. Dark sideburns shape his smooth face, on it a gentle expression. Warm and protective, his arm is curled around my shoulder, and I stop to stare at him with amazement. Honey-sweet inhales and exhales from brown arched lips, I smell his breath. But that's not what's startling. It's the familiarity of his face underlined with distinct features.

The sun, shot high in a rich blue sky, is free from traces of clouds. Trees are alive, air lush with a million things tingling all around. There's a sweet smell of strawberries, moist grass and wet earth. There are colourful flowers and buzzing bees. Petals rise from the ground and sway in the wind as if they were kites. Children are laughing and screaming in the playground across the street. Cars with rolled down windows spill out loud beats of music as they drive by. An elderly couple walking their dog are watching everyone and everything. And mums, normal-looking mums in summer dresses and sandals, chatter amongst themselves along the pavement. They nod when they see us coming. He stops pushing the buggy and tells the child nesting inside the cocoon not to suck on its thumb. A short pudgy woman with wide hips wrapped in a pink apron and plastic slippers says, you all right, Nad? My father nods, his gait a notch faster as we pass by.

My father smiles calling me '*meri beti*', my daughter. He died when I was young, and whatever memories I had of him are gone. I wish I had known him and that he was alive. It is odd that I think of him on mornings like this with such love and longing. I can hear Mum calling out for me. The images in my mind dissolve. I don't want to get up. I want to dream a little longer.

5

AFRAH

I'm wearing a green sari, laughing at a joke someone is telling on the television. My gold bracelets – three on each wrist – clink while I eat pickled mangoes and wait, the main meal still sizzling hot on the plates. The front door creaks open. I hear rain sweeping into the hallway, splashing the floor. Five o'clock and he saunters through, impeccably dressed as usual. Compact and sturdy, his tall figure underlines the slightly wide belly protruding beneath his tight shirt, a sign of good homemade food.

He likes to walk twenty minutes to and from the school where he teaches. He takes off the silk tie knotted around his collar, puts his velvet coat on the rack, and asks what's for supper. Bushy eyebrows knitted tight, there's a trace of tension that I suspect is down to hunger. Before I can reply, the phone rings. I don't want him to answer it. Straightening his back, he picks up the receiver. Now, it will take another twenty minutes.

I scrape the food off the plates, place it back onto the pan and switch the stove back on. I've been meaning to tell him to buy a microwave or gas hob. Maybe when he gets that pay rise next year. He's mentioned before that I shouldn't be sewing clothes for other people. He wants me to do an English language course. But I don't mind sewing. I make my own clothes from the fabrics I brought with me. Silk, chiffon and cotton. Mother had said Scotland is a cold country: 'You'll need to wear cardigans in summer.' I didn't believe her, but she was right, as mothers often are. She packed wool and linen into my suitcase. The season for wearing chiffon and cotton will soon come.

We don't sit and eat at the dining table. Instead, we have our supper in front of the television and huddled over the coffee table, metal plates perching on its edges, brushing our knees. I bring in a plate of samosas filled with mincemeat and peas, and tell him I made another batch and stored in the freezer, ready to snap and eat some other rainy day. But he's not bothered and talks instead about the extra hours he does on the weekends, tutoring children with learning difficulties.

We also eat the hot cumin lamb skewers with coriander chutney that I made the night before. Delicious, he says, popping another one into his mouth. With a napkin, I wipe away the sauce from his moustache. He touches my wrist and the bracelets slide down my arm. He asks if the sari I'm wearing is new, says that the parrot green colour looks good on me. 'No,' I say, smoothing the pleats. 'It was a gift from my mother when I got married.'

Before leaving Lahore, I was teaching orphan girls in the Madrasa and didn't have the time to doll myself up. Now I make it my duty not to look a mess when he comes home from work. I keep the house tidy, but it's not my husband I worry who'll complain. He's not one of those men with high expectations of his domestic wife – presuming all I should be doing is his cooking, cleaning and ironing, and that when he comes home food should be ready to be served.

He's perfectly happy eating beans on toast, and said I shouldn't spend hours preparing traditional meals for the two of us. Fish and chips would do just fine. Growing up in Scotland, I suppose that's what he's used to. I, on the other hand, crave the street food from Old Anarkali. I want to eat bun kebabs and parathas filled with coriander and spices while seeking shade from the scorching sun.

It was after coming home early from the Madrasa one day that Father asked me not to go next door that afternoon. I was to go straight into to my room and stay there and wait for Mother. I didn't ask why, lowered my head and went in without looking back. The sweet aroma of Kashmiri chai and jalebi trailed behind me. I could hear voices, low whispers from the sitting room. The clinking sound of teaspoons against saucers.

Moments before Mother came in, I heard her calling the servant – telling him to run down to the sweet shop and pick up a box of mithai. She told me to get changed and come down to the second sitting room, which is bigger than the first sitting room, and used only for rare occasions to cater for important guests. My heart started to pound. I knew this meant that a boy was interested in seeing me. He was the second. Last year the first had been a librarian who saw me come in one day to borrow books. My parents had rejected him. Not only was he not Kashmiri, but also from a lower caste. I never went back there to borrow books again.

I changed into my finest white cotton shalwar kameez, re-braided my hair tightly, the plait flowing down to my hips, and lined kohl onto my lids, making sure it didn't smudge. I stood outside, sweat coating my forehead as I listened to Mother say, 'She also sews very well. She made the kurta her father wears.'

There was a long silence. Then a female voice asked, 'Can she cook all the traditional meals?'

Without hesitation Mother replied, 'Of course,' and lined up my favourite dishes. Korma, saag aloo, tandoori chicken.

I had to stop myself from laughing. I was seventeen and had just learned how to perfect rotis – no more squares or triangles. Small round flatbreads straight from the tandoor. The list of dishes I still had to learn to cook suddenly seemed long. I entered the room: three unfamiliar people were perched on the other side of the coffee table, their eyes casting looks of approval. One pair of eyes lingered longer – hazel brown, on fair skin, along with a thick moustache and jet-black hair. A sharp nose on a youthful face with noticeable masculine features that was now turning red. He wore a green shirt and brown wide leg trousers. When I crossed the room to take a seat next to my parents he cleared his throat. I was aware of his gaze, his curiosity, as he was of mine, sealed behind the shy girl I was in that moment.

A long awkward silence hung in the air, and I must have only been in there what seemed like a short while, inhaling the soft tinge of his spicy aftershave, before Mother had asked me to return to my room. I did what I was told, trusting my parents, never questioning their decision. Not even when they informed me I was to spend the rest of my life with this Pakistani man in Scotland. Nadeem Malik.

It was only days before the wedding invitation went out. The Mehndi ceremony was big, crowded with relatives and giggling unmarried girls admiring the pattern tinting my hands. I had signed the marriage certificate in what used to be my parent's bedroom, as they had slept in separate bedrooms for some time. I had long nails and plump lips coloured in bright red, and my body was tangled into an embroidered maroon lehenga. My hair was pinned up high in a tight bun circled with flowers. A gold-plated pendant necklace with red stones decorated my neck, and matching earrings hung heavy in my earlobes. Kashmiri women don't get their noses pierced so I agreed to wear a fake nose ring. My wrists wore six gold bracelets that clinked as I repeatedly wiped at the humidity that polished my face. The bracelets were a present from my parents. I had cried on departing their home, knowing that my life was about to change forever. I was no longer Afrah Bhatt, but Afrah Malik.

After dinner, I get to the dishes. Like a true teacher making sure his student does her homework, I hear him pull out papers from the drawer in the living room. He calls for me, and I stop, my hands covered in sudsy foam. Water dribbles from the tap. He says the application for the English language course is on the dining table, adding: 'Don't forget to fill it out first thing in the morning, Afrah Bibi.' His footsteps move across the hallway and up the stairs. The bathroom door creaks open and shuts. I hear the heavy clunk of the lock twisting. I'm surprised he calls me Bibi, another word for wife, and I do like the way it sits on his tongue with a sweet accent. It makes me feel like a respected woman, a woman with integrity.

6

AMIRA

Friday, 18 October 2019

I wish my life could be normal again.

Last week Mum slipped out of the house without me noticing. She forgot the name of our street and which house we'd lived in our entire lives. The elderly retired officer who lives across the street brought her home. Mum was apparently shouting, 'Let go of me, let me go, you silly old fool.' She tried to bite him.

I've been in denial about her situation, *our* situation, for years.

'No, Ami,' I said. 'No one is talking. No one thinks you're crazy.'

'Who will marry you now, Mimi? People don't marry girls from defected families.' Her conviction shocked me.

I push the memory out of my mind and sit up to check my laptop for any incoming messages from Meena. We've not chatted this week and I am anxious to talk to her. I've deliberately not told Mum about Meena. Mum has always disapproved of my friends.

When I was young, I used to sneak out to see my best friend without Mum knowing. It was such a thrill. The excitement of doing what I wanted when I wanted.

I sigh. No new message from Meena. I put my laptop away.

'Mimi, what are you doing?' Mum asks climbing up the stairs. My bedroom door screeches open. Mano's ears are sharp. He leaps from the bed with ease while Mum stands in the doorframe and watches him disappear, a frown on her face.

She comes in and strangles the space between us and mumbles unrecognisable words in her Urdu dialect that I can't make out, because lately she has started jumbling up the words. Mum and I find ourselves speaking two different languages these days. I talk to her in English and she will sometimes answer back in Urdu before switching back to English again.

She draws back the curtains and gazes back at me.

'How many times must I tell you that the stray cat is not permitted to sleep in your bed,' she says in a scolding voice. 'Look, he leaves his hair everywhere.'

'Will you please make sure there's food in his cat bowl?' I fail to control my annoyance. 'Do not feed him any of your leftovers. The dry mix is in the pantry, top shelf.'

'Why are you sleeping so long today. Are you too lazy to get up?' She opens the window. A cold draft wafts through and rattles the frame.

'No, Ami.' I cross my arms over my chest.

'Then what's the matter?' Coming closer, her icy hand smacks against my forehead. 'Is everything OK with you?'

'I just told you, I'm tired. I want to sleep in.'

'Can I bring you anything?' she smiles. 'A nice cup of Kashmiri chai?'

'No Ami, I don't need anything,' I say as patiently as I can.

She looks at the bookshelf in silence. Her gaze fixes on the wood carved frame. I can tell by the glassy look in her eyes she doesn't recognise my father. 'Why do you keep picture of that Hollywood actor?'

'You gave me that photo, don't you remember?'

She shakes her head. 'Areee, don't be silly, Mimi.'

Every day, it becomes harder to be around her.

When I was little, she'd wake me up in the mornings and hum Urdu songs she'd learned from the cassettes she played. She would massage my shoulders before loosening my braid and brushing my hair with long, sweeping strokes. She floated back and forth with ease when she'd draw the curtains to let in the daylight. I would watch her admiringly, listening to the familiar clanking sound of gold bangles from her wrists. She was a beautiful woman with fair skin and an oval-shaped face, with a thick, black braid that sloped down the narrow back that still frames her thin figure.

She would fold over my cover and brush my legs. Her fingers lingered in search for the spot under my calf that is my smooth scar, which she'd then rub gently with freshly slicked coconut oil. I've had that burn mark for as long as I can remember. Mum says she doesn't know how I got it. Perhaps this routine was carried out to help bring back an old memory. She'd then give me a smile, telling me it was time to rise and shine. I don't get to see that part of Mum anymore. The idyllic image of her past self is long gone and replaced with a woman I do not recognise.

Mum detects my irritation and chooses to ignore it by nudging me roughly with her elbow. My patience has reached its peak. I think I'm going to lose my mind.

'Why you in bed?' Mum says, again 'Get up. Late. Very late. Almost night.'

'Ami,' I look right at her. 'How many times have I said—'

I fall silent. Mum fidgets, bringing her nails to her mouth and biting some more. It pains me to see her do it. I don't make a comment. I've lost count of all the times I had to stop her from biting her nails.

The silence draws like an invisible line between us.

'OK, OK,' she says. 'For supper, I make your favourite dish. Korma.'

'Ami, no! Don't attempt to cook when I am not in there with you, OK?'

'But you like korma, Mimi. I make it for you.'

'I'm not going to eat it so don't bother cooking anything, please.' I can't remember how many times I've told her korma is not my favourite dish. But she keeps insisting it is.

'Where did you put my poppy seeds and the cumin masala powder?' she arches her brows. 'Always putting things away where I can't find them.'

When I checked on Mum yesterday, she'd left a bundle of fresh coriander and mint leaves half chopped on the cutting board.

44

Dirty dishes lined the sink and mincemeat sat smelly and grey on the counter. 'I was only making a batch of samosas for lunch,' she said. 'Rest to save for rainy days.'

Thank God she didn't have another attempt at the gas hob. I still don't get how she managed to put it on that day. She has forgotten to switch the hob off, leaving pots and pans to burn, which is unusual as fire makes mum nervous. The extra smoke alarms I had installed were of no use. She pulled them out of the ceiling to muffle the loud beeping sound. I found her sitting in the kitchen chair quietly looking out the window with no reaction to what was happening around her as if a part of her brain had stopped working. She simply went numb.

'Please Ami, there's no need for you to cook. I'll order food from the curry house.' I reach for my phone and pull up their app. I ignore her. She hates takeaway food.

'But why pay someone when I can cook? And God knows what things they put on the food. Tasteless spices and dry herbs. No!' she swipes at my phone. 'No need to order takeaway.'

'What would you like to eat? How about pizza or—'

'Yuck!' she sticks out her tongue and screws shut her eyes tight.

'Fine,' I don't look at her. 'Aloo palak, veg biryani or dhal?' I keep the choice limited to vegetable dishes.

'Then order me chicken tikka, extra hot, OK?' she snaps. 'I don't want the firangi version without any proper desi flavours, so disgusting.'

'The doctor said you should be cutting down on meat. What do you want instead?'

She folds her arms over her chest. 'I want nothing,' she says, and strides out of the room.

7

Friday, 14th March 1986

Dear Diary,

Mum says dinner is ready and is calling me from downstairs. I'm not hungry. I don't want to eat yesterday's leftovers or any of the other traditional Pakistani dishes she likes to cook. Korma, saag aloo, tandoori chicken are all mum's favourite foods. Just one time I told her I liked the Korma she made and now she thinks it's my favourite. But it's not. I want scream in her face:

'WHAT ABOUT MY FAVOURITE FOOD?'

I can hear her panting like an angry bull. Mum does that sometimes to show me she's close to exploding. 'Don't let the food get cold,' She says and leaves the door to my bedroom open.

I hate having my bedroom door open. It is too loud with the little brat around. Why isn't she back at Mrs Singh's? Mum uses me to babysit the little brat, but since I told her I am very busy with homework, she looks after her herself.

I can smell the strong spices and it makes me feel sick. What I really fancy is a burger with fries from McDonald's with a large chocolate milkshake! That's what Naima sometimes eats. Her mum never cooks. They order take away most days. Chinese noodles and prawns, pizzas, kebabs with mint sauce. They have a large kitchen with a bar around the island where they sit and eat. It's so cool. I love eating at their house. They always have cola and other fizzy drinks and one of those big American-style fridge-freezers with buckets of ice cream.

When Mum found out I had eaten pizza at their house she went mental, and I know why. I wish she hadn't done what she did to Naima's mum, it's sooo uncool. I mean, who does that?! Mum thinks I don't know what she did. That I am just an ignorant little girl.

'Silly ladki' she calls me. She would never call me by my real name, she doesn't like it. She told me that she had picked such a beautiful name for me but Dad decided to change it. Mum's got me a nickname and I hate it.

'I like it, Ami,' I lied. 'Call me whatever you want to. I'll be a good girl.'

She smiled then and began humming. There was this look in her eyes that believed me. And just for a moment, I almost felt bad for lying to her.

Tonight, Naima wants to take me to the cinema and watch Thelma & Louise. She said her mum would drive us there and pay for everything. She'd even pay for the popcorn and a bag of pick and mix sweets. I told her to meet me around the corner of our house after eight so Mum wouldn't see their car.

I know, I'll have to be very careful not to get caught when I sneak out.

I wouldn't want Mum to go mental again.

8

AFRAH

Saturday, 26 October 2019

Creases gather on Amira's forehead. She's waving her hands rapidly in front of me.

'Hello, Ami? Answer me,' she shakes my shoulders. 'Are you there?'

'What's the matter?' I swallow a clump of air. 'Did something happen?' I wipe sweat from my forehead. My heart is pounding. I had a dream. Somebody called for me.

'You've been blank. Are you awake or dreaming?' Distress draws across her face. 'Not the first time it's happened. But you don't remember, do you?' Amira glares down at the main article in the newspaper strewn in front of me. 'Promise me you'll stop reading the garbage they write in the papers, OK? It's messing with your mind.'

I think I was reading about the young girl who went missing. It was front-page news. Everyone said it was a tragic accident. The police, the investigators all say she is probably dead. I turn the pages. Where is the article? It's not in here. Gone. How can it be gone?

'Mimi, have you read anything about the fourteen-year-old girl?' I ask.

'Yes.' She grabs the newspaper without even looking at me and chucks it into the bin. 'Nothing has been written about it in here. It's pure fiction, something you must have read in an Urdu fairy tale. Do you get that?'

I go blank. Feel the flush of embarrassment of not remembering what we were just talking about. I don't tell her that. She'll start telling me I am forgetful. But I am not.

48

'A little boy nearly drowned in the lake in our neighbourhood,' she says. 'Terrible, can you imagine?'

'Oh yes, yes,' I say. 'Just terrible.'

'You used to go there with Shafi all the time. We've not gone out in days. If only the rain would stop. It's time I took you for a walk down to the beach again. What do you think?' Her voice is kind and patient. She appears to be in a good mood.

'No, it's too far.' In my mind, I see the broken seashells that she used to collect and store in her silver tin.

'It is not,' she smiles. 'We were there last weekend, remember?'

I don't remember when I last went out. I feel like a certain kind of madness has come over me, as if I have been locked inside this house forever.

Looking down at my left hand, I'm trying to make out the smeared words drawn onto my palm, that I think I wrote this morning. I remind myself: I do this so that I don't to forget to ask Amira to get me what I need. I can still just about make out the words.

'Mimi, listen . . .'

Amira is not paying attention. She is buzzing around the sitting room searching for something. I can hear a beeping sound, and it is getting louder. She looks underneath the sofa, shoving the stray cat to the side. It meows and strides out, grumpily.

'Bloody hell, where is it?' she hunches over to move the pillows about and sighs. The beeping stops.

'Badtameez ladki,' I call out. 'Listen to your mother, now!'

'What's the matter?' She's not looking at me but at the device glued to her hand. One of her fingers swipes the screen while she nibbles at a shortbread biscuit. Crumbs dust the coffee table, but she doesn't sweep them away.

'Can you get me the newspaper? I want it, I want it now!' If only I could remember the story I was reading. Something, some-one. Someone is missing, presumed dead.

'We talked about it – do you recall me saying you get it biweekly?' She throws me a look that makes me feel like a dotty old village woman. 'The answer to your question is no.'

I bite my lip hard to stop it from trembling. 'Silly ladki, when have I asked you?'

Amira looks away as if I don't exist. She walks right past me to the kitchen and comes back with a cloth to clean the crumbs from the table. Then she takes the tin with the shortbread and puts it in a drawer. I say nothing. I sit there, feeling the way I do when I'm around her. Redundant. She frowns at me like a wolf tormenting a lamb. What does my daughter think of me?

'Don't worry about me. I'm perfectly capable of going out and buying whatever I need for myself.' Hot tears spill over my cheeks.

'Ami, please! I'll switch on the telly so you can watch the news, alright? No need to be so dramatic.'

There's no point in switching on the television, I can't remember the programmes I watch. I keep the newspaper because I can highlight the articles to jump back and forth between stories in a sort of makeshift timeline, as I do with my diary.

'I don't want to watch the news.'

'What *do* you want, Ami?' she asks.

'What I want is, I want . . .'

She watches me go quiet again.

Wednesday, 30 October 2019

The armchair makes a creaking sound when I shift and adjust myself to a comfortable position. I turn the pages of the book in my lap and highlight words as I read. I forget everything almost instantly. I try to read the words once more. But I am distracted. I hear a voice – a child's voice – coming from my memory, flickering by like a flimsy film. I listen to the tapping of footsteps getting closer. Then, someone is standing right next to me and leans in close, jabbing a finger at my arm.

'Nano, tell me one of your stories, pleeease.'

'Not now Shafi,' I turn the page in my book, marked in bright yellow. Why don't I remember anything I've read? I start all over highlighting the sentences again and again.

'Oh, but pleeease?' his voice is louder than before and he tugs my arm hard, but I pull it back, continuing to mark the page in a yellow mess. 'Pleeease, Nano. Pleee—'

'Fine,' I say. 'Stop saying pleeease, please.'

He smiles, elbows resting on the arm of the chair, his little chin cupped in his hands.

And so I leave the rest of the pages unmarked and place the book on the tufted ottoman. I start the tale about a boy named Joseph with eleven jealous brothers who want him dead. Halfway through I forget what I had been saying. Is Joseph a prisoner, a prince or both?

Shafi remembers things.

He picks up on the smallest detail, reminding me that I've been retelling the same stories to him ever since he was a baby.

'Joseph,' he says, 'was the prisoner who became a prince. Just like in the tale of Aladdin.'

'Who is Aladdin?' I ask. Shafi scratches the wrinkles on his nose and watches me suspiciously.

'You were the one who read it to me from *One Thousand and One Nights*.'

'No I did not. Never mind.'

He wants me to continue with Joseph. But I can't get back to the knit of it and feel utterly lost in the tangled wires of my mind. Hot flashes tighten the muscles in my face and sweat dapples my skin.

'It's not your fault, Nano.' His sleeve wipes my face. 'Mum and Dad say it's because you're getting older, and . . .'

Silence.

'And what?' I look for clues as to why his chin is now glued to his chest. 'Wiser?'

'Are you going to die soon?' he asks in a low murmur.

'Who told you that?'

I tilt his chin up to gaze at him. A handsome boy with typical Kashmiri features, he watches me with a steady look, lashes long and curled. I stroke the thick hair sitting heavy on his head, and pull the strands back behind his ears. His cheeks are rubbed red.

'You are, aren't you?' He shrugs, doesn't look at me. 'Going to die soon.'

'Look at me,' I smile. 'I'm alive now, am I not?'

'I never want you gone. I want you to stay with me forever.' His arms curl around my waist. Soft fingers clutching tight. 'Let's go down to the lake. Pleeease, Nano. Pleeease.'

Unclutching his hands, I nod. 'Stop saying pleeease, please.'

'Let's go, now, now!'

'Not a word to your mum about this or she will have a go at me.' We have our secrets from Amira and she doesn't like it.

He gets dressed. Wears his wellies and yellow raincoat, and waits in the kitchen, his coconut brown eyes boring into mine. 'Promise you will never leave me.'

'Promise,' I say, sniffing at the flicks of his black hair that give off a soft smell of jasmine. The front door unlocks; keys rattle followed by the clack of heels.

'Ami?' I hear Amira call out. 'Are you in?'

We head out through the backdoor, giggling.

'Hurry Nano,' he whispers. 'Or Mum will notice we're going.' Several steps ahead of me, he walks out the garden gate. I slip into my cardigan and twist the chador around my neck. A strong wind blows in from the east, shaking the trees. The gate swings wide open then shuts against the fence. I close the door and turn around. There's no sign of Shafi.

I fetch the door handle and suddenly it's hot with curls of steam. I take a step back. I look back at the house and it is blackened and smouldering. It falls apart, the ashes turn to dust. I breathe in smoke. It fills my lungs. I can't see. The smoke has blinded me. 'Somebody help!' I shout.

'Ami?' Amira opens the door. Her expression weary. 'What are you doing outside? Who are you with?'

She looks suspiciously over my shoulder. No one is there.

'Were you doing that thing again?'

Twitching irritably, she stands rooted in the doorway, arms crossed over her chest.

'What thing?' I push right past her.

'Talking to yourself, having one of those moment where you go blank.'

The door swings to a close with the shift of her foot.

'What?' Shafi wasn't here? 'Don't be silly, I did not.'

'Ami, you were talking to yourself.' There's a coldness to her voice. 'Don't deny it, just admit it.'

'I wasn't. I was . . .' I look behind her. Every brick of the house sits in its place. My home is right there. It's not gone.

'What?' she demands.

I don't think we've ever been this distant. We used to be mother and daughter. We used to laugh with Shafi.

'Where is Shafi?' I ask.

'He doesn't live with us,' her words are curt. 'Shafi lives with Haroon now.'

'When did this happen?' I'm oblivious of the black hole in my memory.

'You saw him in Anaya, your favourite Indian restaurant. Don't you recall? We celebrated your birthday.'

She shows me the pictures on her phone. I am dressed in my finest shalwar kameez and am wearing gold earrings and bracelets. There's a cake with lots of candles on it. I nod but don't remember any of it.

'How is he?'

'Shafi is busy doing an internship over half term. He was sorry he couldn't stay long. He came to give you this.' She passes me a card.

He's written me a poem. I read it to myself in low voice. It's about a boy and his grandmother going down to the lake for an afternoon picnic, and it's beautiful.

'I never knew what the two of you were up to,' she says. 'Sneaking out the back door, thinking I didn't notice.'

'You read it?'

They all said Amira would have a girl when the edge of her kameez flared up revealing a protruding belly. But I knew when life began forming inside the dark cave of her womb what she was having. I miss his smile, his charming dimples like the marks left behind from fat fingers pressing into dough.

'Shafi did, and it brought tears to your eyes.'

'How old am I?' Fifty-five, sixty? I'm a grandmother to a little boy.

'You turned seventy-six, Ami.'

I stare blankly at her. 'No, I didn't.'

'Yes, you did. Ask Shafi if you don't believe me.'

'Why doesn't he live with us?'

'It doesn't bother me that he's decided not to live here anymore. He is thirteen – too old to share a room with me. It got cramped and the sofa was giving me backaches.' Her expression turns dull, her shoulders heavy.

'But you should have insisted he stayed.'

'How could I keep him?' She pushes back the tears rolling in the corners of her eyes. 'You know how teenagers are. He's far better off living with his father. Now, can we please stop talking about it?' She stomps out of the kitchen mumbling, 'I'm not a failed mother.'

Thursday, 7 November 2019

I take the newspaper. The fresh smell of ink uncurls from the pages when I open it. I can't read the headlines. The words are blurry. 'Mimi, have you seen my reading glasses?'

'Why don't you try your head?' Her voice is charged.

'Oh, I see.' I pull down my glasses and my vision improves.

Night-time trouble caused by rebellious group of teenagers. I begin marking. There's another headline. *Growing concern over missing person with links to Inverness.* There's a picture of a handsome looking man in his thirties perhaps. No mention of the young girl. She's been gone for too long now. Something bad happened to her. I know it did.

Amira gets three different plastic bottles from the shelf. 'Here, take your medicine.' She places a pile of pills on the table in front of me along with a glass of water. Amira is emotionally detached. Lost in a world of her own.

'What's this for?' I push the pills away.

'Stop pretending you don't know,' she snaps. 'I'm sick of telling you things over and over. What's worse, you don't appreciate anything I do.' She snatches the newspaper.

'Give it back, it's mine! Give it back.' My stomach drops. 'I never ask you to do anything for me. You only do what you like.' I take the paper out of her hand.

'Sod it.' She presses at the points of her temples. 'What were you doing outside this morning? Tell me, were you attempting to drive off again? A little trip to the shop, perhaps?' There's a level of panic in her voice. 'What if someone would have seen you or reported you again for strange activities. Ami, we can't risk anything. Do you understand?'

'What are you talking about? I was not trying to go anywhere. I've been in here. Locked up in this house FOR EVER.'

Hands on hips, she takes a deep breath. 'I had to get you because you were pestering the neighbours. Were you bothering Mrs Nesbit again? Because if you—'

'Silly ladki, whatever you're accusing me of it wasn't me.' I stick my tongue out.

Amira is shouting. I cover my ears and face the other way so I don't hear her.

'Ami.' She turns me around pulling my arm. 'I am speaking to you!'

'You are hurting me. Stop it, you're not my mother.'

'I feel like I am losing you.' She releases her grip around my arm.

Why is she so upset? Face all swollen like a balloon. The cat comes in. He curls his tail around my leg. 'Are you hungry, stray cat?'

'And stop feeding Mano. He is not a stray and gets sick from what you give him. I suggest you throw your breakfast out if you don't want it.' She looks at the untouched plate of food sitting on the table. Then moves her looks towards a bowl littered with fruit peels.

'Who is Mano?' She pretends not to hear me and turns away as if setting sail and slipping into a deep blue sea. I wish she wouldn't go too far. I wish I could be her anchor.

'Mimi?' She doesn't turn around and leaves the kitchen, banging the door shut behind her. The thud makes me shudder. Where did she go? Will she be back? I feel anxious and throw away the pills, not knowing what sickness it is I'm suppose to be curing myself from. I call out for my daughter several times. But there's no answer. Then I hear heavy steps thump up the stairs and a door slam shut.

I hear the clock on the wall. The dial makes a mechanical sound. Tick tock, tick tock. It's three o'clock. I don't know how long I've been sitting at the kitchen table or what I've been doing all day. A table, four chairs and all sort of electronic appliances. A microwave, a gas cooker, a blender and a kettle. Everything arranged in its place. I glance at the gas cooker. It's off and I want it to stay off.

There's no sun in sight, only clouds. It might rain soon. It often does in weather like this. Before it starts pouring down, I should go out. Perhaps pay Nisha a visit. We both enjoy eating mithai and I could get a box with barfi and ladoo for us to share while having tea on the terrace overlooking the garden and the line of birch trees growing on black earth. Or perhaps they're pinewood on brown soil? I don't remember.

It's eerie where Nisha lives. The path from the house leads into the gloomy heart of the forest. The horizon, long and lonely, has dark shadows travelling over the quiet hills capped by mist. I could be imagining things, but I may have seen a red stag, majestic and broad shouldered with button-blue eyes roaming out there. Or I may have seen two or three, or more. Ten, twenty. A flock of hundreds.

Nisha is the only friend I have. She said she doesn't get many visits. Not from her daughter, especially. Her son shows up sometimes with his bundles of children wrapped in red and yellow striped scarfs, whatever trend that may be. The occasional postcard arrives from an exotic holiday that she hangs up on her wall among drawings of butterflies and sailboats with faded colours. She doesn't have a board like mine that says Life Story Work or pictures of her family. Nisha says her memory is *just fine*. Except, sometimes she doesn't know who I am. I wonder if she's happier living in the new home? I wonder if she stopped feeling like a burden to her family?

Looking down at my wrists, I notice they are bare. I can't visit Nisha without wearing my bracelets. She'd tell me to get myself one of those big, broad bangles Indian women wear in the heaps of bridal magazines she keeps. Nisha likes to spend hours talking about jewellery. My days of grace and beauty are over. I was a bride long ago, and have passed most of what I had on to Amira. Along with the bracelets, necklaces and earrings, I gave her a large nose ring – no piercing; it's strictly forbidden for Kashmiri women. Amira doesn't respect the views I hold onto about our customs and says I didn't used to be traditional. But she doesn't understand that traditions keep our culture alive.

Other traditions like food are rooted in our belief and customs. She doesn't respect that either, and makes me cheese on toast even though I don't like cheese on toast. When I was young, I'd have roti for lunch and rice for supper, wrapped up nice and cosy in my pashmina chador and blanket. I sneak in dried fruit when she isn't around. Doesn't make me fat. I'm still tall and slender, and even Nadeem wondered how I maintained my figure with a sweet tooth. He's been gone for decades, but his name still echoes in my ears like in a Bollywood movie – nothing romantic or anything like that, just intimate and silent. Like a series of bookmarks, I want to go back and forth in time through the pages of my life. Be able to remember events. Some spindling memories are still waiting to be born, while others are buried in the graveyard of my recollections.

The stray cat strides across the floor with an arched spine.

'Poor slob, we still haven't given you a name. How about Mano?' He purrs. I think he likes it. I get up and open the bread-basket. I take one slice of toast out and pop it in the toaster. When it's done, I spread it with butter and a slice of cheese and take a seat at the table. Mano quickly jumps into my lap, nestling with ease. He purrs along to the strokes from my fingers. I give him some toast and look at the gas hob. My heart starts pounding. I want to, I don't want to. I shouldn't attempt to cook. Things could catch fire. The cat glares at me and meows. 'Are you hungry? Me too. I don't think I've eaten anything today.'

9

AMIRA

Sunday, 10 November 2019

Something wakes me, jerks me out of my dream. It is the sound of wind seeping through the open window. The pillow is damp, and I know I cried myself to sleep last night after pouring my heart out to Meena. I just can't take it anymore. Mum's getting worse. Sometimes, I wish . . . I erase my thoughts. I shouldn't think that way. Meena calls it 'immigrant daughter syndrome'. And she is right. I feel guilty. I could spend my entire life trying but I will never be able to repay Mum for all she's given me. I'm her daughter, her carer. Mum needs me.

Meena told me to rest and recover. 'How will you care for your mother if you don't look after yourself first?' she said. And she's right. I check my laptop for new messages. At midnight, she wrote: 'Night, night Amira. Sweet dreams.' I must have passed out right before.

My eyes feel swollen and my head hurts. A fever, hot and tender, pulses through my body. With one hand, I push myself up from my bed and prop myself up on my elbow. I slept badly and dreamed of being with Haroon. He was lying beside me in bed, hand touching my growing belly, listening patiently as I complained for the hundredth time how many times I visited the bathroom in a day. I told him about my cravings for sour and spicy foods, foods with lots of ginger, lime and garlic. Feeling a kick, he pressed his hand firmer against my stomach and smiled, a glow in his eyes.

'That's one hard punch!' he said. 'Does it hurt?' I shook my head and looked down at the sheets, where a solid streak of brownish blood signalled the birth of a new change to enter our lives.

My dream isn't just a dream, but also a vivid depiction of how my life used to be before Shafi was born. Down to the smallest detail, I still remember the studio flat we rented above a loud restaurant – the only place we could afford close to town. Cigarette smoke smudged the windows, and men in button-down shirts and straight pants chattered endlessly in Italian as if they were bored old women hanging about in an empty cold square, only their 'square' was the restaurant's empty outdoor seating area above which I used to stare out. In winter, Christmas activities and festive decorations would light up the streets, which saw scarves and hats of all colours carried through it, the cobblestones icy with clattering steps.

Weak and tired, I try to swing my legs over the bedframe, but they don't budge from their stubborn position. I call out for Mum, but there's no answer. The house is quiet, she tends to sleep in on Sundays. I adjust the pillow, letting my head sink back into its warmth. I throw a glance at the clock against the wall. The minute hand is stuck on twelve, tick-tocking back and forth. Haroon used to be the one to fix things in our flat. He changed batteries, set the clocks back and forth twice a year. Since I've been back living with Mum, I do everything.

My heart flounders from the dreams and memories stirred by my fever. Haroon busy with his finals, me sitting first-year exams when unexpectedly one day two pink streaks lined the blank spot of the pregnancy test I bought from the pharmacy, certain that no one would recognise me. Impatiently, I went into the nearest coffee shop I could find to use their loo. I was shaking while peeing on the stick and still shaking as I left with it clutched between my fingers. It was a coincidence that Auntie Nazia ran into me on my way home.

'How are you, beti? Everything OK with Mum?' The test slipped and she bent down at the same time as I did to hand it over. 'How's studying going? You done giving exams?' I could tell by the way she was stalling the conversation that her gaze was fixed on the two pink lines. The whole time Auntie Nazia threw her questions at me, she wasn't actually looking at me, but at the positive pregnancy test. I told her I had to leave. By the time I got home Mum stood waiting for me in the hallway. Eyes puffy, tears running wild down her face.

Gossip travelled fast among Mum's friends. Of course Auntie Nazia rang her straight away to inform her how worried she was on seeing me today. By the colour of my face, a sickly yellow, she knew that I was sick, as in, pregnant sick.

I remember how hysterical Mum was.

'Who is he, what is his family background?' she demanded to know.

I didn't bother clarifying any of the questions and told her I didn't know and didn't really care. She tugged my shoulder back the moment I tried to walk past her.

'Is he Kashmiri? What caste is he from?' Mum's words rang in my ears.

Then, I was screaming.

'Why is that so important?!'

These things didn't used to matter to her, but suddenly they had started to, and I couldn't wrap my head around why that was. I once read in a psychology book that immigrants can feel guilty for leaving their country. When they grow old, they tend to go back to their old traditions as atonement. Mum never raised me to care much for our culture. Not in the way she does now.

'Amira Malik, answer me.' Mum demanded how long it had been going on for. 'Has it been months or years? How long?'

She felt betrayed.

'Why do you care?' I didn't have to put up with her and talk about my personal life. What did she really know about me, about what I wanted? I grew up listening to her ideas of life as she dumped them on me and suffocated my needs.

'Mimi, I care. Now, tell me, how long have you been dating this boy for?'

I shrugged. Was I dating Haroon? It felt more like a foolish crush on a boy who'd shown interest in me and asked me to meet him down by the lake one evening.

'Do you plan to marry him?' The last sentence knocked the wind out of me. I had just started my nursing degree after a dramatic argument with Mum who couldn't understand why I didn't want to become a doctor or a lawyer. She accepted I wasn't going to rise to her expectations. And I was determined not to let her criticism doom me to fail.

There was no time for a wedding, not even a small ceremony. Haroon's fingers shook as he filled in the marriage notice. Without thinking twice, I went straight to the local registrar and said we were in a rush to tie the knot. That hasty moment in time, I remember in slow motion. Haroon standing in the registration office in a beige collarless shirt and blue jeans. Black locks, cut short, he looked nothing like a happy groom. His look was fixed on my tummy, soon to become an illustrious bump.

Mum wanted me to go back to finish my degree after Shafi was born. 'Don't you worry,' she said. 'I'll look after him. Concentrate on finishing what you started. Go back to university. You will be grateful that you did.'

It was a difficult choice to leave my newborn baby at home pretending he was a mistake. I didn't want to carry that feeling, or the feeling of being a failed mother. I refused to run away from what was my responsibility and told her that I wouldn't leave him in her care. Shafi needed me. *I will look after him myself*, I told her. She turned her back on me, didn't speak to me for days.

Wednesday, 13 November 2019

Mano is lying in bed next to me, his sharp teeth stuck on a piece of chicken bone. He is so busy gnawing it that blood and marrow spill out on the sheets. 'Where did you get that from?' I rub the sleep from my eyes. 'Did Mum give it to you?' I twitch like a spider. How long has Mano been chewing on the bone? He meows when I shove him away and leaves, tail swishing, through the narrow opening of my bedroom door. I hear a noise coming from the kitchen downstairs, and I know that Mum is in the process of making a mess. I need to stop her before matters get out of hand again.

Burning hot, my body doesn't move, doesn't get out of bed. I look for my phone and find it under the duvet. I snatch it and tap in the passcode. I scroll through my numbers and punch in Shafi's. He's not answering. I try again. *Please Shaf, pick up.* Nothing. I leave a message: 'Ring me when you get this. It's urgent.' The tip of my finger slides down to 'Haroon'.

'You need to stop calling me like this,' he said. 'We are no longer married.'

'I'm so sorry,' I said. 'But there's no one else. I am all alone with Mum.'

I plug my phone into the cable next to the bedside table. The battery is almost drained. I need it charged when Shafi returns my call. And he will, I'm certain of it.

I flip over the duvet and force my legs to move. Weak and dizzy, I drag myself over to the door. I hold onto the panel and lean against the frame. I think I smell food. I am not sure, my nose is blocked. Taking a deep breath in, I stand up straight and move into the hallway. I grab the banister with sweaty palms, my body quivering from the fever. Don't let go, keep moving. At the landing, I rail myself down the steps carefully, keeping my feet tight, toes curled as if grabbing at the floor with a hook.

'Ami?'

I hear her sing a familiar song, the sound of her voice appeasing. I smell the different aromas coming from the kitchen. A rich smell of meat, coriander and cumin float in the air and it makes me feel sick. I make it to the door and push it open. Thick smoke stands like a curtain in front of me. I can't see anything. 'Where are you?'

With arms stretched out, I reach through the smog, coughing. Wafting my hand, I open the window and call out for Mum again. I don't hear her anymore. I hear roaring sounds as if something is about to explode. I try not to panic when I see flames rising inside the oven. I get the extinguisher out from underneath the sink; a blow and the screen breaks, spitting glass all over the floor. I point the nozzle towards the fire, taking it out. I don't stop till the foam runs out. The bottle slips to the floor. I'm stepping onto pieces of glass but there's something else. Round plastic shells. Ripped wires hang from the ceiling above my head. Mum has pulled down the smoke alarm again. Where is she?

The smoke is clearing, and through the light veil I see the back-door smacking against the frame. A gust of wind slips in, whips my hair around my face and I gather the long twist of it in one hand. With the other I push the door fully open and rush outside and around the side of the house. On the front stoop, I notice a pale body undressed and shivering. It's Mum, arms hanging loose at her side. The spinal bones stretched across her back like a rope. I freeze, shocked to have found her like this. I take off the cardigan I'm wearing and push her arms through it. Her legs are covered in goosebumps. Her feet and toenails lined with mud, splashes of dirt stain her ankles. I find her chador lying on the ground, pick it up and wrap it around her.

I look up. Neighbours have come out. One of them is on the phone. He speaks in a loud voice while laughing, 'You won't believe this mate. She's gone mad. Sitting naked in front of her own house as we speak.'

'Ami, come with me,' I pull her close. 'Let's get back inside the house.'

'No,' she shoves me away. 'House burning, on fire. Flames, smoke. Come, come Mimi. We must go, must leave. Dangerous!'

'It was an accident. I took out the fire, it's OK to go back inside again.'

'Terrible accident. Do not to blame me. Not my fault house on fire.' Mum's words come out all jostled. I've never seen her this way before.

'It's alright, it's safe now.' I cuddle her, feel the beating of her heart next to mine and begin to cry. 'I'm sorry. I'm so sorry that

I haven't been able to look after you the way you deserve to be looked after. This is all my fault. If only I had been there for you and not been so dismissive.'

She wipes my tears away. I take her hand to my lips and kiss the tip of her fingers.

'Don't be silly,' she smiles. 'You are meri beti. And you don't cry. You safe. You close to my heart.'

I bring Mum back inside the house. Long curls of smoke follow me like fog. Hot air sinks into my lungs. I can taste carbon, from the charred kitchen. In the living room I place Mum carefully in her armchair. I soak a towel in warm water, and clean the mud and dirt from her feet and ankles with the towel. Her hand rests on my shoulder, it feels warm and protective.

Outside our window, I notice that Mrs Nesbit is now standing opposite holding her phone. She is gathered by other neighbours. A well put together stay-at-home-mum bouncing an infant on her hip. The elderly retired officer who never greets me in the street. Others peek through their drapes, their prejudice clear. I sense their eyes poking and staring suspiciously at me, with pale faces. I feel as if I don't fit into the narrow-minded neighbourhood I grew up in. I can read their lips: '*Bloody Pakis. It's that crazy old woman causing trouble again. And the daughter can't ever seem to control her.*'

There's no time to get my phone from upstairs. I need to ring Haroon and tell him to come to the house. I reach for the landline. I press Haroon's number. It goes straight to voicemail. I call the hospital and tell the secretary to put me through to him.

'May I ask who is calling?' she says.

'It's his wife.' Immediately, I feel stupid. 'I'm sorry. Please tell him it's Amira, his ex-wife. I need to speak with Doctor Khan right away as a matter of urgency.'

I'm put on hold, and bite my lip so hard it bleeds.

'Mira what's going on?' says Haroon. 'Is it Shafi?'

'No, it's Mum.'

'What's happened? Can you call Shafi?'

'He's not answering. I didn't know who else to call. Please. I need your help.'

'Can it wait? I'm in the middle of something.'

'No. Just come to the house. Please. It's urgent, or I wouldn't be calling!'

'OK, don't panic Mira.' There's a long pause. 'I'll be there as soon as I can.'

'And Haroon, do not tell anyone about Mum. You know what happens if you do.'

'I know,' he says in a calm voice. 'Stay in the house. I'll be on my way.'

I hang up.

'Ami, how are you feeling?' I unfold the shalwar kameez I took from Mum's drawer in her bedroom and begin to dress her.

'Look,' she says, pointing at the window. 'Blue and yellow lights blinking. Christmas. It is Christmas.'

Mum's dupatta hanging over my arm slips down.

'No Ami, it's not.' I draw the curtain and see a police car parked next to the kerb of the house. Two men dressed in uniform approach the house. One brings out a notepad. 'Don't move. Stay where you are.'

Mum covers her ears and looks at me. A distant siren that is getting closer is upsetting her. 'Make it stop Mimi!' she cries. A fire engine pulls into the road and halts next to the police car. Mum takes my hand, lowers her head and shakes it. 'PLEASE. Don't leave me!'

'I'll be right back. Promise.'

'No! Please, don't go. Pleeease. Pleee—'

I tug her close to calm her down. 'I'm not going to go anywhere. I'll stay right here next to you. Alright?'

'Promise you will never leave me.' she repeats, clinging to me.

The doorbell rings. Mum is still not letting me go when I tell her I need see who's at the door. I stroke her head with gentle

66

movements and tell her I will be back. She squeezes each one of my fingers hard, and I let her.

Haroon's car pulls into the driveway. Nadia is in the front seat and Shafi is at the back. Another car is parked behind Haroon's. I recognise it from last time it stood in our driveway. The same woman who has been here before from social services gets out. And she isn't alone. She's brought someone else with her. It's John Buchanan from the Carers Support Group. I don't want any of them to see Mum like this. But it's too late. Soon they'll all know how I failed caring for my own mother. They'll judge me and say I am not good enough.

I pick up the dupatta from the floor and set it around Mum's shoulders. She slumps back into the chair; her body suddenly seems lifeless. I want to tell her I am terrified. I don't know what's going to happen to her.

The doorbell rings a second time. I open the front door and am met by the unsmiling faces of the policemen. I show them into the living room and leave the front door open for Haroon and the rest to follow.

Mano jumps into Mum's lap. She strokes him and begins to hum the tune of a familiar song she used to sing for me when I was a little girl.

10

AFRAH

'Where are we going, Mimi?'

I don't think Amira is paying any attention to what I'm saying. 'Are you listening?'

Flurries of rain whirl in the car headlights. She drives off the highway and takes the left lane, long and winding, where the trees stand like burned sticks thrashing against the wind.

'Huh?' Fingers clutching the steering wheel, she bites her lip. 'Don't worry.'

'Why do you say that?' Now I am worried. Above us, giant ravens fill the ink-coloured sky in plumes of powerful dark feathers, and a ridge of cold clouds rise above the morning mist. I peer out of the window. There's no mistaking it, we're somewhere rural, in the Highlands.

'Ami, you are going to be so *happy* where I'm taking you,' she smiles reassuringly. But behind her smile, my daughter reveals doubt. 'It's a beautiful place on the cliffside and close to the sea. You can go for walks and get plenty of fresh air.'

'What was wrong with the air I was breathing before?'

In my mind, I see her walking by the beach and licking the drop running down her ice cream cone. She collects broken shells.

'Nothing,' she smiles again. 'Wait and see, it's going to be—'

'Do you mean we are going on a holiday?'

'Yes, exactly. It's like a holiday,' she laughs. 'I'm taking you to a safe place, where you can rest. Where you will feel better. Like a hotel.'

She thinks I am not well. Is something wrong with me? Amira believes I am pagal. I know I am not. I bite my nails. She puts her hand onto mine and lowers it.

'Stop the car!' I shout out. 'Can't you see the dead animal lying in the road?'

She slows down. Brakes to a halt in the middle of the road. Majestic and big, a pair of button-blue eyes glare straight into my soul. The cold blood is so dark, a mucous brown dried on the black tarmac.

'Poor deer,' she says. 'Must have run blindly into the road.'

'It's not a deer. It is a stag,' I tell her. Monarch, to be precise, with sixteen antler points. Nadeem loved walks in nature. He taught me about Scottish wildlife. Eagles, wildcats and red deer.

Amira puts her foot down on the accelerator and turns the wheel. Swinging right around the mud-covered animal, she drives off at full speed. I turn to watch the dead creature shrink in the distance.

'I heard it on the news,' she says. There's a deer problem in the Highlands.'

'What do you mean?'

'There are too many of them, and accidents appear to be normal. Drivers don't even report them to the road commission. Can't blame them. You get close to little or no reception out in this isolated part of the Highlands.'

Nadeem and I had looked over at the woods, our bodies in sync with the cold earth beneath us. Ahead of us the grass grew patchy, mingled with weeds and leaves. At the hem of the woods there was a vast wilderness. A space belonging to no man. Only deer. Antlers and large unblinking, curious eyes. Nadeem looked over his shoulder. I think he wanted to say, *Look dear, a deer.* But there wasn't just one. Another appeared next to it. And another. A flock. Dozens, and more kept coming. We sat there in silence and watched the herd grow larger with each blink. Must have been hundreds. They just kept coming.

'As I was saying, Ami. There's no need for you to feel worried. Did I mention they have a garden, and right next to it there's a forest and—'

'What about you?' I try to make eye contact again, lean in closer. 'Are you not staying with me at the hotel?' I put my hand on her shoulder. She jumps, eyes still focused on what's ahead. A bleak landscape and fallen leaves scattering the pavement The grey getting closer to the mist that we're driving through.

'Mimi, answer me.' She is quiet and I lose my trail of thought. 'Have you read—'

'No, nothing has been written about a missing fourteen-year-old girl, OK?'

'Silly ladki, of course, it was front-page news.'

'This is crazy,' she cries. 'You sure it was front-page news?'

I hesitate before nodding.

Amira glares at me suspiciously. 'What happened to her?'

I say nothing and glare out the window.

'Please try to understand. I need to feel well,' she says. 'You get that, don't you? I'm only going to be better when I have some time for myself to recover from—'

I touch her forehead. It's cold. 'Mimi, you look pale. Are you sick?'

'No, not exactly,' Amira's expression fills with worry. 'Ami, it's important you try to remember what I'm about to say. Maybe write it down in your black diary, so you don't forget we spoke about it, OK?'

Amira knows about my diary. Has she read the blue and yellow bookmarked pages? Or the grey bookmarked pages? Does she know about my memories, about my dreams?

'Ami, did you hear me?' Her eyes have turned deep and dark like a cave. 'Please, it's very important.'

'What did you say we spoke about?' Amira's face is clouded with something else. Something she isn't telling me.

'This new home I am taking you to. It is going to be so good for you.'

'What home? I thought it was a hotel?' Safe, rest, feel better. The words jumble inside my head and I get a feeling something isn't right. 'Where are you taking me?'

'We talked about this so many times,' she bites her lip hard. Fingers curling tighter and tighter around the steering wheel, the webbing becomes visible on her white knuckles. 'You agreed that it was fine to move out of the house.'

'I did not.' I raise my voice. 'And will not.'

'You said you wouldn't be making any trouble.'

'Why would I do that?'

'You have to accept that you're going to live with others who have the same condition you do.'

What does she mean, my *condition*? Frustration bubbles up inside me.

'I don't know what you're talking about. I never agreed to anything of the sort.'

'You said you want to leave because you don't want to burden me anymore. But I never considered you a burden, Ami. Never. I have no other choice right now. Please try to understand.' I watch her tears drop and soak into her jeans.

The words come pouring out of Amira's mouth, but I have no clue what she is on about.

'The decision is out of my hands,' she says firmly.

'What decision, what are you talking about?' I take a deep, shuddering breath.

'You don't remember things—'

'Why are you making me do this?' I shake my head. 'I'm not leaving. Not going on a holiday. Don't want to be in a hotel.'

'Ami, if it was up to me, I'd have you stay with me. But for now, you'll have to go. There's no other solution. The lady who came to the house when you had an accident in the kitchen, do you remember her? She was from the social services and decided it's best that you be in a care home. It will be much securer because I can't always be around you to make sure you're safe.'

'I'm not going to any dumb care home.' I wipe away the tears pouring down my face. 'Please, don't leave me in a place that isn't my home. Do you hear what I am saying? Do not leave me in any

71

safe place where I must rest, feel better and go for walks on the beach. I don't want to be in a garden next to the forest.'

'It's going to be for your own good,' she says with a level of mistrust as if she doesn't believe what she's telling me. 'Nothing bad will happen to you there. You'll have people who care for you all the time. To make sure you're well looked after.'

'I don't want that. I want *you* to look after me. You are meri beti. Why can't we continue to live together the way we always have? I am not pagal!'

I don't want to leave my only daughter to live with complete strangers who have my condition, whatever that may be. I know I cause trouble because I don't remember things. But I can't help it. Memories I don't want to remember disturb me. I want to know why they disturb me and why they linger somewhere in the back of my mind. Fear is growing slowly with my denial of it all. Fear that I may be responsible for what happened to her.

I screw my eyes shut. I remember bit by bit Amira telling me something about going away while packing. The rain drummed on the roof. Amira's voice came from the other end in my bedroom.

'I've also packed your cotton salwar kameez,' she said. 'I'll leave the wool, I know how it sometimes can make your skin itch. I bought you a new cardigan, you know, something nice to go with your chador. You like wearing that and you like wearing your gold bangles, don't you Ami? I'll pack them too, and your rings and earrings. But please wear them, don't take them off or you will lose them. OK?'

'That's all very nice,' I said.

'I also packed enough warm socks, ordered a new pair of leather shoes from Amazon, which will arrive in couple of days. If you need anything else, I can always bring it when I come for a visit. We'll talk all the time on the phone. You have nothing to worry about.

'Finally, we get to go through your things,' she said, catching her breath. 'This one is heavy, what's inside?'

Her eyes penetrated mine. A curious deep look. I swelled with irritation.

'It is mine,' I said. 'Leave it.' My box filled with old memories. The only few things that reminds me of my past. Old photographs, original birth certificates, news clippings and tapes. The silver box containing broken seashells. And then there's her diary. I took it and hid it in the shed so she wouldn't find it and wouldn't write nasty things in it again. Amira can't see that. She would ask questions.

The rain was slamming harder against the glass. It knocked open the window. Wind whirled in, stirring the papers in my box. Amira grabbed the newspaper clipping that flew out. She was about to read the yellow marked headlines. I snatched it quickly out of her hand and hurriedly shoved it all back in and pushed the box back into the cupboard. I made sure to hide it at the back where she wouldn't find it. Amira said nothing. She stood watching me, arms crossed over her chest, mouth half open as if lost for words. Outside the rain came down. Splat, splat on the windows and on the roof.

Amira changes gear with one hand and with the other she wipes away the moisture on her cheeks. No words come out, but I know she's been crying. The car goes faster, doesn't turn. Doesn't swing into any street for there are none. The white smoky veil lifts and reveals the road, which is familiar. Tall swaying trees with wind-beaten branches arch to the side. I'm sure I've been down this road before. I know where it ends.

The dark forest and the misty sky close in on us. We climb the track that passes big black gates that swing open to the house on the clifftop, and the car sweeps into the drive. It's a long way up to the red brick house with two tall towers on each side.

I straighten my back, peering out towards the sea ruffled by strong winds. My breath quickens. We stop at a sign that says Ravenswood Lodge Care Home. Amira cuts the ignition, sits drumming her hands on the wheel. The engine ticks.

'We're finally here.' She looks over her shoulder. 'And look, look how beautiful it is.'

I roll down my car window. The cool breeze travels in from the coast. I taste salt in the air. Hear the slapping of water against rocks.

Yellow light suddenly floods over us from the arced windows of the house. A dark shadow is standing inside the tower on the left looking out, watching me. It disappears behind the shifting curtain. I have been here before. It's not a hotel but a house with high walls and dark panelled walls. 'Have you brought me to see Nisha?'

'That's right.' Behind the sadness there's a smile on her face. 'She lives here, too.'

Amira tells me to step out. I don't move a muscle and stay inside the car. I wrap my chador tighter around my body like it's a lifebuoy. If I leave the blow from the ocean will ambush me, sweep me right with it to the bottom of the sea.

'I'm not leaving. Do you hear me?'

The wind seeps through the car window. A blowing gale travels over the house. To the left, there's a terrace shielded in glass with benches and tables. It slopes towards the garden to the end where a pond is circled by stones. Beyond the edge of the garden is what I at first think looks like a row of giant men, but is only a line of birch trees standing shoulder to shoulder rooted in the soil, black like midnight.

'Ami, come out.' Amira turns around to face the house.

A tall, thin woman dressed in a white uniform appears in the doorway of the house. Arms crossed, she starts walking briskly our way, galloping down the steps, crossing the lawn. She stops in front of our car and lowers her head, looks in and smiles. She has an ashen face. Her skin is gaunt, teeth stained yellow. The wrinkles form hard lines around her mouth as if carved into her skin.

'Well, a very pleasant good morning and welcome to Ravenswood Lodge Care Home. We've been expecting you Mrs Malik. My name is Myrtle Brown and I'm the head nurse of our beautiful and unique care home.' Her cold silver eyes dart at me. I reach out to grab Amira's shoulder. She's already skirted round the side of car. Her hair, thick like ropes, whips around her face. She tucks it in behind her ears several times. It spindles loose like long black flames.

Amira opens the boot, removes my suitcase. I hear her chatting to the woman in white uniform with the cold grey eyes. I don't know what she is saying. The woman doesn't smile. Doesn't look at me. I roll the window back up. Through the nylon stockings tight around her milk white skin, thick green lines push out as if screaming to cut lose from her body. She tries to open my door. Yanks the handle. Holds back and smiles. I'm not leaving the car. I'm not going anywhere.

A white van with blinking lights takes off to leave through the black gates. Its wheels crushing the path, spraying stones from beneath the tyres. I watch the sharp yellow and green colours blinking at the sign. The R in Ravenswood is black and bold slanting forward like a bow, the L in Lodge is formed like an anchor. The other two words, Care and Home look like dead bodies hanging from a rope. I don't want to go in there.

Across the sky, gulls wheel in an effortless glide. I wish I had their wings. I wish I could fly.

I can see Amira gesturing I should come out. I shake my head and look away.

The morning sun throws a line of gold into the heart of the forest. The hills in the distance are embraced by the fog. Nothing moves out here except the fallen leaves dancing in the wind.

The van disappears into the morning haze and I wish I was sitting inside it. I am willing to go anywhere so that I can flee this cold and lonely place, which is nothing Amira said it would be. A hotel?

I have a feeling my daughter has not taken me on a holiday.

Nor has she taken me to visit Nisha.

Amira is abandoning me.

PART TWO
Separation

11

AMIRA

Seven days earlier

Wednesday, 13 November 2019

I tap my fingers on the mahogany desk. The picture frame on it depicts him with his wife, her long spider-like fingers curled around my son's shoulder. I've seen the same one hanging up on the entrance wall of their home – a top-floor flat that some would call a penthouse. I've glimpsed inside it occasionally, but today as I dropped Mum to be with Shafi I had a better look. The windows stretch from floor to ceiling. Outside, a balcony, its empty chairs overlooking the stillness of the River Ness.

How I used to walk along Bank Street dreaming of the day we'd be living in this neighbourhood, where misty mountains can be seen in the distance. I wasn't sure we'd ever be able to afford a Victorian stone-built house in the Crown conservation area. That perhaps we wouldn't fit in. The small place we rented above the Italian was little bigger than a prison cell, and there was always the fresh smell of tomatoes and basil coming in, and the sing-song voices of the Italian waiters made for a chaotic symphony hanging in the air. There, we fitted in. We were happy during those years we spent in our cell with Shafi bouncing between our knees while the tea kettle whistled, and hot cross buns toasted in the mini electric oven.

Haroon is on the phone. He hangs up and the phone rattles against the base. Sighing and scratching his chin irritably, he throws me a stare that reveals an austere uncertainty. 'Don't be discouraged by what I am about to tell you.' I feel as if I am one of his patients waiting for bad news. That anytime now Dr Khan will inform me I only have two months to live.

'Matters are quite convoluted, Mira. The process appears to be harder than I thought it would be.' He continues to scratch his face, moving his fingers across his cheek.

'What do you mean?' impatience floods me. 'There's got to be something you can do,' I lean forward. 'Please, I beg you. Try harder.'

'My hands are tied Mira. I've spoken to all the medical professionals I know in the field.'

'Speak to them again!' I shout. 'Get a second evaluation from someone else. Just do something. Anything! They can't take Mum away. I am her daughter, her carer. I've looked after her all these years. I know what she needs. Does that mean nothing? Are they suggesting—'

'No one is suggesting anything,' his voice is calm. 'Now, please, try and relax. You have to accept the decision that's been made about your mum.'

'I'm sorry.' I stare down at the white linoleum floor. 'I can't believe they are going to take her away.'

'The case is with social services. A John Buchanan, who you spoke to at the Carers Support Group for Alzheimer's raised a red flag some months earlier. He reported that you appeared to be under severe stress during your visit and he was worried when you never showed up again.'

'That's *rubbish*. I wasn't stressed. He asked me questions that I openly and honestly answered. That's what people do in those groups.'

Haroon pauses.

'What's the matter?'

He hesitates to tell me more. 'Never mind.'

'Please, Haroon. I need to know what you know.'

'Well, if you must . . .' he says in his soothing voice. 'Mr Buchanan believes you are incapable of looking after your mum. You told him that you feared something like what just happened at your home *would* happen, which it did, suggesting—'

'Bloody hell, nothing happened. I was sick in bed and Mum went on one of her typical cooking missions. She lost a little control, forgot what she was doing, that's all. I was there in time before matters turned worse.'

I knew I shouldn't have gone to the Carers Support Group when Meena first brought it up. I told her it was a bad idea, but she reassured me it would help offload the feelings I've been carrying around for years and help me connect with carers in a similar situation. And John. He encouraged me to speak. Ensured me the group is there to help. Confidentiality my arse. 'You know I'm more than capable of taking care of my own mother.'

'Mira, please.' His eyes rest on mine. 'It's not what I think that matters. People talk, and apparently he was tipped off anonymously by someone who knows you.'

'Who?' I curl my hands into fists.

'Do you know a Sylvia Nesbit? She contacted social services to file a complaint. Apparently, she's been filing several since early this year.'

Fuck!

'I knew it,' I slam my fists on the desk. 'Mrs Nesbit lives across the street.'

'She claims you kept your mum locked inside the house all day. And sometimes left her there alone. That's the reason she would run out and behave strangely around the neighbourhood, knocking on doors, pulling on door handles.'

'That's not how it happened—'

'Other neighbours were concerned something wasn't right,' he says. 'And after Shafi moved out there was even stronger reason to believe being in isolation and looking after your mum may not be healthy for your own mental well-being.'

'What do they know about my mental well-being?' I crack my knuckles.

'Mira, don't be too hard on yourself. Everyone can feel a little mad in a situation like this. Have you considering speaking to a therapist?'

'Bollocks,' I say, and laugh. 'Why should I speak to a therapist? I don't suffer from any sort of mental health issues.' He gives me his full attention.

'Take my advice and speak to Mr Abdullah. He's a retired doctor living in Glasgow.'

'Why would I do that?' I say through gritted teeth.

'You can trust him. Mr Abdullah is a friend of my family. His wife was a lovely Sikh lady. She also suffered from dementia and recently passed away. It helps talking to others.' Haroon spots my uncertainty. 'If you change your mind about talking to a professional—'

'I took your advice about joining an online chat forum for carers. I have a support network. I don't need to speak to any professionals. Especially not some retired old doctor.'

He expresses his apologies. 'I never meant to offend you.'

'You're the one who suggested Mum be reassessed. Said the new memory loss clinic next to the hospital could help, and everything else bundled into the dementia package that came with it.'

'Well, didn't it?'

'No!' I touch my flushed cheeks. Mum answering stupid questions over and over about what year and month she was in. She had to repeat her name and address, and then count backwards from ten. 'Those exercises made it worse. Had I known, I wouldn't have agreed to any of it. What a load of rubbish.'

'Mira, you're clearly upset. Try to control yourself. I have patients outside, waiting.'

I cover my face, suppress the tears. I can't blame Haroon. He has nothing to do with any of it and is only trying to help. I'm angry with myself. How could I have been so stupid?

'I didn't mean to. I'm so sorry. They said journaling could improve her memory. In the end, nothing did. Mum kept getting worse over time, and it's all my fault.'

He sits next to me and puts his arm around my shoulder. 'You mustn't blame yourself. You're a wonderful carer. And mother.' There's a touch of relief in his smile.

How could I have let it come this far? Perhaps I should have spoken to Mrs Nesbit, and I should have told the neighbours and people who know Mum that she wasn't well. But instead, I kept her dementia a secret, as if she was carrying a dangerous illness I wanted nobody to find out about. I was embarrassed. Felt too ashamed to talk openly how forgetful she was becoming, as if she was defective. If only I had had the courage to raise awareness, Mum would have been accepted and not rejected. Perhaps even in Asian communities where dementia doesn't have a name and mental health doesn't get addressed.

'I didn't want anyone to judge us. So I decided to keep it a secret.'

'But why?' Haroon tilts his head to the side. 'It's nothing to feel embarrassed about.'

It's like Mum said, 'The Pakistanis in our community would pass judgement. Spread lies and say her willpower has failed, or even worse, they'd start believing she is defective. Mentally ill. Call her pagal, mad. I didn't want that. I was only trying to protect her.'

'When we first met, you cared so little about what other people thought.'

'If only I had listened to Mum. Not been so dismissive of what she was telling me, then she may not have gone down to the kitchen that day. I didn't do enough. I failed her.'

'You can't change what's happened. The council wants your mum admitted. I've been told they have a place for her at a care home called Ravenswood Lodge. A patient sadly died. Your mum will get the room, and I highly recommend you take her there. It's a first-rate private facility. I was also informed you are eligible for funding support. The grant you will receive is enough to last a couple of years. You don't have to worry about anything for now. Isn't that at least some relief?'

Ravenswood Lodge. I remember the glossy brochure John pressed into my hand that day I went to the Carers Support Group. *Speak to them. They are like no other facility. They might be able to help you.* How promising his words sounded. And how stupid I must have seemed telling him everything that bothered me about Mum. He used the situation against me to take her away.

'You don't understand. Mum doesn't belong in a care home. She is not familiar with the customs. A new environment will only make her anxious.'

He swings back into his chair behind the desk. 'What makes you say that? Your mum has lived in this country her whole life, has she not?'

'She has become even more traditional now. Mum will not like it there.'

'Mira, your mum will adapt over time. Most patients do. And besides, traditional views are changing. More Asians are going into care homes. It's not the children's responsibility to look after their parents. Don't feel guilty.'

'She isn't like most patients. She's a proud Kashmiri woman. Her views about traditions and culture don't fit among—'

'Goreh, white people. Is that it?' he says stroking his beard.

I am surprised at how Haroon has neglected his cultural values. 'If anyone should understand what I am saying it should be you. Would you ever want to put your own mum into a care home?'

'From a medical point of view, I would, if she needed to be in one,' he says. 'I know this is hard for you to come to terms with and accept since you've been caring for her all these years. A place like Ravenswood Lodge was created to care for people like your mum.'

People like my mum? His words are unaffectionate. 'It's an institution,' I say raising my voice. 'A cold, clinical care home for people nothing like Mum.'

'Have you been out there, have you seen it?'

'I have.' I twitch my nose. 'I don't like it.'

'It's a very privileged place for the elderly. Beautiful, actually. Unlike any other care home I have ever seen with a rich history and traditions. And they don't only care for patients with Alzheimer's—'

'Blimey, Haroon! You know I don't care about all of that.'

'Look.' He draws in a deep breath. 'If it's any consolation a friend of my distant relatives from Glasgow now works in Ravenswood Lodge as a carer. According to her it's the best place for people with dementia. They are well looked after. It will do her good to be there.'

'What do you mean *do her good*?' I arch my brows.

'Alzheimer's is a serious brain disorder and requires medical attention. You know how lucky you are that your mum has been given a space out there? I know people who'd kill for their parents to be in Ravenswood Lodge, that's how well regarded a facility it is.'

I look out the window. It's a dull day and I think it will rain soon. I get up, help myself to a glass of water. The nurse dips in and tells Haroon he has patients waiting. She stares at me for a while, an unfriendly look. Then shuts the door and leaves.

'I need to prepare Mum for what's coming. I hope she will remember everything I tell her. Most of all, I hope she agrees to go or else she might cause trouble.'

'She will agree, Mira.' Haroon types on his keyboard. 'Your mum is a reasonable woman, strong-minded. For someone with dementia, she is still quite independent.' He stares at his computer screen, contemplating something for a minute, then skates the tip of his finger on the mouse.

'How long do I have?'

'Six, perhaps seven days.' He glimpses with uncertainty towards me.

'But that's so soon,' I say. 'They're not making this easy, are they?'

'Try to cooperate as much as possible when bringing your mum to the care home. Don't let them believe you don't want her to be there. Show that you are willing to do whatever is best for her.'

'I'll take your advice and try my best.'

What will I tell Meena when she asks about Mum? We chatted online every day when I was sick. She was so worried about me.

Haroon clicks on the mouse, gets up and takes a slip of green paper from the printer and offers it to me as if it's a precious present.

'What's this for?' I stare at him.

'It's a prescription that will help calm you down, and cope with the changes ahead.'

'I don't want it.' He shoves it into my hand anyway. Then he hands me a card with Dr Abdullah's number.

I gather my things and prepare to leave. I tie my shawl tightly around my neck. I feel suffocated – not from the soft fabric touching my skin but from all that was said. He puts his hand on my shoulder, taps it twice. I feel like that patient again who has been given bad news. News that's spreading like a bleeding tumour, killing me quicker than I can imagine.

'It's all going to work out fine, Mira.' He locks eyes with me, giving me a warm assuring look. I wish he'd put his arm around me again while he says the same words over and over.

'Will it?'

I hear the clacking of heels approaching the door and I know it is *her*, Nadia. The woman who stole my husband. A swish of air blows at me. The sweet smell of apples escapes from the corridor.

'There you are,' she says, a smile spreading on her radiant, glowing face, a marker of her pregnancy. She beckons me with her hand. 'Not to worry, Afrah is fine now, it was only a tiny cut on her finger that was shedding more blood than necessary. Don't get mad at her for nothing. You did the right thing leaving her with us. She shouldn't be alone, not in her state.'

I stare at her.

'Did you not get the message?' she says.

'No.' I pull out my phone and notice three missed calls from Shafi and a voice message.

'I am the one to blame. I allowed her to eat apples. I shouldn't have. I had no idea she likes to use a knife to peel them.'

'How would you know?' I don't bother taking off my boots. I go straight into the main hall, crossing the tiled floor, sure I am leaving a trail of dirt behind. I don't look twice at the 'wall of fame'. Pictures of holidays, happy, smiley faces. Soon there will be more. Haroon and Nadia are expecting their first child. The knot in my tummy tightens. I untie my shawl, letting air fall on the coat of sweat around my neck.

She takes hold of my arm. 'I'm truly sorry about the decision that's been taken regarding Afrah's care. I really am. You must be shocked. Poor, sweet woman. She depends so much on you.'

I turn to look at her. 'Thank you,' I smile. 'That's very kind.' I depend on her, too. I need her in my life.

'Shafi is also devastated, poor boy,' she creases her forehead, smooth as a baby's. 'He's been through a lot, hasn't he? It sure doesn't show. Don't go thinking he ain't sad. He is, if you ask me. Very sad. Now, I've been giving this some thought and if you like, he could come stay with you before,' she pauses . . . searching for my approval. 'You know . . .'

'That would be lovely. But given the situation with Mum it may not be such a good idea. She will be anxious dealing with the stress of what's coming and I'm not sure Shaf would want to be around her.' I hear the landline ring. Nadia's eyes shift and she excuses herself to answer the phone.

'Hello darling. Sorry, my mobile must be on mute . . . Yes, she is here to pick Afrah up right this minute.'

'Afrah is fine.' Nadia looks in my direction. 'Just fine now.'

I see Mum outside on the balcony standing next to Shafi. I slide open the balcony door. She points at the ducks swimming in the river. Shafi doesn't say anything. He seems happy to see me.

I go out and pull him close. He wraps his arms around me. 'You alright, Shaf?'

He pulls away and shrugs. 'Think so.'

I look over his shoulder. 'Ami, it's time to go.'

'My name is Afrah Bibi,' she says. The look in her eyes is distant.

'That's right,' I double-fold her chador around her cold body.

'If there's anything we can do,' says Nadia, standing in front of the balcony door, 'anything, please don't hesitate to ask. Afrah is welcome to come anytime she wants to visit Shafi.'

'Next time, Nano, we'll go down for a walk by the river. OK?' Shafi hugs her.

Mum whispers into my ear, asks why the boy keeps calling her Nano. That's not who she is. That's not her name. 'Tell him, tell him. I am Afrah, Afrah Bibi.'

Shafi pushes his hands into his pockets. Chin on chest, he lowers his gaze. They used to be close. No more. Not since she was diagnosed.

We step into the elevator. 'Thank you so much, Nadia, for everything.'

'Oh, you are sooo welcome.' She turns towards Mum, smiling carefully. 'Afrah? Aren't we forgetting something?'

I notice Nadia's stare fixed on Mum's wrist, bathing in a large gold bangle.

'That's not yours. It's Nadia's bangle, Ami. Give it back.'

Mum tucks it under her armpit and mumbles in Urdu, 'but she let me have it. I wasn't going to steal it. I want to keep it a little longer. Please!'

'No, Ami.' Softly, I pull it off and give it back to Nadia. Heat creeps into my cheeks; I can hardly look at her. She says Mum went into their bedroom. She opened all the drawers and took the bangle from her jewellery box and asked if she could wear it.

'I didn't want to upset your mum,' says Nadia. 'I let her wear it on the condition she would give it back when she'd leave.'

'Nadia, I am so sorry about that.'

'Don't be. It's forgotten.'

'I don't want to take more of your time,' I take courage and glance at her tummy, which she keeps stroking. 'After December, you'll be busy with . . . other things.'

She nods, delivers a soft smile. Shafi stands like a shadow behind his stepmum and adjusts his hair in a typical teenage manner. I can see why he likes her. See why he'd rather be living with them than us. Nadia is kind, compassionate. She treats Shafi like her own son, and soon he will become a loved brother.

The door shuts. I see Nadia's beautiful face one final time contorted in a true state of worry. I know she meant what she said. She really cares. I hate her for it.

Outside the building, I wipe my tears. *Busy with other things? Way to go Amira.*

Mum keeps asking, 'Who was that nice-looking lady? Will we visit her again?'

Shafi comes down, holding the newspaper. He hands it to me and smiles showing his beautiful cute dimples. I smile back and the tears become visible. He kisses me on the cheek and tells me everything will be fine.

'Oh, and Nano kept saying,' he whispers, '"Mona is missing. Mona might be dead." Who is Mona?'

I glance at Mum staring into the blue.

'Don't worry,' I say. 'It's no one.'

'Sure?'

I nod. I don't tell Shafi about Mum's obsession with the missing girl. He has enough on his mind as it is. 'Just some girl from Mum's imagination.'

'Right.' He leaves, doesn't turn back around.

'You can read your newspaper now.' I pull down her glasses sitting on her head.

'Will we or won't we, Mimi?' She takes the paper and I open the car door. She sits next to me at the front, hooded eyes fixed on mine.

I stare at her puzzled. 'What?'

'Visit your friends again?'

'No Ami, I don't think we ever will.' I start the engine and give gas to the pedal reversing the car. I turn the steering and clutch the gear. 'Why do you ask?'

'She said I could have it, she put the bracelet on my wrist. I told her I don't want it. I should have said something when she accused me of being a liar and a thief.'

'Who, Nadia? I don't think she has. You are mistaken. You borrowed the bangle from her, remember? Besides, you have yours are at home in your bedside drawer. All four.'

My cheeks are hot. I don't want to hear another word about those stupid bangles. I feel so ashamed of what she did. What will Nadia think? She pities Mum. *Poor Afrah*. I don't need her pity. I should never have left Mum with her.

'I wasn't going to take it.' Mum seems all muddled. 'Really, believe me.'

I put a hand to my chest and nod. 'Ami, listen, I have something very important I need to speak with you about, and I need you to remember it. Don't forget, OK?'

'What is it, Mimi?' She searches my face for an answer. And already, I detect the worry in her eyes. How on earth am I going to break the news to her? How will she react? She'll go mad.

12

AFRAH

Seven days earlier

Wednesday, 13 November 2019

I feel a tight sensation in my chest. I wonder where Amira has gone and why she has left me with the nice-looking lady and young boy who keeps calling me Nano. I wonder when she'll be back. I wrap my fingers around the warm cup of English breakfast tea the nice-looking lady made. She smiles at me from the open plan kitchen, asks if I am alright, if I need anything. 'Maybe you'd like a muffin, or how about a fresh doughnut?'

'I don't suppose there is any mithai?' I slurp burning my tongue. 'Hot.' I blow softly on the surface of the steaming cup of tea. 'I could really do with a small bite of barfi.'

'I'm sorry Afrah, we only eat mithai on special occasions.'

'Call me Afrah Bibi.'

I crane my neck to scan the clean space in which I find myself. There are no plants or books. A sculpture of a naked dancing woman in the corner of the room and bizarre looking figures and empty vases decorate a nearby shelf.

She brings a plate of biscuits over. I take a round piece, crushing the sweet sugary powder between my teeth.

'What is this place?' I ask.

'Would you like a tour of our home?'

She flattens the pleats of her embroidered, colourful dress. It's patterned with, not flowers, lily pads, I think. Underneath is a bulging belly. She twirls her necklace with her fingers, moves it around and around her long neck.

The nice-looking lady starts to show me around. 'Here's the guest toilet if you need to use it.' She opens the door to a white marbled restroom, which smells like lavender. The boy shepherds us around, keeps calling me Nano. I'm not his grandmother. Perhaps he says it out of respect. We go down the long corridor, where bright lights stream like glistening water over the stripped wooden floorboards and across the white walls. The door to a room is left ajar. I ask her what's in there.

'That's my room,' says the boy as he heads inside.

There's a bed, desk and wardrobe. Shelves with books and frames. An armchair in the corner with a laptop on it, which he opens and starts typing into.

'We'll leave you in peace, Shaf.'

'You sure?'

'Absolutely, come along now, Afrah Bibi.'

At the end of the corridor there's a large mirror. I stare at myself as I stride down. I'm wearing a blue shalwar kameez loosely around my body. My neck, ears and wrist are missing jewellery. I feel naked.

The door to my left is open.

'What's this room?' I don't remember if she already showed me the loo.

'This is the master bedroom.'

She is about to close the door when my hand lands on the surface. 'It's alright, take a look inside.' It's a large room with a king-size bed and velvet pillows. In the corner, there's a dressing table and a chest of drawers. I open a drawer and look inside. Silk clothes and silk underwear. She gently closes it, watching me carefully. I sit at the dressing table and she allows me to open her jewellery box. I notice a beautiful gold bracelet sparkling with pearls and diamonds.

'My momma gave me this when I married Haroon.'

I hesitate before asking. 'Can I try it?' There's this look in her eyes like she pities me.

Care For Me

'Go on then. But please remember to return it by the time your daughter comes back to pick you up,' she smiles. 'This piece is very precious to me.'

'I won't forget,' I say, and slip my wrist into it. 'I only want to try it on.'

13

AMIRA

Wednesday, 20 November 2019

'Give me that. It's mine, mine!' Mum snatches the bag and clutches it close to her chest. 'And don't touch my chador, leave it, will you? Just leave it, I said. What am I here for?' She makes a break for the door. 'You can't keep me captive. I want to go home. Take me back to my house. Now!'

'Afrah, calm yourself down,' Myrtle blocks her way, holds Mum back. 'No one is going to take your belongings away without your consent. You are not a captive here at Ravenswood, isn't that correct?' Rolling the 'r' in Ravenswood exaggeratedly, Myrtle throws a cautious glare over her shoulder. I nod.

'My name is Afrah Bibi!' Mum shouts out loud.

She starts walking back and forth, throwing things on the floor; pens, papers, books and magazines from the table. Anger draws across her face. I tell her to stop but she doesn't listen, and I'm afraid what it means if she doesn't. Meena mentioned her friend's mum was detained for being aggressive. I wouldn't want the same thing happening to Mum. 'Ami, listen,' I reach out to hold her hand. 'Please try to understand that this is now your *new* home.'

'Liar,' she raises her voice. The echo rings back in my ears. 'This isn't *my* home.' She pulls her hand from mine.

I try not to show her that I am distressed. 'You have to stay.'

Mum reaches for the door, but Myrtle slams it shut. Her sweaty fingerprints quickly dissolve from the door's surface. Mum pushes her away and Myrtle trips. 'Get out of my way, silly woman!'

Myrtle finds her footing and stands up tall, facing Mum. 'Behave yourself.'

Mum opens her mouth as if to bite Myrtle who quickly steps back. 'Did she just—' Myrtle cocks her head to the side and glares at me.

'Stop it,' I say. 'There's no better place for you. Do you hear me?'

'Don't leave me! Mimi, I will never forgive you if you leave me.'

I shut my eyes and whisper, 'You've got be cruel to be kind.' I say it over and over. I know she can hear me.

Myrtle throws me a hard, unnerving glare. 'If she continues to behave in such manners, we may have no other choice but to consider give her medication.'

'What?' I say. 'No, please Mrs Brown. That doesn't sound right, she's only—'

'There are certain things which we do not tolerate here at Ravenswood Lodge.' She flutters her lashes. One falls loose and gets caught in the corner of her eye, which she catches with the tip of her finger. 'Shouting and aggressive behaviour is out of the question.'

'I assure you Mum will settle.' I take a deep breath and focus on the positives just like Haroon said. I take a few more deep breaths and try to relax the muscles in my face. I put a smile on. 'She's just a little upset.'

'A *little* upset? What happens when she is *very* upset? We are a highly respected care home. We have rules patients must follow.' The thick line in her forehead pulses a beat. 'Our waiting list is rather long, given we are a private facility. A stroke of luck placed someone like your mother in our care. Surely you understand that?'

'I do apologise on behalf of my mother, Mrs Brown. This is a new environment for her and she will need time to get used to being at the care home.'

'I understand Afrah needs time to settle—'

'I'm not sure, do you, Mrs Brown.' I raise my brows. 'Because you're implying—'

'Of course, I do. Naturally, she is upset. But there's no need for her to be aggressive.'

'Why don't you tell her what she has to do,' I say firmly. 'She might listen.'

'Stop talking of me as if I am not in the room, Mum says. 'As though I am invisible.'

'We at Ravenswood Lodge fully understand most patients require time settling in,' says Myrtle. 'That's why we encourage—'

'Patients? I am no patient. And I am not ill.' Mum glances around.

I look at Myrtle. 'My mother has a friend living in Ravenswood Lodge. Isn't that right, Ami?' I smile reassuringly. 'Her name is Nisha, Nisha Patel.'

Myrtle clears her throat. 'I know Nisha quite well. She's been with us since early June. We've had no issues with her stay. Lovely old woman. Happy as a clam.'

'Perhaps my mother—'

'Call me Afrah Bibi.'

'Perhaps Afrah Bibi could see Nisha later sometime soon?' I feel my eyes swivel.

'I'm afraid Nisha tends to have a rather busy schedule. She attends physical therapy daily. Since her stroke, we've been working every day to mobilise her left arm and leg.'

'I want to see Nisha.' Ami clutches my arm hard. 'Take me to her.'

'Please, perhaps Mum can quickly say hello to Nisha?'

Myrtle nods. 'I'll see what I can do.'

'Thank you, Mrs Brown.'

Mum's face lights up. 'Bring me to her now. I want to see Nisha.'

14

AFRAH

Amira's eyes lock with the woman she keeps calling Mrs Brown. There's nothing brown about her. Brown is a soft, romantic colour. It reminds me of chocolate, cinnamon and other warm spices. I look at Mrs Brown. Her skin is so white, it lights up like a torch.

'Afrah Bibi,' Mrs Brown takes a step closer to face me. 'If you promise to settle in without causing trouble then you can see Nisha as often as you like, given that she isn't tired from her therapy.'

Sparks of joy rise inside me. 'I promise.'

'Doesn't that sound wonderful, Ami?'

'Amira, you mentioned outside that your mother is quite the foodie.'

'What will I be having for supper?'

The woman looks at me and smiles. 'I believe you are having chicken with—'

'My favourite dish is korma with peshwari naan.' I say.

'Oh, Ami.' My daughter giggles like a schoolgirl. Places kisses on both my cheeks and whispers, 'I will come back to see you soon. Be brave.'

'Do bear in mind we have strict visiting hours,' says Mrs Brown. 'We don't want family members meddling too much with the life patients have built here for themselves.'

'You don't have to worry,' says Amira. 'I'll stick to the visiting hours.'

'Afrah Bibi, soon I shall give you a full tour of Ravenswood Lodge and introduce you to our key staff. But first, make yourself at home. Settle into your room.'

Amira reaches for the door. I tell her not to leave, over and over. But she's not listening, and slips out of the door with Mrs Brown. A tight sensation pulses through me.

I am alone. My daughter left me.

I go to the window. Amira leaves the building and doesn't turn around. The door to her car slams and she heads off, driving down the twisty road and becoming a tiny dot till I see her no more. When will she be back? She never said.

I feel a sense of dread, which leaves me feeling numb.

I sit by the windowsill and stare at the line of trees in the garden swaying in the wind. Their flickering shadows darken the cobbled stones leading up to the house. Circled by a pool of fallen leaves, a tall and lanky man with a shovel in his hand is digging. He stops and wipes his forehead, shifts his ginger matted hair out of the way. Behind him the shrubs show a range of dahlia. Long stems hold heads of purple, red and pink. The man squats, takes out a gardening fork and ploughs it into the earth beneath him. He grabs a bundle of marigolds from the wheelbarrow, and sink them into the black soil. He stands, leans against the trunk of the tree and looks up. He watches me watching him. He gathers his tools and throws them into the wheelbarrow without looking up again.

Black clouds drift above me, hovering like death. Darkness is descending now. I cannot see the ocean, but I can feel the salty air slipping thorough the cracks of the window, the draught gently rattling the frame. I feel a gush of cold air prickling my spine. The hairs on my neck stand up, It's a strange feeling, ghostly. I hear the padding of footsteps and realise I am not alone.

'That's Liam, our gardener. Soon you'll know everyone at Ravenswood Lodge.'

The woman speaking to me is not Mrs Brown. 'Soon you will feel like you are at home.' She has a warm and comforting voice, honey-like.

I blink and level my eyes with her. She smiles at me. She has soft brown eyes like chocolate and cinnamon. Words dry on my tongue when she curls an arm around my shoulder, squeezing it softly. A light feeling sweeps over me. I am less afraid. 'Hello . . .' I have trouble finding the right words. 'Are you—'

'A beautiful good morning to you Afrah.' Her face lights up like an angel.

'Do I know you?'

The woman isn't wearing a uniform. Her clothes are colourful. Pink sweater and green trousers. Yellow scarf with flowers tied around her neck.

She shakes her head. 'I thought it was about time we get acquainted.' Standing beside me, she is tall, with a glorious air about her. Hair, tied into a tight black braid. Gold earrings glimmer in her earlobes. 'What do you think?'

'Who are you?' I feel tempted to touch her face. She has a small nose with a piercing. I hesitate. She is skinny, birdlike. Her complexion is fair with long curved eyelashes. She swishes her narrow hips to the side and sits by the windowsill staring out. Her head turns towards me.

'My name is Zahra Akram. I will be your primary nurse at Ravenswood Lodge.' She moves across the room and begins to unpack my bag. Exhaustion takes hold of me and I lay on the bed my eyelids heavy with sleep. 'From now on, I will take good care of you. You are safe now.'

I am in the dining room having supper. Chicken and vegetables. I look around and see unfamiliar faces. The light is dim, the walls panelled. This is a strange hotel, and the staff aren't very friendly towards me. No one asked me what I want. The cook comes in, a woman with a gold chain around her neck. She was here before and plated what's in front of me. But I never asked for it. She keeps looking over her shoulder, never smiles. Her hair is ginger like a cat and she has small green eyes. I don't know her name. Doesn't matter. I don't like her anyway, I don't remember why. I push my plate away. I've not eaten from it. I don't think I am hungry. She takes it and leaves.

'Are you ready for your bath?' says a gentle voice. I look at the woman with chocolate brown eyes. She notices my confusion and tells me her name is Zahra.

'I don't want a bath. I am having dinner,' I say. 'And I don't do baths. I have a shower every morning. I had one today and I do it myself.'

'I thought it could be nice if you had a bath before bedtime,' she smiles. 'It might help you sleep well in your new bed. What do you say Afrah?'

'Call me Afrah Bibi.'

The cook looks at me from across the room. Her face furrowed. No wonder I don't like her. Who does she think she is? I never wanted chicken with vegetables. I stick out my tongue to show her.

'Come on, Afrah Bibi,' Zahra pulls me gently and we go to the elevator. 'Up we go.'

'Where are you taking me?'

'To your room. You will like it.' She speaks loudly as if I can't hear her. But I hear her perfectly well.

'I don't want to go up. I want to go home.'

She pays no attention. Something must be wrong with her. Perhaps she's deaf. She takes me down the hall and into my room. I think it's the same one where Amira left me. 'Where is Amira? I want my daughter.'

'It's just me now.'

She pushes the door to the bathroom open. It's damp and there's water inside the tub. I shiver. 'From now on, I will care for you.'

'I'm not going in there,' I turn around ready to leave. But she stops me.

'Let's get you undressed.' She strokes my hand.

'I am not taking my clothes off.' What kind of hotel is this?

'Please, Afrah Bibi. You need a bath before bedtime.'

'No I don't,' I cross my arms over my chest. 'Who are you to tell me what to do?'

She begins to undress me, and I slap her wrist. She thinks I can't care for myself.

'Be nice. I am only trying to help.'

'I don't want help. I want you to go away.' I try to move past her but she pulls me back.

'Stop saying that.' She puts an arm around my shoulder. 'You don't mean it.'

I want to go home.

'Help, somebody, get me out of here!'

A woman with a pale face comes into the bathroom. 'What's the matter?' she asks in a strict voice. I know her. I forgot her name. Brownie, cookie. Something sweet. But she isn't. She is bitter and she doesn't look very friendly. She squeezes my hand.

'Ouch! Quit hurting me, silly woman.'

'Nonsense. I am helping you.' She tightens her grip and tugs at my clothes. I twist my head and pull back. She reaches out, but I threaten to bite her hand. 'Stop this behaviour.'

'Badtameez aurat. I don't want a bath, now let me go.' I scream.

'Myrtle, let me try. I am after all Afrah's primary nurse.'

Myrtle Brown. I remember her now.

'Very well.' She glares at me. 'I'll let Miss Akram handle you.'

'It's all going to be fine,' Zahra puts her hand on my shoulder. 'You'll feel so much better after your bath.' Her voice is calm. She pulls me close to a tight warm hug.

I instantly feel better. I feel safe. 'I will?'

She nods. 'How about you lay in the water for five minutes. I'll wait outside.'

They both leave and I shut the door. There's no lock. I sit on the edge of the tub and stare into the water. Steam rises and I touch the surface. There's a knock on the door.

'Do you need help?' A woman with chocolate brown eyes dips her head in.

'Who are you again?' I ask. She has a small nose with a silver ring glinting in it. Amira always wanted one just like that.

'I'm Zahra, your primary nurse.' She smiles hesitantly.

'From now on you're going to take good care of me, aren't you?'

She smiles again. 'That's right Afrah Bibi.'

I take my clothes off and let her help me to a bath.

15

Sunday, 20th April 1986

Dear Diary,

Mum would kill me if I ever had my nose pierced.

'Our kind don't do it,' she said, raising her finger at me. Like I was some dumb little schoolgirl in a classroom, Madrasa or whatever. Mum often tells me she used to teach orphan girls in Lahore. I am not one of her orphan girls I told her and ignored everything she said. It's so stupid. I wish she would get over herself.

Sometimes when Mum isn't around I look in the mirror holding a pen pretending it's a cigarette, mimicking Naima's style when she smokes. And I imagine how my nose would look if it was pierced.

I didn't want to listen to her. She puts me off with her dumb comments. Naima is like a sister to me. It's not my fault Mum doesn't speak to them anymore. Naima's mum said Mum is a common girl who likes to wear wool. I don't know what she means, but I just laughed with her.

I wish Naima was my real sister. I wish I could stay in their house. Her mum gets her all sort of crazy new and shiny things. Her room is littered with stuff. Glittery dresses. Shoes in every colour and every shape. She's even allowed to wear nail polish, and keeps a secret make-up kit inside her bag.

I can't wait for when I get to wear nail polish and make-up someday. I've seen the older girls at school wear lip gloss and lipstick. Soon, I'll be in year ten. Well, not soon, after the summer. Naima is six months older than me. Her birthday is not until July. But she is already planning a big party and wants me to have a sleep over. It's going to be just AH-MAZING. All the cool kids, and some of the much older ones are also going to be there. Her *dad said he would even book a band. I don't care what Mum says, I have to go even when it will get me into trouble.*

Tomorrow Naima suggested we skip class and head to the shopping centre. I'll make up an excuse she's taught me and say I have a 'tummy' ache. Fake period pain always works. With Naima, I feel I have a sense of belonging. I want to be just like her. I may even buy a nail polish for myself from Boots. Ruby red, like the one Naima wears. I'll make sure Mum doesn't notice. I'll keep it a secret.

16

AMIRA

Thursday, 21 November 2019

I woke up at three o'clock in the morning and went into Mum's bedroom to check on her. It was an empty shell. As I lay in her bed, curled up with Mano, I felt her presence and saw visions of her sleeping, resting, reading. And then I heard her voice call out for me. I couldn't get out of her room fast enough.

I want to avoid going back in there. Avoid having to deal with the things she left behind. Piles of newspapers and old boxes.

The guilt of leaving Mum at the care home sits heavy like a stone on my heart. I tried several times to see if Meena was online today, but there was no luck there. And I still haven't told her what's been going on. I could really do with a friend right now.

I put the kettle on and take out my phone from my pocket, type in Shafi's number.

'How's it going? . . . I'm OK,' I lie. 'I was wondering if you want to come over this weekend? It's just me and Mano now . . . Sure, I understand . . . Really Shaf, it's not a problem . . . OK, let's try next weekend . . . Really? Would you want to come with me to visit Nano sometime? Well, speak to him and let me know . . . Love you, too.'

My laptop is open. I'm waiting for Meena to show up online. Someone else sends me a message. 'Hi, I'm new to this forum.' Mike66 writes. I don't reply. I snap the laptop shut.

I miss speaking to Meena. Where is she? Why hasn't she been online?

Mano jumps into my lap and I stroke his soft fur. I feel a tight sensation in my throat. Tears build in my eyes. I feel so alone and the house is empty without Mum. 'How about I go visit her on Saturday,' I say aloud to Mano. I'll bring her a fruit basket and the new pair of leather shoes that arrived for her this morning.' Mano purrs. 'Me too, I think she'd like that.'

17

AFRAH

'Don't touch me, let go. I said let go of my arm.' I try to untangle myself but she keeps holding on, yanking me along.

'I'm not going to hurt you,' she says adjusting her hair. 'Now, please come along and do behave yourself, Afrah Bibi.'

'It hurts. You are pinching me.' I glare at her pale face, shrivelled like a raisin.

'I was not.' She lets loose her grip around my elbow. 'Don't you want to see Nisha after we're done with the tour of the house?'

'What about my breakfast?' I smell rich flavours wafting in the air, buttery, savoury and sweet. 'I am hungry. I haven't eaten anything. Not even had a cup of tea.'

'You missed the gong. Did Miss Akram not explain what it means?' She sighs, removes a patch of hair from her forehead. 'You must come down to the dining area at once when you hear the gong chime.'

'Who is Miss Akram?'

'Zahra Akram,' she says. 'The tall dark haired woman. She is, well, also Pakistani.'

'I remember Zahra.' The woman with black hair. She has the face of an angel. Kind voice and polite, she hugged me. 'What about her?'

'She's your primary carer.'

I stare at her for a long moment.

I don't tell her I was up last night unable to sleep. I went to bed in the morning and heard the bell chime, which reminded me of being in a beautiful Hindu temple. The only one I ever visited when I lived in Lahore.

'You see, we're not like any other care home and that's what makes us very, very special,' words are crisp on her tongue. 'We truly care about our patients. Make sure they are cherished and well looked after. Our community is based on trust, which is why we do not have any security cameras installed. All we ask of you is to cooperate and follow procedure like all the other patients living here.'

'I am hungry. I want breakfast, I want it now.'

'Zahra will meet you in the dining hall after we're done with the tour.'

'Why can't I meet her there now?'

'Because she is preparing your lunch. A special Pakistani dish, chicken korma I believe. Doesn't that sound marvellous?'

The light in the hallway outside my bedroom is soft. Every single door is closed, except for mine. I turn and slam it shut, twisting the knob to make sure it stays that way.

'Listen carefully to what I am about to say,' she pinches my arm. 'If you decide to misbehave, I guarantee your food will land straight in the bin and you shall starve, my dear.' I swallow my pride. It's been replaced with a sense of dark fear. I follow her hesitantly.

'Why are you taking me down this way?' I bring my feet to a halt. It is darker down this hallway, it has heavily panelled walls and tall windows similar to what they have in churches. The carpet is a blood red, the lamps old and dusty. My imagination may be playing tricks on my senses. But I smell something burning.

'Nisha's room is to the left of this corridor, also known as the Morton Wing. You reside on the other end of this hall.' She looks back. 'In Mill Annex. Twelve rooms in Morton and twelve rooms in Mill.'

Beads of sweat trickle down my face. I snatch a deep breath, control my body from trembling. I don't want to walk down Mill Annex. The air feels thick and smoky and I do not like it.

'Good,' she smiles with glinting teeth. I notice a red smudge on her front tooth. Possibly stained from the dark colour smeared over her lips.

The wooden railing stretches down both ends of the hall. In the middle, it divides into two pairs of stairs. We go down, each step creaks underneath the carpet. To the right, the main door leads out to the front of the building. I don't have any memory of coming into the house or going up the stairs and it worries me. What else don't I remember?

'The house has two floors for the patients to enjoy freely. Private rooms, common areas and the garden. You have plenty of room to move around, except the basement and attic.'

'What's in the basement and attic?' I ask. She motions for me to move further down the staircase.

'Kitchen staff work in the basement and it is where we keep all our food supplies. The attic was converted last year to house sleeping facilities for the nurses and carers of Ravenswood Lodge. We're in quite a remote location and it becomes necessary to have our full-time staff around, if you know what I mean.'

I shake my head. 'I don't know what you mean.' And I don't know how I feel about the staff staying under the same roof. Did she say they don't have any security cameras installed? Does that mean the house is safe, or is it merely a way of covering their tracks should anything happen? I know how Amira hates it when I read tragic stories. I highlighted the article in the newspaper. Something about carers who abuse their patients. I am sure it said several deaths had been reported. I can't be too sure though. I may be wrong. My daughter would never leave me in a place that wasn't safe.

She presses the tips of her fingers hard against her temples. 'Certainly, you will forget what's been said. May need daily if not constant reminders about our rules. The gong isn't just for food so don't panic. You will soon learn what's expected of you.'

'What's expected of me?' I ask.

'First house rule,' she says strictly. 'Patients are not to go into the basement or the kitchen at any hour of the day. Do I make myself clear?'

I nod with a level of schoolgirl diligence.

'The second house rule.'

I seem to already have forgotten about the first house rule. But I don't tell her that.

'On three strikes of the gong, all patients must return to their rooms. Nine p.m. sharp.' She stares at me as if to confirm I have understood what she's said.

'Third house rule, which I mentioned. The gong goes off three times a day to serve breakfast, lunch and supper.'

I nod and follow her into a different room with a musty smell. The cold air sweeps through it, and outside the wind howls like a wolf. The unusual ornaments, the oil paintings and carved wooden furniture in the room feels old, ancient. I drag my fingers across a statue, lifeless like this house. There are floor-to-ceiling bookshelves lining the walls, with a rolling ladder stacked neatly at one end of the room. The books are all in leather binding, some with gold spines.

'In here we have the library, and down there,' she points her finger straight ahead, 'is the common area, which also leads into the lounge. To the left,' she peers over her shoulder, 'you will find the little reading room and what used to be the old music room. Nowadays we prefer the patients to use it as common area to read, watch television and play board games. They quite enjoy that.' She stops and looks at me. 'Do you like television and board games, Afrah?'

I shake my head. 'I like to read. Can you get me the newspaper? I need to know what the police and investigators are saying about her disappearance.'

'I'm not the paper boy.' She stiffens her spine. 'I am the head nurse, Myrtle Brown. You may address me as Mrs Brown. See if you can remember that Afrah Bibi.'

'Can I?' I ask. 'Get the newspaper?'

'Special treatment requires you keep up your manners. Understood?'

I nod and follow her into what she keeps referring to as the music room. But it's not called that anymore. I learn it's the little reading room. In the corner by the window there's a large piano. She tells me it belongs to the house and is more than a hundred years old.

I walk behind her, imagining what it feels like sitting in one of the armchairs reading a book while burning logs crackle. The image doesn't form. All I see is rising flames burning down my house. That's not all. I hear screams and feel the urgent need to scream too. Instead, I curb my voice to a soundless whisper. *I am coming. Where are you?* I'm blinded by the smoke.

'As you can see,' she says, 'we keep an open fireplace. The house gets cold, even in summer. Patients appreciate sitting here, supervised, of course. Nisha certainly likes it.'

I tighten my chador around my body. The room has high ceilings and old lamps pinned against the walls. The arched windows throw in daylight, but it still feels dark in every corner.

'Michael, our caretaker, makes sure we have enough wood logs regardless of the season. Come and say hello to Afrah, Michael.' She waves her hand at a man wearing a black suit and white shirt. He nods then smiles walking towards me. I fret and shy away.

'Nice meeting yer, Afrah.' He inches forward. 'Don't be shy. Let me know if I can help yer with anything.' I notice he is missing a front tooth. I look at him and nod. 'Heard yer saying yer a reader.' He thrusts his tongue between the gap in his teeth. 'I'm one meself. We have 'em classics stacked up at the top in the library. Dickens, Brontë sisters that sort of thing if yer like.'

'Michael can get you any book from the library, Afrah.' She interlaces her fingers. I notice a very red colour splashed onto her nails. 'We're very proud of our well-maintained collection.'

'I read books that are in Urdu,' I say. 'Do you have any?'

'Erm,' the caretaker clears his throat. 'I'll ask at the town library if they can get yer some . . . what did yer say again? Urlong?'

111

'It's not *Urlong*,' I reply. '*Urdu*. Related to Hindi and spoken by millions. It's poetic and beautiful.' Michael scratches his head and shifts towards Mrs Brown.

'That will not be necessary,' she says in a strict voice. 'Afrah must first read what is available to her. Any sort of special treatment must be earned. Hold on, a little Myrtle sneeze is coming.' She sneezes into her elbow, an awful barking sound.

I stare at her. She swings me into the hall. I step onto the red rug embroidered with blue flowers.

'Where are we now?'

'Like I said, the first floor is where the patients roam free outside their private rooms, and we have twenty-four, including yours. Not many here, considering care homes are often flooded with sick and elderly people.' A change of expression presses onto her lips, which curl upwards.

'Roam free?' The phrase makes me think of cattle.

'Yes, yes, you see, the house is rather large, more than 9,000 square feet without counting the garden and terrace. Patients are encouraged to *move around*.' She pulls me along towards the entrance. 'The garden is maintained by Liam, our gardener. He has just finished planting flowers in the circle. Aren't they beautiful?' She gazes across the lawn. 'We do accompanied walks to the beach, forest and surrounding areas. Soon you'll be able to enjoy the natural environment of the estate, which brings me to our fourth house rule. You must never leave the premises of Ravenswood Lodge by yourself. Always notify Zahra should the need to step outside arise. For your own safety, you must be accompanied.'

'I am not sure about going out alone anyway,' I look beyond the garden towards a steep path that turns and zigzags into the woods. An untamed wilderness, it frightens me. 'I prefer being in small places.' I see my home before my eyes in flames. I am reminded I don't live there anymore. I live in Ravenswood Lodge, a very special care home with lots of rules.

'Well now,' she folds her arms over her chest. 'We wouldn't

want you to get lost. Don't worry if you do, it happens to most of the patients living here. All you will be required to do in a situation like that is to call out for any of the staff. The nurses and carers will be on duty around the clock so you can always reach out to them for anything you need. Everyone is helpful and friendly at Ravenswood Lodge.'

She shepherds me back in, swinging right into another hall, which is long and dim. Wood ceilings with corners decorated in cobwebs preying on flies. The walls are framed with paintings of quiet faces. Faces that hold stern expressions and look like they were royalty and lived a long time ago. One is larger than any of the others, depicting a man wearing a black hat with a feather shooting through it. He is seated in a velvet chair in a red uniform. The dog resting at his feet reminds me of the stray cat in our home.

'Ravenswood Lodge used to be an extravagant manor previously owned by Lord and Lady Fairfax, where they lived with their two daughters, Victoria and Florence. Great balls and parties were held here to honour royals and the like. The Fairfax girls grew up protected from the world inside these walls. We still keep their portraits as a memory to honour the history of Ravenswood.'
She points towards a wall with a gold-framed oil painting. The pale faces of two beautiful girls poke out. Blue eyes, blonde locks. They look identical in their frocks with frills tightened by a brooch.

'What happened to them?' I stare a moment longer at the girls. Sadness lurks in their eyes. A deep blue ocean of melancholy. I fight the instinct to cry when a memory of Amira, just a little girl, sweeps through my mind. She was so upset, crying out, '*Ami, help.*' I hold myself responsible for the fact that the scar on her calf never disappeared, even after all these years.

'Florence, the youngest, married Laird Arthur. Victoria remained unmarried. She lived out the remainder of her days in the manor.'

'Why didn't she marry?'

'It was believed to be down to mental illness,' she says. 'Some believed she was schizophrenic. Lord and Lady Fairfax thought it best she be kept at the estate, isolated. The west wing, Morton, caught fire. It was only many years later that it was fully refurbished.'

'Morton Wing,' I say. 'It smelled like something burned there.'

'Nonsense,' she says. 'You couldn't have.'

'How did the daughter die?'

'She died in the fire. Some say she caused it and tried to kill herself. Rumour has it her body was recovered and buried in a closed coffin. The sight was simply too painful. After her death, the house was passed onto other members of the Fairfax family. Florence believed it was haunted. After the death of her sister, she refused to set foot inside,' she says. 'Claimed she could hear her sister's screams, see flames. The house was abandoned. It stood empty a long time. People started silly rumours, said it was haunted.'

'Is it?' I feel a cold chill travel down my spine, 'Haunted?'

She gazes at me in silence. Shakes her head. 'Of course not. In the early 1950s the estate was bought by a Scottish duke, Frederick MacGregor, to facilitate private care for his mother, Lady Ivy, who was experiencing a decline in her memory. He was sure the fresh ocean breeze and natural environment would do her good, with its calming, healing effect. One certainly cannot dispute with that. If you look out over the fields beyond the garden, you will see the crystal snowflakes capped around peaks of the Highland mountains. it melts into the bay, the sea. It's also known as Echo Ben. Do, you know what Ben means?' she looks at me as if I am some foreign object.

I shake my head.

'I'm not surprised. Not many do. Mountains in Scotland are called Bens. Echo, the one we can see from the house, has been climbed by many hikers. Last year, we had a young couple down these parts who were famous. The guide lost them and weeks later their bodies were washed up on the shores. We couldn't take the patients for walks. Crowded with photographers and journalists, it was quite a disturbing scene as you can imagine.'

I stop my feet from carrying me any further. The wind is cold and unsettling against my skin. I feel the hairs on my neck rise. I don't know what part of the house I am in. Don't know how I got here or how I will get back to my room. Mrs Brown is still talking and it feels like she never stopped, even for a second. I have trouble placing all the pieces of information she's said out loud in my memory.

'Upon the death of Mrs MacGregor, the house was refurbished again. So you see, my dear Afrah Bibi, you couldn't have smelled anything burned up in Morton Wing. It was repaired and painted many times over the course of time.'

'That doesn't mean—'

'What it means is that the house was converted into a private facility to treat Alzheimer's to accommodate the wishes of the MacGregor family. Not all our patients suffer from it, though. Take Carol, for example.' She looks across the room we're in. At a table, a large woman is playing chess and smiles over at us. Steam rises from the cups in front of her. 'She is diabetic. Although she, too, tends to forget things. Don't you Carol?'

'Is that the newbie who's taken Alice's room?' Her eyes linger on me curiously, looking me up and down.

'Yes,' replies Mrs Brown. 'Meet Afrah. Afrah, meet Carol.'

The heavy woman stands up to take my hand. 'You look so exotic! And what nice clothes. Mind you, you look a lot like one of the other nice ladies who lives here. Nisha is her name. She came in June. But I've been around long before that. Tell me why are you here? Do you remember anything? Are your children tired of caring for you? Did they leave you without telling you anything? Mine did. It was not pleasant at all, I admit. Was it your son or daughter who dumped you?' She stares at me with brows arched, expecting an answer. I don't know what to say. She has asked me so many questions already.

'I don't know what you mean.' I release my hand from hers. 'My daughter would never *dump* me. I'm here on holiday.' I know I must stay on holiday till Amira comes back. I have to.

'This isn't a holiday,' she laughs. 'Carol, my name is Carol. Don't forget it, most people do, and I don't see why. It's an awfully easy name to remember, like Kate or Katie. Anne, Anna. I should consider changing my name so people can remember it. What do you think, Myrtle? Your name is very uncommon.'

'Nothing wrong with your name – or mine, for that matter. I am sure Afrah will remember it with time.'

'Afrah, why are you here again? You never mentioned. Don't tell me. Your daughter left you. Am I right? It's always the daughter. Nisha's left her too. She wants to be here, unlike most of us, and says she never wants to go back to her family.'

'Plenty of time to chatter away later. Afrah is not going anywhere. She will be staying at Ravenswood.'

Mrs Brown takes me down a corridor where I see an empty dining hall. I turn back and see Carol still standing firmly on her feet, looking at me.

'The Council grants places only on very rare occasions. You do understand you are privileged to be here, don't you?' Mrs Brown stops to stare right at me. I can smell her breath, sour, tinged with raw onions. 'And about Alice . . . don't believe what anyone tells you. Especially Carol, that curious creature. You see Afrah, Alice's death has nothing to do with the history of the house, or anything else. At the age of ninety-seven, Alice died peacefully in her sleep. It was simply her time to go.'

'There you are. I hope you didn't get lost,' a soft voice says. I turn and a wave of relief washes over me when I see the woman with chocolate brown eyes. She smiles, puts her arm around my shoulder. 'I've been waiting for you Afrah.' Her voice is kind and patient.

'You have?' I feel a childlike excitement.

'Myrtle told me what you like to eat, so I made your favourite dish.' She takes me away from the room I am in. I sit at the table and smell the spiced flavours rising from the plate sitting in front of me. 'That's not all. I also made peshwari naan, just for you. But don't tell anyone.' She brings her index finger to her lips, then unpacks the soft dough bread hidden inside layers of foil. I tear a piece of the naan and dip it in the masala sauce. The flavours explode on my tongue.

'How does that taste?' she asks, adding a fresh sprinkle of coriander leaves on top.

'Beautiful, just beautiful.' The mix of spices hit the back of my throat. Warm and wonderful, I taste the chilli, cumin and turmeric followed by a strong after-taste of garlic and ginger.

'Now, try this,' she says and puts a perfect round chapati on my plate. The sweetness of the roti – a fresh crispy dough with puffed up burned blisters. I pop each one. I'm eating with my fingers, licking the tips after each mouthful. The woman puts a glass of mango lassi next to me. I bring it to my lips and gulp down the cool liquid. Cooking traditional Pakistani food from scratch takes time. She must have spent hours in the kitchen preparing.

Some of the other patients smile at me. Another appears to be intrigued when he sees me and says, 'Hello, good to have you with us.'

'They are excited about your arrival,' she says. 'And so am I. It's so nice to finally have you stay at Ravenswood.'

A man leaves his seat and comes up to me. 'The food you are eating looks wonderfully fresh,' he says. The woman standing next to him whispers, 'It smells invigorating, it must be delicious.' I look over my shoulder. Their plates carry dry bits of crust from their sandwiches. I turn to the woman with the chocolate brown eyes sitting beside me and place my hand on hers.

'Thank you,' I say. 'I've not had a proper korma in a very long time.' I must have tried more than a dozen times to make it, but each attempt was a failed disaster, with Amira telling me off.

'There's no need to thank me,' she says back, warmly. 'It's my pleasure. I learned to cook from my auntie, an expert in the kitchen. I never order takeaway and rarely eat out,' she explains. 'Homemade is the best. I love it.'

'So do I,' I smile, taking joy in each bite. 'You mentioned your aunt taught you how to cook. What about your mum and dad?' But she looks away and shakes her head.

'I lost both my parents when I was young. My auntie raised me.'

'I am sorry,' I squeeze her hand. 'I know how it feels to lose someone. My husband passed away many years ago.'

'Do you have children? Or any other family?'

'I have one daughter. I raised her all alone after the passing of Nadeem. And it's just been the two of us. We have no other family here.'

'Was that the name of your husband?' she says, this time in fluent Urdu. 'Nadeem?'

I nod. 'After he died, I needed a new start. I took Amira and moved to the Highlands.'

'How did you manage to raise your daughter alone with no family nearby to help? I can't even imagine.' She looks at me sympathetically like she understands my pain. I don't know why I am telling her this. I don't even remember her name. I feel ashamed to ask her.

A girl chewing pink bubble gum comes over to us. 'Zahra,' she says. 'Can you take my evening shift tomorrow?

Zahra, Zahra. I must remember her name.

'Not a problem,' she smiles and looks at me. 'Your daughter—'

'Her name is Amira. She said she will visit me.'

'Of course she will,' Zahra's eyes glow. 'I have relatives in Pakistan who I visit. There's no distance far enough to keep family away and, in your case, it's just your daughter.'

I examine her close. She has elegant features, fair skin. Her nose is pierced. I don't ask, but I know that from this she is definitely not Kashmiri.

'Tell me more about your daughter,' she says. 'About Amira.'

'She is like her father, with a much sharper edge. My mother was a lot like her too, although she was a happy person.'

'And Amira isn't?'

'She is strong-minded, with a will of iron. We used to be close. I don't know what happened. Amira is less forgiving than her father. She has his brain, but not his compassion.'

'I'm sure things will change. Mothers hold a special place with daughters.'

'Yes, they do.' Perhaps if I were closer to Amira, I wouldn't be sitting here chatting to Zahra. I would be in the comfort of my own home.

'I'd like to meet Amira next time she's here.' She undoes her ponytail, hair swinging onto her shoulders. One corner of her mouth tipping upwards as if pulled by a string.

'I am not sure that's such a good idea,' I hesitate. 'Let's see what happens.'

Zahra smiles when I finish my plate, wipes the sauce from my mouth with the napkin gently. 'Something sweet for the sweet lady.' She opens a tin that's full of golden ladoo. I take the biggest I can find and push it into my mouth at once. Yellow crumbs gather in my lap and I laugh with her as we both look at the mess.

'I love mithai,' she picks a ladoo and eats it in the same way I have done.

'Me too,' I take another without hesitating. Amira isn't around to tell me off.

'How about I save the rest for a rainy day? I'll bring it to your room.' There's a glint in her eyes. 'I wont tell anyone about it.' I nod. I know we are going to get along just fine.

Saturday, 23 November 2019

The daylight is sharp, and I bring a hand in front of my face, shielding my eyes from the sun. I'm sitting in the garden with Nisha. A teapot is on the table with two saucers and a plate with assorted biscuits. Nisha pours tea into our cups. She's in a wheelchair, her legs covered in a blanket. No gold bracelets glint around her wrists.

'What have you done to your bracelets?'

She shrugs. 'Diya took them because she was afraid they'd get lost.'

I know how much Nisha likes wearing jewellery. It's the only thing that makes an Asian woman shine with age. She presses a biscuit between her teeth. I don't feel like eating anything sweet today. My mouth is moist, filled with the taste of sugar and ghee.

'They said it will rain in the afternoon. That's when Margaret was meant to take me out for a walk.' She holds out her palms. 'No one wants to walk in the rain except for Carol. She likes the rain.'

'Who is Carol?'

'You must have met Carol. Big girl, talks a lot. It's impossible not to notice her.'

'I remember who she is. I saw her sitting in the library. I think she said call me Kate, Katie. Anne, Anna.' We both laugh.

There's a long silence. Nisha looks at me. 'Michael said he will light up the fireplace in the little reading room. I like sitting in front of the fire, reminds me of the time I married Anand. We walked the seven rounds around the Agni.'

'Michael?' I see a man with a missing front tooth. He looks after the house – the caretaker. He said he was going to get me an Urdu book from the library in town.

'Diya doesn't want to re-marry. Still, I let her keep my bangles. The Pandit warned me. Her janam kundali didn't match with that man she wanted to marry. Now I'm waiting for her to do the seven peras again to fulfil Saptapadi.' Nisha pulls the blanket close to her chest. 'Join me inside if you like? It will be cosy and warm.'

I shake my head. 'No, no I don't like sitting by the fire.'

'You prefer being in the garden?' She laughs, a sharp bark. 'Don't catch a cold.'

Nisha babbles on and on about the weather. The freshly

planted flowers. Colourful and lovely. Suddenly, she speaks to me as if I am a stranger. We stop talking about our usual things. Jewellery. Food. Family.

I ask Nisha if she knows who I am. She laughs loud this time and says, 'Don't be rude. How can I forget you, Afrah Bibi?'

'Nisha, I want to go home. This place, I do not like it. I can't explain what it is.'

'Nonsense.' Her mouth falls open, shapeless like a bag. 'Why would you want to leave? It's wonderful. Calm and serene. Here, people look after me. Here, I can do what I want without anyone complaining. I'm at peace.' She takes another biscuit, covered in thick chocolate, dips it into her tea and eats it in one mouthful.

Words begin to spin inside my head. Rules. Two or three gongs for bedtime or supper, or both? I don't know, it's unclear and muddled. What was her name, *little Myrtle sneeze?* No, it was Cookie, wasn't it?

Nisha shrugs. 'I, I don't remember what I was saying. Tell me, what was I saying?'

'You can stay. I want to go home. Is there a way out?' I look at the black gates. I am trapped. There's no way out. Even if there was, I wouldn't be able to go far. Beyond the garden, the line of trees is endless. A thick forest, dark. The sea hugs the cliffs and a barren landscape. Where would I go, and how would I reach home? There is no escape.

Looking out and beyond, a vast emptiness surrounds me. The quiet valleys and cold hills, with their dramatic, flat ridges, they inhabit the dark and uncontrolled borders of the woods. At the brink of it sits this old Victorian manor, resting like a silent grave. The narrow drive up to the house is bordered by old limbs of large swaying trees. Out here among the untamed wilderness, I feel restless like an animal. The wind ruffles through my body and my mind. The weather is changing.

Nisha drinks her tea. 'You miss your daughter. I hate to admit it, but I also miss Diya.'

I almost forgot to tell Nisha. I smile leaning closer. 'Amira rang,' I let out the excitement filling my voice. 'I can't remember when—'

'What did she say?' Nisha licks the chocolate from her lips.

'She is coming to visit me today.' I hear my own silly grin ring in my ears.

'Did you forget already?' says Nisha. 'Amira has already been.'

'When?' I trace my memory back, but nothing comes to mind. 'No she hasn't.'

'She was here this morning, and brought you a basket full of fruit and the new pair of shoes snuggled around your knobbly feet.'

I look down, only to realise I am wearing a pair of shiny shoes. The leather tight, yet soft. I have no memory of how it came to be that I have new shoes.

'Where's the fruit basket?'

'Carol ate most of the apples. I didn't touch the grapes. Diya never brings me anything. Why can't she be more like Amira? Your daughter is so sweet.'

I don't remember Amira being here. It must have been a short visit.

There's a scraping sound. The gardener uses a rake to gather fallen leaves.

'Liam was complaining about the strange smell coming from the kitchen,' says Nisha. 'I think he meant the smell came from your Pakistani food.'

'He probably never had a good curry,' I say.

The gardener stops, holding the shaft with one hand and resting his chin on the handle, staring in our direction. A cold unnerving glare.

'Who is he?' I wonder what's wrong with him since he looks so miserable.

'*That's* Liam. He looks after the garden. Thinks he owns Ravenswood Lodge.'

I know he's the gardener. I wonder *who* he is and why he is unfriendly. 'Tell him not to stare like that.' I find most of the staff to be unfriendly. All orders and rules, no smiles. Except for Zahra. She always smiles.

'No use,' says Nisha. 'He doesn't like *our* kind. Calls me Gandhi when no one is around. I told Margaret. She insisted he meant no harm. Sometimes I don't remember what he says. This Liam, he says some very strange things.'

'He said something to me passing by, if only I could remember his words. Harsh, like the look on his face.' I try not to let his glare bother me.

'If he ever speaks to you again, ignore him,' says Nisha. 'I try writing things down to remember them better. But it is simply no use. I have scribbles with Post-its in my room with no clue what I write down. When and why it matters, or what I did. Maybe it does. Maybe it doesn't. God knows.'

I tell Nisha about my diary and how I bookmarked it using colours. 'It's how I recall important events like memories and dreams. It's how I sometimes differentiate between what's real and what isn't.'

'Show me,' says Nisha. 'I want to see this diary of yours.'

'You can't,' I say and twist my hands in my lap. 'It's private.'

I don't want Nisha to know the things I write. About my dreams.

An old gentleman in a tweed jacket strides speedily over in our direction. His arms flailing up and down. He steals a biscuit from our plate and goes down to the garden next to the gardener. He loops around and pulls down his trousers and pees all over the flowers.

'Get him, Liam!' a woman in a blue dress shouts.

'Aye.' Liam drops his garden tools and walks down the gravelled path. 'Stop yer doaty old fool.'

The woman runs in the old gentleman's direction. She is out of breath. Her face puffy and red like a pig's. 'John, how many times have I mentioned, you are not allowed to do this.' She yanks him to the side. He pulls up his trousers. She grabs his arm and ushers him back towards the house, shaking her head the entire time. He has wispy hair and is almost bald. He stares at me as he passes. Shouts, 'My biscuits. Give it, give it!' He runs back and scoops the plate clean.

'Stop it,' the woman says tugging him towards her. But he isn't listening. His mouth darkens from the chocolate smeared all over. He laughs. 'Stop stealing, John.'

I turn to Nisha, cocking an eyebrow. 'Still think it's calm – serene?'

'Ignore that old idiot,' Nisha laughs out loud. 'When he's not snooping into other people's rooms, he has this nasty habit of peeing outside.' She pours another cup of tea.

'Did I tell you, Amira is coming today.'

Nisha shakes her head, drinks from the cup, slurping slowly.

'Clouds are gathering, time to go,' says a woman who's just come outside. 'We expect heavy rain anytime now.' She pushes Nisha's wheelchair inside. I sit back and sip my tea. Down the hill, I see the zigzagging track. Through the faint light, a head bobs up like a giant rock. It's the gardener. He comes up to me and barks something. His expression cold. 'Excuse me?' I feel ashamed for not understanding what he's said.

'Yer kind make me wanna—'

'What?' I demand.

'Nothing.' He stomps away without turning around.

The iron gates open and a car drives onto the twisting road. Smoke rises from the chimney of the house, curls with the mist. Grey clouds scud across the sky above. A woman, fresh-faced with chocolate brown eyes, steps out of the car and walks in my direction. I see a wide smile spread across her face.

'Let's get you settled inside.' She has the face of an angel. 'It's getting cold.'

'Tell me, who are you?' Water touches my skin. I am getting wet. Her arm is around mine. And we walk inside. Heavy rain splashes against the windows. 'Do I know you?'

'It's me, Zahra, remember? I'm glad I made it in time.

Otherwise you would have gotten wet sitting out there in the cold and in the rain, you poor thing. You look so tired. How was supper? Did you hear the gong? Have you eaten?'

I nod. I think I have. I don't remember what I ate.

'Let's get you in bed early, skip bath time. OK?' She seems tense.

'But I am not tired.' I turn as we walk up the stairs. 'Where has Nisha gone?'

'I'm sure Margaret is giving her a bath,' she says in a feathery voice, and I know who she is. 'I'll check on Nisha for you tomorrow.' She strokes my arm gently.

We reach the top of the stairs and the sign on the wall reads Mill Annex. We turn into the corridor and she stops in front of a door with the number nine on it.

'This is your room, Afrah.' She pushes it open and places me on the bed. Her features are familiar. Graceful. Smooth and fair skin. She looks Kashmiri, like my daughter.

'Is that you?' I feel a tear draw down my cheek. I touch her face. She smiles.

'Yes, it's me, Zahra, and if you promise to be good, I'll give you the treat I went to town to get you. It's something we don't keep here.'

I feel my childlike excitement spark into life. 'What is it?'

'Something very special. You will like it,' she says with a sweet smile.

'How do you know what I like?'

'Your daughter told Myrtle and Myrtle told me.' She tears open a plastic bag with dried kiwi, apples, bananas. I take it from her and lay down, smelling the sweetness of the fruits.

'Thank you,' I say in a low whisper. 'Can I eat it?'

'Go on.' She gives me the treat.

Zahra is so kind to me. She draws the curtains and puts a blanket over me, humming a sweet lullaby. I feel myself drift away while listening to the rain drum against the windowpanes.

'Amira said she would come, but she hasn't been to see me.'

Zahra stops humming, 'Are you sure about that? I think I caught a glimpse of her this morning before leaving my shift. Does she drive a blue car?'

'How should I know? She hasn't been. She doesn't love me.' My voice is loud. 'Why else would she leave me here?'

'Calm down, Afrah Bibi.' She touches my hand, but I yank it away.

'Get away from me.' I get up, trying to push her. She steps back.

'Please, stop screaming,' she says. There's hurt in her chocolate brown eyes.

I get up and start throwing the dried fruit at Zahra. She tells me to stop, to be kind.

'Silly ladki.' I go back to bed and pull the duvet over my head. 'She doesn't love me.'

18

Saturday, 24th May 1986

Dear Diary,

   Mum doesn't love me. She caught me smoking. I know I should never have done it at home and it was a stupid, stupid thing to do. I opened the window to my room and sat on the edge of the windowsill to try one of the new menthol flavour cigarettes Naima gave me. Mum must have forgotten something because she came back to the house one minute later. She saw me from outside blowing smoke out of the window. Her eyes were wide like saucers. She rushed up the stairs, threw open the door to my room and totally freaked out.

   What is this? And who are you? she cried. What have you become? Where is my daughter?' She shook my shoulders hard. I am your daughter, I said it's me. Don't you recognise me? But she kept yelling No, no, no like crazy. Then she turned and said something very nasty. You're just a dirty and shameless girl. And I wished she wasn't my mum. I wished she could just go away.

   She made me wash my hands thoroughly with soap. The entire time, she hovered over me, breathing down my neck. She asked me if I had more cigarettes. I shook my head. But she didn't believe me and went through my things, pulling open all my drawers, throwing everything onto the floor. There was a madness about her that scared me.

   My room was a mess! I hate it when it's a mess. Mum knows that I like all my things to be tidy and organised. She didn't care. She did it to upset me and to make me feel horrid.

   Mum told me to brush my teeth. I want that filthy stink gone from your mouth, she barked. Then she began shouting and

127

crying about what a disappointment I was. That I had betrayed her trust. I told her to stop and covered my ears. But she wouldn't. One of the neighbours must have heard her yelling because the police came knocking on the door. Mum's face went pale when the officer began questioning her. He looked at me and asked if I was OK. I nodded. But I wasn't OK. My face was burning hot from the anger bubbling inside me. After he left, Mum leaned with her back against the front door and stared at me angrily.

Mum was so annoyed. Now look what you've done, silly ladki. She pulled my arm and dragged me back into my room. She locked it from the outside. I was crying, begging for her to let me out. She didn't. I jumped out of the window and ran all the way to Naima's house. I was hysterical when her mum opened the door. I couldn't stop crying. I felt so horrible after what she did. Mum scared me!

Naima said Mum was a real nutter. She called her pagal. We went up to her room and she leaned her head against my shoulder and said I shouldn't even bother going back home. I should stay with them and her parents could adopt me. I told her Mum would never agree. That's when Naima looked at me and said, There are ways, you know. My dad knows about these things and could sort out all the paperwork and get it done. Your mum wouldn't even have to know anything about it.' She had this mysterious look in her eyes, dangerous almost. She told me to think it over. I nodded. My life would be so different if I moved in with Naima and her parents. It would be better because I would be loved.

Naima showed me her new pair of shoes. White Nike sneakers. She told me to try them on and said that they were mine if I wanted them. I hesitated at first. Shoes like that cost a fortune. But we don't talk about money. I asked her if she was sure. She nodded and handed me the shoes. I slipped my feet into them and it felt sooo good being treated nice. She said I deserved them. No one should have to put up with a pagal mum like mine.

I told Naima I was going to keep the shoes. This time I didn't care what Mum would say. She nodded and said from now on whenever I want something I need not worry. We're practically like sisters, and Naima is so right. We are just like sisters.

19

AMIRA

Sunday, 24 November 2019

My laptop is on the kitchen table, bathed in a pool of light. I pry it open and visit the chat that's just pinged with a message appearing on my screen. I put my tea down.

> Thelonelymouse: Hello lovely.
> Nursemira: Meena, where have you been? I've been trying you for days.
> Thelonelymouse: Sorry love, but my father passed away. It's been so hard coming to terms with his death.
> Nursemira: I'm so sorry. How are you now? Is there anything I can do?
> Thelonelymouse: Stay online. Chat.
> Nursemira: Of course, anything you need.
> Thelonelymouse: How is your mother? Is she doing better?
> I pluck up the courage to tell her the news about Mum.
> Nursemira: She is in a care home now. I saw her yesterday. It's a long story . . .
> Thelonelymouse: I have time, tell me what happened. After everything you told me about her, I feel like I know her.

I realise I am meant to meet Haroon in town to speak about Mum. I feel the sound of the clock move through my body like deep breath. I'd love to sit and chat with Meena. I don't want to disappoint her. After all, she has been like a sister to me. But on the other hand, I can't cancel on Haroon last minute. He has already taken a lot of time out of his busy schedule to speak with me.

Thelonelymouse: Are you still there?

Nursemira: Yes, I'm still here.

Thelonelymouse: Now, tell me what happened.

Nursemira: It wasn't my decision. Mum was forced to leave. There was an incident with fire. The oven was in flames and the glass exploded. She gets very distressed when it comes to fire. Mum was fine but it alerted the neighbours and someone called the police. Somehow the social services were informed too. I suspect that my next-door-neighbour made the call. She complained about Mum before. You may remember I mentioned her.

Thelonelymouse: Yes, you told me about the old dotty Mrs Nesbit. What a nosy old woman. I'm so sorry to hear about what happened. It sounds dreadful. How do you feel now?

Nursemira: I'm fine. But I miss having her around the house. When I saw her yesterday, she seemed happy. I think it's the right decision for her to be in a care home. Now and then I can't help feeling, well . . . guilty.

Thelonelymouse: Don't, Amira. You know, this new change might be just what you need. My father was a wonderful man. I miss him every day. In the end, I was glad he went to live in a care home. It was a hard decision, but it made me appreciate him more.

Nursemira: I must confess, I have been feeling less stressed and more at ease with Mum gone. Though I still carry the load of guilt like I've somehow disappointed her.

I move my fingers away from the keyboard and sip my tea. I realise as I sit here chatting to Meena that I can't let my feelings of failure betray me anymore. Meena is right about the new change in my life. It might just be what I need.

Thelonelymouse: You are still a good person, Amira. Don't let the guilt of not caring for your mother upset you. What happened wasn't your fault. Try and take pleasure in the little things and think about what you can do now that you no longer care for your mother.

Since Mum's been away, I've been sleeping in. Mano wakes me now and then licking my fingers. He misses the treats she used to feed him. I still have to go through her old boxes, a feast for the charity shop. I'll take it slow and get rid of her things.

Thelonelymouse: Are you still online love? Take her a nice present, things you told me she likes. Perhaps her favourite food. It will make her happy. I did when I visited my father. Hello, Amira? Are you there?

Nursemira: I'm still here. Funny you mention it. I brought her a fruit basket and new leather shoes. It made her happy . . . I think!

Thelonelymouse: What's wrong?

Nursemira: I didn't spend enough time with her.

Thelonelymouse: Which care home is she at?

I hesitate before typing. But then this is Meena. I can trust her.

Nursemira: Ravenswood Lodge.

Thelonelymouse: I heard about them. It's supposed to be the best care home in Scotland. Quite a beautiful place, too. She is very lucky to get to live in such a sought-after location. People I know would do anything to have their parents in a care home like Ravenswood Lodge.

It makes me feel good hearing Meena say that. It drowns out the constant guilt.

Thelonelymouse: How do you afford it? I struggled paying for my father. I had to sell our family home in the end to pay the bills.

Nursemira: I guess I'm very lucky because the council is paying.

Thelonelymouse: That's wonderful.

Nursemira: I am so sorry for all you've been through, Meena. How are you?

Thelonelymouse: I guess you can say I am managing. I've kept busy applying for jobs. Never thought I would have this much time. I went for an interview with a family. Live-in position. They're looking for someone to help take care of their disabled son. A seven-year-old boy. He's a real sweetheart.

Nursemira: I hope you get the job. When will you know?

There's a pause. Meena starts typing, pause, then appears to retype.

Thelonelymouse: They called this morning and offered me the job. I start right away.

Nursemira: That's wonderful news. Congratulations, I am so pleased for you. And a live-in position, too! That's so exciting. Where will you be living?

Meena knows everything about me. But I've never even asked where she's from.

Thelonelymouse: I'll be moving to Inverness in couple of days. Isn't that where you live? Anyway, I want to thank you. You helped me through a hard time when I was looking after my father. The conversations we shared meant a lot to me. I stopped feeling lonely. Made the right decision getting him into a care home. I've accepted life as it is. I am moving forward. We need more carers like you, Amira. You've been such a lovely friend to me. Someone I trust.

Nursemira: Thank you. You've also been a great friend.

Thelonelymouse: What are you going to do?

Nursemira: I'm thinking of going back to university.

Thelonelymouse: Really? That's great!

I am about to say I have to leave but then I see Meena is typing a message.

Thelonelymouse: A friend just messaged me asking if we can have lunch together. I'd better go. I'll be busy moving and in my new job.

Nursemira: It's time for me to go too. When are you online again?

Thelonelymouse: Try me next week.

Nursemira: OK, will do.

Thelonelymouse: When are you paying your mum another visit?

Nursemira: Not sure, why?

Thelonelymouse: We could catch up in person next week when I'm in Inverness. Gotta go, love. Take care xx.

Nursemira: Bye Meena. Xx

She logs out, and I feel excited about meeting Meena. I have no idea what she looks like. We've only chatted online. Next time, I'll ask for her number. It's about time we met in person.

Haroon walks into the restaurant and the wet air sweeps in with him. The rain that follows him in hits the glasses of an elderly man sitting nearby. He takes them off irritably and wipes them clean against his shirt, his stony grey eyebrows raised.

'I do apologise, sir,' he says in his usual polite manner. Before the elderly man puts his glasses back on he gazes into Haroon's big brown eyes and murmurs. 'No harm done.' Haroon carries the innocent look of a deer: gentle and handsome.

'Have you waited long?' he says, as if he's expecting me to be angry.

'No, not at all.' I watch him wipe the raindrops from his face. 'I ordered you a coffee.' He puts his coat on the chair before sitting across from me.

'I can't stay long.' He leans in close and I feel his breath on my face. A soft tinge of something sweet and sticky. 'I am on call from the hospital.' He stares at the black liquid cupped in white ceramic.

'I know, I am sorry,' I sip my tea. 'Thanks for coming. I'll keep it brief.' I stare at the large clock on the wall, my eyes fixed on the ticking. He slurps his coffee, his pinky finger raised.

'I've heard back from Myrtle Brown this morning. She's the head nurse in charge of running Ravenswood Lodge.'

'We've already met, and I saw her again yesterday when I visited Mum.'

'You've been to see her already?'

I nod. 'What did Mrs Brown share with you that she's not sharing with me? Medical related worries I presume?'

'Not at all. In her professional opinion, your mum seems to have settled in well. She says it's all down to her personal nurse, a Pakistani woman. Do you remember me telling you she is a friend of my family down in Glasgow? He takes another slurp of his coffee. 'Have you met her? Lovely lady.'

I feel the pulse in my throat beat faster. 'Oh, isn't that nice.' I tighten my grip around the mug. 'She was off duty when I was there. But Mum spoke very highly of her. I can't wait to meet her.' I dunk the teabag a few times and watch the movement of water in my cup.

'Things turned out well. Myrtle Brown sees no reason to be concerned. It's the early phases of a change which normally causes fear and anxiety in the patients settling into a new environment. Right now, your mum is getting the best care anyone could ask for.'

I sigh, feeling relieved that the news about Mum is positive. 'And you were right from the start. I'm sorry I was ever in doubt about the care home. Mum could be happier living there than with me.'

'The care home is very traditional, Mira. Close-knit community built on trust between the patients and the nurses. It's a really calm setting.' He sips the coffee and wipes his mouth. 'It provides patients with framework and regular routines.'

'You are right, after being out there and seeing things for myself—'

'Your mother is lucky,' he says.

'When do you think I should I visit Mum again?' I still feel bad about leaving her yesterday and the feeling that I somehow failed to care for her is still there. I glance at my phone. Nothing. I'm itching to give Mum a call. I'd like to meet this carer of hers. I cross my legs, unable to stop fidgeting. I finish my tea in one long gulp.

'Give her some time – a couple more days. Maybe even a week.'

'What?' I shake my head. 'Mum will go mad.' Or perhaps I will. I feel curious about her carer. Is she as good as they say she is? No one cares for Mum more than I do.

'I understand you've been caring for her a long time, just . . . try not to contact her at least for another day or two. She needs time to adjust. If you keep interfering with regular visits she may not fully settle.'

'I see your point, but I already said I'd see her soon, perhaps—'

'The more familiar she gets with the new change, the less she will depend on you. Once she accepts her new environment you can start to increase the visiting time.'

I feel horrible for not calling her today. That's the least I could do to fulfil my duty as her daughter. Part of me is terrified of what she might say. She will blame me, tell me she wants to come home. I wouldn't know how to respond or what to say anymore. Her words still echo in my mind. *Mimi, I will never forgive you if you leave me.*

'I won't contact her then,' I say. 'If that's what is best for her.'

'And for you. Try to move slowly and steadily on from your mum.'

Haroon knows the toll Mum's presence had on our marriage during the early onset of her dementia. 'Who are you and what are you doing with my daughter?' she'd say. She'd then turn to me. 'Why is this man sleeping in your bedroom? Who is he?'

I pull out a glossy brochure and show it to Haroon. He widens his eyes then stares at me. He tilts his head to the side. 'What's this, Mira?'

'I think I want to go back to uni.'

'That's wonderful news,' his fingers brush mine as he turns the pages. 'It could be good for you to get your life back on track.' His face turns red. 'I'm sorry. I didn't mean it like that. You know what I mean.' He hands back the brochure.

'I understand and you're so right,' I deliver a soft smile. 'I need to focus on myself.'

'Nothing will give me greater joy than to see you go back to study.' He meets my eyes with a deep, intense look.

'Me too.' We sit in a moment of silence gazing out the cobbled streets with people running, seeking shelter from the rain. 'Nice of you to come here to meet me.'

Haroon gets up, ready to leave. 'I have to go. Do you still want Shaf to visit you next weekend?' He furrows his brows into a tight knit.

'Actually, I'll be sorting the house out.'

I have to rearrange things. I'll start with Mum's room, go through her boxes. Clear out the junk. It's time I realise she isn't coming back.

I could turn her bedroom into a guestroom for Shafi so he can start staying with me again. On second thought, the house will be too big for just one person. Perhaps I'll sell it, move into a small flat near Bank Street. I'd be closer to Shafi.

'I'll tell Shaf to call you. FaceTime.'

'I miss him so much. Can you believe he's grown up so fast?' I smile.

'He's good at heart,' says Haroon.

'He gets that from you,' I say. 'Thank you for checking on me.'

'See you around Mira.' He starts off quickly down the street.

I sit back a while staring at the brochure.

20

AFRAH

Friday, 29 November 2019

The room I am in is strange. I do not recognise the shape of it. Certainly nothing familiar and nothing like home. It's like some daunting space swallowing me. I wonder where I am. And I wonder how I came to be here. I don't know how long I've been sitting on the edge of the bed, keeping my body from falling into a slumber. I feel more tired than usual, and let myself slump into the mattress, the material itchy against my skin. My chest is wet. I wipe the layer of sweat into my chador and press it against my face. I'm hot. I had a bad dream. The images flicker in my mind where the same voice screams for me over and over.

I open the bedside drawer. It is different. Spacious. Inside, I find my diary, gold bracelets and reading glasses. Quickly, I jot down my dream before it slips away. A tight feeling snakes around my chest. I put down the pen and bite my nails. Amira's voice plays inside my head. *Don't do that Ami, please.* I can't help myself. Whenever I have a bad dream, I turn to my fingers like a child searching for comfort.

I put on my glasses, shut the drawer. I yank back the pillow. No dirty knickers hidden behind it. I see a wardrobe and open it. All my shalwar kameez are on the hangers, and my other clothes neatly folded in the drawers. The bathroom door is ajar. I go in. There are pictures against the tiles of me and Amira. Damp and curled at the edges. Life Story Work pinned with my memories.

I turn towards the mirror. My hands dig into the edge of the sink, strangling a scream. I look terrible. My hair is loose, flaring up on all sides. I touch the birthmark on my neck. I notice a purple bruise on the side of my cheek below my earlobe. How did that get there? I go out and scan the room again. I am not in my home. And this is not my bedroom. But why are my belongings here? I look for boxes on the top shelf. Boxes that contain fractured pieces of my memories. My past life. I panic. I want to scream. Instead, I let out a groan. They are not there. Where are the boxes? *Amira!* She must have taken them. Someone is turning the handle. I rush towards the door. A woman steps inside. It is not my daughter.

'Where is she? Where is Amira?' I realise I am shouting. Panic surrounds me. 'And who are you?'

'I'm your carer, Zahra,' she says and looks at me with compassion. 'You have been living at Ravenswood Lodge Care Home for just over a week.'

'What do you mean?' I want to make a break for the door but she has blocked it.

'This is your new home. You live here now.' She says in a calm voice.

'This isn't my home.' My throat is tight. 'I don't live here.'

'Do you remember your friend Nisha? She is also a patient of Ravenswood Lodge. Nisha has been with us since—'

'I don't care.' I try to push past her, but she doesn't let me. 'Let me go.'

I feel the blood drain from my face. The room is spinning and I lose my balance and fall flat on the floor. She steps towards me. 'Afrah, you tend to forget things, but don't worry. I am here to help take good care of you. You are safe.' I feel her presence next to me and do not move as she puts her arm around my shoulder and pulls me up gently. She takes me into her arms and I sit up straight. She brings me a glass of water. I drink it quickly and wipe my mouth with my sleeve.

'The breakfast you had yesterday, pancakes with maple syrup, you liked it very much. How about I tell the cook to make it again this morning for you?'

'Chup karo . . . shut, up!' I scream. 'I don't like pancakes.'

139

'Then I'll make you traditional Pakistani breakfast myself, paratha and omelette.'

'Will you do that?'

She nods. 'Everyone in the care home is talking about the new food smells and colourful flavours. Even the cook. She said, Zahra, what do you think about doing a curry night once a week?' She delivers a kind smile. 'And guess what you will be having for supper this evening? Korma. That's right. It's just for you.'

I touch her face. It makes me feel better.

'You remember me now don't you, Afrah?'

'Yes,' I say feeling at ease. 'I remember who you are.' She has the face of an angel. She reminds me so much of my daughter, Amira.

'Don't worry about anything,' she says in her politest Urdu, 'ap fikar na kare.'

Zahra places a cup of tea in front of me. The smell of cardamom and saffron. The colour bright and pink.

'It's a special blend from Pakistan.' She pours herself a cup from the pot. 'I just love Kashmiri chai, don't you?' I nod and blow softly on the surface of my steaming cup of tea. It instantly makes me feel calm. 'How about tomorrow we have tea in the garden? It's meant to be sunny, blue skies.'

'I'd like that very much.'

She gives me the plate she's arranged and sits across from me. When I ask her what it is, she says she is worried about me. I've not eaten breakfast or lunch from the kitchen. I remember that's because I don't like what the cook makes. Cold food. I stick my tongue out.

I roll a ball of paratha with egg in my fingers and tease it around my plate.

'Why are you here?' I ask.

'I've always wanted to be a carer.' There's elation in her voice. 'I can't tell you how much I enjoy working at Ravenswood Lodge,'

'Why is that?' I say.

She shrugs. 'I don't know. Caring for people just fulfils me.' She smiles, and her company puts me at ease.

'You are a good carer, Zahra,' I look into her chocolate brown eyes glinting with joy.

'I do my best.' She lets out a sweet laugh. 'Do you like your room? I took the liberty to unpack the things you left in your suitcase. I want you to feel at home,' she says, looking slightly worried.

I turn my head and see the man who works in the garden walks across the hall wearing black wellies edged with mud. I forgot his name, was it Larry? No, he doesn't look like a Larry. I wonder what business he has inside the house. He's the gardener and not the caretaker. Liam – that's his name.

'Well, do you?' she smiles.

'What was that?'

'Your room, is it nice?'

'I like it.' I look down at my plate and eat every single bite of my food. I drink the tea, asking for more. The taste is thick and creamy.

'We can frame some more pictures on the wall if you like, of you and your daughter. Do you have any other family? Or is it just the two of you?'

I wipe my mouth with the napkin she passes me. I feel itchy, restless, and get up. 'I have no other family.'

'Are you ready? says Zahra. 'Time for your bath.'

I cringe. I don't like baths. We don't take the lift up, and I feel tired walking the stairs. Zahra holds me by the arm. 'You didn't nap this afternoon. Spent all day with Nisha chatting first in the common area, then in the music room having an attempt at the piano. Do you remember?'

'You mean the little reading room,' I say. 'Where is Nisha?' I don't remember seeing her all day.

'Nisha loves her bath time. Margaret is helping her to one.'

The air is stale and damp in the dark hallway. At the top, I rest against the panelled wall. Zahra tells me she is sorry the house is old with very little modern facilities. But a little exercise is good. Next time, we'll take the lift.

Inside my room there's mud on the carpet. Zahra examines what appears to be the trail of footprints. 'Don't worry, I'll get rid of it,' she cleans it with a dry cloth. 'Might have been one of us. Happens all the time. Look, all gone now.'

'It wasn't here when I left,' I say.' I'm sure of it.'

She holds pills in her palm and asks that I swallow them. I hesitate.

'It's your medicine.' I notice my pill boxes sitting on the desk. Next to them there's a picture of Amira.

I do as I'm told and then lie down in bed.

'Not too fast. Bath time, remember?'

I shake my head. 'I don't want to. I want to sleep.' I feel drowsy and shut my eyes.

I open my eyes. Zahra is sitting in the armchair reading a book. I open the bedside drawer and hold my breath. 'My bracelets, my diary. They are missing.' I look across the room. My pill boxes are not on the desk. Neither is the framed picture of Amira.

'Are you sure you put them in there?'

I nod. 'Someone has been in my room. Someone stole my things.'

Zahra tells me to calm down. She looks around and finds nothing.

'It was the gardener. I saw him,' I am shouting. 'He did it. He stole my things.'

A woman barges into the room. 'What's the matter?' she asks in a strict voice.

'Myrtle,' says Zahra. 'Afrah's valuables are missing from her room.'

'So? We haven't had a day where the patients haven't lost something.' She glares at me and I recognise that pale face and those cold silver eyes. 'Afrah Bibi, you ought to take better care of where you put your things. That is, if they really were there in the first place and you haven't misplaced them yourself.' She leaves without showing any concern over what's happened.

Tears well in my eyes. Zahra puts her arms around me and gives me a warm hug. My voice comes out broken. 'The bracelets were a wedding present from my parents. The diary had all my memories in it.' Tears tumble down my cheeks. Why would anyone take the photograph of Amira? And my pill boxes. I need my medicine, don't I? Who would do such a thing?

'You had a little nap while I was in the room with you. No one was here.'

'I'm not lying, I am telling the truth.'

'I believe you Afrah. And don't worry, fikar na karo,' she pats my shoulder. 'I will get to the bottom of this. I'll check with everyone. I will look for your things.'

'Shukriya, thank you.'

A heavy woman appears in the doorway, peering in. 'What happened? Who stole what from whom and when?' I find her annoying and want to shout, *Get out*.

Zahra shakes her head. 'Not now Carol.'

Red patches of defiance appear on the woman's cheeks. She breathes in sharply, 'It was probably John. He stole my purse the other day. And I saw him snooping in Afrah's room before.'

'Please, give us a moment in peace.' Zahra waves her hand telling her to go.

Flabs of her body spill over her sides when she pushes her jeans higher up to her waist. 'I was only asking.' She twitches her nose, left, right. 'I want to help. I can look for your things if you tell me what's missing.' Zahra shakes her head. The heavy woman disappears behind the door. Stomps down the hallway. I hear her say out loud, 'Afrah probably forgot where she put her things.' But I didn't. I am not imagining things.

'I understand how you must feel right now,' Zahra pulls back my hair neatly and wipes my tears with her sleeves. 'How about we skip bath time and I bring you a cup of warm milk with honey.'

I peer into her eyes. Mellow, the colour warm like the autumn sun. She is trying her best to care for me. I nod, leaning my head against her shoulder.

'The gardener doesn't like me. He stole my things!' I think he's out to get me.

'Liam is narrow-minded,' says Zahra. 'but I don't believe he would steal from anyone.'

'Then how do you explain the mud on the carpet?' I saw him. It was from his wellies.

'I don't know.' She folds her hands in her lap. 'Perhaps Carol is right. It could have been John. Or perhaps you forgot where you put them.'

'I want my daughter. Call her. I want her to come. Now! Abhi! Abhi!'

'It's too late to call your daughter now, OK Afrah? I'll ring her in the morning for you.' she says mildly.

'Amira hasn't been to visit, has she?'

Zahra shakes her head. 'Not in a while. She's probably busy.'

'How long has it been since she last came?' I raise my voice. 'How long, I said?'

Zahra looks away but I catch a glimpse in her eyes of shame. 'We'll give her ring first thing in the morning.'

I lose my trail of thought in the silence between us. I feel as though I am awake, but dreaming. Something is wrong, terribly wrong, but I can't put my finger on it. I feel the pounding of my heart, a slow beat inside my chest. A sudden jerk back into my consciousness when I notice the vase full of roses by the window-sill. The wind flickers the fallen petals. Somebody has put the flowers in my room.

'I saw the gardener,' I don't know when, but I did. 'He went straight into the house.'

'What are you saying Afrah?'

'He's been in my room,' I smell the earthly scent wafting the air. 'He was here.' I point at the roses with long stems and sharp thorns. Words fail to slip out from my mouth.

Zahra is quiet. The look in her eyes a combination of worry and discomfort.

21

Sunday, 15th June 1986

Dear Diary,

Lying is beginning to come easy to me. It's like acting. When I lie, I get what I want. Lying is a skill. The more I practise, the better I get. So I use it as a rule.

Yesterday, I didn't feel like going to Urdu school. I can't stand the teacher. He's a bald, skinny little man who always picks at his nose. I said I wasn't feeling well and faked a fever. Naima does it all the time. She taught me. I held the thermometer under hot water, stuck it in my mouth and let Mum pull it out. She saw my flushed face (from jumping up and down) and ordered me to go lie in bed.

I could hear her mutter to herself, maybe I should call the doctor and ask him to take a look at her? She stared at me strangely. Later, she brought me a tray with food and all my favourite snacks. She kissed my forehead. Held my hand when I pretended I was going to be sick. She's not been this nice to me in like, forever.

Lying works. I can be anyone. Do anything without having to worry about picking a fight. Lying keeps me out of trouble. But sometimes, when I am not careful enough, like yesterday, it doubles the trouble.

Mum found out I had sneaked out of bed to go to Naima's. She showed up at their house and went mad. She was pounding on their door. I know you are in there, she said. Come out, come out now! Her voice was so dark and she reminded me of the big bad wolf huffing and puffing to blow the three little pigs house down.

Naima was so embarrassed and so was I. Thank God her parents weren't home.

Mum was shouting, get out, get out, this instance. And I did.

She looked at me and said, don't you dare set foot in here again. She dragged me into the car and we drove home.

She said I can never see Naima again. Never go to her house. When I asked her why not, she said because her parents are bad people. Whatever does she mean by saying that? I protested. Told her they are not bad, they are nice people. They treat me like I was their daughter. They love me.

Mum raised her brows and asked if I knew that Naima's dad is involved in shady business. She called him a fraudster. He is not, I said. I told her to stop lying.

But Mum said she wasn't lying. She insisted that Naima's dad takes money from people and gives them false identities. Passports. Drivers license. He forges all sorts of documents and gets paid a lot of money for it.

I still don't believe what she said. Naima told me he owns a shop and sells electronics from Japan and other countries. That's why he has to travel a lot.

Mum just laughed. She said it was a cover-up. She told me to stay as far away from Naima and her family as possible. I was very upset. I wanted ask her the reason for their fall out, but she told me never to mention it again. When I insisted, she looked at me angrily and said in her strict voice, not another word about the Pashtuns. I want nothing to do with them. Not anymore. Not after—And then she was quiet.

She didn't speak again till we got home.

I know why she doesn't want to talk about it.

I know what she did.

When I told Naima what Mum had said, she got super mad at me, told me never to say that again. I have never seen her this upset before. Not even when Oliver broke up with her a week ago. I promised never to talk about it again. We talked about boys – Naima has a new boyfriend. A Pakistani boy from school. She tells me what they do when no one watches. So disgusting. She said everyone does it.

After school, Naima came to the house with her new boyfriend. She was standing outside my window. Mum was cooking in the kitchen. I couldn't go out the front door, so I tried to sneak out from the bathroom window. It was a bad idea. A very bad idea. She caught me, made a huge fuss.

Mrs Singh came running from across the street. She didn't even close the door to her house. She pulled Mum back and told her to calm down. But she wouldn't listen. She was shouting at Naima don't you come near my daughter again, or else. Mum went nuts. Or else what? said Naima. She wasn't bothered at all. She called Mum pagal auntie. She looked right at her and said you can't tell me what to do. Can't keep me from seeing her. Naima isn't scared of Mum.

Back inside the house, Mum completely ignored me. She then didn't speak to me for days and it made me feel horribly guilty.

I wish that Mum wouldn't always make me feel so guilty.

22

AMIRA

I fiddle with the radio, but the connection is bad in the rural parts of the Highlands. I keep my eyes on the road, don't want to hit another deer. They jump out of nowhere, wide eyes blinking in the headlights. I wish the drive back wasn't so dark and lonely. That way I could visit Mum more often. She was quiet today, hardly spoke, and I wonder what was on her mind.

'You OK, Ami?' She looked at me with hollow eyes. 'Say something.' Her face just shrunk as if she'd suddenly aged.

'I'm fine. Zahra cares so well for me.'

I nodded and tried not to show my annoyance.

Zahra is lovely and I can see she's formed a special bond with Mum. Pouring Kashmiri tea for her, bringing her chador. She is attentive. Whenever I looked at her she smiled and asked if I needed anything. Haroon was right about her when he said that Zahra is sweet. It makes all the difference she is Pakistani, too – a friend of his family. Zahra doesn't judge me for not coming to see Mum every day. She said Mum was doing great and has found new friends. Nisha said Mum gets special treatment from Zahra. Traditional homemade food and other treats. Nisha moaned her carer doesn't even sit and have tea with her on the terrace.

I called Mum every day the week I didn't visit her. But she was hardly available. Either she was napping, out for a walk or having tea on the terrace. Sometimes when she'd get on the phone she appeared distracted as if she wasn't interested in talking to me.

'Who are you again?' Mum didn't know who I was. I hope she doesn't forget about me now that she has Zahra to care for her. I kept calling her *Ami,* so she'd recognises me. Mum's always been a strong and independent woman. She had to be, a widow raising her daughter all alone.

Mum kept saying her things are vanishing. Jewellery, photographs, and pill boxes. Zahra told me not to worry. And I'm not worrying. I know Mum is forgetful.

Before leaving, I did something I should have done long ago. I told her, 'I love you, Ami.' I haven't said that in a very long time. She stared at me and bit her nails. 'Are you OK?' I wanted to give her a cuddle. She pushed me back and looked away.

'Why wouldn't I be?' I sensed her mood darkening. 'Silly ladki. And where is Zahra? I want her to take me back to my room. I want to nap.'

I don't know if she was angry or just being moody. But it made me feel horribly guilty. Like I had done something wrong. Perhaps I am being overly sensitive. Mum's mind was probably elsewhere.

She was arguing with one of the carers – a young man. Mum's words were muddled. She was speaking to him in Urdu. I don't think she knew what she was doing or what was happening around her until Zahra came over, and before she took her upstairs to her room she told me: 'Your mum is a little tired. You don't need to worry. I am here to care for her.' Mum didn't even turn around to say goodbye. She has settled in very, very well. I worry that soon she'll forget all about me.

The radio comes on. Finally, reception is back. I'm leaving the rural Highlands. I don't like the gloomy drive out here. The long black roads, the endless arched trees. It's deadly quiet.

23

AFRAH

Monday, 9 December 2019

It's chilly out on the terrace. Yellow and red leaves pave the soil in the garden. Zahra puts a blanket over my legs and tells me not to worry about the incident, which happened on Sunday. These things are common in care homes. She detects the discomfort drawn across my face. But I have yet to understand what it is I am to feel upset about. I furrow my brows and ask her if I did something terrible. She shakes her head and delivers a soft smile. Her subdued manners make me at ease.

'Give me a moment Afrah, I will be back shortly.' She disappears from the terrace carrying a scent of lavender with her.

I peer out through the glass shielding me from the garden where the gardener uses his rake to gather the leaves. He stares oddly in my direction and it makes me feel uncomfortable. He is the reason I am upset. It hits me so suddenly that something isn't right about him. Why else does he glare at me as if he wants to murder me? Perhaps I was rude to him. I don't recall that. But I do recall what it was he said to me in passing. He mumbled something like, *if you want to eat curry then go back to where you came from. This isn't Pakistan.* I think I said, *I am from a big city called Lahore.* I could be wrong. I could be imagining these words. I could have dreamed it.

'Yer all right little lady?' says a curt voice.

'Huh?' I turn around and a man stands next to me holding a book. He pulls back a chair and sits beside me. 'Oh, hello . . .'

'Michael is the name.' He points at badge pinned against his suit jacket.

150

'I remember you. Have you found any Urdu books in the town library for me?' I gaze at the one he's hugging to his chest.

His face reddens. 'Sorry, I haven't inquired, can do this afternoon if yer like?'

'That would be nice, thank you.' I try my polite manners with him.

He unclutches his fingers and passes me the book. 'Meanwhile, how bout yer read this? Was Alice's favourite. She won't mind. Go on, have it.'

'Shukriya—thank you.' I take it and pull down my reading glasses. '*To the Lighthouse*, by Virginia Woolf.'

'Set in Scotland. Isle of Sky.'

'I've lived here most of my life,' I say. 'Always wanted to go.'

'Was Alice's fave book. Go on, have it little lady.'

'Who is Alice?'

He says she was the oldest patient who lived in Ravenswood Lodge and lived here the longest, more than thirty years. Came when she was sixty-six years old. Healthy as a bull. One morning she never woke up. Liam was very close to Alice. She knew every flower and every tree he planted. He was devastated when she died.

'She used to be in my room. That explains why he hates me. He thinks I am replacing her.'

'Aye, some of the patients still think Alice is around,' he says. 'One is even thought to have seen her wandering around at night,' he chortles. 'Liam took it the hardest. He wasn't happy when he heard someone was moving into Alice's room. He had a violent argument with Myrtle about keeping it vacant for a while before filling it. *Let her memory live*, he said. But Myrtle wouldn't hear of it. We have a long waiting list. Only the privileged patients get to stay here. And so you were brought in, lucky little lady.'

The gardener walks with a brisk pace towards the terrace. He snorts, an awful gurgling sound. Presses his face against the glass and glaring in with wide eyes, murmurs something I can't hear. Michael gets close. 'Yer all right Liam?'

The gardener pulls back and cocks his head to the side. 'She's trolley. Stay away.'

The caretaker waves his hand. 'She's bonnie.'

'The gardener doesn't like me,' I say. 'He wants to hurt me.' I touch my tender cheek, it hurts. I think I saw a purple bruise in the mirror. How did it get there?

'What in devil's name makes you say that?' He turns around, his bushy brows raised.

I wring my hands nervously. 'Tell him to stop looking at me like he wants to kill me.'

'Oi,' the gardener says in loud voice. He motions for Michael to come.

Michael ignores him and sits next to me. 'Liam's a wee crabbit. But no murderer.'

'I think he stole something from me.' I look out the window. He pushes the wheelbarrow down the zigzag path. He wears wellies covered in mud. 'There was black dirt on the carpet in my room.' The rain pours down and the wind howls blowing shuddering gusts against the rattling windows. He turns out of sight behind the trees. 'I know it was him.'

'Carol is always pokin' aboot patients' rooms. Myrtle caught her red-handed. And John. He snatches things not his. Don't remember where he buries them. What yer missing anyway? I can keek for yer. I know all the corners of old Ravenswood Lodge.'

'Well, my gold bracelets. They mean a lot to me. And my black diary with all my memories. Now, I have nothing.' Something else is missing, but what? My pill boxes perhaps. Or is it still on the desk next to Amira's photograph? I can't remember.

'Don't mind 'em folks here, little lady. Forgetful, but harmless. They'll grow on yer, like the Scottish weather does.' Thrusting his tongue between the gap where he's missing a toot, he chortles. 'Most go aboot forgetting something every day. You may have forgotten too. John forgets where 'e puts his teeth. Barks Myrtle took 'em. Stuck a fist down her throat pulling at 'em. Liam found

152

his teeth buried in the garden where John pees. Bullocks 'bout marking a safe territory. He is a lazy bugger. Truth be told, John don't remember the way to the bathroom. And if yer ask me, Ravenswood has 'is own ghosts.'

'What do you mean? Can you explain it so I could understand perhaps?'

He strokes his beard and sighs. 'The estate used to be a horrible place, a hollow shell for decades after being abandoned by the MacGregors. I read it meself in the library papers. Lady Ivy hung herself. Before her, the Fairfaxes left their daughter. Burned to death in the Mill Annex. Rumours of witchcraft for 'em folks before used to burn witches on the very grounds we stay. I swear, sometimes I see their wrath.'

He lowers his voice. 'It ain't only 'em elderly folks. Believe me, the black soil still carries blood, and a raw feeling of smouldered flesh sometimes taints the air. Yer gotta be mad to be out in this barren land with dark forests and angry cliffs bowed into the sea. Mad.' He widens his eyes. 'Spirits haunt this great manor bleeding at the 'eart of the bleak and earthly witch tormented land. Don't let the ben surrounding the estate fool yer. At night yer can 'ear 'em. They are screaming from the pain. The suffering. The wounds bleeding with the witches burned to ashes.'

'Will you be joining us for tea, Michael, or are you busy taking care of the house?' Zahra has turned up holding a tray, which she places on the table.

'Gave Afrah Alice's book,' he says, motionless.

'How nice of you. I am certain Afrah will enjoy reading it later this afternoon. Seems like she's not the only one who likes to read. You're quite the storyteller yourself.'

He salutes, gets to his feet and leaves.

'Was Michael being naughty sharing gossip and ghost stories with you?'

'He was.' I untangle my neck from my chador, heavy and drenched in sweat. 'Don't remember what he was on about, something about witches and ghosts.'

153

'It's a small community at Ravenswood. Don't let what he said bother you.'

'I don't. Have you brought—'

'I made a fresh pot.'

She pours the pink tea into two cups. Serves me a plate of shortbread. 'What's the matter? Why so quiet?' she asks in Urdu, placing her hand on my lap.

'Nothing's the matter.' Heaviness surrounds me. 'Let us drink our tea or it will go cold.' Any hope I have to leave this old haunted house vanishes. And where is my daughter? Why hasn't she come to see me? I lean my head back and close my eyes. I see Amira's face. That's not all. Next to her I see someone else. A dark burned face and hollow eyes. It frightens me.

'Time for lunch Afrah, didn't you hear the gong?' She walks right past me spinning like she is a ballerina.

'Leave her alone, Carol,' says Nisha. 'She's *my* friend.'

I turn around and stare at Carol. There's something strange about the way she looks today.

'Recognise these, do you, do you, huh?' She jingles the bracelets around her wrist like some crazy dancing monkey.

'What are those? Wait . . . Are those mine? Give them back, you thief!' I get up, kick the chair with the back of my heel. 'It was you, you stole them from me!'

'Did not. Somebody put them in my room.' She places a hand in front of her mouth and giggles. 'I didn't steal anything. I am not a thief, Afrah. Stop calling me a thief!'

'What's going on?'

'Myrtle, Carol stole Afrah's bangles,' says Nisha. 'Look what's around her arm.'

'Someone is always stealing things around here. How many times must I remind you all to put your valuables away?' says Myrtle. 'Are those the bracelets you made a fuss about?'

'I made no fuss,' I say. 'She stole from me.'

'Did not.' Carol hands me my bracelets. 'Here, take them. Don't want them anyway.'

'It's time for your lunch Afrah.' Someone puts an arm round my shoulder. I can't see who it is. 'Come with me. We'll find your diary too. It's only a matter of time.'

I walk down the hallway hugging my bracelets close to my heart.

'She stole them from me,' I whisper.

The icy wind blows in, a strong current, from the window that knocks over a vase. It drops and breaks. Water floods over the broken pieces. I look down the dining hall – no one is there, and I am alone in this chair, in this room with empty plates and glasses decorating the table. I think I have been sitting here for ages. I've been left alone. Amira must wonder where I am.

'Somebody get me out of here,' I say aloud to make sure I'm being heard. Nothing. 'It's getting dark. Where is my supper?' I've not eaten. My tummy is growling and I am so hungry I think I will faint.

A young girl dressed in a blue uniform appears out of nowhere. 'Afrah, what's the matter? You OK? What were you saying?' She turns her head and looks at me curiously.

'Nothing,' I lie. 'I said nothing.'

'Something about supper, I think? You've been served already. It's time to go to your room.' She motions for me to leave. I stand up staring at her as she starts down the hall.

'I've got to eat something,' I say under my breath.

I go down to the basement and yank on the door handle in front of me. It's locked. The same girl appears.

'Please leave,' she says. 'You are not supposed to be down here.'

'Badtameez ladki.'

'What did you call me?' Her words are pointy. She takes one step closer.

'Nothing,' I lie again.

She pulls me along and I tell her to let go of me. She is not listening. Is she crazy?

155

'Pagal, pagal!' I shout. Her face turns red. 'Where are you taking me?'

'I've had enough of you,' she says and shakes her head. 'This stops, alrighty?'

I mimic her voice mockingly. Three strikes of the gong chime in my ears. I've been hearing it every night. That's when everyone goes to their rooms. That's when I sleep.

The grandfather clock strikes the hour. 'Nine p.m.,' says the girl. She presses the button to the elevator, her face awash with emotions. She turns and I walk off. I swing into the corridor, and find myself getting lost.

Now I am in a different room. It's dark and the curtains are flickering in the wind. I shiver and turn around. A tall man with a pale ghostly face with wrinkles stares at me. He pushes me, I stumble. I roll over on my stomach. I feel his heavy breath on me. I shield my face with my arm and crawl, pushing my elbows forward.

'Where the hell do you think you are going?'

He looks down on me and spits.

I wipe my face with my sleeve and get up. I walk without turning as fast as I can. I am in the library, the musty smell is awful, it makes me feel sick. I turn into the common area and knock my knee against the table full of board games, now falling over. A dice escapes, rolls and spins to a stop. I turn and there's another room, and another room. I am in the little reading room . . . music room . . . or whatever it's called. I stagger against the piano; the keys spill out dark clunks of noise.

I stand still, my chest moving with my breath. Something is burning. A charred smell assaults my nostrils. I cough. I hear heavy footsteps; someone is talking, whispers and voices. A door slams shut. I jump and feel too afraid to call for help. Where's Amira? I wish she was here. I need her. She will be worried. I need to get out of this crazy place. It's *making* me crazy. Somebody is getting closer. Somebody is out to get me. Thick curly waves travel down my throat, hot like fire. I let out a scream, 'Help!'

'You are really trying my patience,' says the same girl. 'Go to your room, now.' She yanks me hard by the arm. I don't get a proper look at her. She wears brown shoes with black laces. 'If I catch you out here again, past bedtime, I'll tell Myrtle.'

'I've got to get home. My daughter is worried about me.' I cut loose but she runs ahead and blocks my way, arms spread out wide. She shakes her head.

'This needs to stop. Up we go.' Her shoes squeak. 'Alrighty?'

'But what about my daughter?'

'She's already been to see you today.'

'Don't lie. Amira wasn't here!'

Now, she is talking to herself, mumbling that she can't wait to be off night duty next week. Me too – I don't want her bossing me around. We are in the room, number nine. There's a desk, a chair, a bed. All sorts of newspapers and books. I sit at the edge of the bed and glare into the empty space. My emotions feel caged. I need to get out of here. The girl is outside chatting to someone. I catch a glimpse of a tall woman with blonde hair.

'Afrah called me something in that language of hers. I bet she swore at me.'

'I'll tell Myrtle so she can make a note of it. Where's Zahra?'

'Off again, I think Afrah hasn't had her meds. Do you mind? I'm knackered.'

'I'll see to it, give her an extra dose to knock her out,' says the second voice.

That's when I remember my pill boxes are missing. But that's not all. Somebody at Ravenswood Lodge is playing games with me. Someone wants me gone.

Wednesday, 18 December 2019

The front door clacks open and slams shut. Someone is in my room. I see the shape of a tall woman skirting gracefully around the desk. 'Wakey, wakey. It's your favourite carer, Zahra.' Hands draw the curtains with ease. I don't want to get up. I am comfortable in bed – sleepy, warm.

The light stings my eyes and I see the shape forming clearly now. Zahra wears a long skirt, white blouse and scarf with flowers tied around her swan-like neck. 'It's a beautiful day. You slept in, even missed breakfast.' A radiant face, straight lined lips and pony-brown eyes with fluttering lashes smile at me. I don't know how it is I feel light-headed. No amount of numbness will blur the dream. 'Did you have a good night's sleep?' She stares at me for a long time and I wonder what's wrong.

'Yes, I slept well,' the Urdu words roll out on my tongue.

Fiddling around with one hand I search for my reading glasses. And my diary. It isn't beside me. When did I last write in it? It's difficult to keep track of anything without it. How do I feel? Blue or yellow? No bookmark to dictate my mood. To tell me how I may or may not have been feeling. I don't want to use grey. Lately, I have had a lot of bad dreams. I find myself roused in hot flashes and my clothes are clammy.

'Zahra, have you seen my diary?'

'You don't remember?'

I shake my head. 'Remember what?'

I wipe the thick layer of sweat from my chest and bite my nails till I can't anymore more and hide my ugly fingers behind my back. Shoved behind my pillow, I pull out the newspaper. She comes closer and hands me my reading glasses from the drawer. 'Is this what you were looking for?' She places them on my nose and pulls back strands of hair flaring behind my ears. 'There we go.' Her voice is kind, and she smiles like a politician's wife. I re-jig the pillow behind my back.

The articles are highlighted in yellow, scribbled with words in my own handwriting that I cannot read. She peers over my shoulder. 'You asked several times if you could have the newspaper. And so, Myrtle agreed you can have it. But don't tell anyone.'

'She did?'

'Don't be so surprised,' Zahra arches her brows. 'She may not appear to be, but the woman is butter mellow, underneath that hard skin of hers.'

I uncurl the scrawled pages and lay the paper flat. All I see is ink on paper. The words seem smeared, as if flying off the page. I feel dizzy and lean back. My heart is beating at a slow rate underneath my saggy flesh.

'You've mentioned several times now that you are following a story in the papers about a young girl who went missing after a tragic accident. I did an online search. Nothing came up in this area. Perhaps if I knew how old she was, or where she lived I could look it up. What was her name? Was it national news?'

'Please stop,' I put my hands over my ears. 'Too many questions.'

She detects my discomfort when I look away. 'I'm so sorry.'

'I can't remember the details.'

'Never mind,' she says, and smiles. 'I'm sure it will come up. I'll keep an eye on the papers for you. Is it an important story?'

'It is, or it was.' Bad feelings well up inside me. My eyes cup with water. I feel Zahra's gaze, but I can't look up. 'She was so young.'

'Sounds just terrible. I can't begin to imagine how the girl's parents must be feeling.'

I look straight into Zahra's eyes filled with bright light. 'She was only fourteen.'

She shifts page after page. 'Does it say that in here?'

'It was front-page news. Now there's no mention of her anywhere. Some say she is dead. She has been forgotten. Not by me. I still remember her.'

Zahra puts the newspaper to the side. 'I understand how some stories can have a long-lasting effect on some people. Especially tragic stories mentioning the disappearance of children. Stories like that never give closure. Try not to read anything that may upset you.'

I don't tell her that for years that's all I've done. Skimming papers, collecting articles, keeping her alive, but she is long gone.

Zahra notices my damp clothes and sweeps across the floor. 'How about you get out of bed and get changed?'

I shake my head. 'No, I really don't want to.'

She opens the wardrobe and pulls out a hanger which holds a green sari. 'This is nice. With your height, I would love to see you wear it.'

I stopped wearing saris a while back, and I don't think Amira would have packed it. So how did it creep into my wardrobe? 'Put it away,' I say raising my voice. 'Don't touch anything.'

She comes close and sits at the edge of my bed. 'I never meant to upset you. Nisha wears them and I got curious. I hardly wear any Pakistani clothes unless I attend weddings or funerals, which I rarely do.'

'Me neither,' I can't recall the last time I attended an event.

'How about this.' She pulls out a beige wool shalwar kameez. 'This looks nice. Try it on.'

'Where did that come from?' I ask. Zahra looks confused. 'It's not mine.'

'Are you sure?' she says. 'It was in your wardrobe. You must have brought it with you from home. You don't remember packing it?' She brings it over.

I shake my head. 'As I said, it's not mine,' I touch the material and it itches. The memory cuts me. Crawls into the crevice of my mind like an insect. I press on my temples to calm myself.

'I'm so sorry. I shouldn't have bothered you about getting changed.'

My clothes suck at my skin. Zahra hauls me up and I swing my legs over the bed frame. My feet search for my slippers. The skin lumpy with thick blue veins running under it like ropes push into the shoes. I shove my shoulders back. My muscles crack like old wood.

'Nisha said she will take her tea in the old music room should you want to join her.'

'You mean the little reading room.' I swing my cardigan over my shoulders.

'One month in Ravenswood has served your memory well, Afrah.'

I can't believe I have been here so long already. Has my daughter paid a visit? I don't know. I have faint memories of the past few weeks. Zahra releases the hatch and swings open the windows. I get it, my room needs airing. She moves swiftly around, humming, and begins to tidy up, nursing my things with great care.

Outside, the sky ripples away in a hurry. Trees with black branches sway and creek. The wind comes in strong, and my hair flows across my face. The rain stops and dead leaves fall soundless to the ground. I notice a hairline crack running against the glass. If I push it hard enough it would break. The thought makes me shiver. Glass exploding, flames tearing down these old brick walls. I shut the window carefully. I need it to provide me with the illusion of safety.

'Where are you off to?' asks Zahra.

'I want to see Nisha.' I pull my cardigan on.

'Wait,' she says, and takes out a powder foundation and a brush. 'First, let's cover that nasty looking bruise you got yourself. You don't remember getting it, do you? You were up in the middle of the night banging your head against the bathroom wall with your eyes shut.'

I touch my forehead. I feel the ugly lump pounding, the pain swelling, and spreading into the dark corners of my consciousness, into all the places I do not like to think about.

'There, all lovely again,' she says. 'We'll go for our afternoon walk when I am done.'

I walk down the dark hall, down the stairs and into the little reading room. I'm out of breath and feel my hair clinging to my neck. Nisha rests in the big armchair with her head leaning back, her body wrapped in an emerald floral sari. Busy flicking through her phone, she is unaware of my being in the room. At random, I pick a book from the shelf, flip through the pages, not knowing what I read. I smack it shut.

Nisha looks my way. I sit in the corner, away from the unlit fireplace. Carol towers over me, asks what book I've got this time. I ignore her. What I cannot get used to is Carol snooping. I imagine she marches into my room and shuffles my things around when I am not there. A curious creature, Mrs Brown calls her. Always hovering about and meddling in other people's affairs. Asks all sorts of questions. I don't remember what I may or may not have told her about my life or about my daughter. Amira has not dumped me in a care home. Nor has she left me without the promise of a return. She will visit me, or perhaps she already has. I ask Nisha if Amira has been around. She shakes her head.

'Diya never visits, she rarely calls or sends messages. Besharam girl. I have to keep up with her on Instagram.'

'Insta-what?' I ask.

'Social media,' says Carol. 'It's a platform for sharing pictures. You don't use it?' She shoves the screen of her phone in front of my nose and flicks through picture after picture. 'You're better off without it. Terrible connection out here anyway.'

I take deep breaths. 'I don't have a phone and I don't have pictures to share.'

'Yes, you do.' Nisha empties her cup, slurping the last drop of tea. 'Whenever I called, you never picked up. Besharam woman.' She uses her index finger to wipe the crumbs from her plate of food and licks it clean with her slate-like tongue.

I'm amazed Nisha remembers my life more than I do.

'I was very lonely and afraid when they first placed me in the care home. You came once to visit and then didn't show up again. Why didn't you take any of my calls?'

'My phone was broken.' I remember now that I kept it in my bag among loose coins, old receipts and scrawled notes. 'I think I threw it out.'

'Ranveer shows up with the girl and the boy. My grandchildren.' She faces the screen of her phone towards me. I see the image of a chubby boy wearing a baseball cap and a skinny girl in braces smiling broadly. I tell her I have no grandchildren. 'But you do,' she reminds me. 'Amira was married to a handsome doctor. They have a son. He must be a teenager now.' I shake my head. 'Shafi left. He never came back.'

162

'Well, *your* handsome son hasn't been here in a while now, Nisha,' says Carol. 'He looks like a Bollywood actor. He really does. Gorgeous. Just gorgeous.'

I deliver an awkward laugh.

'Why is that so funny, Afrah?' Carol rolls her eyes.

'My daughter has a picture framed in our house of that famous Hollywood actor. Daniel Day-Lewis. She says it's my husband. Silly ladki, where would she get that idea from?'

'My Ranveer takes after his father,' says Nisha with a gleam in her eyes. 'He studied engineering in Cambridge and in Oxford. His wife is an advocate. A very important woman.'

'What about *your* daughter Afrah?' Carol offers me a cup of tea. She sits on the arm rest next to me. Bits of her white skin roll out from underneath her tight top. 'When do I get to meet her again? Not seen her around in a while. Did you argue? Nisha said you did.'

'Did not,' Nisha sticks her tongue out.

'Did, too,' Carol mimics her.

'Shut up, Carol, you moti cow.'

'What did you call me?' Hands on hips, she looks at me as if I said something offensive. Then she laughs and reaches for the pot. I don't want tea, but take it anyway, and feel the steam warm my face when I cradle the cup in my hands.

'What's the reason she hasn't come? Is she also a very important woman?'

I say nothing. I rub my forehead and a swelling pain breaks out.

Carol cranes her neck lowering her head. She examines my face, creases gather between her brows. 'Afrah, what on earth happened on your forehead? There's a nasty purple bruise. Haven't you noticed? Looks like you've walked straight into a door.' Her expression turns stone cold.

Nisha puts on her glasses. 'Oh yes. Very nasty bruise.'

I touch my forehead again and feel the tender lump pulsing like a nerve. 'How did that get there?' I shrug and look away. 'I don't know what I did.'

'My thigh is bruised. Big purple bulge like an aubergine,' says Nisha. 'Margaret said I fell from my wheelchair. But I don't remember falling from my wheelchair or from anywhere. I really don't.'

'Are you saying Margaret pushed you?' Carol looks suspicious. 'Mind you, I once saw her shoving Alice. Poor lamb, she was so fragile. Couldn't get out of bed for days. Margaret said she tripped. But I know what I saw,' she whispers.

'I must have fallen off my wheelchair,' says Nisha. 'If Margaret says so.'

There's a long silence. Gusts of wind seep through the windows. A blowing gale. Suddenly it is as though I see hairline cracks everywhere. The house feels shaky, like it might collapse. Ashes in the fireplace rise and fall light like feathers. The room feels chilly. In the corner of the room, the grandfather clock strikes the hour, leaving a mechanical noise inside the case before continuing to tick-tock away.

Nisha asks Carol for a biscuit from the tin hidden underneath the table. A secret stash. She opens the tin and releases a sweet powdery sent. 'Would you care for one, Afrah?' I shake my head. I have no appetite. 'Nisha?' Carol waves a hand. 'Hello? Are you in? She's gone blank again.' Carol chortles. The saggy flesh underneath her chin jiggles. 'She does that sometimes, the poor lamb. Disappears into a world of her own.'

I look right at Nisha, still as a statue. Eyes wide open and mouth shut. The biscuit is clutched tightly between the tip of her fingers. I call her name again and again. She could well be dead. 'How often does she—'

'Space out?' says Carol eating with her mouth open. Crumbs dust her lips. 'Dunno. Not often. Oh wait, I could be wrong. She has her moments where she forgets faces. Don't recognise anyone around here. Wears off quickly though. She'll be back to normal soon. Last time it happened she woke thinking she was on the moon. Can you believe it?'

'There,' says Zahra appearing in the doorway with a big smile on her face. 'I am all done. How about we take our afternoon walk now?'

Done with what I wonder? I am relieved to see her so I don't ask. I put the cup of tea down and go out with Zahra, who holds my coat in one hand and shoes in the other. She shepherds me out the front door. A tall man with a pale ghostly face and wrinkles stares at me. He moves quickly in my direction. He runs into me, his sharp shoulder bumping mine. He throws me a murderous glare and mutters words I don't understand before rushing off.

'Are you OK?' Zahra says, placing her hand on my shoulder. 'I am so sorry about that. Liam is a loner. You know how his type are. Loners are often . . . eccentric.' Zahra plants her remark like a sprouting seed.

'He's plain rude,' I murmur, hiding my hurt.

'He can be. But you mustn't let Liam's brusque behaviour be a bother.'

'That's not it,' I feel shaken. 'Liam doesn't like me. I think he wants me gone.'

Zahra says: 'How can anyone not like you?' She says I've brought life, a fresh breath of air to Ravenswood after Alice. She curls her arm around mine. 'I'm so happy that you came.'

We head down the slope, passing the belt of trees and circles of flowers. The grass is moist, the air fresh. We walk a while, till the ground underneath me changes to pebbles and rocks. We are near the coast now. I taste salt in the air, and hear the sounds of waves slapping against the shore. There's a view out to the sea that cradles a fishing boat, and the bay's cliffs wrap around the beach, touching the soft sand. We go down a winding path, and I panic and almost slip. Zahra holds me tightly so that I stay upright. I steady my feet, crunching sand and sea algae.

'We've been coming out here daily.' She bends and collects broken seashells, locks them into her fist. 'Do you remember?'

I shake my head. 'Nadeem and I went out for walks on cold days like these.'

'Was that before your daughter was born?'

I look out towards the raging ocean. 'We took her with us. She liked running around, chasing paper bags flying in the wind. A wild spirit.'

'Do you miss her?'

'Every day.' The wind slips into my eyes, and a tear drops. 'There isn't a single moment when I don't think of her.' I feel lonely, hurt and betrayed.

'She's probably giving you time to settle into your new life. It's a big change for both of you. And I'm sure she will soon pay a visit.' Zahra pads my arm. Clouds have gathered and thunder rumbles, then silver lightning cracks the sky. We draw back towards the house, passing sandy slopes with half-buried shells. I pick a broken one, remembering how my daughter used to collect them in her silver box.

'How can I forgive myself for what I did to my daughter?'

'Did you have a quarrel?'

'I don't know.' That's what Nisha said, and Nisha remembers things better than me.

We sit on the terrace. The view to the garden is dominated by shades of grey.

'Ever since she was a teenager, she was a rebel, with such a fiery temper.'

'What happened?' Zahra adjusts the scarf around her neck. 'What had she done?'

'She had her nose pierced when I told her she couldn't, and I caught her smoking and spending time with a girl I thought was a bad influence, and showed no shame throughout. No guilt.' The memory blooms in my mind. 'I was so close, I wanted to slap her.'

'Why would she do that?' Zahra looks at me, her eyes small and watery.

'She did it all to defy me. She had a friend I did not approve of.'

'Who, a boyfriend?' She arches an eyebrow.

'No, a girl from a Pashtun family we used to know,' I take a deep breath. 'We stopped talking after they accused me of something I didn't do. Of course, I wouldn't let my daughter go and hang out with theirs. They spread lies, spoke ill of me. None of it was true. They were bad people. Involved in shady business—'

'What did they accuse you of?'

I twist my naked wrist. 'Stealing.' The memory fails me. 'It happened long ago. My daughter never understood why I didn't want her going to their house. She would argue with me, throw tantrums. That girl, her so-called friend, had a bad influence on her.'

'And what did she say when you told her the reason she couldn't be friends with the girl? Did she understand your reason?'

'Who?' I lose my trail of thought.

'Your daughter?' she says. 'You were telling me about the fall out with your friend.'

'Where is Amira? Has she come to see me?' I stand up. I told her someone stole my things. Told her what's happening. Sometimes, I don't feel safe. My breath a fog against the window. The black gates are shut and the long drive leading to the house is forlorn and misty. Grey clouds scud across the sky above. Heavy thunder rolls through the heavens. A flash of lightning.

'No, Afrah,' Zahra stands behind me and I turn around, looking into her big brown eyes. 'No one is here to see you.'

The sky releases another sharp clapping sound. Water falls from the sky and tumbles over the glass roof like a monsoon. 'Can I call her?'

'Of course, we can give it another try.'

Zahra puts down the receiver. 'Still no answer. Try her again tomorrow.'

24

Tuesday, 29th July 1986

Dear Diary,

Today, Mum went mad. She was screaming at me telling me to pull it out. How could you? Didn't I tell you are not allowed? I told her to back off and not touch me. It was only a joke, a fake ring in my nose. She knew it wasn't. It was real. She got so upset she started crying.

I told Mum, I don't care what you told me. I told her it's my nose, not yours.

She wouldn't listen, and went on and on about what a disappointment I was to her, to our family. I told her plainly to shut up, and she raised her hand. She didn't strike me, but I could tell she was very close to. I went up to my room and turned the key. She was banging hard on my door telling me to unlock it. I just covered my ears. Go away! I yelled.

I looked in the mirror. The ring was barely noticeable, a tiny silver thing glinting innocently. It was Naima's idea anyway. She dared me to get it done. What's the matter? You chicken? Scared of mummy?

I had to show her I wasn't scared this time, not like that day one the beach. This was a different kind of pain. It was totally worth it. Oliver's friend kept smiling. He said it would be so cool if I did it.

Naima paid for the piercing. She also paid for three new nail polishes. Black, purple and red. I took one out of my bag when I was in the bathroom. Black. Naima suggested the colour and said it was sexy, and I went for it. I did my toenails and put on socks so Mum wouldn't notice. Tomorrow, I will do one finger. The day after tomorrow I'll do two, and so on. She'll eventually notice, but I don't care. She's got to stop telling me what to do. It's not fair.

Naima's mum never interferes with what her daughter does. She's such a cool mum. They are close and do everything together. I wish Mum was cool, too. We aren't close anymore. I wish we could do more of the things we used to do. Go back to how we were. Mum would take me to the beach and we'd collect broken seashells. Now we never talk or go anywhere together except for Urdu school or the masjid.

Later, Mum came knocking on my door telling me to come down and eat. I didn't answer. I knew what I had to do. Fake sobs to make sure she heard me. I wanted her to feel horrible for making me upset about the piercing. She sighed and left.

I forced myself to cry so hard my eyes were red. Then I went down to show her. That usually does the trick. Mum was quiet. She made me a paratha with saag aloo, which I didn't eat. It made me feel good watching her feel guilty. When she had gone to her room, I looked at myself in the hallway mirror and smiled. I love my piercing. I just hope that Mum doesn't ruin it the way she ruins everything else.

Mrs Singh brought the little brat over and I knew I had to babysit her. What's that funny thing in your nose? she said pointing her little finger at me. I grabbed her hard and told her to shut up. Her lips puckered and a tear dropped from her eye. She's so sensitive and always cries like a baby. She moaned I was being mean again. Pinching her when she's annoying me doesn't make me mean.

I could hear Mum stomping down the stairs. I thought I heard you she said and smiled at the little brat. What happened little baby? Was the silly ladki being mean to you? Was she? Mum glared at me then back at the little brat whose apple cheeks were wet with tears, Don't cry Mum said and gave her comfort. Come, we'll play a game. The little brat stopped crying, leaping like a *monkey onto Mum's hip as she took her upstairs. She lets her play with my old toys and it upsets me.*

Mum doesn't love me anymore. She loves the little brat now. Sometimes I wish she would disappear. When I look at her, I want to smash her head against the wall.

25

AMIRA

Thursday, 19 December 2019

The estate agent has put a 'for sale' sign up outside and arranged for a young newlywed young couple to view the house on Sunday evening. I never thought I would be selling my childhood home. A home where the memories of playing tag and skipping rope with children in the neighbourhood flood the pathways of my mind.

'Buyers are looking to live in good neighbourhoods,' he says. 'In areas like these with families and great schools around – properties tend to sell fast.'

We start at the top of the house and he scoots up the ladder. 'It's a good size loft which could easily be converted into a bedroom with a walk-in wardrobe and bathroom.' He climbs down with a gleam, as if his sale pitch got easier. 'People are always looking for reasons to create more space. And your home has potential for it.'

I smile. I never considered this to be an option, not even when Shafi lived with us.

He opens the door to Mum's room. 'This must be the master bedroom. Decent size.'

I nod and show him my bedroom. 'This is the second bedroom, also a decent size.' But he doesn't seem interested in my diversion. 'Ensuite bathroom?' That gleam appears on his face again.

'Yes, and the mosaic tiles are new, done early this year.' I haven't been in here since Mum left except for this morning when I quickly rammed everything into the wardrobe to make sure her room looked tidy. I've been avoiding going in there, avoiding dealing with her things. The guilt of leaving Mum sits heavy like a stone on my heart. I still feel her presence. Visions of her sleeping, resting, reading. And then I hear her voice call out for me. I couldn't get out of her room fast enough this morning.

'Excellent space,' he says going through his checklist. His head dips into my room. 'Perfect for a child.' He looks at me expectantly.

'Oh, my son is a teenager now. He lives in town with his father.' Thinking of Shafi makes my heart feel warm. I can't wait to see him on Sunday. We've been planning a trip to Ravenswood Lodge. He's finally ready to visit Mum.

'This house will make a lovely little home.' He climbs down the stairs and eyes the place with curiosity. 'We *just* need to find the right family for it.'

His shoes clack against the kitchen tiles. His nostrils flare, he doesn't say anything. I spent all morning cleaning the surfaces, leaving the windows open to air the smell of burning still rubbing off the walls. *The gas hob is brand new*, I tell him. He peers out the window on the side of the kitchen Mum used to sit in. I see her in a state of ease and of comfort. 'It's a very quiet neighbourhood as you can see.' I blink, and in a flicker, her shadow disappears.

'Wasn't there an incident in the local papers?' the estate agent asks. Mano curls his tails between the man's legs. With his foot, he pushes the cat gently to the side. 'About a fire in one of the houses on this very street some time ago?'

I shake my head innocently. 'Not that I know of.' I lift Mano, nursing him in the nook of my arms. 'You see, not much happens around here. 'I live in a—'

'Very quiet neighbourhood. You mentioned.' His finger touches the tip of his lips, pondering. 'I'm sure it was this street.'

I caress Mano in quick strokes. The estate agent isn't stupid. He is on to me and must have read the local paper depicting a clear picture of our house and of Mum in her state of stupor. 'We had a tiny accident some time ago but really, it was nothing—'

'I thought your house was familiar,' he looks at me. 'But you're not the old Asian woman who tried to burn down your own home, are you?' He has been waiting for this.

I feel the muscles in my face tense. 'My mum lives in a care home now.'

When I went to see her yesterday, she kept saying she has no house. It's burned down.

'Makes sense you want to downsize. The house is too big for just one person.'

He goes into the living room and whispers what sounds like an affirmation. 'This is the right size for a lovely home. I will find the right family for it.' He scrapes dust off the wooden frame hanging on the wall and looks at me, darting the inevitable question. 'Is this Daniel—?'

'No,' I say. 'It's not Daniel Day-Lewis. It's my father.' I want to say I never knew him. He died when I was still young. But I don't think he would care to know. He cares only about whether or not he is able to sell my childhood home.

'Are you sure, because that looks a lot like—'

'I think I know my own father.' I bite my lip. I didn't know him.

'Handsome bloke with a striking resemblance to the actor, wouldn't you say?' the edges of his lips curl. 'Wouldn't have thought he was Asian—'

'Pakistani,' I say.

'Pakistani, Indian, Bangladeshi, Asian . . .' He stops, looks away.

I want to shout into his face. *What the fuck do you mean?*

Mano jumps and places himself in Mum's armchair, tail wagging. There I see her stroking his fur gently. She looks at me and says, 'I am proud of you, of who you are. You are not a failure. Not a disappointment. I love you no matter what'. I press the tears back.

I open the front door and lean against the frame, watching the estate agent sneeze into his elbow. 'Cat allergy,' he says, inhaling the cool air. I nod and smile. Can he please go now?

On the way out, I hand him Mum's set of keys to the house,

now clutched tight in his fist. I tell him there's a playground on the other side of the road, and two miles walk will get you to the barren beach. I used to head into the woods alone to skim stones at the lake. Sometimes they would bounce off the surface, other times they would sink into the water, never to be seen again.

'It really is the perfect place to raise a family,' I say.

Another pondering gaze. He looks around as if to take my word for it.

Behind the net curtain on the other side, I see Mrs Nesbit watching me. Her pale blue eyes move rapidly from side to side. I want to knock on her door and ask why she called the social services on Mum. Why didn't she inform me first? I still see the image in my mind of that day. How the entire neighbourhood stood watching us with poised expressions.

The for sale sign flaps in the wind. He adjusts it, pressing the stick deeper into the ground.

'Where will you be moving to, Miss Malik?'

'Huh? Oh, I'm looking for a one bedroom apartment or closer to town.'

'Let us know if you need any assistance. My colleague has had some great new properties come to the market that are not yet listed,' he hands me a card.

'Thank you, I will.'

He shakes my hand and tells me he will be in touch. I thank him again for coming out and say that I hope the fire incident doesn't put buyers off. *It may*, he says, in which case I need to consider a lower asking price. He gets into his car and drives off. On my way in, I don't turn around. I can feel Mrs Nesbit's eyes burning the back of my neck.

26

AFRAH

'Where are they?' I open and shut the drawers. Shuffle papers on the desk. 'My bracelets?'

Zahra looks at me blankly.

'Has she been here?' I shout. 'Did she come here to steal my bracelets again?'

'Give that back!'

I snatch the newspaper from Zahra.

Throw it up in the air. The pages scatter all over like bits of debris.

'What's the matter?' She stands back against the wall.

I throw the cover and pillow off the bed. The pulses in my temples feel like they're going to explode. The heavy woman yanks open the door, asks what's happening. I turn to the wardrobe, pull out hangers with clothes that do not belong to me. 'Not mine,' I shout. 'And also, not mine.'

Zahra skirts around the desk. She grabs my wrist, but I throw her off, push her back so she staggers backwards and stumbles.

'Should I call the security guard?'

'Carol, no! I'll talk to Afrah, get her to calm down. Please, leave, now!' The door slams and heavy footsteps thunder down the stairs.

Zahra gets to her feet. I pace across the floor, and she reaches for my arm. I scream. She holds me close and I can't move. I sob, the tears catch in her blouse.

'Do you remember? I told you before. I searched all the rooms with permission from the patients. No one has seen your bracelets.'

What is she talking about? I push her away, hard. 'She stole them from me. Nadeem believed me when I showed him the photograph. He went straight to her house and brought back all six bracelets. She refused at first. But she was the thief, not me. She denied everything. Insisted they be hers. She never stopped to accuse me of lying and stealing. I did no such thing.'

'Afrah, when was this?'

'Before she was born. I was pregnant. I stopped wearing my jewellery because of the swelling. Not because of shame or guilt like she said. Time didn't heal any wounds. We never spoke again, not even after she was born. It is custom that daughters get their mother's jewellery. She didn't want them, didn't care. So I gave Amira two of my bracelets.' I swallow the hard knots in my throat. I feel lost in time. 'Where am I? And who are you?'

'It's where you live Afrah, in a care home. I am Zahra, your nurse.'

I shake my head. 'Leave me alone. Just go!' she turns and slips out of the door.

My room is a mess. Pillow and duvet off the bed, feathers flying in the air. Clothes out of the wardrobe and unfolded. The newspaper is scattered across the floor, I gather the pieces and scrunch them into the bin.

Somebody is outside my door. 'You've gone mad, haven't you? Gosh! Look at the mess you made again. Just look at it.' The large woman shakes her head. I hear her footsteps fade away. I pick everything up, putting it straight. I shake, bending down, hands on knees. My throat is dry as if I have been shouting.

'Stay here,' says Zahra. 'I'll be right back.'

'Why don't we go out and get some fresh air? A walk will do you good.' Zahra gets me dressed and we go out in the garden. 'Wait here while I grab my jacket.'

Some of the other patients are talking to me, but I only hear the toothless man say he enquired and didn't get any Urdu book from the local library. I shrug, don't know what he is talking about. The tall man with the pale wrinkly face makes a snarky remark and walks past me, punching my shoulder hard. I lose my balance and stumble.

Zahra grabs me and asks if I am feeling OK.

'Did you not see that? He pushed me,' I point a finger, but the man is nowhere to be seen. 'He wants to hurt me, fool of a man.'

She shakes her head. 'See what?' she says with a smile. 'Who wants to hurt you?'

'I saw Liam push you,' says Carol. 'If you ask me, he hates you. No doubt.'

'Liam doesn't hate Afrah,' says Nisha, rolling over in her chair. 'He despises her.'

'He's a nasty bastard,' says Carol. 'Stole your gold bangles and sold them.'

'He did what?' I touch my empty wrist. 'When?'

'Maybe the old idiot John took them and buried them in the garden,' says Nisha. 'He's taken my pills. Flushed them into the toilet. Idiot. Idiot.'

Carol laughs. 'Planting gold thinking he'll grow it. There he goes peeing all over Liam's beautiful flower bed.' We all watch John run down the path and hide behind a tree.

'Stop this circus at once.' Mrs Brown hisses. 'Everyone, get inside.'

Zahra pulls me close and we stroll down the slope and past the yard. We walk a while, and I can see the ocean towards the end of the house. Rocks jut out of the water. No trees out here. Only a grey landscape and windblown bushes and shrubs. Dead plants, with dry stems dangling downwards. In the distance, there's a clutter of cottages and the odd fishing boat bobbing in the water, as if made of paper.

I keep thinking someone has been in my room, gone through my things. I've noticed a strange smell, earthy, burned. Zahra doesn't seem to be paying attention. Why isn't she taking me seriously? She thinks I am forgetful, that I can't remember things.

'Why so quiet?' I say. 'Has something terrible happened?'

Zahra looks at me so suddenly. 'You were upset about the jewellery earlier so I went looking everywhere again and found these.' She takes out four gold bracelets. 'I wanted to hand them back to you when we had a quiet moment.'

'Where did you find them?'

'In Carol's room. There's your thief.'

'I don't understand, why would Carol do such a thing? She reminds me of—' I stop. I don't want to say her name.

'Who does Carol remind you of?' she says sweetly. 'A friend? Someone you knew in the past?'

'No one,' I say, and bite my nails. Thinking of her brings back bad memories. 'I want to go back. Please take me back, now.'

'Sure.' Zahra smiles.

We make a turn, my feet crunching on half-buried shells. 'I don't like it out here. My daughter used to drag me to the beach to collect broken seashells. She kept a silver box for them, which was in the garage. That's where we stored things. Photographs, documents and files. My unused saris in the suitcase. My husband's tools. I also kept her diary there. We lost everything in the fire except for what was stored in that garage.'

'What do you mean? What fire?' Zahra asks. 'How did you lose everything?'

I sense Zahra has an appetite to know more. She wants to hear the story I am holding back and keeps looking at me curiously.

We are back at the lodge and I have tea with Zahra in the little reading room. The fireplace is all smoke and ashes. I don't like the smell of anything burned. Ashes, smoke – even dust – can stir my emotions. I ask if we can sit in the library. She leads me by the arm and I sit on the sofa facing a shelf with leather-bound books. She brings the tea over and pours me a cup.

'You mentioned losing everything in a fire,' says Zahra.

'Did I?' I laugh. 'I don't remember.' Zahra looks at me unbelievingly. 'Tell me more about yourself. Do you have any family?' I ask in Urdu.

'I do,' she hands me a mug.

'Where are they now?' I sip too quickly and the tea scalds my tongue.

'In Scotland,' she says. 'I try to visit whenever I can.'

'You mean your parents and siblings?' I ask.

'No, just my auntie. She raised me all by herself. I have no siblings. It's always been the two of us after my parents died in a car accident when I was little.' She looks away, and I trace sorrow in her eyes.

'I'm sorry for your loss,' I say. 'Sorry you had to grow up without a real family. Losing someone you love is a hard grief to carry.'

'I was devastated for a long time,' she says. 'The pain of losing someone you love never really goes away. I think of my parents every day. Do you think of your husband often?'

'I do,' my hands interlace. 'He was a good man. He didn't deserve to die young.'

'I know how it feels to be alone. Without a proper family. We Asians build our entire lives around our families and our communities. If I may ask, how did your husband die?'

Tears fill my eyes. 'It was a tragic accident. I don't want to talk about it.'

'That's fine. We don't have to talk about things that makes you feel uncomfortable. Losing a spouse and raising a child alone is not an easy thing to do.'

'It wasn't my fault,' I say. 'His death wasn't my fault. There was nothing I could do.'

'Why would it have been your fault?' She looks right at me.

'That's what they all thought. And then she began screaming: "*You killed him. You finally killed him.*"'

The echo plays in my ears. I drop my cup. It breaks between

my feet. Zahra sweeps the glass away and throws the shards into the bin.

'They never liked me,' I mutter.

'Who?'

'My husband's friends. They were like family to us. At least I thought they were until—' The memories fill my mind. Her stern look. Her cold arrogance. She wanted revenge. 'We stopped talking. There was nothing left to say.'

'Do you mean the same Pashtun family you had a fall out with?'

'What difference does it make now? I have no one. Amira has left me. She hasn't returned my calls or visited. She doesn't care,' I stare into Zahra's glowing eyes. 'Does she?'

'Give it some time, I'm sure she will come visit you soon.'

'She hates me. My daughter hates me.'

'Who hates you?' says Carol snooping into our conversation from nowhere. 'Liam. Yes, Liam hates you. He told me he doesn't like foreigners. He says they smell of garlic. I didn't say it, he did. You know what he also said? That you should go back where you came from.'

'Carol that's enough now.' Zahra stands up. 'Please, leave!'

'Yeah, yeah,' says Carol mockingly. 'I'll leave.'

But she doesn't. She hangs around and watches us, carefully listening to every word we say. I throw a book at her.

'You are one crazy old lady,' she says.

'Come on, Afrah, I'll take you back to your room.' Zahra leads me to the lift instead of the stairs where Carol stands watching us.

'Leave me alone,' I say, glaring at Carol. 'Go, chalo, jao!'

'What are you so mad for?' asks Carol with annoyance. She turns away and I go to the windowsill in my room and look out. A vast emptiness surrounds me. The quiet valleys and hills embracing the rain. This place is abandoned with nothing except the manor resting here like an empty tomb.

'Nadeem would have liked it out here. He was a nature lover. And so was she. The beach was her favourite place as a child, and I'd take her out there most weekends. Things changed and we stopped going. I wish she had never befriended that girl.'

'Your husband's friends,' Zahra draws the curtains and places a jug of water next to my bed. 'Have you ever tried to make contact to them?'

I shake my head. 'No, I didn't want them to find me when I moved away. I guess I was protecting Amira. For so long I carried the secret in my heart. It's a burden getting heavier with time. It's a secret that follows me wherever I go.'

'What secret, Afrah?'

I pull out the newspaper from the bin. 'Nothing gets written about her anymore. From front-page news to nothing, nothing! Fourteen, so young. Vanished. Disappeared. No trace of her anywhere after the fire.'

'The girl you keep talking about. Did you know her? Who was she?'

I nod and turn back to the windowsill. I touch the glass, scratch at the hairline crack. It rains as though it's never going to stop. That drumming sound. I wish it had rained that day. Nadeem might still have been alive.

'Next to my husband's tombstone, there's another grave. I have been collecting the stories in the newspaper ever since she disappeared. The police, the investigators. Everyone was talking about it. How did it happen? Was it an accident or did somebody do it? It was my fault. I left the rice to burn in the kitchen. The fire from the candle had spread within seconds. I didn't react when I should have.'

'Afrah, who lies buried next to your husband?'

'She is presumed dead,' my face twitches, 'but I still dream about her.'

The incident plays on a loop in my head. I left without telling anyone. I had to get away. The fire took everything away from me and there was nothing left for me to stay behind. I only had scraps of memories, that had survived in the shed. Photographs, original birth certificates, news clippings and old tapes. The silver box containing broken seashells. And then there's her diary. A trail to the past. I kept it all in the box.

A fresh start was what I needed for myself and for Amira. So I ran away.

'Who do you still dream about, Afrah?'

I turn around and wipe away the tears welling in my eyes. Zahra stands in front of me, her face awash with sympathy. 'I am to blame. I did something unforgivable.'

'What did you do?' There's no judgement in her voice. She draws close with a sympathetic look in her eyes. 'Afrah? Don't be afraid. You can tell me.'

I release the tension from my mind. 'There was a fire, a terrible fire with flames everywhere. Our house burned down. It was my fault. My husband didn't survive. Only Amira and I made it out alive. She was with us in the house. It was front-page news. Her picture was everywhere. She had disappeared after the fire. We looked for her everywhere for weeks. The police, the search parties. There was no trace of her. Everyone presumed she was dead. I never got over it.'

'Who is presumed dead, Afrah?' says Zahra. 'Please tell me, was it the girl who had a bad influence on your daughter?'

I shake my head.

'Then who was it?'

'She destroyed my old cassettes with my favourite music on it that was precious to me. Showed no shame. No guilt. I shouldn't have, but I couldn't help myself. I struck her so hard she had a nosebleed. I regret what I did.' I place my hands in my lap and look up at Zahra. 'I used to call her something else. I had this name for her. Meri—'

'Meri what?' Zahra takes my hand and holds it in hers.

The name slips from my tongue. I haven't said her name out since that fateful day.

'Afrah,' says Zahra. 'Sometimes it helps to talk about things.'

'I never told Amira about it because she would ask questions.'

'What don't you want Amira to know, Afrah?'

'That I had another daughter, Mona. She was only fourteen years old. She was in the house when it caught fire and has been missing ever since. It was front-page news.'

I can hear someone running down the hallway, away from my room. Someone who was listening in. Someone else who now knows my secret.

PART THREE

Confessions

27

Sunday, 10th August 1986

Dear Diary,

I'm so angry with Mum for lots of reasons. But mainly for what she did. She took the piercing out while I was asleep. The hole sealed overnight. She denied it and said in her mocking voice, I don't know what you are talking about. And it just made me even more angry. It's my nose, why does she get to decide what I do with it?

Mum said I was a role model to my younger sister. I squirmed. The little brat does my head in. I wish she would stop coming to my room, nagging me all the time. She always, always leaves a mess, so I told her I'd bury her bed with spiders while she was asleep if she ever set foot in my room again. Her eyes doubled. I hope she stays away.

Dad took me out — we went for ice cream and a drive along the beach. I was so happy I could spend time with him. He's been so busy tutoring privately on the weekends and in the evenings. I've not seen him like in forever. He asked me what was going on between the two us? As in Mum and me. He looked frustrated and said we used to be so close. And I told him she doesn't care about me. All Mum cares about is herself. Dad just put a hand on my shoulder. He smiled like he didn't believe me. I told him it's true. Told him Mum hates me! She also hates that I hang out with the Pashtun family and says Naima has a bad influence on me.

Dad said Mum doesn't hate me. She's just a little stubborn sometimes. But why can't she be more like Dad? I hate that she is so stubborn. Why does she always have to ruin everything? I told dad that I wish she would be normal. Dad smiled again and told *me not to be so hard on her. He gave me a warm look and said that deep inside Mum loves me.*

Dad talked nonsense. What does it mean to love 'deep inside'? Mum just keeps the love I deserve locked away. What's the point in that? I told Dad. It's the same thing as not loving me. Dad pushed Mum's tape into the cassette player. A silly song spat out an annoying melody: It's a sunny Sunday. A fun day.

Mum likes listening to Hindi and Qawwali songs and often hums along to ones like this. I told Dad I don't like listening to Mum's cassettes. I wanted him to play something else. Jennifer Rush, Whitney Houston, Michael Jackson. Anything else but Mum's cassettes.

I also told him I don't understand why she listens to it. He said it connects her to her culture. She grew up in Pakistan and holds different views. She is traditional. Whatever that means. If she is that traditional why doesn't she go back I said. Dad laughed and said tradition is also to be close to your family. He said when he and Mum get old they want me to be there to care for them. I stared out the window, ignored what Dad went on about. I never want to care for Mum. She never cares about me.

After we came home from the drive along the beach, I went to Mum's bedroom and reeled the tapes of all her favourite cassettes and put them in the brat's room. I left them on the floor. Later, I saw Mum chucking them in the bin, and when she wasn't looking, I took them out. I waited for her to say something. But she never said anything. She protected the brat. She always protects her. I wish she would go away. I wish she'd never been born. We were fine, before she arrived. The day she was born, Mum changed. She stopped loving me.

Mum put on the radio and listened to English and American songs. Finally, I asked her, What happened to all your favourite cassettes? Mum didn't say anything. That's when I told her it was me. I destroyed them. I threw the broken cassettes at her feet. I couldn't help it. I wanted to hurt her back.

That was when Mum lost it. She went nuts and slapped me so hard I had a nosebleed. Even Dad told her she was overacting. She dragged me up and slammed the door to my room. Mum said I had been a very, very silly ladki. Dad came upstairs later and said I should make up with Mum. I used my rule. I lied: 'Okay daddy. I'll be the daughter she wants me to. I'll be a good girl.'

But I wasn't.

Last night, a black spider with thick legs scurried across the wall. I didn't even shiver when I saw it. I knew exactly what to do. It was twitching irritably as I pinched it by its hairy leg. I opened the door to her bedroom and put it on Amira's little face, numb with sleep. 'Sweet dreams, little brat.' I nudged it with my finger. The spider didn't move. Next time, I'll need more. I'll get a bunch of them. I nudged it again before it scuttled down her perfect little Kashmiri nose. Her hand wiped like a windscreen all over her face. She scratched her nose and felt the itch. She opened her eyes and screamed. Mum came running out. I was already in my room watching them through the opening. She held Amira close to her heart, her little eyes wet with tears.

I wish she'd hold me like that when I cried.

I wish Mum would love me the way she used to.

28

AMIRA

Diya has offered to help me search for flats online. She scrolls through property sites with me, putting in my search criteria.

'If you could sell for asking price, chances are you'll get a good one-bed in town.' Diya is savvy and knows the market and neighbourhoods in and around Inverness well. She sold Nisha's house in a bidding war and spent months searching for her dream home, a beautiful house in the Highlands overlooking Loch Ness. She calls it her 'settlement reward' after getting divorced from Jim.

'What about a studio?' I bite my lower lip. I don't tell Diya it is likely the fire incident will knock down the asking price. A studio is not ideal. I wanted Shafi to have his own room when he stays with me. But he can always sleep on a sofa bed.

A flicker of doubt appears in her eyes. 'You plan on staying single?'

'For now I am.' I don't care to think about marriage, or family. I want to study something creative instead. Design, fashion or, perhaps, art.

'What's the mortgage on a studio like?' I ask.

'Depends on the location. How central do you need to be? Don't tell me you want to stalk your ex living right next to him.'

'You know me better than that. I respect Haroon.'

'He cheated on you with the woman he worked with *and* left you while your mum suffered from dementia. How can you still be talking to that bastard?'

'He also helped me a lot,' I say, in his defence. 'When Mum was diagnosed, it took a hard toll on our marriage. I don't blame him

190

for leaving.' Mum stopped recognising Haroon. She would push him out of the house and shout, *Stay away from my daughter*. He felt rejected and hurt. His masculinity and ego shaken. It wasn't her fault she didn't recognise him anymore. Just like she can't recognise Shafi or the man in the frame as her husband.

'Don't tell me you are accountable for his screwing another woman.'

'It's not like that – you wouldn't understand. Haroon cheating was a result of what went on in our marriage. But I have forgiven him. He's done enough to redeem himself.'

'Like what?' Diya tilts her head.

'Arranged for Mum to see specialists, made several appointments with the memory loss clinic. Appointments I missed. He even recommended Ravenswood Lodge. What ex-husband does that? He checked in on Mum to make sure she's settled.'

'Has she?'

'Haroon said she had. And she seems happy whenever I visit. Why do you ask?' I don't mention Mum losing her things. She is forgetful and it's nothing to be worried about.

'The place gives me shivers. Ranveer suggested Ma be there, I agreed, and pay my share every month.'

'You don't want her to be there?' I ask. 'Is something wrong?'

'No, it's just not that cheap to keep her in a first-class private facility. Yes, they care for the elderly and for people with physical disabilities, including Alzheimer's – and so on, but to be honest—' she hesitates to go on.

'But what?'

'Ma's memory is fine. Sometimes she forgets faces and places and disappears into a void. It takes her a while to return to normality. The doctors said it's the effect of her stroke and I shouldn't worry.'

'But you do, don't you?' I think of how much I worry about Mum.

She nods. 'Ma is old and vulnerable. She is unable to recall whatever goes on in the timeframe she blacks out. And that really worries me. In the freefall of her moment of blankness anything could happen, and she wouldn't be able to remember. I took her jewellery. I don't fully trust the people working at the care home. What do you think of it?'

I don't tell Diya I packed all of Mum's jewellery. I shouldn't have. Mum said her things were missing.

'I don't like the idea of Mum being in a care home. The location is rural, and it takes a while to drive out there via those winding dark roads, lurking with deer and other creatures. And that old Victorian manor – you're right. The place also gives me the shivers. But I had no say. Mum was granted a place by the council. They have carers and nurses to look after patients around the clock; a community of their own. Like you said, it's a first-class care home. I wouldn't be able to afford to keep Mum there. I don't expect to pay frequent visits. I'll be going out there once a week when she's settled, to see how she's doing. I really am in no position to make any complaints.'

'Expect complaints if you swing by once a week to visit her. Ma complains all the time that I never visit. You know what it's like. I somehow can't get over Ravenswood's dark history. I started looking into it. Believe me, some spooky things went on in that house.'

'Like what?'

'The killings. They used to burn witches out there. Ma has trouble sleeping. She said she saw a woman in white with a veiled face wandering around the halls at night holding a candle. She was sure it wasn't a patient or carer. I mean, who would do that? Disturbing, don't you think?' Diya shakes her shoulders.

'What are you saying? That the house is haunted?'

She shrugs. 'An article was featured in the papers about the care home. One of their patients died in her sleeps. Alice Clark. I find that bizarre. What's also bizarre is that they have installed no security cameras in or outside the care home. A "very traditional place", or so they say. Who knows what goes on when no one is watching.'

Alice Clark . . . I remember Haroon telling me when I met him at the café that Mum got her room. It's what made it possible for her to get a space at Ravenswood Lodge.

'Why should they, when it's such a small facility? They trust their staff. Haroon tells me Mum's been lucky. She has a Pakistani carer looking after her, a friend of his family. That's one of a few reasons I've kept off from contacting her too much. She's bonded with her.'

'Oh, don't get me wrong, Ma is happy with Margaret, it's just—'

'You are giving me reason to worry! Should I?' I raise my brows.

'No,' she smiles. 'Of course not. When are you visiting your mum again?'

'Tomorrow – time doesn't work in the same way for her as it does for me.' I pull out my phone to see if Ravenswood Lodge sent an email back confirming my visit. Nothing.

'Well, you'll see she's doing fine. If anything, it helps make the guilt go away.'

'What did you do?'

'I stopped visiting her. Ma would call me every freakin' day. She mainly calls to complain. Ma never accepts me for who I am. I wish she'd look at me and say, Diya, you are enough. I love you as you are. But no, instead she stalks me on Instagram and posts bad comments on every one of my posts.'

'Really?' I raise my brows. I can't imagine Nisha would do such a thing.

Diya nods. 'My friend's mother, a widow, decided to move back to India and live in an ashram. Ranveer didn't like the idea when I made the suggestion. He's always been her favourite. "Ma needs care," he said. "The best she can get. We owe it to her." How did your mum take the news when you broke it to her?'

'Mum wasn't keen when I first told her. You know how it is in our culture. We look after our parents when they are old. We do not abandon them. Guilt is one thing. Another one is blame or even shame. Mum started saying, "I am not pagal." She believed I was sending her to the care home because she had become a burden. As I was about to leave she kept saying, '"Don't leave me! Mimi, I will never forgive you if you leave me."'

'Gosh Mira, I'm so sorry you had to experience that. How did you cope?'

'I had to keep telling myself, you gotta be cruel to be kind, and then I left.'

'No wonder you feel guilty,' says Diya. 'I've had Ma push the emotional switch. It doesn't matter what I do, she's always disappointed. And then it is always *my* Ranveer this and *my* Ranveer that. You're lucky you never had to experience any sibling rivalry.'

'I always wanted to have a sister or a brother. Someone I could talk to.'

'Be happy you didn't. It took a lot of therapy and self-help books to accept who I am,' says Diya. 'Now I tell myself I am not a failure. I am good enough no matter what.'

We both laugh; who would have thought we would be sitting and sharing the effects our cultural upbringing has had on us? Diya's words evoke my feelings that I've kept suppressed for all the years I cared for Mum. I love her and I loathe her for the same reasons Diya lined up.

A message pops up on the laptop screen from Meena.

Thelonelymouse: Hey love, you online?

Diya looks at me suspiciously. 'You seeing someone called *Thelonelymouse* and haven't told me?'

'It's not what you think! She is a friend of mine who works as carer.'

'And so is Bob,' Diya folds her arms over her chest. '"We're friends" he said.'

'You need to stop dating Americans.'

'I'll date any Dick and Harry. For I shall never marry again.' We both laugh.

I check my phone again.

Thelonelymouse is typing.

Thelonelymouse: I have a favour to ask. Could we meet somewhere and talk? It's sort of urgent. I really need you, Amira.

'What does your friend want?'

'Nothing,' I snap shut the laptop and smile. 'So, what flats have you arranged to show me this afternoon?'

Diya pulls out her phone and swipes through a list of homes. She has been busy.

It's late at night when I unlock the front door and hit the light switch. I hang my bag on the hook. I am exhausted after the flat viewings. I saw five cold and clinical little cells that I couldn't imagine living in. I want something warm, homey. I guess I have to keep looking.

I go into the kitchen and pour cat food into Mano's bowl and switch on my laptop again. There's a message being typed from Meena. I pull up a chair and take a seat.

Thelonelymouse: Amira, hey love, you online?

She must have been waiting for me since her last message.

Nursemira: Are you OK? Sorry I was busy, couldn't speak before.

Thelonelymouse: I'm so sorry. I didn't mean to worry you, but I really need your help.

Nursemira: Has something happened? You can tell me.

Thelonelymouse: I'm struggling. You know the family I am living with, I don't think I can stay with them anymore. I mean, I adore the little boy I'm looking after, but something has happened and I think I have to leave. I am so afraid. Thought maybe we could meet in person – we've been meaning to anyway. You've been such a good friend to me.

Nursemira: Sure. Anything.

I bite my lip. I feel so sorry for Meena and hope it's nothing serious. She seemed so happy about the live-in position when we last spoke. I wonder what's happened? Did she regret her decision? I need to be there for her. I have to help her.

Thelonelymouse: Tomorrow morning? Meet me at the Caledonian Canal. We'll find some place to go for breakfast. My treat.
Nursemira: I'm sorry. I can't tomorrow.

That's when I plan to take Shafi out to visit Mum. I want to take her out for a walk on the beach.

Thelonelymouse: Please Amira. You are the only person I can trust. I really need to talk to you as a friend. As a sister. Please! I am desperate.

I think of Mum and of her disappointment when she finds out I am not coming. I don't blame her. I have only myself to blame. Perhaps I am a failure after all.

Nursemira: Don't worry. I'll see you then.

Meena types a message with her number in case I need to reach her and says she'll meet me at eight o'clock. I save it on my phone and log out. I go upstairs and fall into bed, but I don't sleep. I stay awake, worried. Guilt surges through me like a sharp sword. What am I doing? Failing Mum to meet with a stranger I met online.

I check my phone for emails. Nothing. The care home never confirmed my visit. Perhaps it's because I said I'd bring Shafi with me. But that shouldn't matter, should it?

Mum may not even remember I am coming tomorrow. And I can always pay her a visit the next day. I'll just have to tell Shafi we'll go some other time. It's not like Mum remembers him anyway.

Mano jumps into bed and lays next to me. He looks at me with sleepy eyes.

'I will make it up to her,' I tell the cat. 'Over the holidays, I'll have Mum stay for longer. She can stay an entire week.' He meows and places his chin on his paws.

It will be just like before.

Me, Mum and Mano.

29

AFRAH

Saturday, 21 December 2019

I drift through the room like a stray cat, my hands touching the surfaces around me. I caress the walls, pieces of old furniture and lifeless oil paintings. I don't feel anything. Things are just things, and these things do not belong to me. The memories they carry are blank. I look around. This is the life I live now.

A draft slips in and the lamp swings in the breeze. I shut the window tight. I turn.

My heart almost stops when I hear a strange tapping. There's a sound of footsteps outside the room. Slow and deliberate. I swing open the door.

No one is there. The hallway is empty.

My fingers trace the walls as I travel down Morton Wing I imagine the deep blue sea bashing against the cliffs in the perpetual cold rain outside. How soothing it would be to be carried along by the waves, a gentle rock of comfort.

'What are you doing out here?' asks Nisha. Wrinkles bunch together as she creases her nose. 'You shouldn't be out at this time. The woman in white might see you.'

'I couldn't sleep.' My mood darkens. 'Who is the woman in white?'

The house feels cold and lifeless. An icy sensation itches at my spine.

'I am going back to bed.' She adjusts her nightgown and closes the door to her room.

I wander back to my room and creep under the duvet. I don't sleep. The window is open and the wind rattles the room. A bad feeling wells up inside me. I hope that nothing bad has happened to Amira. And I pray my daughter pays me a visit soon.

We walk down the winding path that leads us out of Ravenswood Lodge and into the quiet of the forest. A flock of deer pass through the other side of a creek. I tell Zahra how Nadeem and I once saw thousands coming out of the woods like an army of soldiers.

We walk in silence towards the bay hugged by cliffs. Now at the shoreline, cold nicks my skin. The bitter sea wraps around us like a blanket. The current blows in strong and draws back towards the horizon. I look out at the sea under the shadow of the umbrella Zahra holds above our heads. We sit down on a tree trunk. Shoes nestling into the pebbles. Black, grey and white shiny stones wet from the rain.

'When she was little, she loved coming to the sea.'

'Which one of your daughters? Amira or Mona?'

I stare at her in surprise. 'How do you, did I—'

'You told me about your other daughter, Mona.' She digs out a piece of paper from the inner pocket of her coat. 'You said she was fourteen when she was with your husband in a fire and went missing. I went to the library and got this for you.'

I take the paper from her and unfold it. It's a front-page news article describing the tragedy.

'It took me some time to find it. Afrah, it happened over thirty years ago.'

Zahra relates to my pain. She knows how it feels to lose someone you love.

'The night of the fire I lost everything.' I press a hand against my lips, strangling my sobs. The heavy burden of their loss presses hard against my chest.

'You still have your daughter, Amira. But I understand, losing your daughter and your husband is a deep wound, which can never heal. When I lost my parents, I was devastated. I was fortunate I had the love of my auntie. But there's nothing like the love of parents.'

199

Wind blows in from the sea, the article ripples in the wind and sweeps out of sight. Zahra runs to catch it. But it's too late. It is gone with the wind.

I struggle to breathe. 'I never told Amira. She doesn't know—'

'What are you afraid of, Afrah? Did something else happen?' She looks at me disbelievingly. 'You ought to tell her the truth.'

I shake my head. 'I was afraid she'd ask questions. Afraid she might try to contact Nadeem's friends. I didn't want her to have anything to do with them. They'd tell her lies – turn my own daughter against me like Mona turned against me.'

'Is that because you felt mistreated by them? You mentioned you were accused of stealing?'

'Sultana, the mother, with her pride, her arrogance. She looked down on me, on us, for not having money. We were an ordinary Pakistani family. Just happy and living within our means in a working-class neighbourhood. Nadeem didn't have a fancy job. He was a teacher in the local school. I was taking small jobs, like sewing. We weren't good enough in their eyes. The more I wanted Mona to stay away, the more time she wanted to spend with that awful girl, Naima. She was so angry with me for not seeing her. I couldn't I tell her about what had happened. She wouldn't have believed me.'

'What do you mean, tell her what?'

'Have I told you the story? The allegation was absurd. I never laid hands on Sultana's jewellery. We had an argument. I never told anyone about it.'

'What was the argument about?' She gives me a sympathetic look. 'It's okay, you can tell me, Afrah, don't be afraid.'

'I'll tell you. I'll tell you everything about that fateful day she came to the house.'

30

AFRAH

Saturday, 15 August 1970

I raise my head from the toilet. Wipe clean my mouth with the sleeve of my wool kameez. I pull myself up to the sink. The cold water pouring from the tap feels soothing against my skin. I hear Nadeem call out for me.

'What's taking you so long, Afrah Bibi?'

I tell him I am coming and rush out like a dutiful wife to attend to his needs over mine. He removes the sleep from his eyes when I draw the curtains. A sunny day breaks through.

'This ongoing morning sickness must be terrible for you,' he says.

I touch my belly. 'I'm fine. Except for too much spicy food. Those green chillies you bought from the market, I was generous using them in every chutney and every dish.'

He laughs, I think, to fill the empty vacuum. 'Whatever you do, do not use chillies in anything you prepare for lunch today. Hashim isn't particularly fond of spicy foods. Neither is Sultana.'

I almost forgot his friends were coming over. 'Will they be alone?'

'No,' he replies. 'Sultana's parents will also be joining. Pashtun families are close, and ever since they had their baby her parents —'

'I get it.' I swallow hard, remembering Sultana's words. 'When are you going to have a baby of your own? It's been three years already. I say, go to our family doctor – Dr Mohsin – and have yourself checked out.' I didn't tell her I was pregnant. 'What is worse, people are talking. Asking all sorts of questions, like:

"Is Afrah barren?" Well, are you?' She stroked her matka-like belly with one hand while the other was pressed firmly against her back. I didn't answer.

Baby Naima was born in July. Milky skin and a head full of light brown hair. And those green eyes must be a result of their Pathan genes, according to Nadeem, who mentioned it with a hint of admiration. After she was born, Sultana kept her hidden for days, swaddled tight in a blanket where only a scrap of her pink skin was visible. When she had the special amulet made to protect Naima from Nazar, the baby was shown to the world. And what a show it was. They hosted a magnificent party at their house. Hashim arranged for a singer to perform. Waiters served exotic food on silver platters. Sultana wore the most beautiful white silk sari I had ever seen. And her ears, arms and hands were adorned in gold.

'Don't worry,' I say to Nadeem, and spread a fake smile across my face like a clay mask. 'I'll cook an impressive meal to their liking.'

Nadeem looks happy. He's not worried. Why should he be? He's not pregnant, with swollen hands and feet, having to cook all day in the kitchen.

At the front of the house, a black car parks in the free space. *Mercedes-Benz S-class*, I hear my husband mumble.

'Who do they think they are,' says Nadeem. 'Showing off like that with their new car? Just because they have money doesn't mean—' I nudge him.

'Areee, kush nahi hota, it doesn't matter,' I say.

I open the door and put on a big smile. My muscles ache. I release the tension from my face when no one smiles back. Sultana carries a rich and sweet scent. I think she smells like jasmine. She walks straight in, nodding at me. Several rings sit on her fingers, embellished with red and green stones. Gold earrings with pearls and diamonds swing from her lobes. The gold bracelets on her wrist clink when she adjusts the pehlu of her peacock blue silk sari, embellished with gold strings. I can tell by the design that she is wearing another one of her Banarasi. Purple, red, green, in shimmering treads.

They all sit at the dining table, baby Naima nestled in Nadeem's arms. Sultana corrects him, tells him not to hold her daughter that way, but *this* way. Hashim glances over but doesn't really seem to care. He writes something down in a notebook.

'Always working,' Sultana's mother shakes her head. Her father reveals sleepy eyes under a bushy set of brows.

We perch around the coffee table after lunch and I serve mithai and jalebi. Hashim helps himself to gulab jamun. Sultana hands him a napkin, a gesture to wipe the grease from his beard. She takes a ladoo from the tray, eats it in one mouthful. I offer to refill her tea, remove the cosy from the pot, its threads shredding. She declines.

'No thank you, I need to lie down to feed baby Naima. She is hungry.' Tiny red lips puckered in search for milk, press against Sultana's bosom.

I take her upstairs to our bedroom. 'Please can you hold her while I untangle my sari? She hands me the baby and takes off some of her many pieces of heavy jewellery. I stare at the girl's face, plump and puffy. Light as a feather, she's in a white cotton dress. She smells sweet like honey. She clutches onto my dupatta when I pass her back into her mother's arms.

'The wool, isn't it itchy on the skin?' asks Sultana. I don't reply. I look down at my plain clothes. 'It must be, just look at her.' she shows me the baby turned red. 'You've given my daughter a rash.'

'I'm sorry. I didn't mean to—' I shut the door, catching a glimpse of Sultana's cracked nipple, large as a pointy fingertip. I feel a tingle in my own and I shiver.

Sultana's parents are taking a nap on the sofa. Heads resting against one another. Outside, Nadeem is chatting to Hashim while he peers over the rose bush looking bored. I join them, absorbing the sun smiling in a cloudless sky. The grass is soggy from last night's rain, roots sinking into brown squelchy mud. I don't lift up the bottom of my shalwar, drifting in patches of mud. My body begins to itch. I will change into something else. Now, I have reason to.

Sultana is done feeding baby Naima. She puts her on the bed, her little chest rising and falling with soft flows of breath. Sultana puts on her jewellery, smoothly slipping on her gold bracelets, six on one, and six on the other wrist. She also puts on a heavy looking gold necklace, earrings and several rings.

I open the wardrobe and take out a blue cotton sari, which I quickly wrap around my body. She notices the muddy edges of my shalwar, which I shove into the laundry basket. I don't tell her I think the wool itches. That would prove her point about what she said earlier. Sultana only wears silk and chiffon.

'Soon you will also have your baby in your arms. Make sure Nadeem gets you something nice.' She shows me her bracelets. 'Hashim bought them from Saudi, twenty-two carats each. A gift for having Naima. I have a kada cuff also. Special custom-made design. What do you have?' I show her mine, a simple set of six gold bracelets. 'You should have them melted into one big bangle. I can show you the design of my kada.'

'I like what I have,' I say.

'Here, why don't you try them.' She hands me her bracelets. 'They are much nicer.'

'No, no.' I pull back. 'I said, I like mine.'

'Nothing beautiful about plain and simple jewellery. So boring.' She takes offence in what I said, her nose twitching from side to side. 'What's to like?' she laughs. 'You barely have fifty grams worth of jewellery. Here, give them to me.'

I refuse and hide my arm behind my back.

'Even baby Naima has gold bracelets worth more than yours.' She shows me the baby bracelet, beautiful with black beads and diamonds. 'See, twenty-two carats. Custom-made and costs more than £1,500 . . . Probably more than what Nadeem earns in a month.'

'My husband makes enough for the both of us.'

'Does he now? And when you have children, then what?' she says curtly. 'Would you like to have my kada? Here, have it. I can buy ten just like these.'

'Really Sultana, that's very kind of you but—'

'But what Afrah, huh? What?' She stares at my bracelets. 'Give them to me. They look shameful. At least wear something decent.' She tries to force her bangles onto my wrist again. I tell her to stop, but she doesn't listen. Jewellery is a woman's treasure, her safety gifted by her parents when she leaves their home upon marriage. They may not be fancy but my bracelets have an emotional value that cannot be measured in any amount of money.

'No,' I push her back. 'I don't want your charity.'

'What did you say? *Badtameez.* Is that how you treat my kindness?' Sultana's breath is heavy. 'I would have thought you knew how to behave around your husband's friends. You are nothing but a common girl. You will never be of our standard. Who do you think you are in your itchy and cheap wool clothes, and worthless jewellery?'

I want to leave, but she blocks my way.

'You have no idea what I can do to you,' she says, smiling predatorily.

'Sultana, why would you say that? We are like family.' I feel my heart twist as if she's stabbed me with a knife.

She laughs, glaring at me. 'That's why you treat me like this in your home? Like a stranger. You barely look at me or speak to me. Are you jealous?'

'I am not.' I look right at her. 'I'm sorry if you feel I ignore you. Let's forget this incident,' I reach out for her and apologise.

'No, Afrah.' Her cheeks are pink. 'And don't *ever* think we are like family. The only reason we remain friends is because Hashim feels sorry for Nadeem.'

'Well, he has nothing to feel sorry about. We are happy.' I try to leave the room, but she pushes me away. I fall to the floor, but don't do anything. I sit there while she goes through my things.

'Pitiful choice of clothes, don't you think?' she laughs, an evil cackle.

Her words crawl over my skin and climb through my flesh. I get up and tell her to stop. I grab her wrist and push her away. 'You are nothing, Afrah. You have no style or taste. I will make sure—'

Tears burn my cheeks. 'Let me go.'

She blocks the door when I try to leave. I force my way past her, through the doorway. I hear her say, 'I will make sure everyone knows what a common girl you are.'

I stand at the end of the landing, my head raised. Sultana frowns at me with pure malice. The look in her eyes tells me she isn't going to let this go. She is thirsty. Thirsty for a fight.

That night Sultana calls to announce she is on her way back to our house.

'What for?' I ask. 'Everything OK?' I glance at the clock. It's almost ten o'clock.

My husband shakes his head, puts down the receiver. She forgot something in our bedroom. Have you noticed anything? I tell him I haven't. Creases form on his forehead. His hand scratches the back of his neck. He heads upstairs without a word.

Sultana goes straight into our bedroom while Hashim waits in the Mercedes-Benz.

'I left my gold bracelets on the nightstand,' she says, pointing to the vacant spot, illuminated by a pool of light from the bedside lamp. 'They are not there. Afrah where are they?'

I look everywhere. Under the bed, beneath the bedding, in the drawers. 'I haven't seen your bracelets, Sultana. Sure you left them in here?'

'Of course I am.' She makes a hissing sound. 'Why would I otherwise be coming here at night? Afrah, you saw me take them off so I could nurse baby Naima. Didn't you?'

I nod, fold my hands tight behind my back.

'Well?' Her voice is shrill. 'Where are they?' She fixes her eyes at me for longer than necessary and it makes me jittery.

Suddenly I feel like a servant accused of stealing from the lady of the house. Except this is my home and I have not stolen anything. Why *is* she accusing me? Sultana searches the entire room herself. She squats, bends and rushes around. Her hand reaches the bottom drawer where my clothes are neatly folded. She pounds each item and throws it onto the floor. Nadeem's hand reaches for her shoulder, but he pulls it back when he too hears the clinking sound of jewellery. Eyes rolling wildly, she clatters six gold bracelets between her fingers.

'If you haven't seen my bangles, then what are they doing in your drawer?' She holds them up to show me. I want to say something, but the words don't come out.

Nadeem stares at me disbelievingly. 'Afrah?' He wants an explanation.

The realisation of what she is doing shakes through me like a tremor. I'm shocked. Why would she deliberately do such a vicious thing, tampering with my mind?

Sultana stands up, her hand high as if about to strike me. She lowers it and hisses, 'Liar. Thief.' Then leaves without saying goodbye.

My insides are twisting. Nadeem reaches out and pinches my arms, twisting the flesh between his fingers. 'Did you take Sultana's bangles?'

I shake my head. He releases the pressure, his face red with shame, and walks out the bedroom, thundering down the stairs. I can hear them talking. The engine starts. Doors slam. Nadeem doesn't come up.

I lay in bed and pull the duvet over my head stifling my sobs. The bracelets Sultana took are mine. They belong to me. The six gold bracelets my parents gave me on my wedding day. She's taken them. Taken them because she's wrongfully accused me of having stolen hers. I will not let her bring shame onto me. I will clarify matters. I will get my bracelets back, even if it means breaking all ties with the Pashtuns.

In the morning, I show Nadeem our wedding pictures.

'Look,' I point at my wrists.

He notices I wear the exact six bracelets Sultana stole last night. But he doesn't seem to care. His spirit is down when I tell him what happened. Men don't like to get involved in matters between women.

Nadeem doesn't eat his breakfast. He tells me to stay at home till he returns.

'Make sure she gives back my bracelets.' I shove the picture into his palm.

His head hangs, shoulders slumped. He knows and I know this changes the relationship we have to his friends. They will start spreading lies. Let them say what they like. I know I am no thief. My heart races when Nadeem leaves the house. I stroke my tummy. Soon we will have a family of our own, and no child of mine will ever have anything to do with that Pashtun family. That, I swear by.

31

AMIRA

Sunday, 22 December 2019

I'm at the Caledonian Canal, standing on the Bridge of Oich. It's an unusually misty morning, and the fog has covered the water. No one is in sight. I check my phone. There's an email in my inbox sent late last night from Ravenswood Lodge, confirming I can visit Mum today between nine and eleven o'clock this morning. I am also welcome to bring Shafi along. In a note below it says: 'We encourage you to make the visiting time and avoid cancelling as most patients anticipating a visit from relatives and friends may become distressed and highly agitated.' Mum is expecting to see me. I have to make it. I'll listen to what Meena has to say, pick up Shafi and drive straight to the care home.

A jogger, dressed all in black, runs briskly towards me. Plumes of cold breath escape his mouth. He wears a hood that covers most of his face. I hold onto the rail as the jogger passes by. I pull out my phone and text Meena: *'I'm here!* No answer. I wait before calling her. I tuck my hands in my pockets, my shoulders raised to my ears. The cold is getting to my bones. Where is she? I am sure she will be here soon. She is probably running late. Meena is not the type of woman who's going to stand me up. I tell myself, she is a friend, a *good* friend.

I walk back and forth, rock on my heels. It's eight-thirty. I think I see somebody coming through the fog. I rub my eyes – is that someone's shadow? I'm starting to feel nervous. I hear the slow clacking of heels. It's a woman, or perhaps it's a man? I think I see a sharp red colour. Is that somebody's coat? Could it be Meena? I don't have a clue what she looks like, and it's probably different to how I've pictured her. The figure has quickened their pace towards me, seemingly carrying an air of stress. The fog is getting thick now. I think I see a woman passing me in a hurry, her head turned to the side. I can't see her face properly. I can't see anything in the fog. The clacking stops and I feel my heart race inside my chest.

I must be imagining things again. Nobody is here, just me. I widen my eyes and still believe somebody could be at the other end of the bridge. 'Meena? Is that you?'

I hear the sound of heels clacking aggressively now. But there's nothing, I can see very little through the fog.

'Is anyone there?' No answer.

I hear something that sounds like sniffles and imagine them belonging to a desperate woman.

'Are you OK? Can I help you?' No reply. I hear a scraping sound. Like nails as if scratching the rail of the bridge. I walk back, stumble and run.

A ripple breaks the silence. A splash, a loud burble in the water. Then it's silent again. I turn. The fog suddenly seems thicker. I don't believe anyone is there, but I need to be sure. 'Hello? Is anybody there? Hello?' No answer. I must have imagined the whole thing. Another figment of my imagination just like the spiders in my bed. That's what lack of sleep does to the mind, it plays tricks.

Trying to control my cold hands from shaking, I dial the number Meena gave me and after countless rings, there's still no answer. I decide to wait. She sounded so worried about the family she is living with. I hope nothing has happened to her. Oh God! I stop my thoughts from spiralling out of control. I ring her number again. I have a bad feeling about this. What should I do? I can't even contact the police. What will I say? Still no answer. I decide to leave a message.

'Meena, hi, it's Amira. Are you there? Pick up. I am here at the bridge and I was wondering if you were OK? Please call me back.' I sound worried. I am worried.

It's almost nine o'clock. I should go, get out of here. I walk off and a message appears on my phone. It's from Meena. 'Sorry couldn't answer. Wait for me. Don't go. Will be there shortly.' I text her saying I have to leave, but she begs me to wait, and I root my feet to the ground.

I fidget and keep staring at my watch. A message pings from Meena. 'Hey love, I'm here. Can't see you anywhere. Where are you?'

I look around. The fog has surrounded me. But I am sure no one is here.

'I'm on the bridge,' I crane my neck all around me, feeling the muscles twist.

'So am I, Amira. Why don't I see you?'

I type as fast as I can. 'Meena, what bridge are you at?'

'I'm waiting at Fort Augustus,' she replies. 'Where are you?'

'Stay there,' I type. 'I'm at Oich. I am coming over.'

It was late at night when we spoke. I don't remember what she said about where to meet her and assumed it was Oich. Fort Augustus is only a short drive away. I rush back and get into my car and drive as fast as I can towards it.

The fog is blinding me, I'm not even sure where I am going. I see headlights beaming from the opposite side of the lane. The mist feels like a thick smoke. I slow down, squint. I hope I am driving in the right direction. I continue at a slower pace, following the straight road. My phone is vibrating, so I reach inside my bag to pull it out. Suddenly I have to take a sharp turn and swing into what I believe is the parking area. I stare at the screen, it's an incoming call from Meena. I look ahead, when a jeep out of nowhere hurtles right towards me. A crash reverberates in my ears. My head hits the airbag, bounces back. I taste blood inside my mouth. It smears the frames of my car. Everything turns black.

The light behind my eyelids is sharp. A sheet is pulled over my body, the smell clinical, sterile. I know I am in a hospital. I wiggle my fingers and wince in pain. My bones feel like they're rattling. I open my eyes, panic and confusion spreads through me. I hear the sounds of hospital machines – that's when I remember I had an accident. A car drove into mine. I try to get up, but a familiar voice is telling me not to. His hands press a plastic cup close to my lips. I swallow the cold water and it softens my cracked lips.

'How do you feel, Mira?' Haroon's deep brown eyes rest on me. I know by the look of it that he's going to give me some sort of lecture. I nod to signal I am OK. A lump on my head is pounding, pain swelling through my body.

'That was quite a nasty accident you had. Luckily nothing happened. The driver you crashed with drove off. Not to be found anywhere. And no one saw anything due to the heavy fog. The police came around when you were asleep. I gave them your details. They have questions. Do you remember what happened? What were you doing out on Caledonian Canal? I thought you were picking up Shaf? He was looking forward to visit his Nano. We called and called. Fortunately, we were able to trace you through the location of your phone. Mira, please answer. What happened? Why were you out there? Should I be worried?'

Fuck! 'I am so sorry,' my raspy voice cuts in my ears. 'I was meeting a friend.'

'On a Sunday morning?' Haroon crosses his arms over his chest. 'Look, Shaf is worried and missed his cricket match this afternoon when he heard what had happened. The trainer was pissed. Didn't believe we had another family emergency. They seem frequent now.'

'Haroon, please.' I don't look up. Heat washes over my face, and I let it. Why is he so angry anyway? It's not like we're married anymore.

Haroon is about to leave the room.

'Wait,' I say. He stops, doesn't turn around. 'I have to go, can you sign the release papers?'

He draws in a deep breath. 'Are you sure? I can take a look at your bruise and examine you myself. I want to make sure you're OK, Mira.'

'Really, I feel fine.'

He stares at me incredulously. 'Mira, you got lucky, a little bump on the head and no major injuries. But I'd really feel better if I could take a look at you.'

'No need for it, can I go now?' He knows I don't like hospitals. 'I'll make it up—'

'Fine,' He rolls his eyes. 'I'll sign the release papers so you can go home after you speak to the police.'

'What happened to my car?'

'It was sent to the garage. Will you be OK ordering a taxi?'

'Yes.' My throat is dry. 'Thank you.'

Someone is at the front door. Two police officers, one tall and one short. They introduce themselves. But I don't register their names. I still feel I am in a daze, still standing on the bridge surrounded by the heavy mist. They ask if they can have a moment with me. I nod and show them inside the living room.

Mano meows and curls his tail around my leg. I place him in Mum's armchair and notice the men are already sitting at the dining table, examining every corner and every nook of the house.

'Miss Malik, can you give us a description of what happened this morning? What were you doing on Caledonian Canal?' the short one asks.

'I was meeting a friend. She needed to see me. I think she was in trouble.' I take a seat across from them. I hope Meena is okay. I've still not heard a word from her.

The tall one takes note. 'What kind of trouble was this friend of yours in?'

'She didn't say.' Heat is building in my cheeks. 'Is everything OK?'

The short one asks for details so they can run my story. I give them Meena's number and tell them how I met her. I open my laptop, ready to show them the log of conversation we had in the chat forum for carers. But as I log in, a message says the user *Thelonelymouse* does not exist and though our conversations are still on there, I can't send any more message. I tell them that the account existed until just this morning. My friend Diya can testify I chatted with *Thelonelymouse* yesterday.

'What's her full name?'

'Meena, Meena Bashir, I think.'

The short one nods and I notice the suspicion in his cold blue eyes. The tall one is calling someone. He glares at me, unsmiling, when I try to show him the messages we exchanged this morning. He doesn't appear interested.

'You don't think meeting a complete stranger – who you've never met before – who you know only from an online chat forum for carers was dangerous?' says the short one. 'This person could be anybody. Were you not afraid going out there alone?' His voice is full of tension, and I avoid looking at him.

Feeling judged, I shake my head. 'We started chatting online – it's been about a year, I believe. It was harmless. She was a carer like me, and she supported me in my time of need. When she wrote to me last night she genuinely seemed worried and frightened about living with the new family she was working for.'

'Did she say what family? Did she leave an address or anything we can check?'

'No, nothing. It all happened so fast. We only chatted occasionally. I wasn't expecting to ever meet her. In the end I agreed because she sounded desperate. I didn't know what else to do. I just wanted to help. Wanted to be a good friend.'

'Burner phone,' says the tall one. 'Can't trace it. Seems like it was ditched after use.'

Something has happened to Meena. She must have been afraid and deleted her online account. Why else hasn't contacted me again? No incoming messages or calls. It's not like her. Meena wouldn't leave me worried.

Now he glares closely at my exchange with Meena. 'Where did you say, you were meeting her?' He holds my phone, scrolling through my messages.

'There was a misunderstanding about what bridge we were meeting at.'

'Let me get the facts right. You drove out to Caledonian Canal this morning to meet your friend whom you met in an online chat for carers?' I nod. 'Can you state the exact location on Caledonian Canal where you met her?'

'That's the thing, I didn't. I waited for her at Bridge of Oich. She never turned up. She was waiting for me at Fort Augustus.'

They look at one another, brows arched.

'Is something wrong?' I ask. 'Is Meena OK?

'How long were you at Bridge of Oich?'

'About an hour, I believe. I'm not sure.'

'And then you headed to Fort Augustus, which is where you had an accident?'

'Yes, like I said, I was waiting for her at the wrong location.'

'Why did it take you so long before you realised you were at the wrong meeting point? Wouldn't you have agreed in advance on the exact place?'

'Like I said. It all happened so fast. There was a misunderstanding. I couldn't get hold of Meena and decided to wait at the Bridge of Oich in case she was running late. I called and left her a message. I drove off when she told me she was at Fort Augustus. But before I could get there, a car out of nowhere crashed into mine.'

'Did you get a look at the driver?'

I shake my head. 'It was unusually foggy this morning.' He asks if I am sure. 'Yes, I couldn't see anything.'

'Do you remember what sort of car drove into you?'

'I think it was a black jeep, but I am not sure.' They exchange worried glances. 'What is this really about?' I sense something else is going on. 'Please, I need to know. Is it Meena? Has something happened to her?' I think of the incident on the bridge, the shadow, the strange sounds of heels clacking. Did I see somebody? No. It wasn't real. It was just another figment of my imagination. A crazy fabrication of my tired mind.

'Are you planning to leave the country anytime soon?'

'What? No. My family is here. My mum, my son and my husband.'

'Ex-husband, correct?' The tall one says. I nod and look out the window. The moon appears through the broken clouds. Its waxing yellow shade casts a pale light on the pavement. 'You were married how many years?'

I tell them, though they already know I was married to Dr Haroon Khan for nearly twelve years. They've obviously come prepared and done a full background check on me. I look at the short one who seems ready to shoot another question across.

'Miss Malik, why are you selling your home?'

'I'm down-sizing.'

'Will you move away from Inverness?'

'No, I have no reason to. I've lived here my entire life – I was born here.'

'Are you sure about that?'

'What are you suggesting? I think I know where I was born.'

'Our records show you were born in Glasgow at the Royal Infirmary.'

'No, you must be mistaking me for someone else.' I try to stand up, but gravity pulls me down. 'I've never even been to Glasgow. Never had any reason to.'

'You are the child of Afrah and Nadeem Malik?' I nod. 'Our records show you were born in Glasgow.' The tall police officer scribbles something down in his notepad.

'What's where I was born got to do with anything, anyway?' I shake my head.

'It's procedure, Miss Malik,' the short one says. 'Is it correct your mother was recently placed into care by the council because you were unable to look after her? Because there was a fire inside your home?'

'Nothing happened. She lost control in the kitchen.'

'And where were you when she *lost control* in the kitchen?'

'Look, I've already gave my statement to the police about what happened that day. I was in bed, I wasn't feeling well. I was down with a cold.'

'So while you were ill and in bed, your house nearly burned down.'

This is a statement and not a question.

'No!' I feel my breath getting short. 'I took the fire out before it could spread.'

The same exchange of glances. They've already framed a picture of me, and I read the mental headline: *Divorced Pakistani carer unable to care for her mother nearly burns down family home and crashes car on historic bridge.*

I shiver. I don't want Shafi to suffer anymore as a result of my mistakes. I keep quiet. I don't even consider mentioning that I may have seen a woman on the bridge this morning. They might think I'm mad.

'Can you please tell me what this is *really* about? Why are you asking me all these questions? I was meeting a friend. I had an accident. That's not a crime, is it?'

'Miss Malik there's been an incident at Caledonian Canal. We believe it happened during the time you were present. We can't be too sure, the fog clouded—'

'What kind of incident?' Beads of sweat trickle down the back of my neck.

'A young woman has been found dead.'

I feel the ache in my body swell. 'Is it Meena?'

'We haven't identified her body, and can't disclose any information at this point. Can you state the time you arrived at the Bridge of Oich this morning?'

'It was around eight o'clock I think. Or just after eight.'

The front door unlocks. The estate agent comes in with a young merry looking couple who suddenly don't look so merry when they see me sitting in question with two officers. We all look at each other, faces surprised and embarrassed. How could I have forgotten about the viewing this evening? I sink back into my chair and look away. Heat spreads to my ears.

'Well, this is a surprise,' says the estate agent. 'I think we will have to come back another time.' He ushers the couple out as fast as he can and leaves the front door ajar. Outside I can hear him say how deeply sorry he is. If they are still interested, he will rearrange the viewing.

'That's not going to be necessary,' says a male voice. I sink deeper into my chair. The estate agent says he has a list of other homes he can show them. Homes in a good neighbourhood. And I know he means homes that weren't on fire and mentioned in the local newspaper. Homes that don't have police officers questioning its owner.

My phone vibrates – it's from the care home. I need to take the call if I want to make a new appointment to see Mum. The tall one clears his throat, suggesting I don't take the call. I wish the floor would open up and swallow me. I put the phone away. It doesn't stop vibrating. I dig my nails into my palms, scoring my flesh.

'Miss Malik,' says the short one. 'Do you happen to remember what time you arrived at Fort Augustus after you left the Bridge of Oich this morning? We believe the body of the young woman was dumped in the canal somewhere between the two bridges.

Body? Dumped? Was she murdered?

I look right at him. 'No, I don't.' I really don't want to speak to anyone. I want to be in bed. I want to disappear.

32

AFRAH

Sunday, 22 December 2019

I'm awake, my eyes blink rapidly. I had a bad dream and the images flicker like dust. I wipe clean the sweat from my chest, and touch my matted hair, pulling it back. I open the bedside drawer. My diary isn't in there. I search for paper, but there isn't any in sight. I have to write down my dream. I orientate myself and stumble as I get up. The room is somewhat dark, I can't see much except for the wide windows staring right back at me as if I were a lost soul.

Fresh cold air wafts through the windows and cools my skin. I reach out waving my hands and knock over the bottled water, which smashes on the floor. Glass scatters over my feet. I move back and sit on my bed staring into the darkness. Waves of light begin to seep through the windows. It's a pale autumn light. I hear the rain lashing down, splatting against the windowpanes. I want to go out. I want to walk on the beach and collect broken seashells.

I hear footsteps outside and fumble to switch on the light. 'Who is there?' No answer. I call out again and get to my feet, taking slow steps towards the door. Someone is breathing heavily on the other side. I open the door. The corridor is black, and I feel an icy chill travel down my spine when I see a shadow is standing there. It gets closer and closer, and I can make out the shape of a woman dressed in a white dress. There's light, a candle in her hand, and her face is veiled. She moves slowly in my direction. I slam my door shut and lean against it. The handle rattles. Someone is trying hard to get in. The door shakes, I turn around and keep pushing it back and begin to cry out loud, *Go away, leave me alone*! I feel my body turn weak. My arms fall to my side and I collapse onto the floor.

Carol, with her black widow-like claws pokes at the food in her bowl. I take a seat across from her, and watch the daylight flicker against her pale face. I am having porridge for breakfast. No omelette, no paratha. I peer over my shoulders.

'If you're looking for Zahra, she's not here. No special treatments for you. Oh yes, we know all about them treats she's been giving you. Why should you be given special foods when the rest of us get beans on toast? Doesn't sound fair, does it now?' Carol puts a spoonful of porridge into her mouth and swallows hard, her eyes never leaving mine. Why is she being so mean to me?

'Where's Nisha?' I ask.

'She's not down. Margaret says she's not well. Better leave her be.'

Mrs Brown stares down at me. Her presence makes me instantly feel cold. 'What's the matter, Afrah Bibi? The food not good enough for you?'

'They don't eat porridge in Pakistan,' says Carol. 'Liam told me that.'

'Did he now?' Mrs Brown interlaces her fingers behind her back.

I open my mouth to say something but the words don't come out. I feel dizzy.

'Hold on,' she says. A sneeze is coming. 'A little Myrtle sneeze.' She shoves her nose into her elbow. She sounds like a barking mad dog. 'Zahra is back in the afternoon. She's on night shift today. I suggest you go to your room after breakfast and stay there. You don't look well, you need to rest.'

'Can I call my daughter?' I ask.

'Still hasn't come?' Carol says curiously.

'Mind your own business, Carol,' says Mrs Brown sharply.

'This *is* my business. Afrah is my friend. Aren't you, Afrah?' she says mockingly.

I get up. 'I'd like to call my daughter.'

'Has Zahra not informed you? Your daughter is due to visit you this morning. But do help yourself. The phone is in the lounge.' She turns and leaves, leaving a trail of cold air behind. I go down the hall, my vision becomes blurry. I think I see someone. A tall man with an ashen face. I leap to one side, and hide my face behind the curtain.

'Yer OK?' a voice says.

'Leave me alone.' When I look, no one is there.

I don't know where I am. I lost my way. I hear the ringtone of a dial phone like the old days. I need to follow that sound. I turn to my left and find myself going down some steps, they creak beneath me. The walls are made of red bricks, and I smell cement. A single bulb dimly lit swings lightly in front of the door at the end of this corridor. I push it open. Inside the air is damp. I smell something raw. Chicken or fish.

What is this place? I walk into a table and knock my knee. The pain is excruciating, and I gently rub it away.

Where am I? Some kind of basement. There are pots here with herbs, dried meat hanging from hooks. Baskets with vegetables. Someone shouts, 'Get out, out of here! Go before I knack on yer.' A woman is skinning an animal and chopping the meat with a butcher's knife. Blood is on her hands and she licks it off one finger slowly while glaring at me. I cover my mouth so that I don't scream.

'Afrah, wake up,' someone shakes me gently. 'Wake up. Nap time is over, rise and shine.' I take a moment to establish whether this is a dream or reality. My chest heaves, sweat lines my hair. I find I am in my room. I pull the duvet down reluctantly, on edge. The room is dark, curtains undrawn. I want to go back to sleep again. I tug the duvet close to my chest.

'Go away. Who are you anyway?' I peek out at a woman with chocolate brown eyes.

'It's your favourite carer, Zahra.' She places a hand on my arm and shakes me gently. 'Come on, I'll help you get out of bed.'

'No,' I say. 'I'm asleep. I don't want to get up.' I close my eyes.

'You are awake now, open those beautiful eyes, come on.'

I take a look at her. She sits on the edge of the bed and says I must have been sleepwalking again because I was lying on the floor. Two male nurses found me and carried me to bed during a routine check. I tell her I can't remember what I did. I breathe in sharply and something hurts. I pull the cover down and bring a cold hand to my nose, which feels swollen and blocked. I notice I am now taking even sharper breaths through my mouth. I stare at Zahra who detects my confusion.

The tips of her fingers draw down my face, a gentle caress. 'You sweet thing, what is happening to you?' She comes back with a cold compress and wet cloth. She wipes dry blood from my lips. 'Look at that terrible bruise you've gotten. Does it hurt?' She tells me to keep the cold compress on my nose to reduce the swelling. 'What happened?'

That's when I remember the vision, something between a dream and reality. 'There was a woman outside my room.' I think it was this morning, I am not sure. 'I saw her walking down Morton Wing. She must have done this to me she, she—' I catch my breath.

My thoughts get muddled. In my memory, I now see a woman skinning an animal. She had blood on her hands. What's happening to me?

'What woman? Could it have been someone who came from the outside? We've had some contractors come in to do fix-ups around the house.'

'No, I don't think so. Somebody was trying to get into my room. The door was shaking. Please believe me, I am not lying.'

'Afrah, are you saying someone from the care home did this to you?'

'I don't know. I didn't see her face. It was veiled. I, I—' I'm stuttering. The words won't form on my tongue. I feel exhausted. I touch my swollen nose and start to cry.

'Try to remember who she was. Did she say anything? What did she want?'

I shake my head. 'I don't know. Leave me alone!'

Zahra looks at me with worried eyes. 'Afrah, are you sure it wasn't a dream? We both know you sleepwalk. That must be how you got those nasty bruises. Now, it's nothing to feel ashamed of. I've seen it happen plenty of times before. It's quite common among most of the patients I cared for. I think you ought to stay in bed. You could do with some extra time resting.'

'I know what I saw.' I hear the gong. 'It was a woman, she was dressed in white.'

'That's lunch. Would you like to go down?'

'I am not hungry.' I remove the cold compress. 'Please, will you call my daughter? I want to speak to her. I—' Unable to utter words again, I swallow hard. My throat feels tight.

Zahra searches for water and notices the broken bottle underneath the table. She twists the lid of another and pours water into a cup. I can't drink it fast enough.

'I'm thirsty. More,' I say, feeling a line of water dribble down my throat. She refills my glass and tells me she has unpleasant news. Amira never came to visit this morning.

'I don't know what's happened. Myrtle has left her a message. I am so sorry Afrah, I don't want to worry you. I'm afraid to tell you that something may have happened to her.'

A jolt of energy pulses through me. My stomach turns over with nerves.

'Afrah, I will do all in my power to see if I can get in touch with your daughter.'

'Would you really do that for me?'

'Of course I will,' she says. 'Perhaps you should take a shower and get dressed. It will make you feel better. Do you want me to help you?'

'No, I can take my own showers.' I get out of bed and I walk around in circles. I open the wardrobe and close it again. I want to look nice. I will take a shower, braid my hair. Decorate my ears and wrists. I bite my nails. 'Do you really think Amira will be coming?' Blood drips from my nose, tinges the carpet. I lean my head back and Zahra puts cotton into one of my nostrils.

'I worry about you,' says Zahra. 'You seem a little shaken today. How about you stay in, and take your meals in your room today. Have a lie in to calm yourself down. I'll let Myrtle know you won't be coming out.'

'That would be nice, thank you.' I don't feel like seeing anyone except for Amira. And I don't feel like being with anyone except for Amira. My daughter will be OK, nothing would have happened to her, and she will come and see me.

Zahra smiles and tells me she'll get a pot of tea up for me. 'Are you sure I can't bring you anything to eat? You've become so pale, so thin. How about mithai? There should still be some ladoo left in the tin I bought you.' She opens the box but it's empty.

'Naughty,' she says with a sweet smile. 'Have you finished it already?'

I shake my head. 'No, I haven't.'

'No need to feel ashamed,' she says. 'I can always get you more from town.'

'I haven't eaten the mithai!'

'Then who did?' Zahra puts the box away. 'Let's forget about it. Doesn't matter.'

'But it does. Somebody has been in my room. I don't know who. My things are missing, I think my earrings—'

Zahra touches my earlobes. 'You are wearing them now,' she gives them a gentle rub and I feel the gold joined with my skin. 'Don't worry, I'm sure that very soon the rest of your things will show up. Was it a black diary you were missing? Myrtle said—'

'I don't care what she said.' I lean into the armchair. I close my eyes and see the woman in white coming towards me. My heart sinks to the bottom of my stomach. I can't help but feel I am being punished. That somebody in Ravenswood Lodge has it in for me. 'Somebody is out to get me. You have to believe me.'

I open my eyes. Zahra isn't there. I call out for her and the door creaks open and then slams shut. I tell myself it's a draft of wind, nothing more. I crawl under the blanket, my body shivers. I stay in the armchair.

The curtains draw and I hear the sound of clinking cups. I peek out and see Zahra placing the teapot on the table. She hands me the mug. She swivels around the room as if searching for something. She opens and closes the drawers. Comes out of the bathroom looking confused. 'I always put your pills on the desk. They are not there. Have you removed them?'

I shake my head, blowing on the surface of the tea. The steam warm against my face.

'Then where could they be?' Zahra looks into the bin. 'There they are. Emptied into the waste basket.' She looks at me, poised and careful as a cat.

'I didn't do it! Somebody has it in for me.'

'You know that's not true.'

The tall man with a pale face. *Larry?* He's the gardener. He does not like me.

'Where is the gardener?' He must be hiding. I don't recall having seen him in a while. 'He hates me. Carol said so.'

'I wouldn't believe a word of what Carol says.' Zahra pours herself a cup of tea. 'She's been snooping in your room. She had your bracelets, do you remember?'

I shake my head. Could that be the reason she's cross with me?

'Has the gardener come in?' I go to the windowsill. He is not in the garden and there is no sign of his tools. The spade, the rake. I wonder what he's digging when no one watches. I've seen him standing by the tree with the wheelbarrow as if hiding something.

'Myrtle said Liam is running errands in town. He needed new tools for the garden to trim the trees. Don't let his rude manners cloud you. His behaviour is no different with any of us.'

He sold the things he stole from me. 'Perhaps he's buried my diary.'

225

'Why don't we get you a new one? That way you can write things in it so that you don't forget. Isn't that what you've been using it for?'

'The diary had my memories, my dreams. Things I can revisit.'

'Like what?'

'Some arguments with Amira and some laughter with Amira. We don't have many joyful moments, but one thing is for sure. I disappoint her. She is embarrassed of me.'

'What makes you believe you embarrass her?' Zahra places her hand on mine.

'She says I am forgetful, and I can be sometimes. I won't admit it to her because she'll think I am unreliable. A superfluous woman. No one wants to feel defective like something is wrong with them. I believe something must be wrong with me. That is why she's left me.'

'You are here to receive the best care.' Zahra takes a sip of tea and then looks at me with her large eyes. She lowers the mug and says, 'You are not defective.'

All mothers at some point in life feel judged by their daughters, not once, but several times. It is unavoidable. Mothers try not to judge their daughters. The love we carry is unconditional. I don't mind the judgement. After all, what girl wants to become her mother? Everything we say and do disgusts them. But what they don't realise is that they are destined to turn into all what they hate. Their mothers.

I may have failed as a mother. I wasn't prepared to raise daughters in the West, with my Eastern traditions. In my generation things were done differently. Times were harder. I have never said that to Amira, and perhaps that's why she stood up to me. She knew deep inside I didn't take her for granted. What she doesn't know is how proud she makes me. If only she knew how much I love her. If only she knew what sacrifices I made.

There's a knock on my door. 'Afrah, we've found your diary,' says the big-chested woman at the door. 'It was in the little reading room. Nisha said she saw you leave it there and we all believe her. Nisha never lies.' She passes it to me and leaves. My cheeks feel hot.

Zahra doesn't say anything. Lowering her eyes, she says she will come back in a while to check on me. She walks out without turning around, without smiling. I know what she thinks of me. I hold myself back from screaming: *I am not pagal!*

The black gates remain shut. They've not opened since I've been on watch for Amira's car to haul in. My eyes are getting sore from looking at the zigzagging road paved with dead leaves. I close them briefly and see her. She is five years old, tucked in tight and fast asleep. Every night she'd scoop in between us, saying she had a bad dream.

'Spiders, Ami, they're crawling in my bed.' I let her sleep next to me. I liked having her close to my heart.

'You still here?' says Mrs Brown. 'The visiting hours have passed. We allow guests, friends and family members to come between 9 and 11 a.m. on Sundays.'

I don't pay attention. And I don't move. I sit in the chair and continue to wait for my daughter to show up. Zahra said she was coming. She could be here anytime now.

It seems like I've been sitting out on the terrace for hours dressed in the green sari I found in my wardrobe. I even showered and wore the new cardigan Amira bought me.

'Still no sign of her?'

'Go away, Carol.' I wave my hand at her. I feel tempted to call her a liar, a thief. But I don't want to aggravate her. Who knows what she might do.

'Why don't you make me?' She pulls up a chair, sits across from me. 'Nice out here. Cold, but nice. We're expecting snow anytime now and it's going to be a white Christmas. Do you celebrate Christmas, Afrah? I bet you don't where you are from. We are all preparing to go home over the holidays to visit our families. Even Nisha. I think you'll be the only one left out here all alone.'

'She will show up,' I say. 'Amira would never leave me hanging like this.'

'Don't be so sure.' She keeps her face set in a smile. 'I heard Myrtle tell everyone that your daughter stopped answering her phone. No one knows where she is. She's gone, disappeared. Who does that? That's just bizarre, isn't it?'

I take several deep breaths, feeling my emotions break me, one by one. My head falls back, my eyes looking up towards the sky. Grey clouds scurry across the landscape and I know it's going to rain soon. I get up and toss my chador around my shoulders and go back inside, kicking everything down that comes my way. Pots of plants, flowers in a vase.

I stop. The air falls short in my lungs. I don't even realise I am screaming now.

'My, oh my!' says Carol. 'She's gone mad again. A complete nutter.'

Mrs Brown yanks me by the arm. 'That's enough, Afrah Bibi. Stop this instance. I said stop screaming.' She slaps my wrist. I feel heat in my face.

'What happened?' I drop to the floor and hug my knees and begin to weep like a child.

'This cannot go on,' says Mrs Brown. 'We do not accept aggressive behaviour.'

I look up at her and wipe the tears hanging in my eyes. 'What are you talking about?'

The rain bashes hard against the windowpanes and I wish I was out there dancing, getting wet. But instead I am in bed with the duvet pulled tight on my sides. I can't move my legs and I don't know how long I've been lying here. The window blows open, hits against the wall. The wind fresh from the sea funnels into the room, a cold bite. Strands of my hair twist loose and I don't remove them from my face. The water bottles begin to shake, glass clinking. I laugh. Zahra comes running in and shuts the window. She pulls back the hair from my face and puts my chador over my shoulders. I stop myself from laughing and stare at her.

'She's not coming, is she?' My eyes fill with tears.

'Oh Afrah, I'm so sorry. I tried to tell you but—' She turns around and begins to fold my laundry.

'Don't be.' I shift the pages of my diary searching for the blue bookmark. It's not in there. I notice some of the sheets have been torn out. I notice that all the bookmarks are missing. I show her. 'Look, do you see that?'

'Bizarre,' she says. 'Who would do such a thing?'

I get out of bed and shuffle my feet into my slippers. I am going to speak with Nisha. I told her about my diary, about the bookmarks. 'Nisha did it.'

'Afrah, wait.' She pulls me back by the shoulder. 'Are these your missing pages? I just found them behind your pillow.'

I snatch them out of her hand and rush out.

In the lounge, I hear Carol cackling. I climb down the stairs and see Nisha wearing an amused expression. *What's so funny?* I ask. One of the patients holds up a bundle of papers. He is reading with a mocking voice. I recognise the words. My skin puckers with goosebumps. 'Stop it,' I say. No one is paying attention to me.

'Listen to this part. It is oh, so scary! I push open the gate and enter a mossy track that leads me straight to the misty graveyard, where a tombstone sleeps beneath a yew tree with branches stretched out like claws. They reach for me with their hooks. Grab and pull me towards the open grave. I do not want to look and yet I do. A blackened corpse rises from the dirt, eyes hollow, hair thinned and flaring in the wind. It is rotten and has been dead for decades, but still comes to life most nights in my dreams. It looks at me and screams, saying the same thing over and over. Now look. Look what you did to me.'

'You have no right,' I push him away and grab the papers from him. 'Give it back.'

Zahra is standing across from me, her eyes shining with tears that don't fall.

'We're just having some fun,' says Carol. 'Don't be such a bore.'

'What's going on?' Mrs Brown glares at Zahra then back at me. 'Afrah, are you causing trouble yet again? Because if you are—' Her voice is shrill.

'I haven't done anything. They are mine.' I show her the copies from my dairy. 'My stolen dreams.'

'What atrocity,' says Mrs Brown looking around. 'Who did this? I demand to know.'

The toothless man comes forward and says he found the copies of my diary entry in the library. He has no clue who put them there. Mrs Brown frowns, but I detect a smile as she tells everyone to clear the lounge.

I turn to Zahra. 'Now do you believe me? I am not pagal.'

She nods, pats my arm and leads me back up the stairs.

33

AMIRA

Monday, 23 December 2019

I peek through the curtains occasionally to see what's going on outside. I am sure Mrs Nesbit saw the two policemen last night. She notices everything, and probably alerted the entire neighbourhood that they went into the house carrying suspicious looks and now this . . . the breaking news about the woman found dead in Caledonian Canal.

I draw back the curtain and switch the telly back on. My knees fidget and are perched against the coffee table, which begins to shake. It has gone viral. Every channel is about her and her identity is not yet revealed. I still worry it could be Meena. The police officers think I have something to do with what happened on the bridge. I trace my memory back: what did happen on the bridge? Nothing. What I saw was a brisk jogger and the illusion of a woman. She wasn't real, she couldn't have been.

I think of Mum, and her fixation with one particular story about a missing girl. She became obsessed with it, and I can see why it's easy to get hooked. I happened to be at the wrong place at the wrong time and somehow I'm getting involved with the death of an unknown woman. It makes me think, why was Mum so keen to read about the fourteen-year-old girl? Was her story a fact or fiction? Mum asked me every day to get the newspaper, which makes me speculate the incident of the missing girl may have happened a long time ago. What if Mum had something to do with it? Why else would she collect the newspaper clippings and still be looking for it?

The phone rings and I let it. Now somebody is leaving a voice-mail, and it takes me a while to realise it's Haroon's raspy morning voice.

'Hi Mira, it's me. Are you there? You're probably asleep, in which case I don't want to disturb you. I'm going to drop off Nadia's car. You won't get yours back for a while from the garage, and I know you need one to get around. I'm worried about you and I want you to get some rest. Sorry if I was a little reserved yesterday, I was shocked, that's all.'

Outside, a car pulls into my driveway. It's Haroon, he's come to give me the keys. I feel a spark of joy. He's the one person I want to see, to speak to. A taxi waits at the kerb. My heart sinks into my stomach. Haroon drops the keys into my letterbox and slides into the backseat of the taxi and it drives off. I know he said he doesn't want to bother me. He wants me to recover from the accident. But something tells me he's had enough and doesn't want to get involved in what's going on. He must have heard the news. He knew I was at Caledonian Canal yesterday morning. He doesn't want to see me. Doesn't care if am well. I don't blame him. After all, we are no longer married.

I open the door to Mum's room and pull out the old boxes from her cupboard. They're heavy and I empty everything onto the floor and scatter the mess around. I find black and white photographs of Mum when she lived in Lahore. Folders full of papers, letters and brown envelopes. Tons of newspaper clippings, circled, highlighted. Rubbish news.

There are several photos of Mum with a man I do not recognise. He reminds me of the man from my dreams. Long hair, juvenile features. He is well proportioned, with broad shoulders, and has a funny looking moustache which makes him look like a circus director.

There's an album with pictures of a girl who looks very similar to me. She is wearing a school uniform that says QE, Queen Eleanor. I flip through. Mum is with the same man and the same girl. In some of the photos, she is wearing a sari and holding a baby. This makes no sense. Why wouldn't she have shown me these photographs? And who are these people? Friends, relatives? Mum is captured in different places – London, Edinburgh, with this man and this girl. I recognise them from somewhere, perhaps from my vivid dream when I was ill.

I get an email from the care home. My heartbeat quickens. I've not been I touch with them to let them know why I couldn't make the visit. I've been dreading telling Mum what's happened. She would get worried.

Myrtle Brown is saying Mum has been causing a lot of trouble – there have been several disturbing incidents now, incidents that put their reputation at risk and are highly disruptive to the other patients. She is urging me to show up today, or else she will have no other choice but to put Mum away. She's also written a reminder that from tomorrow, no one is expected to be at the Ravenswood Lodge. Most patients go home to either their families, relatives or close friends. They tend to close for two days over the holidays. Under rare circumstances, and should a carer agree to care, patients are left behind. But it's never been done. All the patients have families they stay with.

Fuck! How could I have forgotten? I try not to panic. I need to go out there as soon as possible.

There's an incoming call on my mobile. 'Please can you come down to the police station? Miss Malik, it's urgent that we speak with you.'

I try to breathe but cannot seem to catch my breath trapped in my lungs. Something awful has happened. I can feel it. My heart feels like it's going to explode. 'I'll be on my way.' The phone nearly drops from my grip so I prop it against my ear and shoulder. 'I am not going to be long.' I grab my bag and shoot out of the front door.

I meet the short police officer who brings me to a meeting room. He is joined by the tall one who places a file on the table and flicks through the pages. The short one glances over it and says the woman who died was identified as Meena Bashir. She worked as a carer in Glasgow for a while for a wealthy Pakistani family looking after a disabled mother. She left her position in what we believe was caused by an unresolved dispute between her and the family accusing her of theft. No charges were made, and she moved to Inverness early this year to care for another family looking after their young boy. We spoke to both families where she worked as a carer, who stated she was a frail and very nervous type. It turns out she had a medical history of mental health issues and suffered from depression and anxiety. We believe her death was by suicide. A letter was found inside her coat stating she was going to end her life. We've checked her laptop and can confirm she had an active account on the chat forum for carers as *Thelonelymouse*. This account was recently deleted.' He shuts the file stares at me.

'What about her father?' I say. 'Meena told me she cared for him.'

'We don't have information about that.' says the tall one. 'Miss Malik, did Miss Bashir ever talk to you about anything else? What she was afraid of? Why she suddenly wanted to meet with you?'

'I don't know. I had little information about her personal life. All she told me was that she looked after her father, also a dementia patient who recently died. She said she was then taking a live-in position with a family to care for their son in Inverness. That's all I know.'

'When was this?'

I shrug. 'Just recently.'

'The information you've given us doesn't match with what we have on record of Miss Bashir. She had no relatives, no family. She moved to Scotland from Bangladesh to care for the family in Glasgow. She was with them for two years before she moved to Inverness to look after a young boy.'

'What was the family called, in Glasgow?'

They exchange glances. 'I'm sorry, that's confidential information.'

'If you come to think of anything else she may have—'

'I already told you everything. Can I please leave now?'

'Can we check the messages again that you exchanged with her?'

I pull out my phone and give it to them. He looks sceptical. Says there's no way of knowing if these messages really are from Meena Bashir. They could be fabricated.

'I don't understand,' I say. 'What do you mean?'

'There's a log of messages sent to you at 9.30 a.m.: "I am at the Bridge of Oich. You are not here. Where are you?" And again, at 9.40: "Amira, are you OK? Where are you?" 9.45: "I really needed to see you. I needed a friend I can trust." 9.50: "I am sorry. I am sorry for everything. Don't hate me." How can we even be sure Meena Bashir wrote these messages? For all we know they could have been from anyone. We have no way of tracing the phone number.'

'Are you suggesting I am lying?'

He looks at his partner, his expression worried. I ask to leave and he gestures towards the door. I depart from the building as fast as I can. Inside Nadia's car I drop my head between my knees and feel the tears fill my eyes. Somebody is knocking on the car window. The tall police officer is looking in, and I roll down the window.

'Have I forgotten something?'

'No,' he says. 'But I thought you might want to know that a search on Meena Bashir's laptop showed she had looked up Ravenswood Lodge. Isn't that the care home where your mother, Afrah Malik, was placed recently?'

'I mentioned during our chat that Mum was there.'

'When?'

'I don't know, couple of weeks ago.'

'Miss Malik, Meena Bashir had applied for a position there earlier this year. What our records also show is that she made contact via email to the social services several times under the name of a Silvia Nesbit. She wrote complaints about Afrah Malik of 22 Denver Street. Requesting to have her removed. That's your home address, correct?'

I nod. I feel the ugly lump on my head pounding, the pain swelling.

'Why would she file a complaint under a different name? Doesn't it seem odd to you?'

'I don't know, but I may have . . .' I pause and control my voice from trembling. 'I may have given Meena the information. Silvia Nesbit is my neighbour.'

'Why did she have a keen interest in having your mother removed?'

'I'm not sure—' Meena must have tried to sympathise with me. She must have thought it was what I wanted. The only logical explanation I can come up with is that she was trying to help me.

'You have no idea why she would give your mother to social services, and at the same time, apply for jobs at the care home in which your mother was later placed into?'

'I told her things about Mum, personal things. She knew I was going through a hard time. I never imagined she would make any formal complaints or use what I told her to try to get Mum removed. It turns out she lied to me. I believed her and thought she was my friend. I believed she was in some deep trouble.'

'The family she worked for in Inverness gave us no reason to believe she was in any serious difficulty. She wrote to you asking for help. Before you could meet, you had an accident, and then she died. Something is missing, doesn't seem right. We were hoping you could help us explain a few things as you were the last person who spoke to her.'

'I really wouldn't know. I am as confused as you are.' My head is heavy spinning with questions. Meena knew of Ravenswood Lodge. Why wouldn't she tell me she had applied for a job with them after I mentioned Mum had moved in there? 'It makes no sense what you told me. I really must go,' I give him an urgent look. 'Please, can I?'

He nods approvingly. 'Miss Malik if there's anything you come to think of get in touch with us as soon as you can.'

'But what does all this mean? Meena's death, was it—?'

'Her history of mental health proves she wasn't stable. We know her GP had prescribed her with antidepressants. She may have had a hard time. Stress, pressure and long working hours living with a family as carer. It all adds up.'

'But why would she lie to me? Why not tell me the truth—?' I thought we were close.

'People forge identities online all the time Miss Malik. It's easy to be anonymous, fabricate lies. Dual personalities, psychotic behaviours. The list goes on. The fact she befriended you online and lied to you, shows how unstable she was. She may have been lonely, and her attempt to speak to you was perhaps her final cry for help.'

And I failed her. I didn't make it in time to speak to her. Now I will never know what she desperately needed to tell me. Why did she contact the social services using Silvia Nesbit's name?

I knock on Mrs Nesbit's door and she opens it, tells me to come inside. She offers me a cup of tea. From the kettle, she pours hot water into a mug.

'How is your mum? We were all worried about her.' I curl my fingers around the cup and blow on the hot surface.

I don't say anything. I am surprised. She appears different, calm and understanding. Watching her for all those years across the road, she is not the nosy woman I imagined her to be. 'Mum's doing well. She's in a care home now.'

'I am glad Afrah is doing better. It was hard seeing her health decline. She used to be such a jolly woman. Would invite everyone over for tea and Pakistani sweets. What are those colourful things called again?'

'Mithai.'

'That's it. She'd cook a lovely big pot of curry and share it among us. We adored her. Such a shame when her memory declined. Dementia can be awful. Changes people. My husband passed away five years ago. He had Alzheimer's. Bless Gerald. He spent his last days in a care home. It was impossible for me to look after him. He hardly remembered me.'

'Mrs Nesbit,' I sip the tea. 'Did you ever call the social services to report Mum asking them to take her away?'

'Why would I do that? I've known Afrah since she moved to the neighbourhood. She was so vulnerable during those early years, a young Pakistani widow, a single mother. I used to look after you when she had late night shifts working at the convenient store. Don't you remember? You couldn't have been older than five or six.'

'No, that's not true. Mum didn't move here when she was a widow – she's lived here with me all her life.'

'Your mother told me she had moved from Glasgow. She needed a new start and wanted to make new friends. She was quite traumatised about something that had happened. Let me think, what was it? Something about friends accusing her of stealing some gold bracelets. Turns out it was hers that got stolen. Poor Afrah, how she loves her jewellery.'

I remember Mum wandering around the house late at night. She'd wake me and say, *She took my bracelets. We must go to her house and get them back.* I thought she was imagining things. Mum's always been obsessed with those bracelets. Even had to try on Nadia's. The nights she woke me up, I looked for them to show her where they were. I assured her no one would take them. She always ignored me and delved into her own little world. I knew she kept secrets. I just never knew what they were.

'Mum never said anything about living in Glasgow or having friends there.'

'Afrah cut them off. Didn't want anything to do with them. She told me that they were close friends of your father's.'

'Did you ever know my father?'

She shakes her head. 'Afrah only mentioned that after he died in the house fire, she moved out to the Highlands.'

'What house fire, Mrs Nesbit?' You are mistaken. Dad didn't die in a fire.'

'Look for the scar on your calf. You got it in the fire Afrah rescued you from.'

How does she know about my scar? I pull up my trousers and run my hand over it.

'Surely you must have read about the fire incident. Afrah kept the newspaper clippings. She even showed them to me. I think there was a young girl, too, about fourteen who went missing after the fire, and if I remember correctly—'

'Are you telling me that for all these years, she has been lying to me?'

I get up and thank her for the tea and make my way to the door.

'Amira? Where are you going?'

I leave Mrs Nesbit's house and go straight back to ours. I begin to sort out Mum's documents, making sure nothing is missing from the boxes. I check statement of the old bills, showing an address in Glasgow, which means Mum did lie to me. Mrs Nesbit was right. She lived in Glasgow before moving to Inverness. Why did Mum keep it a secret from me?

I discover cassettes, and slot one of them into the player. Old Hindi songs stream through the speaker and I recognise the tunes she would hum for me when I was little. I re-examine the photographs of the same two faces I cannot place in the puzzle. It doesn't make sense. Who is the man? And that girl, she looks so familiar, her smile, the way she's running along the shoreline. Who is she? They can't be family. Mum always said we have no other family. It's always just been the two of us.

Something is missing. I stand on the foot stool and search through the cupboard with my hands. Hidden at the back, I find a third box. That's the one Mum didn't want me to look at the day I packed her things. She must have hidden it afterwards. What's in there that she doesn't want me to see?

I pull the box out and uncover a bunch of old newspaper articles. I read some of the headlines. Mrs Nesbit was right. There was a fire – Nadeem Malik, deceased. But the man in the picture is not my father. *Or is he?* I rush down and look at the frame hanging against the wall. I Google Daniel Day-Lewis. I scroll through several images until I find the exact same one hanging in the wooden frame where he is leaning against an apple tree, with the backdrop of an orchard.

Mum used to look at the photograph and ask, *Why do you keep a picture of that Hollywood actor?* I repeatedly told her, 'It's your late husband, Nadeem. You gave me that photo, don't you remember?' She shook her head and said, *Areee, don't be silly Mimi.* It didn't upset me, not as much as it does now. She made up a lie and gave me a photograph and had me fooled into believing that this man was my father. And I believed her. What an idiot I've been. I tear the frame off the wall and smash it into pieces.

I go through the rest of the stuff and find my original birth certificate. I was born in Glasgow Royal Infirmary. I find another birth certificate. I bring a shaking hand up to my mouth.

I had a sister. Mona Malik.

I glimpse at the headlines of the newspaper articles and find the front-page news story, the one that mentions a fourteen-year-old girl of Pakistani origin. I read the full article. *Missing daughter of Afrah Malik presumed dead after a terrible accident during a fire in the family's home in Glasgow.* The address matches the old bills. But that's not all. I now realise that it's her story, a true story that's been haunting Mum for more than thirty years. She lost a daughter, and has ever since has been plagued by her death.

I remember the day I picked up Mum from Haroon's place Shafi told me, *Nano kept saying Mona is missing. Mona might be dead. Who is Mona?*

It all makes sense, and I see the pieces of the puzzle come together. The man in my dream was my father. The girl next to him was my sister. And it was me – I was the baby in the stroller. They died in a house fire over thirty years ago in Glasgow. That explains Mum's phobia of fires. Her need to connect with her missing daughter through the front-page news.

Mum had a fall out, an argument with Dad's friends who accused her of stealing their gold bracelets. Her own obsession with jewellery proves she carried the trauma, which I never understood till now. But why wouldn't she tell me any of this?

What is she really hiding from me?

I look at the photographs in the newspapers – it's them, I am certain of it. It's Dad and my sister Mona. Mum did everything in her power to make sure I would never know the truth about what happened to them. She moved away, started a new life for herself and for me. All these years, I lived on the lie she fed me. How could she do this? How could she betray my trust like this? I deserve to know the truth.

I dial Haroon's number. He's not answering. I leave a message. 'I need an urgent favour. Could you ask your relatives in Glasgow if they ever knew my parents, Nadeem and Afrah Malik? Or may have friends who might have known them? It appears we lived there before moving to Inverness. And, I also had a sister . . .

'Mona Malik. She was in a fire over thirty years ago with Dad and has been missing ever since. I only just found out going through Mum's old things. Haroon, she never told me! She lied to me and I need your help to find out why. I can't trust Mum.'

I hang up and take out Dr Abdullah's card. I dial his number. There's a beep and I leave a message. 'My name is Amira Malik. I have your number from my ex-husband, Dr Haroon Khan. This may be unexpected – I understand if you don't want to call me back, but did you ever know a Nadeem and Afrah Malik? Nadeem was my dad. He died in a fire over thirty years ago in Glasgow. I also had a sister Mona Malik who was in the same fire.' I hang up.

This is stupid. What do I hope to find out? Just because he's a retired old doctor doesn't mean he knows every Pakistani who died in Glasgow. I remind myself that it is in the nature of our community to help one another. We go by caste, by reputation, so that we can check on each other when we need to. There's a small beacon of hope inside me that says maybe Dr Abdullah knew Dad and my family.

My phone vibrates and I instantly take the call. 'Hello? . . . Yes, speaking . . . Now wait a minute, before making any hasty decisions Mrs Brown. I am sorry, I understand what you're saying. No one will be there. Everyone is leaving tonight? OK . . . Sorry, I didn't mean to—I'll leave straight away. Expect me to be there within the next thirty minutes.'

I hang up and stumble over the box. At a closer look, I find a diary in the bottom next to a silver tin. I open the rusty lid full of broken seashells. Mum always liked collecting those. The diary has a musty smell to it. I flick to the first page, which says, 'This diary belongs to Mona Malik'. My heart skips a beat. My sister kept a dairy? I read the first entry. My nerves begin to stir like cut-off wires.

Outside, snow is tumbling down from the sky like cotton balls. The weather forecast predicted heavy snowfall with the chance of a blizzard. Glistening crystals land softly in my hair. It's going to be a white Christmas this year. I start the engine to Nadia's car and wait for it to heat up. I see Mrs Nesbit from the window. I wave at her and smile. Then I drive as fast as I can, heading in the direction of Ravenswood Lodge.

34

AFRAH

Monday, 23 December 2019

I'm in a room where the sign says 'little reading room'. I am sitting comfortably in the armchair, facing an Asian woman. She snores very loudly, her mouth wide open as sudsy drool sloshes down the corner of her mouth. I can't remember what I have had to eat today; my stomach feels heavy. A man in a black suit and white shirt passes me and asks if he should set up the fireplace.

'No! I am leaving.' I try getting up, pushing my hands against the arms of the chair, rolling forward. I slump back, feeling weak and tired. He insists I stay seated and gets me a random book from the shelf. I tell him I don't want to read it. He crosses his arm over his chest. 'No need to be rude, little lady. We've been in quite some mood today, haven't we?'

'I'm not in any mood.'

'I am sorry. I looked for yer diary. I had nothing to do with the missing pages.'

I shake my head. What's he on about? 'Chalo! Jao, jao,' I tell him off in Urdu.

He doesn't like that. 'Oi!' he shouts suddenly. 'Michael is my name.' His finger points at the badge pinned to his jacket. 'I'm the caretaker of this place. Treat me with respect, little lady. I was only trying to be nice.' But he is not. He is rude and right in my face. 'Yer can't read the books anyway, said Myrtle. Yer went mad earlier. Do yer recall?' He shouts 'Oi' again, louder this time. I keep on ignoring him. His face is getting puffier. 'Liam was right, yer nuts.'

'Leave me be,' I say. He turns and shuts the main door to the room so hard the sign rattles. I hear him mumble, 'I can't wait to leave this place tonight.'

There's a loud noise. A drilling right outside the window next to me. The Asian woman wakes and mumbles something. I direct my attention at the gardener, cutting down branches from the tree. Oak? Pine? I don't know anymore. It's large with a thick trunk. He stops and puts down the chainsaw and frowns coldly in my direction. My heart feels frail and sweat begins to dapple my forehead. Larry. That's his name. I remember he hates me. I remember he stole something from me. He doesn't pick up the chainsaw again. He kicks the grass and spits, eyes fixed on mine. I look away, turning a blind eye.

'Where is Carol? Did she leave already without saying good-bye?' says the Asian woman. She folds the pleats of her brown sari then turns, glaring at me with her hazel brown eyes. 'What are you looking at? Cat got your tongue – where is she?' She's in a mood, rubbing me up the wrong way.

'Carol?' My memory associates the name with a heavy woman. 'Who are you?'

'Me?' she laughs. 'Who am I? Who are you? And what are you doing here?'

'I don't know. I think this is my home,' I say.

'No, it's not. It's *my* home. You don't even like being here. You are crazy. The mad woman living in Alice's room. Pagal aurat.' Her voice is thin and small.

'Quit bothering me.' I stride into the hallway. A woman passes me. She goes to the Asian woman who now says she wants to have tea on the terrace. But she tells her it's time to leave soon. Her son is coming to pick her up anytime now.

'Why is Afrah still here? Why is she not leaving? Tell Afrah to leave. She is not welcome here anymore. She is crazy. I want her to leave. I will tell the woman in white to make her. Just the way she made Alice—'

'That's enough now, Nisha. Calm down. We'll get you a hot

cup of milk with honey. It's quiet time now and this time don't even think about not taking your pills, or else . . .' I can hear the Asian woman cry, 'Stop hurting me, you're hurting me!' The sound of slapping echoes through the room, and she goes quiet.

'I'm not hurting you Nisha, you're the one hurting me.' I see them now turning the corner into the hallway. The woman quickly rolls Nisha in the wheelchair and stops at the lift. Nisha's wrinkly face is dappled with spots of red.

'I'll see you get a shower before Ranveer gets here.'

'I hate showers,' the Asian woman gets up, but she is pushed right back down. 'I don't want it, I don't want it.'

'Behave, Nisha.'

'Stop hurting me, Margaret.' She slaps the woman's sausage like fingers.

'Now Nisha, be nice, and stop lying. I was not hurting you, Nisha.'

Nisha, Nisha? She is my friend. 'What do you know about the woman in white?'

Nisha turns her head, sticks her tongue out. 'Why should I tell you?'

Someone walks past me. Someone else walks past me. I don't see Nisha anymore.

A tall man with a pale ghostly face and wrinkles strides speedily towards me. He holds a newspaper in one hand, rolled up, and slams it into his other palm. His eyes are bloodshot.

I turn around and catch my breath. I move up the stairs, up, up as fast as I can.

He's right behind me, walking faster. I run down the corridor, passing the Morton Wing sign, and yank the first door handle I can see. Locked. The next one is locked too. I try door number three. Nisha is inside, facing the woman who is pinching her cheeks while making her swallow a fistful of pills. She cries when she sees me. 'Get out! Get Out!'

I swing left, up the stairs, to the loft, to the loft. I am exhausted. There are voices behind one of the doors, a low whisper. There are so many I don't know which handle to pull. The corridor suddenly turns pitch black. I hear the beams creak, the wind whistle. I stand still and a voice amplifies as if coming from inside my head.

'How quickly can the procedure be done? Because we must all leave this evening. We're closed for two days over the holidays, remember?' says the voice. 'Well, well, aren't they all brain damaged? Just numb little minds that never shut the fuck up.'

I hear loud laughter, and an evil cackle. 'And the new one. That is right. She has been with us for just over a month. Quite a nutcase. I will see to it that she gets sectioned. Her aggressive behaviour has been out of order. I don't want to put our reputation at risk. Well, we could put her up in the tower, we've not had anyone in there since Alice . . . Don't say it! We don't like using the term "mad woman in the attic". Of course, my dear. Safe measures, we always apply safe measures here at Ravenswood Lodge. It's what makes us so unique. Hold on, don't go anywhere, a sneeze is coming. A little Myrtle sneeze.'

I can't believe what I've just heard. Mrs Brown is planning to get rid of me. This woman is mad, *pagal*. I knew something was off about her when I first set eyes on her. That cold, pale face. Stern expression. Strict voice. She is out to get me. I step back, feel sweat trickle down my forehead and sting my eyes. She probably stole my things to play with my mind. Told me it was my memory. Now I know she's wanted me gone all along.

Quietly, I draw back down. The hallway is empty. Where is everybody? No one is here and suddenly the place feels ghostly. I think I was being chased by someone or something. I start to chew my nails. A girl blowing pink bubbles from her mouth asks if I am OK. I say I don't know. She leads me to a room in the other end of the hall.

'Remember, this is your room. Number nine. Mill Annex. Don't forget alrighty?' She slinks down the hall and starts chatting loudly to the tall woman with blonde hair and says she can't wait to leave tonight. It makes me wonder, where is everyone going? They both laugh and look at me now as if I were a dotty old woman.

I push open the door and step inside. Is this my room? It's so dark, and I fumble to find the switch on the wall. Cold wind slaps at my face. The windows are wide open, the curtains flaring, ghostly. Everything is a mess. Newspapers are scattered all over the floor, crumbled and torn. Picture frames broken and photographs ripped into pieces. Clothes are jumbled on the floor, my shalwar kameez and saris. Dirty, pee-stained underwear is spread all over on the bed.

'Who did this?' I look around at the mess again. 'Who was in here?' Myrtle Brown. She did this!

'My, oh my! What have you done to your room, Afrah?' asks the heavy woman peering in. 'You're in deep trouble now.'

'Nothing, I did nothing. It wasn't me.' I push her. She's strong, doesn't move an inch.

'Liar.' She drops the bag clutched in her hand. 'You've been going mad throwing things around all day because your daughter never showed up. Is she not coming to get you over the holidays? Is she abandoning you?'

'Shut up, I say. 'Chup karo.'

'You are crazy. Super crazy. Everyone around here knows. You pushed poor Ed when he was reading for us in the hall. You snatched the papers out of his hand. We all know your secrets. Your wild nightmares. We all know what you *did*.'

'Get out.' I fetch the book and throw it at her. She wails and runs away screaming.

'Myrtle, hurry up, stop her! Afrah's gone stark raving bonkers.'

'Carol, what are you still doing here? I thought you had left already.'

'I am about to, but please stop Afrah.'

I hear footsteps approaching. My door squeaks open.

'Afrah Bibi!' says Mrs Brown appearing in the door. She squints her eyes. 'Goodness gracious, what have you done to your room?

Do you know what we do to patients like you? Well, do you? Answer me.'

I hesitate before shaking my head. She's now right in front of me. I smell her breath. Sour like acid. I turn my head. I don't want to see or smell her. She grabs my arm and I tell her to let go.

'We make sure they leave and don't come back.' She smiles. Her face is calm as it was from the start. 'I've spoken to that doctor in your family. I've informed him about what's happened. But this tops it. We do not tolerate havoc and patients smashing, littering and destroying the historic property of Ravenswood Lodge.'

'It wasn't me. I didn't do any of this.' I want to shout: *'you did this. Liar!'* But I am afraid of what she might do if I said it out loud.

'Then who did? Lying runs in the family. Your daughter is as unreliable as you are. Perhaps it's a thing in your culture. In any case, we are reviewing your stay at Ravenswood Lodge. We simply cannot tolerate this sort of behaviour. Do I make myself clear? You will have no more privileges of Pakistani food and ordering special Urdu books from the library. It stops now!'

'What about the newspaper?' I ask. 'You said I could have it.'

'What?' She arches her brows. 'I said no such thing. Now, if you are you putting new demands on me to bring you the newspaper then it's never going to happen. Never!'

'I want my daughter. Where is Amira? I need to call her.'

'I've been trying to get hold of that daughter of yours. If she cares about you, and I hope she does, then she'll show up today just like she said she would. Otherwise, I'll make the decision without her consent.'

'What decision?'

'That you, my dear Afrah Bibi, should be removed for showing outrageous behaviour and be placed in the tower till you learn how to behave. Never in my history as a nurse have I ever seen anyone quite like you. Now, clean up your mess.' She stares at the walls for a while, then leaves, slamming the door shut.

There's an odd smell in my room and I swivel around. That's when I notice the graffiti paint dripping off the wall. In big letters, it says: I KNOW WHAT YOU DID!

The writing makes my cheeks hot and my heart ache. I go into the bathroom and smack the door against the frame. There's no lock so I grab the shower chair and lean it in front of the handle so no one gets in. I let the water run cold from the tap and splash it onto my face, loosening the tensed muscles that are vibrating with fear. I see several pictures of Amira, hanging loose from the tiles and torn in the middle. One, with the two of us in it, has her face scratched out and the edges are burned.

I begin to cry, loud inconsolable sobs. I sit on the floor with my head dipped in between my knees. Where is Amira when I need her? Something pounds in the middle of my body. I feel cold. Help me God, I am trapped. Somebody is outside, yanking the handle to get in. The door is shaking violently. I feel myself go cold. I am trembling. Somebody knocks. It's getting louder, like a fist hammering inside my head. I draw my knees closer to my chest, crunch my upper body into a ball.

The hammering stops. It's silent. I release my arms from my knees and push myself forwards, coiling and twisting like a snake before I get to my feet. I am losing my balance, and push my hands against the damp tiles to support myself. I think I smell blood. I turn to look at the mirror and cover my mouth, strangling my scream. There it is again, this time scrawled in red across the mirror. _I know what you did!_

35

AMIRA

The flurries of snow whirl in the car headlights along the road leading out of Inverness. I put my foot on the accelerator and drive at full speed. The evening sky spreads like a blanket above the curve of snow-covered patches, the forest ahead naked, the branches black.

I flick on the radio and listen to the presenter's voice talking about the holiday season madness. Last-minute shoppers buying presents to be decorated underneath their Christmas trees. I lower the volume. There's an incoming call from unknown caller, which I answer.

'Am I speaking with Amira Malik? This is Dr Abdullah – you left me a message.'

I keep my eyes steady on the road. 'Thank you for returning my call.'

'This is quite some coincidence, Amira beti, I can't believe this is you. I never thought it to be true that you are Haroon's wife.'

'Ex-wife.' I say, but I don't think he's heard me.

'My late wife used to babysit you when your family lived in Glasgow.'

'You knew my family?'

'Yes, we were neighbours, and I knew your parents very well. Your father was one of my patients. Such a tragedy how he died. He was a good man. Your mother stayed with us after your house burned down. You were little then and may not remember.'

'I don't, I mean I have a vague memory of Dad, glimpses really.' I see him pushing me in the stroller, smiling down on me.

'Can you tell me more about him?' Tears are blinding me, and I dab my eyes with the sleeve of my coat. 'Did you know any of his friends?'

'I knew of one Pashtun family, I suspect many in our community did. They were close friends of your father's. Before, we'd see them a lot. But then they stopped coming around to your house Their black Mercedes used to stop around the corner to drop your sister off.'

'Was that because—'

'Your mother disapproved of your sister seeing their daughter. Her name escapes me.'

'Naima?' My sister mentioned her a lot in her diary.

'Something like that. My wife kept an eye on things, called your mother so she wouldn't be worried. I suppose there had been a few incidents. It wasn't hard to see your sister was mixing with the wrong kind of people. Her friend showed up at your doorstep and your sister ran off several times with her. Your mother would get worried sick.'

'Dr Abdullah, do you remember what caused the fire?' I sense the scar on my calf itching. 'Mum's old now, she has dementia and never mentioned anything to me. I've only just found out I had a sister and how Dad died.'

'Oh wow . . . Well, I remember very well. You don't easily forget incidents like this about people you know. I believe the police report stated that the fire was caused by an accident in the kitchen. They didn't do much investigation. Your mother wasn't herself after that. She was in severe shock, and I treated her while my wife took care of you. She blamed herself . . . But there was something else.'

'What do you mean?'

'Something she wasn't telling us. A pain, a guilt that plagued her.'

'Well of course, she had lost her husband and daughter in the fire.'

'I'm talking about some kind of trauma, which she never spoke of. She naturally would blame herself. But it wasn't her fault. The night of the fire was a warm summer evening. She was expecting guests and had spent all day cooking and cleaning. My wife had offered to take care of you in the morning so that she didn't have to look after you. Your father worked most weekends. He took extra hours tutoring children with learning difficulties. You loved coming to our house and playing in the garden. We never had children of our own. You brought happiness to our lives, Amira beti. But my wife was a little worried. You had so many bruises around your arms and legs.'

'What do you mean? Was I a clumsy child?'

'You'd say: "Meena did this to me." We thought Meena was your imaginary friend. Then your sister showed up on our doorstep once. You pointed your finger at her and said, "That's Meena."'

'Meena? Are you sure it wasn't Mona? I think . . .'

My thoughts try to connect the dots.

Forgotten memories suddenly flood me. And that name sounds so familiar. I think I used to call my sister Meena. I think it was her nickname.

I shudder. My sister has been missing ever since the house fire that killed Dad. She was never found.

She is presumed dead.

'We didn't know what to believe. But it was clear your sister was hurting you.'

My sister mentioned me in her diary. She was unstable and jealous. I think of how Diya mentioned sibling rivalry. I can see why my sister hated me. Her constant clashes with Mum made her feel left out.

'Do you remember?'

'No, I don't.' I take a deep breath. But I think I do. I hear a younger version of myself cry, 'Meena, stop hurting me.'

'I think that "Meena" was your sister's nickname, chosen by your mum.'

'That's very likely, Dr Abdullah.' Mum also nicknamed me *Mimi*. I never liked that name.

Mum has always been controlling. Has always had a strong

mind of her own. But why would she never tell me I had a sister whom she called Meena? I get that she had a fall out with Dad's friends and refused to see them again. She didn't want their daughter hanging out with my sister. But why did she have to spin a lie like that?

'Dr Abdullah, why did you never get in touch with Mum after she moved to Inverness? It sounds like you and your wife were close to her.'

'Afrah disappeared. She left no note to explain why she had gone. No one knew where she went or what had happened to her. We thought that perhaps she had moved back to Lahore. She often spoke about how much she missed the warm climate and the food. That nothing was left for her here after the death of her husband. Your mum was deeply hurt after the dispute with the Pashtuns who accused her of stealing gold bangles. And when your sister sided with them she was devastated. Afrah wasn't a thief. She stayed with us after the fire and insisted paying for everything. Left money all the time for food. Both my wife and I wouldn't hear of it. It's not how things are done among us. Even so, before your mother disappeared with you, she left an envelope with money.'

'But why would she leave without even saying goodbye?' I make a sharp turn into the quietness of the Highlands. The wind rustles through the mountains. Low swinging branches snap in the blowing gale. Snow keeps falling, covering the valleys and hills stretched far beyond the rivers, which run wild between them.

'Like I said, Amira beti, something else deeply troubled your mother. It was like a splinter in her mind that drove her insane. She had terrible nightmares and I'm sure it had something to do with your sister's death.'

'What do you mean?'

'There was a proper burial for your father in the graveyard. But your sister's grave—' His words are breaking up. '—it had a traumatic effect on Afrah. She couldn't get closure.'

'Hello? Dr Abdullah. I can't hear you.'

253

I pull the phone away from my ear and stare at it. Fuck!

'Please can you repeat what you said?' I shout into the receiver.

'Amira Beti, are you still there? Hello?'

'Yes, I'm here. I'm still on the line.'

There's noise in the background. I can't reach him.

I am about to hang up when I get another incoming call.

I thank Dr Abdullah again, but I don't think he hears me. I take Haroon's call. He says he can't hear me, the connection is breaking up. I realise I'm about five miles away from Ravenswood Lodge. I tell him to hold on while I turn the speaker off. I turn my head towards the radio, look up at the windscreen again and see a deer appear out of nowhere. I feel the car begin to skid. I think I'm in a ditch. Blood is splattered all over the windscreen. I touch my forehead. The skin is split open. Warm blood trickles down my face.

'Haroon?' The screen on my phone is crushed. I can hear him say, 'Are you still there Mira? Listen, you will never believe what I found out about your sister Mona—'

I taste blood. My eyelids are heavy. The sound of wind muffles in my ears. I give into the darkness.

36

AFRAH

Monday, 23 December 2019

I hear the ocean striking the cliffs. I call out. 'Hello, is anybody there?' I call out again. But I don't think anyone is here. I am alone. Snowflakes sweep in through the window and land like dust against my face. A storm is brewing outside.

I notice the paint on the walls glowing in neon colours. *I know what you did* written all over in small and big letters. The letters are jumbled, the colours sharp and intrusive. Somewhere in the room, music begins to play. It's a familiar old Hindi song that I would hum to my daughter. 'Is that you, Nisha? Quit it.' I cover my ears. 'I said stop it.' I unplug the cable from the socket, but the music plays on. Its's coming from everywhere.

The door pushes open. I see a person standing there dressed in white. A bad feeling devours me. The room is cold, and more snowflakes fly in, seeking home in the blank surfaces of the room.

'Is that you Carol?' The floor creaks and the tall shadow with a pale face gets closer. 'Who's there?' I try to grab something, anything. My hand fumbles, and I take hold of the book from the table. It must be the gardener. He is out to get me and so is Mrs Brown. She told him to do it. And it was him all along playing with my mind. He wants to hurt me. They both do.

'I will hit you, I am warning you. Stop. Don't get any closer.' If only the music would turn off, it's driving me crazy. What do you want?' Cold sweat runs down the knobs on my spine. 'Do you want gold? Here, take my bracelets. I wrench them off my wrists and throw them into the thin air. The person in the darkness laughs evilly.

The knots in my tummy are getting firmer and I slip into bed. There's a pain growing in my shoulders. I lay on my back, hugging my knees. The white cotton envelopes me. My mind is unable to rest, and I press one hand over my eyes and let the other wander over to the cold side. The music suddenly stops playing.

The bedside clock is ticking. Every minute there's a loud pounding in my ears. I pull down the duvet, my body shivering. I lay watching it as the hand moves around the dial. Outside, the snow keeps falling. Silence.

There's no sound and not a breath of wind, no cold creeping through the walls. I smell something burning. Ashes and dust. Smoke curls like a rope around my neck. The dry air is trapped in my throat. I can't breathe. I creep out of bed and lurch forward, coughing and snatching at breaths of air.

Then, out of the quiet, I hear footsteps getting closer and closer. I feel cold hands tightening the bones in my fingers, cracking one by one. Click, click. Fear has me ensnared. Someone is speaking to me and I look up. It's a woman with long dark hair blowing wildly in the wind. She is dressed in a long white dress and puts the candle in her hand on the nightstand. I have seen her before. Who is she?

'What do you want?' I ask.

'Hello Ami,' she says. Her eyes glint red and amber like flames.

'Is that you, Amira?'

She throws me a hollow glare. No, this can't be. She is not my daughter. I look away, shut my eyes.

'Who are you?' It's a ghost. An evil spirit haunting the house. 'Stay away from me.'

'It's me, Meena. Don't you recognise your own daughter?' she laughs.

'My daughter is dead.' I open my eyes and look right at her.

'I am back, Ami. Back from the dead.'

PART FOUR
Union

37

MONA

I feel so much better now that I am alive again. Well, I was never really gone. I am still presumed dead by the world. I have been for decades. It feels good to bring some part of me back to life, and it's all thanks to Meena. She has done a fantastic job fooling my little sister, who never suspected a thing. Meena, the sweet girl with rosy cheeks and tight black braids, just the way Mum imagined I would be after I was born. Sorry to be a disappointment Mum. But I never was a good Pakistani girl. I have my own rules by which I live.

Unlike most other things in my life, lying comes easy to me, and I always get what I want. Technically speaking, I built my world around a sound web of lies, and it's served me well. I have fooled the world and my own mother into believing that Mona Malik disappeared from the face of the earth after that dreadful night of the fire.

But why? Mum will wonder, when she finds out. I'll tell her again and again, as she's becomes demented and may need reminding. It's just like I told her before the house burned down. She stopped loving me. And what's the point in staying with someone who doesn't love you? You might as well be dead to them. And so I remained dead for decades. But now that I am back, I want revenge.

The way I found out about Mum and the little brat is the way it works in most Asian communities, where gossip travels faster than lightyears. My curiosity awakened when I first heard some girls at a party chatting, saying that a sharif ladki, a decent girl, from a Kashmiri family, had married a doctor – Haroon Khan – after he impregnated her, and who divorced him several years later after he had impregnated someone else. Gossip like this spreads like a tumour among Pakistani circles. Sorry it didn't work out, sis. I could have told you he was a cheating bastard. I know a wandering eye when I see it.

I then spotted Dr Khan at a wedding in Glasgow. He matched the exact description the girls still gossiped about. Tall, handsome, bearded, with a flirtatious smile. What's not to like and to chatter about? On further eavesdropping, I learned that the sharif ladki he had married was a drop-out nurse, an Amira Malik from Inverness. At first, I didn't think much of it. But then I heard that she worked as a carer looking after her mum, Afrah Malik. It was easy putting the pieces together after that.

Was I emotional? Sure. Did I shed tears of joy? Absolutely not. Anger and resentment spiralled inside me. The old feelings that took me years of self-therapy to get over, resurfaced. I began remembering what had happened on the night of the fire. How Dad gave his life up to save me. How I crawled out at the back and escaped death. Naima's mum took me in and, once I was gone, presumed dead to the world, I remained dead. I took on a new identity, a new life, which Naima's dad sorted out for me in the blink of an eye. Naima's mum taught me the important principles of revenge and how sweet it is when put into practice. No one knows revenge like she does, and so I began to work on my master plan when I discovered that Mum had lived a seemingly idyllic life with the little brat somewhere in Inverness. The problem with a life like that is, it gets mundane. I saw it as my duty to make Mum's life colourful.

The first seed of a lie I planted was when I told my circle of people to tell my sister's ex-husband's circle of people that I was a caring nurse. An important first step, which I called the initiation stage. Then I googled Dr Haroon Khan from Inverness, and dropped him an email introducing myself as a friend of his family from Glasgow. I never met his family. But he doesn't know that.

The second seed of a lie was to let him casually know that I was looking for work. Could he please get back to me if he heard of any open positions in health care? I sent him various documents. Highly impressive letters of recommendations, all fake, of course, and easy enough for me to forge. All part of my plan, which worked in my favour. He said, 'She's the best carer out there.' And I particularly needed him to say that to Amira.

He told me about his ex-wife, Amira Malik, who also worked as carer. The third seed of a lie I told him was about the carers support group. 'Make sure to tell your ex-wife to become a member, Dr Khan. We carers need caring, too.' I sent him a traceable link to the forum site and sat back watching the online activity patiently. Who joined, who wrote what, who was caring for whom. I did this for months under different names and spoke to a bunch of very depressed and desperate carers. None of them were Amira Malik. I cracked my fingers every day and typed to random people online, scanning for any new members that had joined. Then I saw a new member, who went by the name *Nursemira*. And bingo. The link I had sent to Dr Khan traced back to an email from amirakhan@onlinewebmail.com.

I typed a message. 'Hey love, welcome to the forum, nice seeing a new member join.' She replied hesitantly, apologising for being new. 'Don't worry, so am I. Where are you from?' She said she lived in the Highlands. Our chat went on and on – I call this the 'warm-up' stage. I wanted to gain her trust, and dropped in that my name was Meena Bashir. I told her it felt so impersonal not giving out your real name. There was a long pause before she wrote back. 'I'm Amira Khan, nice to meet you, Meena.' I knew that wasn't true. I knew she was *the* Amira Malik after she had revealed bits of information about Mum and how it had always just been the two of them and no one else after her dad died at young age. But she didn't know that I knew who she really was. Just like she didn't know I wasn't the *real* Meena Bashir.

Meena exists only as a fictional echo. She was the idea of a good girl with a bad side. And I know all about how to create a good girl gone bad. When I was little, Mum nickednamed me Meena, and used to call me Meri Meena all the time. She disapproved of Mona, thought the name was untraditional and brought shame to her Kashmiri heritage. She never called me by my real name. So in her eyes, I remained *her* innocent little Meena.

Being someone I am not comes easy to me.

A while ago, I hired a timid Bangladeshi woman called Meena Bashir to look after Naima's mum who became my new mum, Sultana. It was easy sorting her visa and papers to get her from Bangladesh to Scotland. Before Naima's dad died, he taught me all about forging documents. That's how I stayed alive, not as Mona Malik but as someone else. Mona died after the fire in Glasgow. May she rest in peace.

Meena Bashir is my new cover up, a stolen identity I am using to execute my plan. We'll get to that later. I wanted to give Meena Bashir all the qualities Mona Malik never had. Sweet, gentle and kind-hearted. Meena Bashir is understanding and helpful, a real true friend in need. Meena Bashir has a father who suffers from dementia and whom she tenderly and selflessly cares for. That makes her likeable. I typed in, 'Nice meeting you, Amira. What a beautiful name.' I call this the 'forging a friendship' stage. I asked her several questions, and she didn't hold back, like most carers in the chat forum, when it came to sharing her years of frustration our mother had caused her. Mum's stubbornness – her behaviour didn't seem to have changed. I pitied my baby sister and mirrored my own frustration back: 'My dad pees in his bed. He leaves a mess everywhere. He doesn't listen. He is so forgetful.' All the usual tropes I had picked up during my months of activity chatting to hundreds of carers. I call this the 'initial research' stage.

I would glance over my plan and tick off the boxes on my to-do-list.

Step one: Before I set up my account – becoming Meena Bashir in the support group for carers – I will test my skills chatting to other carers to get as much information I can about patients with dementia. Speak to carers. Gather information. Tick.

Step two: pick the perfect name. Something innocent, yet catchy. How about *Thelonelymouse*? Most of the carers are lonely, depressed and suffer from mental health issues of their own. The name *Thelonelymouse* instantly evokes sympathy and I have had hundreds of carers reach out to me. Tick

Step three: once identified, make contact and establish a long-term friendship to gain Amira's trust. It wasn't difficult to gain the little brat's trust. She was always so vulnerable. Tick.

As I sit here in the comfort of my chair, I glance over my master plan and it almost seems too easy. Amira will practically walk into my trap. She has no idea what's coming. All I have to do is lean back and watch the mistakes she is about to make.

38

AMIRA

I wake at the crack of dawn and find myself cold to the bone. Dry blood peels off my forehead, where the split wound aches. Quickly, I try to orientate myself. I've crashed Nadia's car into a ditch. A dead deer lays sprawled on the bonnet, its wide eyes glaring right at me. I switch the windshields off to stop the awful scraping sound. I search for my phone and find it on the passenger seat. Every muscle in my body aches and is stiffened by the freezing temperature. A frigid cold. I grab my phone and push open the door.

'Come on, come on.' I need a signal. Nothing. I have two energy bars left before my phone runs out of battery. I start off slowly towards the care home. The road is dark – only a faint light from the sky is visible, the rest is overshadowed by the wind-blown trees dressed in snow. I have to keep moving. I have to get to Mum. I fiddle with my phone, swiping the broken screen. Still no signal. I can't even reach 999.

The road seems never-ending. Barren and desolate; no one is out here. There's no hope of any seeing any car either. People are home, safe with their families celebrating the holidays with their loved ones. Something is out there in the dark – a four-legged creature moving, rustling through the woods. It's a deer. I don't just see one. I see another and another. Two more join, then three. I must have hit may head harder than I thought. There's a large flock, probably hundreds of them now, and more keep coming with each blink of my eyes. I tuck my hands into my pockets, my ears touching my shoulders. I start to run as fast as I can and skid across the icy road.

The snow keeps falling and falling. I turn around and see no deer in sight. But I keep running. I don't stop till I reach Ravenswood Lodge.

I walk up the winding road and pass through the arched branches. The white trail up the hill leads to the house. I hear the tides slap against the cliffs, and then slowly ripple back to the bay. My breath forms plumes of smoke curling against the distant belt of trees. I go past the black gates, reach a deserted garden. No one is in sight. There is not even light in the windows, except for one – coming from the tower.

'Hello? Can you hear me?'

There's movement behind the curtain. Somebody is inside the house. I reach the front stoop and climb the stairs to the main door and press the bell, but there's no answer. I call again. 'Open the door, if you can hear me.' Where is everyone? I stand outside like a ghost and ring the bell again. Still no answer. Did I miss something? I check my phone. 24th December. Of course. The care home is closed. It's shut down for two days over the holidays. Panic surges through me. Where is Mum?

I hear screams coming from the tower. Somebody shouts, 'Help me. Please help me.'

It's Mum's voice. She is in danger.

I lift one of the flower pots at the front of the house and throw it through the window, smashing it into pieces. I climb through carefully. I am inside the house; my feet crunch on the broken window glass. It's silent. I press against the floorboards, my weight releasing the sound of old creaking wood as I walk into the hallway. Outside, the snowstorm plays hide-and seek. The wind batters the windows, slipping a bitter sea breeze under the quivering doors.

I walk up the staircase and stop in the middle to pull out my phone, which has reception again. I answer the incoming call from Haroon. There's panic in his voice.

'Where are you? I am worried sick about you, and so is Shaf.'

'I'm OK, don't worry about me. I'm at the care home. I need you to drive up here as soon as you can.'

'What's going on, Mira? Didn't you get any of my messages?'

'I had no reception. Listen, something bizarre is going on. I heard Mum screaming for help. No one is here all the staff and patients are gone and—'

'Mira, I can't. I am at the hospital. Nadia went into labour last night. I sent you a message about your sister, Mona. I made some enquires and Mira, the police never recovered a body. There's a grave next to your father in Glasgow, but it's empty—'

'What do you mean?'

'Your father was friends with a wealthy Pashtun family. I don't know them, but a friend of a friend of my relatives in Glasgow knew their daughter, Naima. She lives somewhere in America now, married to—'

'Get to the point, Haroon.'

'They had just one daughter who went to the same school as your sister. I believe they were friends. After the fire, the Pashtun family adopted a girl said to be from Pakistan. She was fourteen years old. The same age your sister was when she was presumed dead.'

'What are you saying? That she's alive, and all this time lived with this Pashtun family as their daughter?'

'Yes,' he sighs heavily. 'It sounds crazy I know, but—'

'Haroon, that's nuts.' Or is it? The diary entries. Mona was close the Pashtun family. She defied Mum, just so she could be with Naima, who she admired. But why would she do that? Why refuse your own mother and pretend to be dead? What did Mum do that was so terrible that my sister chose to fake her death for more than thirty years?'

'You won't believe what's next. I got hold of a picture of the girl the Pashtuns adopted and sent to boarding school. It's a school picture. But I wanted to see if I could spot any similarities between her and you. And Mira, she is a spitting image of you. Mona didn't die. She is alive. I am sending you the photo right now. See for yourself. Do you recognise her?'

I hold back the phone. A picture comes through. But I can

barely see it through my cracked screen. 'Haroon? Are you there? Hello? Answer me.'

'Mira, did you get it? Yes, I am still here. Have you seen the photo?'

'No, my screen is cracked.'

'Mona changed her name and goes by—'

My phone dies on him. Fuck.

'Help! Somebody help me get out of here.' I hear a faint voice.

'Mum?' I rush up the stairs, and swing open the door to her room. My mouth falls open. The walls all have the same writing in different neon colours. *I know what you did.*

'Mum, what the hell did you do?'

I hear her loud screams and turn up towards the tower.

The staircase is dark, there's not a flicker of light. I hold tight against the railing, pulling myself up in all my heaviness as if I were a sinking anchor. In the long corridor, there are doors to my right and doors to my left. One at the far end squeaks open and a tall lanky shadow steps out in the vein of a yellow pool of light. My heartbeat quickens. I want to believe someone is there and that I am not imagining things again. After the car crash, I feel dizzy. Disoriented. The tiredness makes my frustration boil over. I rub my eyes, hot and dry. Someone is definitely there. I stand in the dark hallway holding my breath and listen to the sound from the tower. It is a rising cry coming from Mum's weak voice.

'Help me!'

For a moment, I completely freeze. I want to shout, I am coming, but there's a lump in my throat, lodged with fear. I am unable to speak. I shiver, feeling goose pimples grow on my arms.

I take one hesitant step backwards, and the shadow steps forward. This person is real and not a fabrication of my imagination. Suddenly, I can't seem to quell the unease rising inside me. I clearly see the shadow now slowly stepping towards me. I grab the door handle to my right and wrench it to open, but it's locked. The shadow stops, and I feel glowing eyes through the dark burning at me. It is silent and cold, and the curtains behind me billow.

The wind sweeps in from the open window, slashing ice against my back. It is as though I'm back in the local church, in the Carers Support Group, in the corridor where a shadow stood watching me, just as I am being watched now. I open the door handle to my left, which is also locked. Shit. I am trapped in this house and my fear takes over.

I'm caught up in a new but familiar feeling as I was on the Bridge of Oich, surrounded by the fog, when I heard the scraping noise of nails grinding the rail of the bridge. I hear it clearly again and see threadlike bare arms stretched out. It is that same aggravating sound of nails scraping against the wall. My sweaty hands press against my thighs. A tight blow of energy pulses through me. My stomach flips over as tension rises inside of me. I sense an air of stress in the void. All sort of emotions tumble inside me and I lose my sense of place just for a second before I realise where I am again.

A cold shiver peels down my spine. I am inside Ravenswood Lodge Care Home. No one is here except for me, Mum and the shadow standing across from me at the other end of the hallway. My pulse is thumping, my thoughts shooting off with a mixture of paranoia and superstitions about the house, its ghostly stories, which Diya shared with me. I am looking at no ghost. The person glaring at me is real and not some woman in white haunting the house and its visitors. Plumes of breath circle around the figure whose long bony fingers stretch out at me through the shiny blackness. My limbs go stiff as the person gets closer.

'Who is there?' I call out.

As it approaches, I see the shadow becomes visible, taking the shape of a woman with long dark hair flaring in the wind. I hear the sound of creaking leather and stand face to face with her. She looks right at me and an unkind smile appears on her lips. I move back, grab the curtains, pull them to one side. A stream of daylight casts light on her face.

I take in her features. The crown of her head. A set of rising brows. Her nose, a fine line, with a glinting silver ring around the nostril. She throws back her hair that slides down her back. She gives me a curious glimpse, eyes glittering. There's a pinched look on her pale face. A long silence wraps around us as our gazes deepen. She is taller than me, slim and bony. My heart beats hard inside my chest like it's going to explode anytime now and tear out of my skin.

'Hello, little brat,' she says in a cold distant voice. 'We finally meet again.'

Suddenly I hear Haroon's voice saying:

Mona didn't die. She is alive.

My breath catches in my throat as I stare at the woman.

What is Mum's carer Zahra Akram doing here?

39

AFRAH

Saturday, 15th August 1992

I go through the checklist again, eyeing the groceries on the kitchen counter. Yoghurt and cucumber for the raita. Food colouring – yellow, green and red – for the sweet chawal. And almonds. I'd have to peel them. I thought I asked him to get me peeled ones. Mrs Singh gets hers from the shop, why can't I? I won't go upstairs and wake him. Let him have his nap before they arrive. What else did he get? Raisins. Coconut, poppy seeds. Chillies and curcumin powder. Garam masala. Where are the cumin seeds and bay leaves? I need all the ingredients if I am to cook the perfect chawal and korma. Mona loves Korma. I'll make an extra-large portion. I pull out the diced chicken breast from the fridge.

My eyes shift and I put the list down. The minute hand pacing away on the clock. The guests will soon be here, and no sign of Meena. Where has that ladki gone? I flatten the pleats of my sari. This won't do. I go upstairs and quickly change into the wool shalwar kameez, a new set Mother sent from Pakistan. Although we're in mid-July, it's too cold to wear cotton. It shouldn't itch. It wouldn't. Saeeda Begum wore wool last Sunday when I saw her in masjid. First time I set foot in Glasgow Central Mosque and already they're asking when I will send my children to the Muslim school. Let them ask, Nadeem said. It's what they do.

Saeeda Begum kept asking me about Sultana, of course, the Durrani family know about our fall out with the Pashtuns. Gossip spreads fast in our community. Let them talk. I'll cook a dinner for them to remember. From the pantry, I reach for the crate of yellow mangoes Mother sent, along with the spices and namkeen.

A refreshing lassi goes well served with the sweet chawal. The Durrani family have one son. A handsome boy Mona's age.

I turn back to my list. Fresh coriander, mint and tomatoes. The phone rings.

'Hello? How are you, Mrs Singh? . . . Is everything alright? . . . Are you sure? . . . Can you see her right now getting out of the black Mercedes? . . . I know, you mentioned it's not the first time they stop around the corner of our road to drop her off. Please excuse me, but I have to go back to the kitchen . . . Yes, yes thank you for looking after Amira this morning. She is fine, napping upstairs with Nadeem . . . I really must go, we're expecting guests this evening . . . Bye.'

I feel heat on my face. Nadeem must know what she is up to. He knows everything. Keeps secrets from me. They both do. He spoils that ladki. Had to give her an unconventional name too. Saeeda Begum was asking, 'Is Mona short for Mahmona?' I shook my head, felt the shame creep into my skin. I had chosen such a beautiful name for her, even Mona said, 'I like it, Ami.' She was a little girl then. 'Don't worry, I'll be your Meena. I'll be a good girl.' Look at her now, all grown up and independent. I hope the Durrani family take a liking to her. But first, let her come home. She'll have to answer to me.

I tune the radio to the local station and it crackles with static. I turn and fiddle the button around, trying to find a music station. Something blows through the speaker – it's that Whitney Houston song again. I stand by the window and lift the net curtain. I want a good look at her when she comes down the road. If Mrs Singh's report is correct, she should be here by now.

The English lady next door pushes the pram. All dressed up in her summer dress and sandals with painted toenails. I see her chatter with the other goreh mums on the pavement. They keep amongst themselves. Nod when they see me. The old widow living next to Mrs Singh never nods. Always in her plastic slippers and pink apron, she stands in the doorframe and stares curiously at me like I am some mystical ornament. Whenever she sees

Nadeem, she says, 'You all right Nad?' like he was the same type of goreh living in their neighbourhood. The last time she did that, I said, 'My husband's name isn't Nad.' She didn't look at me, but at Amira crying in the pram. My girls get stared at, and I tell myself it's because they are pretty and like twins, only years apart.

The children in the playground are screaming, laughing. Tomorrow I'll take Amira out for a stroll. Buy her an ice cream. Mona doesn't like it when I spend time with Amira. Tells me I love her more than her.

'I don't, Meena beti,' I say.

'Stop calling me that. My name is Mona.' She gets angry so fast. Takes all the toys from Amira and screams, 'They're mine. Not yours. I don't want to share.'

When I was a child we had to share everything. Mona doesn't understand, she's a desi goreh, and takes after her father. I wish she wouldn't be so angry all the time and I wish she would stop going to Sultana's house without telling me.

'But Naima is my best friend, she is like my sister, and I like spending time with her. Her parents care about me. Naima always pays for everything when we're out and so does her mum. Why can't I see them?'

'How many times have I said this? I will not have you go around to their house behind my back. We have nothing to do with them anymore. Nothing, so stay far away. Understood? I don't want to catch you going there again.'

Her face gets pink, and she thinks I don't know about all the things they buy her. Clothes and shoes from expensive shops like those white Nike sneakers she's started wearing. I don't want their charity.

Boiling with anger, I pull the entire curtain to one side. She should be here now! 'Where in God's name is that silly ladki?'

Upstairs, Nadeem and Amira are awake. 'Where's Ami?' I hear Amira say.

There's noise at the front, keys rattle. I pull back my hair and leave the kitchen.

She comes down the hallway, leaving the front door open. I stand poised and watch her throw her bag onto the floor. Jennifer Rush crooning from the radio in the kitchen. She walks right past me. She doesn't meet my gaze. I'm not sure she even knows I exist. The pressure cooker whistles and a starchy smell of rice moistens the air.

'Where were you?'

No answer.

I catch a glimpse of her reflection in the mirror at the other end of the hall. I catch my own gaze in it as I stride in her direction.

'Answer me. Where did you go?' She turns into the dining room, pulls back a chair and sits at the table set with empty plates and glasses. Her fingers toy with the table cloth, twisting it into a tight knot.

'Don't pretend you don't know where I went.' The candle flickers, casting a shade on her face, which has turned pink. 'You've known all along, haven't you?'

'Badtameez ladki. That's not the way to speak to your mother. Didn't I tell you I don't want you to—' I fall silent and watch her watch me.

'Don't you tell me what to do.' Anger lingers like phantom threads between us.

'What did you say?' I loom over her, but she stands up and pushes the chair away with her foot. The table shakes, knocking over the candle. Thick smoke is coming from the kitchen. The smell of burning rice. But that's not all. Something else is burning. I look down. Small ribbons of flames rise from the table top.

'From now on, you don't have to worry about me.' She's at the window looking out. The hazy summer light slips through the shutters, leaving shadows on the floor.

'Why did you have to go with her?' I go to stand beside her and place my hand on her shoulder. It feels warm, smouldering. Hot air begins to envelop us, makes its way into our lungs.

'Tell me, why?' I adjust my wool kameez.

273

'Because,' her beady eyes look directly into mine, 'you stopped loving me.'

Nadeem comes in holding Amira. He asks, 'What is going on?' I turn to look at him and a rage of smoke curls up behind him. It sweeps in like a wave and everything turns cloudy. The living room is hot. I scream, 'Hurry, get out, now!' He stumbles back and falls. Amira drops to the floor, her head hitting the panel hard. A wound splits open, dripping blood. She cries hysterically and stretches out her little fingers for me to reach. 'Ami, help, help me.' She coughs. The smoke is everywhere, dancing through the flames of fire. The walls are blackened. Flames flickering everywhere. There's no time to get the extinguisher from the kitchen. Amira screams. Fire has caught her dress. Her movements are frantic. Eyes filled with fearful tears. I leap forward and lurch into action. Stamp on her dress, my foot warm from the blaze. I reach out to take hold. 'I have you,' I say. 'I have you.'

I swing around and see no sign of Mona or Nadeem. In the corner by the door, a glow sparks to life. A gaping mouth of fire spreads fast and the blue flames curl merciless surrounding the room. My throat is so dry I can hardly breathe. The sharp hot smoke plumes into the air. The fire begins to consume everything in our home. A black cloud of smoke circles above me. I look up and fear the roof will come crashing down anytime.

'We've got to go! Nadeem? Where are you?'

Desperately, I look around. I hear a distant voice caught behind the thick smoke. 'Meena, meri Meena. Meri beti, is that you?' I stretch out my hand to see if I can grab hold of her, but she is not there. 'Where are you?' There's no answer. Sweat coats my skin, I can taste the char on my tongue.

'Nadeem where are you?' Perhaps they made it out already.

Amira is crying, her calf a scorching wound. I rip a piece of cloth from my kameez and tie it around her leg to stop it from bleeding. I hold her close and pull my chador over her head and hurry towards the doorway. The searing heat throws us back. The frame is black and burning into ashes. The ceiling is lowering, making an awful, thundering sound. I crouch low, tightening my grip around my daughter. I spin around. My mind is racing. The broken windowpane. It's our only option before it catches fire. Smoke and heat suck at the walls. I have to do this. Have to throw Amira out first.

I kick at the glass with my foot again and again, smashing it into pieces. I need to toss her out and lunge out the same way. I whirl round catching a glimpse of Meena's brown eyes glowing with the fire. Then I look down at Amira's eyes glazed with fear. I hold my crying child close. 'You are going to be fine.'

Amira is safe, she is in my arms and I hold her tight, feeling her heart beat next to mine before I let her go.

40

MONA

Sunday, 10 November 2019

Reviewing my master plan, I have been very busy the past couple of months and I am close to reaching my goal, Mission Revenge. I have been chatting to Amira, aka *Nursemira*, for almost a year now, giving her the impression that I am Meena Bashir, a sweet carer who looked after her father till the end of his days. The reason for stealing Meena Bashir's identity was purely to hook Amira, get her to trust me, and also to get as much information about Mum as possible. And it worked. She trusted me with everything I needed to know to get Mum into a care home.

It took three further steps:

Step one: making persistent calls and sending emails to social services to complain about Afrah Malik, a seventy-six-year-old dementia patient whose daughter is incapable of looking after her own mother. I had to pretend I was Mrs Silvia Nesbit. A perfect cover-up. Of course, a nosy neighbour like Mrs Nesbit would call them. Wouldn't anyone, if some crazy old lady acted odd around a quiet neighbourhood? Mum doesn't get any vote of sympathy. Amira, my dear little sister, is terrified what people would think if they knew that her mother, a well-respected woman, had dementia. This makes it so easy to carry out my master plan, a plan that shifts things and forces Mum out of her comfort zone. And I will use Amira to do the dirty job for me.

Step two: making Amira go to the Carers Support Group where I had given John Buchanan an anonymous tip that she was a highly stressed-out carer who was struggling to look after her own mother. A dementia patient who accidently sets things on fire and who belongs in a care home. I mentioned that Ravenswood Lodge would be a suitable place for someone like Amira's mum. A traditional Pakistani woman who thrives in close-knit communities.

I've been busy spreading so many seeds and seeing the little plants of my lies grow. Tampering with Amira's frail mind seemed easy, so it wasn't hard to make her think that she was doing things subconsciously. Like telling her to attend the local Carers Support Group. 'Did wonders for me,' I lied. I had to expose her vulnerability. Make people see that she was simply not fit to be a carer.

I know lots about Mum now, too. Amira's told me how terrified Mum is of fire. That's not her only oddity. Mum's eating and cooking obsessions are checked in my little notebook. I know she prefers to drink Kashmiri tea. I also know she has a sweet tooth, especially for mithai. Mum's always been fond of cooking and prefers eating a curry over Western food.

Amira has revealed more details about Mum to me than about herself. Sure, she touched on the subject of her life. The failed wife. The failed mother. And the soon to become (if not already) failed daughter. She occasionally mentioned how awful she felt for not being able to complete her degree. Shame she never became a real nurse. Mum had such high expectations of her daughter.

Step three: contacting her ex-husband to feed him information about Ravenswood Lodge. A first-rate facility and the perfect home for the elderly with dementia. I had to make sure a space would be available for Mum, and went through a lot to make it happen (including getting rid of Alice: it was time for her to go).

It was also time to plant another seed. So I sent another email from the fake account I had created to Dr Haroon Khan. I had applied for a job at Ravenswood Lodge looking for a position as a carer. I raved about how fantastic a care home it was. Very traditional, with a close community of people based on trust among the carers and nurses. It's in a lovely and natural setting. It's a first-rate private facility. I know people who'd do anything for their parents to be there. I highly recommend it for dementia patients. It is also a perfect place to carry out my master plan. Isolated, few members of staff, no cameras. It even has a spooky history of murders and mad women.

The key figure is Zahra Akram, a friend of Dr Haroon Khan's distant relatives. She is trustworthy and sympathetic. The perfect carer.

So how did I make it all happen, and what's Meena Bashir's role in all this?

Nothing. Meena Bashir has no clue I used her name to cover my set up to trap Amira.

Meena Bashir is a nobody. She was only a pawn in my plan – I met her first of all when I hired her to be a carer for Naima's mum Sultana. She did a terrible job looking after Sultana and decided to leave after two years as soon as she was offered more money to look after a disabled boy in Inverness.

Sultana was furious and filed a complaint against her for theft. Of course the accusation was false. But she had to be taught a lesson. In the end, I convinced Sultana not to press charges. It would have ruined my master plan. I couldn't have Meena Bashir on police record. She agreed, and let Meena off the hook on the condition she be taught a lesson later. I told her not to worry, and to leave it with me. When Sultana talks about teaching someone a lesson, she means business. And what could be more glorifying than death?

I stole her identity to hook Amira, struck up a friendship of trust. My sister told me everything I needed to know about Mum.

I soon plan to get rid of Meena Bashir and dump her body into the Caledonian Canal. I have no use for her now that Mum is in the care home. I need to get rid of Meena Bashir. Fast.

The police will think it was a suicide. Forging a fake psychological profile of someone only takes one cash transaction. I already have Meena Bashir down as depressive, unstable, frail and very nervous.

Amira works as an alibi. Nothing can or will ever be linked to me. I do not exist, remember? Mona Malik went missing over thirty years ago. I will ask Amira to meet me at the time I plan to dump Meena Bashir's body into the Caledonian Canal. The police will think Meena was depressed and obsessive. Everything will link back to the calls and emails to social services from Meena, as it turns out, and not Silvia Nesbit. The trap will work as a double-edged sword. Meena's mental health issues, her fabricated lie about looking after her father. Her accusation of theft while working as a carer in Glasgow. And her laptop which has all the information the police need. Amira, the little brat, will feel hurt and betrayed. The real Meena Bashir will be dead.

Soon, I can execute the last phase in my master plan: Mum. Amira has no idea what is coming. She'll wish Mum never set foot in Ravenswood Lodge.

41

MONA

Monday, 23 December 2019

It was peaceful this evening as I wandered down the dark hallway of the empty care home and admired the wood panelled walls and the arched church windows, throwing in a gleaming snow-white light over the rooms. I am getting attached to Ravenswood Lodge, it's eeriness and isolated location. While everyone else couldn't wait to get out of here, I couldn't wait to stay behind. Not even Liam, who I consistently fooled into believing Mum dislikes him because he's a gardener, a lowly working-class member of our society. 'It's a caste thing, Liam,' I said, convincingly. 'An old Pakistani woman, Afrah is very traditional about these things. Don't make her cross.' Ahhh, the beauty of reverse psychology. It didn't take much persuasion before Liam started pestering Mum and insulting her with spiteful remarks. He even gave her a little nudge and made the poor old woman stumble. The things I saw . . . the things I chose to ignore.

Liam did exactly what I needed him to do so that Mum felt threatened and vulnerable in her new environment. She believed he stole her things. The more I convinced her he didn't the more she believed it be true. Truth is, Liam couldn't care less about Mum's stupid bracelets and her diary. He was a little resentful about placing the roses in Mum's room as a gesture of peace when I asked him to. And that mud trail on the white carpet, such a classic clue I cleverly planted. All it took was a fistful of the soil from the garden and I sprinkled it like dust when no one was watching. And no one watches around here. No cameras, no fuss. Bless Myrtle, she has the authoritative soul of a woman with strong principles. And principles rule in small thriving communities.

And Carol. Curious, prying Carol, has also gone home to her family in up in Aberdeen. Merry Christmas Carol. She was the easiest piece to spin around my little finger. Carol was just being – what does Myrtle call her? – a 'nosy creature'. That's it. I told Carol Mum wanted her to have her bracelets. 'Go on,' I said. 'Take them – they will look gorgeous on you.' I put them in her room and said Mum left them for her, while I let Mum believe Carol had stolen them. The ongoing tension between them – Carol sparked that herself. The prying, the annoying remarks bothering Mum, generally getting on her nerves. In the end, even *I* got disturbed by Carol and had to tell her off. She just wouldn't leave Mum alone. I didn't want Mum to feel too annoyed, I wanted to scare her. Make her believe she was pagal.

I was getting a little bored with some of the trivial games I played with Mum and decided to raise the stakes. Mum's diary was pretty pathetic. And those silly bookmarks. 'Today I am sad. I had an argument with Amira.' Blah blah. The juicy stuff came from her nightmare entries, which I presumed were about me. I took copies and left them in the library. John, that fool, picked them up, and I convinced him it would be a grand idea to entertain the other patients with a story from Mum's diary. 'Afrah would appreciate it,' I said. 'She loves to read it aloud herself and really wouldn't mind.' Elderly people are so frail. They don't need much convincing, bless their souls.

Although, I do wish John would have hurt Mum a little more when he went after her. He only pushed her and chased her around the house a little when I told him she was rattled about his peeing in the garden. I don't think Mum remembers what he did. She never mentioned anything. But I saw him going for her. It was a true pleasure to watch.

Mum has no idea that her nightmare is about to turn into a reality – and in reality, you can't wake up. And I was only just beginning to trick her mind. I needed to scare Mum a little more, so I created a rumour about the woman in white and made an appearance. It freaked Mum out and made Nisha talk about it, so Mum believed it to be real. Nisha was the toughest person, though, to turn against Mum. In the end, I had to tell her I had heard Mum say how silly she thinks her daughter Diya is. Not just that. Mum also thinks her son Ranveer doesn't look like a Bollywood actor and isn't that handsome. That triggered Nisha, and I had to cover my mouth not to laugh out loud when she had a go at Mum this afternoon. She might have ruined their friendship for good.

The rest was just repeating the existing ghost stories. I told Michael to colourfully explain some of them to Mum as I went to refill the tea kettle. And Myrtle, she did an excellent job too. 'Tell Afrah about the history of the house when she gets here,' I said. 'It belongs to the pride of Ravenswood Lodge.'

Myrtle wasn't sure. I persuaded her that, as a dementia patient, she'd probably forget most of it anyway. I was eavesdropping as Myrtle went on introducing her to every nook of the house. I must say, I was surprised at the level of detail she poured into her narrative. I could see the chills run down Mum's spine. That's right, Ami, welcome to Ravenswood Lodge Care Home. You will be cared for very, very well.

The other odd things, messing around in Mum's room (throwing out her pills, emptying the tin with mithai) and picking the wrong clothes, were easy. Naima's mum always said Mum was a common girl who liked to wear wool, so I put a fresh pair of shalwar kameez into her wardrobe among other pieces, like the green coloured saris she would wear. A little glint from the past, Ami. That made her quite upset.

Then there were all those fake calls to Amira. I never called the little brat. I did email her, stressing to her about the visiting hours. And when she called to check on Mum after I crashed my jeep into her, I hung up. I didn't want her out here vising Mum. Sooner or later, she would have started to suspect that something wasn't right. I couldn't take that risk. The less she came, the better my master plan would work. Amira has to stay as far away as possible from the care home. I am *this close*, and cannot have her meddle with my plan. Suppose she noticed the bruises I caused Mum, or if Mum suddenly remembered things and told her Amira how scared she was? Even if Amira turns up, it'll be easy to get rid of her. The cliffs, the forest, the ocean. The places you can hide a body out here are endless.

After all, it's the reason I chose this place for Mum. And it's all worked out brilliantly. The care home is empty like a shell. Deserted. Dead. I have said my goodbyes to Myrtle Brown and the rest of the staff, assuring them that I would stay and look after the place. Ravenswood Lodge is safe. It is in good hands. And so is Afrah Bibi. As her primary nurse, I will care for her till her daughter gets here. Myrtle was a little hesitant, but I think she trusts me. What a fool. Over stating.

After I redecorated Mum's room into a mess, and made Myrtle and the rest of the lot here believe Mum's crazy, it's time to draw my final move. Mum was scared to death when she saw the beautiful writing on the wall, *I know what you did*. She knows what I mean. She remembers what she did. I tried my best striking up a close friendship with her, being kind and patient loving and understanding.

I was getting a little sick of it. I wanted to shake her by the shoulders and scream in her face: 'Just tell me, tell me why did you did it?' But patience is what Naima's mum has taught me.

I just couldn't help myself tonight as I went into her bedroom to scare her. That look on her face when I told her who I was. Afterwards, it only took some chloroform on a handkerchief to knock her out. When she wakes, she will have no idea what I will do to her. She must suffer, just as I did. The sad part is, she may not recall anything just before she dies.

42

AMIRA

Her voice is emotionless and her mouth curves into a nasty smile. She laughs, a sharp brittle note. She comes towards me and I step to the side, sliding my hand along the rail leading down the stairs. I see her now, the same shadow coming into my room when I was little. She stood watching me as I pretended to be asleep. I would see her from the corner of my eye, creeping around in my room, touching my things. Taking back what belonged to her because she didn't want to share.

Blood pulses in my ears. 'I know it's you, Mona, or should I call you Zahra Akram?'

She laughs and a spiteful grin plasters across her face. 'It took you a while to figure out who I really am. But yes, it is me, sis. I am back from the dead.' She twirls. 'Just look at us. We are practically twins, just years apart. You only notice when you pay attention. And not many people do.'

I shake my head, refusing to believe it. 'Who are you?' I examine her features up close, through the flickering light. She is the sister I never knew. Faint memories of her scratch the surface of my mind. Memories that have been supressed for years.

'Call me Zahra, and if you feel nostalgic, call me sis.'

'How about Mona Malik? That's your real name.' I notice a white cloth is tucked into her hand, which she is twisting hard between her fingers.

'Mona Malik is gone,' she says. 'Dead for more than 30 years thanks to our mother.'

'What happened was an accident. I found the articles. I read

284

what happened during the fire. It was a horrible accident and no one is to blame.'

'That's what you think.'

'Why did you disappear like that?' I bite the insides of my cheek, clamp to the warm flesh. 'Why didn't you come back home?'

'Because, little brat,' she raises her chin and her voice is cold like steel, 'unlike you, I wasn't wanted by our mother. She wished me dead and condemned me.'

'What makes you believe that? Mum would never—' I chew my lip.

'But she did,' She takes a deep breath. 'And I wanted to punish her. So I remained dead to her and dead to the world. But I've always been here. If only she had bothered to look for me. But she never cared for me.'

'Mona, I think all these years you've been under a heavy cloud of a terrible misunderstanding. Mum would have come for you if she knew you were alive. Why did you never bother contacting us?'

'Save your judgement of me please,' her voice is shrill. 'I chose not to have anything to do with Afrah Malik or her daughter – you! It's the only reason I remained dead in the eyes of the world.'

I realise what my sister is. Vicious. No daughter in her right mind would disappear and pretend to be dead and cause grief to her mother on purpose.

'Why come back after all these years as her carer, and not as her daughter?'

'Because I heard about you and your failed marriage through some gossipy girls. I couldn't pity you. I didn't even know you. Then I learned who you were, Amira. Some failed nurse-turned-carer for her mother, Afrah Malik. It brought me back to the past and with it came all the old feelings, which sparked back to life. I had to do something.'

'So you tricked Mum? Made her believe you care for her?'

'I had to. There was no other way. And it was all down to you, sis. You helped me.'

285

'What do you mean?' An uneasy feeling travels through me. 'Why would I help you?'

'I had to be someone you'd befriend and trust. So I pretended to be Meena Bashir. Aka *Thelonelymouse*. Yes, it was me, *the* Meena Bashir in the online chat forum for carers you've been speaking to. Not the dead body the police found. That's the real Meena Bashir. I stole her identify just so I could fool you, and her. What's that saying? Ah yes, kill two birds with one stone. And guess what? You are up next.'

I feel the blood drain from my face. It wasn't a coincidence that the Meena who contacted me online happened to be my sister. She has a twisted mind. I knew that the moment I read her diary. And she hasn't changed.

'How did you know it was me in the online forum for carers?'

'I made sure your ex-husband told you about it. And I waited for months before you finally joined. I knew the instant you came online who you were, *Nursemira*.'

'Haroon? How did you get in touch with him?' I feel the rise of anger, hot and crawling up from my stomach into my throat. 'Most importantly, why?'

'It was easy to get in touch with him after I spotted him at a wedding.' She looks at me, her gaze unflinching. 'Afterwards, I tracked him down online. After all, how many doctors in Inverness are called Haroon Khan? I told him I was a friend of his family in Glasgow, which he believed. Men are so lazy sometimes. Your ex-husband in particular, and so easily fooled, too. Mind you, cheating men tend to be fools. Your ex never bothered checking who I really was. If he had, my plan would have failed. He'd have known Zahra Akram had nothing to do with his relatives living in Glasgow. He believed I was a caring and wonderful nurse, a friend of his family now working at the best care home in Inverness.' She tilts her head forward and her face is stony. 'He believed all that I told him. Lucky for me, my plan worked out.'

'What plan?' My breath is shallow, now harder to draw.

'The plan to get Mum into the care home. And you helped me, sis. You did all the legwork for me to get Mum into Ravenswood Lodge. I played my part of course. I did a lot of research. The care home had to be perfect. A place where I could reconnect with Mum, get close to her and gain her trust without having to worry about looking after other patients.'

'You made those calls to social services. You knew all about Mum. You were jealous, weren't you? I read your diary, I know who you are.'

She laughs. 'So Mum still kept my old diary, did she? What else didn't catch fire?'

'Mum has old photographs of you, Mona. She didn't forget you. If only I had known . . .' I sigh. 'I found your birth certificate. The news about the fire.'

'That's how you found out about me? Birth certificate, photographs and newspaper pieces.' She smiles callously. 'Some part of Mum wanted to remember me. Wanted me to be alive. Too late, sis. She'll get what she deserves. Once I am through with her, people will think she was just another loopy old Asian woman who died of dementia. She will deserve everything she is going to get.' Her eyes are blank and her expression dead in the flimsy light of the dark hall-way. I realise she is not truly my sister. We are complete strangers.

Mona deceived me. Made me believe she was a carer, a friend. She deceived Mum, too, and never meant to care for her. I feel deep pain clutch in my heart. Mona is capable of anything. My sister wants to hurt me and hurt Mum. The air feels dense and my vision turns blurry. I focus on the darkness in her irises. A strong hatred reflects back at me.

'But why put Mum away? Why into a care home?'

'It was the easiest way, really. Once you joined the online chat forum and befriended me, aka Meena Bashir, you handed me all the information I needed to execute my plan. Besides, it's the perfect punishment for someone with dementia, isn't it, little brat? To take the comfort of their home away. In Mum's case, she took away my home, burned it to the ground and killed me.'

'You are a liar.' I want to grab her, push her down the stairs. 'Mum would never do such a thing.'

'You think you know our mother so well. Why did she lie to you all these years? Why did she never tell you the truth?'

I look away. Heat flashes to my cheeks. I think of Dr Abdullah's words. He said that Mum carries 'a pain, a guilt that plagued her'.

What truth is Mona talking about? I can't trust Mona and I can't trust Mum.

'You are no different. You are a liar. Do you have any idea what you've done?'

She nods. 'It took a little muscle flexing, and I had to pull some strings to get rid of Alice so that I could make room for Mum. That's right. Old Alice slept through as I pressed a pillow over her face. Then it was easy. I didn't even have to do anything but sit back and watch the show go on.' She draws a long breath.

'Why would you do that? Go to all that trouble to hurt Mum?'

'You still don't know do you? I've not had this much fun in years. Lying is what I do best. Look at the web of lies I have created. Isn't that some genius master plan, or what? I even had the police fooled. No one saw me coming. Would you have guessed that I was Meena Bashir if I hadn't told you? Did you also know it was me that day in the Carers Support Group – in the corridor coming at you, making sure you walked right back into my trap?'

I hold my breath. So I did see someone in the corridor that day. The shadow. It was my own sister. 'You interfered with my mind, distracted me and made me believe what I saw wasn't real.'

I remember confiding in her through several online chats. I told everything about Mum to the Meena Bashir I thought was my friend. But all this time, it was my *dead* sister using the information I gave her to frame Mum. She wanted her to be put away, somewhere remote where she could get close to her to play her twisted game of revenge. But why?

'And the woman who died. The real Meena Bashir. Why kill her?'

'I had no choice. She was no use to me anymore.'

'You were scared, weren't you? Keeping her alive meant the police would trace you.'

I snatch a deep breath. The police mentioned a family she worked for in Glasgow. I can see the pieces come together. 'Meena Bashir worked as carer for you in Glasgow, didn't she? You are part of that wealthy Pakistani family and she cared for your disabled "auntie". You accused her of theft and went after her because she left to care for another family.'

'You are right. I did what I had to, to get rid of her. How else would I cover up my traces? I couldn't take any risks and have the police come back with more questions. I paid a therapist and GP in advance to hand the police the profile of an unreliable patient suffering with depression. The police saw the history of a woman with mental health issues. Her GP would testify he had subscribed her with antidepressants. The police saw exactly what I fabricated through my clever lies. An immigrant who had a hard time coping with the stress and pressure of long working hours as carer.'

'You killed an innocent woman!' I scream. I feel sick to my stomach thinking about it. She widens her eyes, deep and dark like a tunnel. 'And you used Meena, just like you used me.'

'It was so easy. I contacted Meena, offering up her last paycheck in cash, which she never took before she left Glasgow. She agreed to see me and gave me the address she was living at in Inverness. With the money, I also gave her the laptop I had already used to set up a fake profile in the online forum and the email in her name to contact social services, which showed her interest in applying for a job in Ravenswood Lodge. I knew the police would link her to you and believe her death was a suicide and nothing more. You'd come across believable to the police, telling them exactly what they needed to hear. Meena's betrayal, her secrets, her lies. Sis, you were the perfect victim. I used you to cover my tracks.'

I say nothing and stand back watching her.

'The night before you agreed to meet me at Caledonian Canal, I followed Meena and offered her a lift home. But she never made

289

it back to her family. I threw her body into the canal hours before you showed up. And yes, it was me that morning on the Bridge of Oich, the shadow in the mist. I had to make sure you'd come and you did, little brat. You have been walking into every trap I set out for you.'

'You kept me waiting,' I say. 'Texted that you were on your way when you weren't. You never said where to meet you, did you? And it was your jeep that drove into mine?'

'Who else's would it be? I've parked it down by the beach so no one would notice the front bumper needs fixing. You see, little brat, I've learned from the best how to cover my tracks. Naima's dad, Hashim was a brilliant con artist. He was never caught by the police and specialised in forging identities for decades. And Naima's mum, Sultana taught me patience when seeking revenge. I watched. I learned. When the time came, I used my skills quite cleverly, don't you agree?'

'So that's what this is? A crazy act of vengeance against Mum? Against me?'

'Little brat,' she says in a mocking tone. 'There was no other way to get information out of you and close the case without raising unnecessary suspicion with the police. In the eyes of the world, I am Zahra Akram, the adopted daughter of Hashim and Sultana. I'm a loving and kind carer. Anyone here will testify for that, even Myrtle Brown.'

'You tried to kill me.' I catch my breath. 'Crashing into me with your car.'

'I had to stop you from going to Ravenswood to see Mum. The more I tried to keep you away, the more Afrah Bibi wanted you. She has always chosen you over me. Pathetic. Because from what you told me, you were sick and tired of caring for her. You wanted out and I merely fulfilled your wish. You ought to thank me for putting Mum into a care home. I did you a favour.'

I see the girl from the diary. Mean and unkind. I remember her clearly now from my early childhood. I remember her grabbing my arm, and hard. Blue and yellow bruises appeared on my body. She wanted to hurt me just as she does now, and I realise what she did to me. She is no different to who she was then. She threatened to put spiders in my bed if I would tell on her. She was the reason behind all those nightmares I have.

'I take a step back. 'What do you want from us?

She steps closer. Her breath comes out like rings of smoke. Her gaze is pinned to me. 'She never told you did she? Never mentioned.' Her gaze pinned to me. 'She never told you, did she? Never mentioned my name. I was her Meena, *meri Meena*, she'd call me. A good girl with a bad side. She couldn't even call me by my real name after you were born. How I resented you for it. Mum's been lying her entire life. But this lie, she cannot escape. It has followed her. She destroyed my life, took everything away from me.'

'She is our mother. How can you hate her this much?' I recall her written words. The resentment in her diary for Mum and for me. I want to reason with her. She needs to know Mum doesn't hate her and neither do I. Mum's been haunted by her disappearance her entire life, collecting pieces of information in newspapers. Every day she hoped to read the front-page news about her daughter.

'Mum has poured her soul, blood and energy into raising us without wanting anything in return. She needs you, Mona. Needs you to be her daughter, to love her.'

'How can I love her, when she never loved me? All those years pretending I never existed. I must put an end to this, to what she did to me. But before I do—'

'Wait, stop!' I step back.

She raises her arms towards me and has her hands clasped tightly around my neck. The wind blows in hard, whipping her long hair around me like a rope. I push her back. My teeth grind and pressure fills my jaw. I let out a groan.

'What did I ever do to you?' I shout. 'I don't deserve this.' Tears sting my eyes.

Shock etches across her face. She steps back. The creak of wood expands then cracks. I whirl around, but she grabs my wrist and pulls me close. Her eyes are full of anger. She drops forward and leans in close and presses the handkerchief in her hand against my nose. I push back, but my arms fall to my side. She holds the pressure firmly, and I begin to feel dizzy. Nausea swells inside my stomach. Slowly, my eyes fall shut. I feel myself drop, my body weak. I try not to breathe, but that's impossible. I slip and tumble down the stairs.

43

AFRAH

Tuesday, 24 December 2019

I am tied to a chair and can't move my hands or feet. I look around the room where I have been brought to. It is dimly lit. Something is burning. Candles flicker in the distance. Blue flames are dancing. From my mouth, I cough out mucous. I try to speak, to shout, but the pain allows me only to whimper. My tongue feels swollen. The ropes against my wrists and ankles are tied tight. I am aware of everything around me, aware of the danger I might be in. I see her face, pale, like she's dead.

'Let go of me,' I say. My voice is close to cracking. I feel weak, as if anytime soon I will collapse. I twist, moving my body from side to side. The chair tips back and leans against the wall. A shadow hovers over me. 'Who are you?'

The woman with dark hair steps in front of me. Purple shadows circle underneath her eyes. She laughs, and then a strange smirk sits across her lips. She is familiar. But I can't place her in my memory.

'Don't you recognise your own daughter, Afrah?'

I squint. 'You are not my daughter. What have you done to Amira?'

'It was always her, wasn't it, Ami? You chose that little brat over me, and left me to die in that forsaken house. You even left your husband to burn.'

'Mona? Is that you?'

'Mona is dead. You killed her.' She pulls the chair up and cuts me loose with a kitchen knife. My body buckles in shock. 'All those years I resented you for what you did. If it hadn't been for

293

Naima's mum who took me in, I would have ended up back with you. But I could never go back to you. I know what you did. And you know what you did—'

'Meri beti. You are alive.' I begin to cry. I don't believe my eyes. 'Meena, you are my Meena.' I stretch out my arms. I want to hold her and never let her go. I want to ask her why she went with Sultana? Why didn't she come back to me? Why did she punish me all these years, making me believe she was dead?

'Don't you dare call me that. You have no right after what you did.' She places the knife against my neck and draws a line of blood. I take a deep breath.

'No, please.' She is not the way I raised her. But I cannot blame her. Sultana took her from me. She raised her with the same vengeful spirit she carried. The door is open, and I see the swirling stairwell leading down is narrow. I won't get far before she stops me. The place looks eerie, with candles placed in tall holders as if she's performing some kind of sadistic ritual. She catches the rapid movement in my eyes and cackles, shaking her head.

'Don't even think about running away, Ami.' The tip of the knife touches my chin. 'There's nowhere you can go and there's no one to rescue you. The house is empty. Everyone has gone. It's just you and me.' She pulls my hair and yanks me down.

'Please, I am your mother.' I want to reason with her. 'Let me go! Mona, listen—'

She yells into my face, mimicking my words like some savage beast.

'I told you, Mona is dead. You killed her that night in the fire. You are a murderer.'

'What happened that night was an accident, believe me. I would never hurt you. I have lived with the guilt ever since. If I could go back and change things, I would.' I want to bite my nails. A sudden flash of my dreams sweeps through my mind. She looks at me and throws my black diary at my feet. She says she read the garbage I wrote. There's no guilt, just confessions without forgiveness.

'You say you'd go back and change things, but you can't Ami. Nothing can undo what you did.' She carries such contempt and anger in her eyes. 'All these years, you lived a happy life with Amira giving her all your love. You went as far away as possible forgetting you ever had another daughter. Is that how you dealt with your guilt? You never even mentioned me. Amira knows nothing about me because you never told her. You didn't even bother to visit my empty grave. Truth is, you never liked me, did you? You never liked your own daughter. What kind of mother does what you did?' She twists the tip of the knife into her palm, dripping blood. 'The kind that deserves to die.'

'Mona, listen to me,' I try to wrench free. 'You need help. Please let me help you. We can start over. It's not too late. Fate has brought you back to me.'

'Shut up,' she says between gritted teeth. She quivers, nostrils flaring. 'What do you really know about me? If anyone needs help, it's you. Just look at yourself. Old and demented. Do you think searching for my story, for what happened to me in the newspapers, means anything? I know all about you, Afrah Bibi. This isn't fate. I planned for this day, to confront you with your sin. I shadowed you and waited a year before facing you with the truth, and it feels good to be the one who's in control over *your* life, just as you were of mine. I am now the one who gets to decide if you should live or if you should die. Just the way you did.' She twists the knife again and I close my eyes.

'Please, let me go.' Her mind seems as if it's elsewhere. She grabs me and yanks me up, my kameez in her fist stained with blood. I claw at her fingers, but she laughs and grabs me roughly by the arm and shoves me backwards.

'You're hurting me, stop it!' I push her away, but she swoops down on me and drags me across the room and throws me onto the floor. Bile inches up my throat. I can't get up, I shout for help.

'Naima's mum said you were a common girl. She used to laugh about you.'

I feel an ugly lump swell in my throat, expanding like a living creature inside of me. My own daughter wants to kill me. 'Sultana never loved you. She used you to get back at me. Don't you see? Why else would she —'

'Be quiet. I don't believe a word you say. You are a liar and a thief. You stole Naima's mum's bangles and never told me about it. You deserve to suffer for all that you've done. Do you hear me, Ami?'

'Fine then kill me, kill your own mother. I deserve to die,' I say. 'I was a bad mother and I am sorry I failed you. I am sorry you felt neglected.'

There's a glimpse in her eyes, a familiar look, and she turns around so I can't see her face. Wind batters the windows. A storm is brewing outside and it has surrounding the house. There's nowhere to run. Nowhere to hide. I am captured in this forsaken house with my daughter who has returned from the dead.

'I know you're angry about what I did. You hold me responsible for the accident.' I take a deep breath and throw her a soft gaze. 'But you have to believe me, it wasn't my fault what happened. We can still move on together and be happy again if only you to forgive me.' With ease, I put my hand on hers. My heart jumps to my throat. 'Can you imagine the pain, the suffering I went through, for over thirty years because I believed you were dead? And now you stand in front of me, my own flesh and blood. Thirsty for revenge. We can learn to forgive each other.'

'It doesn't work like that, Ami.' Her breath grows heavy. I look her straight in the eyes. She is playing a twisted game.

'Don't be afraid of death,' she smirks. 'I've seen it. I danced with the flames of fire you put out for me. And now you can be free, too. I'll make your death beautiful and pain free. You won't suffer. Not the way I have.'

'What do you want me to do?' My breath sits heavily in my chest.

'I want you to crawl,' she says. 'Now!'

Instead, I push her with all my strength and run past her, start climbing down the stairs. Halfway, I nearly stumble, and grab the rail. She is getting to her feet, and stands at the top of the stairwell watching me.

'Ami,' she says taking slow steps towards me. 'Where are you going? Are you going back to Amira?' she pants loudly. 'She doesn't love you. She left you here to rot. In a care home. She hasn't been to visit you. She doesn't care if you live or if you die. You are a liability to her. She blames you for all her failures. Her education, her marriage. I know because she told me. You have no one, Ami. No one except for me.'

A sickening feeling envelops me. I stagger and hit my head against the floor. Mona comes down and wraps her arms around me, as if to embrace me. She strokes my hair. I try to get away, but she's forceful and squeezes me tighter.

'Please, let me go.'

'All you had to do was to love me and none of this would have happened.'

Madness shines through her bloodshot eyes. My mind whirs. I don't hesitate. I manage to forcefully slip out of her grip and crawl with my elbows towards the door. I keep going but my limbs freeze. The window is open, a wild wind sweeps in with snow. I don't look back. I keep moving. I can't see anything. The snow blows in hard, a veiled curtain spinning me away from the world. I bump my head against something sharp. I think I am losing consciousness. Everything falls silent. I wet my dry lips, licking away blood from the split wound. I lean back against the wall. I'm paralyzed and unable to move.

'Pathetic, Ami.' Mona yanks my arm, and drags me out and down the stairs. 'You didn't even try to fight, that's how weak you are. But don't worry, it's not over yet.'

'Stop it,' I say. 'Let me go.' My pulse thuds through my veins.

'You're crazy if you believe I am going to let you get away with what you did.' She lunges towards me and roars like a wild beast. The pain burns through me as I fall and hit my head against the chair. I crawl across the floor toward the stairs, but she grabs my ankle and slides me back.

My eyes squeeze shut and I slump between her hands. Just as I lie on the floor, I open my eyes, and shove her away hard. Her head bounces against the brick wall. Her breath is heavy, snarling like an animal. Hissing wildly. She strikes me hard then tightens her hands around my neck. The tears in my eyes build.

'Help,' I shout. 'Somebody help me get out of here.'

My skin itches, and my throat is tight. When I look up again, I see that the curtains have caught fire from the candles, and everything is burning. The smoky air is trapped in my lungs. I crawl across the room, but Mona grabs my wrist and pushes me hard. I stumble back and come crashing down the stairs, the pain is shooting up in me.

Blinded and coughing from the thick smoke, I get up and open the door. I don't see her anywhere. I leap forward, but she jumps in front of me out of nowhere.

'Now, look what you've made me do.'

'We need to go,' I say. 'Or we both die.' I take her hand, and lead her through the black cloud smoke curling around us. I am back in our house on that fatal day when it all happened.

'Help me, Ami, help. Please,' I hear Amira cough.

'Where are you?' I wave my hands, but the fire is getting out of control. The heat seers into my skin.

'Ami?' Her hand is on my shoulder. But it's not Mona. It's Amira. She came for me. She is here. 'Let's go, now.' She pulls me away. But I let go of her.

'Amira stop, we can't leave.' She takes my hand and says we have to. 'The whole house is about to burn down. If we stay, we will die.'

'I can't leave her. I can't leave my daughter.'

A roar shoots through the smoke. I stagger towards Mona and see that fourteen-year-old girl again, crying for help. Amira takes my hand again, but I tell her to let go of me.

'I can't do this again. I can't leave my daughter to die again.'

'What do you mean?' I let go of Amira's hand and walk back. 'Don't Ami, please.' On one side, I see Amira as she was when she was five years old, crying for me to rescue her. And on the other side, I see Mona, left in the flames to die. She wanted my help that fateful night of the fire. She may even have reached her hand out. But I didn't take it. I took Amira and threw her out of the window. She was screaming. I lunged after her and left Mona to die.

With a grunt, Mona launches herself at me. Her body smashes into to mine. I fall back against the wall. I stretch my hands out to stop her. My breath heavy in my chest. I slump, spine curved. I am unable to hold myself upright. The air in my lungs falls short. The smoke from the fire is blinding me. Red and blue flames surround us. Sweat washes down my face. I hoist my body up, stumble into the white smoke and push open the window, exposing my skin to the winter breeze. Heavy snowflakes slap my cheeks, bite my skin. I turn around and see Mona standing in front of me.

'Help me, Ami.' She reaches her hand out for me. Before I can take hold of it, she staggers backwards and falls. Blazing timber panels from the ceiling crash down on her and she screams, and it echoes in my ears. I see her wide brown eyes look at me one last time before they shut.

'No! Mona!' The smoke curls around me and I trace dark flecks of blood from my head. I reach my hand out for her again, but it's too late. Everything turns dark.

44

AMIRA

One month later

Saturday, 25 January 2020

The snow falls like motes of dust from the grey sky, over the pedestrian outside. The house smells of fresh roses. I've brought home a beautiful red bunch and placed them in a vase by the window where Mum sits in her armchair reading a book.

'Did you like the ceremony this morning?' I ask.

'Yes, it was beautiful,' says Mum. 'Was she a friend of yours?'

'You could say that.'

I grab my crutches and look out of the window. The winter sun is out on this beautiful January afternoon. I ask Mum if she wants tea, and she says Kashmiri chai please, meri beti. I bring her a mug and she sips slowly while looking at me.

'Who are you? And where is Zahra?'

'You are home now,' I say.

'Oh,' she peers out. 'Look, it's snowing. Isn't it beautiful?'

Someone is calling me. It's Haroon. I take the call in the kitchen.

'Thanks for checking on us . . . We're doing fine . . . Don't need anything . . . Mum's much better . . . Yes, I'll take her for the check-up tomorrow . . . Thanks for making the arrangements with the specialist . . . No, Haroon, I don't want to give any interviews, I told you already. The police have everything in my final statement. The case is closed as far as I am concerned . . . OK, give Shafi my love. Tell him I'll pick him up tomorrow as planned. We'll head out with Mum to the new facility next to the hospital.' I hang up and scroll through the charity page we set up one week ago. Money keeps coming in and the donations are generous. One anonymous donor has given us £50,000. I wonder who it's from. The transfer came from Glasgow.

'Who are you talking to?' Mum's in the doorway. 'Was it Zahra? Tell her to make korma for dinner. She makes it so well.'

'Ami,' I get close to her. 'It was Zahra's burial ceremony we went to this morning. Zahra was your daughter, Mona. Do you remember now?'

'Oh, how is Mona?' Mum looks confused. 'If you speak with her, send her my regards. Tell her Afrah misses her company.'

There's a knock on the door. Mrs Nesbit has come to visit with her son. She wears a beautiful black dress, tight around her frame, and a sparkling green broach above her right breast. He wears a black suit, white shirt and black tie. They've brought lilies, and give their condolences. I lead them into the living room and place the flowers in a pot.

'Sorry I didn't make it to the ceremony,' she says.

'That's quite all right Mrs Nesbit. Thanks for coming and for bringing the flowers.'

'I hope the burial gave Afrah the closure she needed.'

Mum comes in and asks who the woman is. I tell her it's a friend. I excuse myself and lead Mum up to her bedroom. 'It's time for your nap.'

'I don't want to nap. I'm not tired.'

'Then rest, Ami. OK? Just for a bit.'

She lays down and I put a blanket over her. Her eyes are wide open, staring at the picture on her nightstand. 'Isn't he handsome? Nadeem looks just like Daniel Day-Lewis.'

I shut the door and go down to offer Mrs Nesbit tea. She tells me she followed the story in the news. What a tragedy. I don't say anything. If only I could wipe the past clean. If only I could borrow Mum's memory for an instant. Mum may have gotten closure. But I never will. I will never know what she did. The secret died with Mona, and Mum's memory is deteriorating day by day. But I am glad she is home. I feel privileged to care for her.

'How are you holding up?' asks Mrs Nesbit's son. He carries a smell of coffee and cigarettes. 'Still want to sell the house?'

'Yes, I am thinking of moving further out with Mum. She likes to be close to nature.'

'Aye,' he says. 'Me too. I got myself a little cottage out in the Highlands.'

'Actually, I have someone interested in the house. A couple.' I look at Mrs Nesbit.

'We'll miss having you around,' she says. 'Things will not be the same without you.'

'Have you found anything?' asks her son. 'I can recommend some places—'

'I'm looking at a small cottage in a rural area,' I smile. 'With an hour's drive into town so I can see my son once in a while.'

'He's a handsome lad, like his daddy,' says Mrs Nesbit. 'Smart, too, I can tell.'

'It was his idea to set up the charity,' I say. 'We've raised more than £90,000, which will go to people with dementia. It's a small amount, but it's a start. Shaf feels quite passionate about raising awareness. It's given him a purpose, a way to deal with Mum's condition.'

'You have lots to be proud about,' says Mrs Nesbit. 'Shafi is a fine young lad.'

She gets up and gives me a hug, then leaves. The snowflakes melt into the silver of her hair, and her footprints fill with newly fallen snow. A car pulls up at the front of the house and a man brings me a bunch of flowers and a card. I open it and read:

Dearest Amira, I heard about the unfortunate event that struck your family and I am truly sorry once again for the loss you and your mother suffered. Give her my best regards.
Best wishes, Dr Abdullah.

He's included a check for £10,000 to go towards our charity.

At night, I sit in the kitchen with Mano in my lap and hover the cursor over property sites. I have my eyes on a cottage by the sea. It's small, with a garden, and is forty minutes' drive into town. I can see myself living there with Mum. I can enrol on a long-distance learning programme with the university. Shafi is planning to study in London, so there's no point in staying here. And he's promised to keep in touch and call frequently.

The incident at the care home shocked him. He was by Mum's side the entire time at the hospital, and even came home with us. It's brought us all closer together while Haroon's been busy with his newborn daughter. Three names I told him were out of the question: Mona, Zahra and Meena. He laughed. They called her Nayab. I can live with that.

It was hard explaining everything to the police. But I showed them Mona's old diary. It turns out she was a very skilled con artist like Naima's father. She made money providing people with fake identities. Faking and forging papers wasn't an issue. She was a natural liar, an expert in pretending to be someone she wasn't. That's how she landed herself a job at Ravenswood Lodge and fooled us all. Mona may not have planned to die, but she did plan her own disappearance. She made everyone believe she was to the world and changed her identity multiple times.

Perhaps it's a blessing in disguise that Mum doesn't remember what happened. She doesn't watch the news and she stopped reading the newspaper. How can anyone live with the truth that your own daughter planned to murder you?

Mona went to great lengths to carry out her plans. She bought gallons of petrol to set fire to the care home. Mum and I made it out in time. By some miracle, I managed to find her again and carry her through the smoke and flames, then managed to jump out from a window. Mum was lucky – she landed in bushes covered in thick snow. She doesn't remember anything, of course, and thought her recovery at the hospital wasn't in a medical facility but that she was still at the care home. She kept telling me she wanted to go for a walk out to the sea. Kept talking about Zahra. It's only a matter of time before she fully forgets about her.

I broke my leg, but it could have been much worse. I hesitated before jumping. I had a moment of fear as if I had been in a similar situation before. The fire spread violently, and then I took a leap of faith. I threw myself out of the window and landed on the ground. I heard the snap of a bone breaking. The colour of red turned dark, almost black against the snow. I pulled away and dragged Mum with me.

I saw the whole house burn to ashes as it came crashing down. There was no sign of Mona. She had turned to dust. Sometimes, at night, I still think I see her shadow standing in the distance and watching me.

The wind slips through the window and the kitchen door creaks. Mano meows and arches his spine. His eyes are wide, glaring firmly at the door. *No one is there*, I tell him. For a brief moment, I feel chills run down my neck. The hair on my arms rise prickling my skin. We are alone. I pat Mano's soft fur. It's just the three of us. You, me and Mum.

45

AFRAH

Tuesday, 10 March 2020

The sun is hiding behind the clouds, leaving a red glow across the mauve sky. Feathered wings spread and make a flapping sound. The birds of spring caw loudly as the day turns a shade darker. Sitting in my wheelchair, I let my hands rest on its flat arms. I find comfort and solace in the garden, smelling the sweetness of the daffodils in bloom.

'Ami, I'm going to tilt this back for you so that you are comfortable.' The girl raises my foot rest and my body leans back. She puts a blanket over my legs. 'There, you can take a nap in the sun, isn't that nice?' Light begins to stream out from behind the clouds. The sun is tired of shying away from me now, and it comes out to kiss my prickly skin.

'I don't want to nap,' I say. 'I want to go for a walk down the beach.'

'How about we do that tomorrow?' she says.

'Please, can you take me now?'

'Just a brief walk then.' She pushes the wheelchair out onto the pavement. A woman across the road stares at us and nods.

'Good afternoon, Mrs Nesbit,' says the girl pushing my wheelchair.

'Good afternoon, Amira. Good afternoon, Afrah.' She smiles but I don't know her.

'Who is she?' I ask. 'How does she know my name?'

The girl doesn't answer. And I forget what I had just asked.

On our way, we pass a couple with two large dogs, and a little boy on his red tricycle. His mother shouts, 'Not too fast, sweetheart.' Somewhere in the distance, church bells chime. I peer over to one of the neighbouring houses, red bricks and black roof.

The girl stops to buy two coned ice creams and a bag of cherries, which she places on my lap. 'Try, delicious.' She gives me the ice cream. Cold and sweet against my tongue.

Rays of dimming sunlight gleam through the trees as we get closer to ocean air. I longed to see it, and out here the water is beautiful, a vast cerulean shoreline. Cawing seagulls flap their wings, and steal leftover food from the beach. Smaller birds crush seashells between their claws. Others crowd the pier, the wind sweeping away their songs. I bend and collect some of the broken seashell. Grains of sand sift through my fingers as I close them tight into my fist.

We walk slowly along the beach, my hand in hers. We sit on the bench close to the dock, looking out towards the endless water where boats are drifting. She puts her arm around my shoulder and holds me tight. With her other hand, she brushes the wind-blown hair away from my face. She tells me that soon we'll move into our new home which has sea views. A small cottage with a garden that's also a short walk to the woods.

'That's nice my dear,' I tell her.

'I love you, Ami,' she says, and kisses my hand. Two gold bracelets slip down my wrist. She is wearing the exact same pair around her arms. Must be a trend, I think.

I smile and look at her. The sun is glowing on her skin. I ask her who she is, but she doesn't answer. She just smiles and tells me that soon we will go on a trip to Glasgow to visit my husband's grave. 'Isn't that nice?'

I nod and lean my head against her shoulder and close my eyes. She takes the blanket and covers my legs. With her, I feel safe, I feel cared for. We sit a while on the bench together and watch the burning sun sink into the deep blue sea. Then she says, 'Let's go Ami, let's go home.'

Acknowledgements

Deepest thanks to Noor Sufi for her trust and support. Without her this book wouldn't have been possible. I am also immensely grateful to my editor Sara Adams. Her advice and positive energy has been invaluable. Thanks to the fantastic team at Hodder and for their creativity in designing the book cover. I am also eternally grateful to my copy-editor Christina Webb who has a keen eye and knows how to be judicious. I am indebted to my lovely agent Hannah Weatherill for her guidance and support. Thanks for believing in me and for sending your happy vibes my way.

I will always be grateful to my dear friend, Sally Long, for sharing her knowledge on dementia with me. Her emotional insights made me understand what it's like to place your mum in a care home. And my talented friend, the writer Lindsey McGhee who never stopped believing in me since we first met at the University of Surrey during our creative writing course. She believed in me yesterday, today and tomorrow. Thanks for being a true friend. And for always, always reading all my drafts. A deep thanks to Lubna Abbas for sharing her experience as carer with me. Her insights into the Pakistani community and what it means to care for your own mother who has dementia was tremendously helpful.

I want to thank my loving mother, my oldest friend and mentor for listening to me, for praying for me; my sister and best friend for her spiritual love and guidance; my beautiful family for empowering me, for teaching me how to be strong and to be myself; my lovely aunt for sharing her experiences as head of SubCo Trust, a charity that addresses the unmet needs of vulnerable Asian elders in London. Every day, she does a remarkable job helping the Asian community, in particular those who suffer from dementia, memory loss, diabetes and stroke.

Last, I don't know how to thank my wonderful husband for his kind and loving support during hard times. I am grateful that he was there to look after the boys while I worked day and night. My gratitude goes especially for his patience, understanding and eternal encouragement and belief in me.